Genation

Grizz

Rise of the Blackguard

A novel
by

Robert A. Hunt

Robert A. Hunt

ISBN-13: 978-1484135167

ISBN-10: 1484135164

First Wordpainter Books printing April 2012

Dedication;

This story about 'Grizz' is dedicated
to my son, James, for without his brilliant inspiration
this story would not have made it to print.
As the first big fan of Grizz, James
made some suggestions which
brought the character Grizz to life.

FORWARD
...RAGE!!!...

Blind rage has been the choice to reach for power and control throughout the ages. When parts from an alien anatomy is grafted into the body of a human child, slowly replacing his original human flesh, consequences quickly begin to weigh in. Unrest, impatience and an unsettled grasp for establishing dominance not only goes wrong, but such power and energy is not only turned against the boy but the scientists who created him. No one wants to lose control and so begins the battle to regain it. The rage within Domin is a result of being half human and half volk. This rage kindling at his very core was not only a leap in genetic capability; it was what caused a boy named Domin to become known as Grizz.

Here, in this incredible story of a baby who was born into the most unfortunate circumstances only to become the most powerful human of our time, comes the retelling of Domin's tale. This novel is a back story which takes place during the events of Genation Book 1: Earth Volk.

Follow Grizz's rise to power. Find the answer to the mystery of what made him so strong and powerful as a Blackguard.

Chapter 1

"Of all the challenges you've face throughout your career, there is nothing that can prepare you for what I am about to show you now." Sweat beaded upon the brow of the nervous doctor. He had been the mentor of Daniel McNeil since he was a graduate fresh out of Princeton University.

The young assistant was far too brilliant for simple medical opportunities. Doctor Evon had a keen eye for talent such as Dr. McNeil's. He had commitment, qualifications, a character of brilliance and stamina which is rare these days.

Dr. Evon could remember his first encounter with the boy. He was impressed with the depth to which his understanding could reach on so many levels of practice. When Dr. Evon first offered a chance for Daniel to work with him, he declined. Already committed to a path to success, Daniel wasn't interested in other avenues. The moment Dr. Evon mentioned the generous rate of pay, Daniel began to listen.

Since the time they first began working together the two men had experienced many ground breaking medical and scientific mile stones and turning points. They were the best of the best and included in many projects which were all at the fore-front of technical, medical and scientific breakthroughs including stem cell research, disease epidemic studies, political chess and climate change. When the bar was raised higher, these were the men who had a hand in raising the bar.

In the dark of night and through the pummeling shower of wind and rain, Dr. McNeil accompanied Dr.

Evon to the roof of the university. Upon the slick surface of the rooftop's heli-pad, other highly esteemed doctors and scientists eagerly awaited the precious delivery. This specific, and secured, wing of the university was quartered off to limited access. No unauthorized persons were permitted to enter the secured wing under any circumstances. Though the students of the university did not understand the rule, they honored the rule and they rarely questioned it for they were always met with the same short and simple answer, "Access denied, please state your name and student identification number for reporting purposes."

From the darkness of the wind swept night, the blinking landing lights of the helicopter approached. As it landed, Dr. McNeil wiped the rain drops from his bifocals and asked his mentor, "What makes this delivery so unique?" The landing skies of the copter swung back and forth overhead as the pilot wrestled against the turbulence of strong winds.

Dr. Evon leaned in close to Dr. McNeil and spoke so no one else could listen in. "We humans have made a lot of progress here on our planet. You and I have had wonderful opportunities whereby we are partakers of global growth, but this... If this is what I understand it to be, it is way over our heads."

The helicopter touched down carefully where it was quickly stabilized.

"Our challenge, as it always has been, is to overcome our own limitations and be the leaders we are expected to be. We must take control of what is given to us and through our unsurpassable genius, keep one step ahead of everyone else." Dr. Evon couldn't take his eyes off the helicopter. The cold rain was obviously unimportant to the doctor in comparison to the present unfolding event.

"Dr. Evon, please, sir, I'm going to need more details than that." Dr. McNeil blinked as rain trickled over his eyes.

None of the other people with them were sure what to expect from the delivery based on the report they received earlier. Locked to the side of the green military helicopter was a metal framed stretcher with a red blanket covering over the body. It was not easy to see the body who lay perfectly still under the blanket and red tie down straps. The extremities of the body were long and gangly, too long for the stretcher. The burned flesh of hands and feet hung out from the blanket.

The eyes of Dr. Evon held a seriousness in them which was so solid compared to the statement he made next, "It is believed to be a creature, not of this planet."

Judging from the character of Dr. Evon and the strange things they had seen daily in their line of work, Dr. McNeil turned his attention back to the helicopter only now he shared the same sense of awe as his mentor, Dr. Evon.

The heavy stretcher had to be lifted by six men so the Gurney could be wheeled in under it. At the moment the stretcher was placed on the Gurney, it was wheeled off the heli-pad and in through the double doors of the university. With growing eagerness and anticipation, the group of men and women remained near to the gurney. Each one could hardly wait to get the body to a secure location where they could remove the blanket and see the mysterious body underneath.

Within the United States government there existed sections of unofficial or classified divisions. These divisions were not to be mentioned in association with the government. In fact, the level of security was so high it was next to impossible to find any evidence linking such organizations to the government at all. Private, or rather, secret sectors like these consisted of special men and women who were specially trained and trusted to carry out classified projects which were unlike anything of our civilian known world. Within these classified organizations were X-files and classified operating procedures.

Within a secured operating room, Dr. Evon took immediate control of the operation. "Alright, people we have a female burn victim here, so let's not ask too many questions and keep our heads in the game. Janice, check heart beat and breathing. Jerry, I want you to perform a full body survey and document all burns and or injuries."

Janice began to report, "I'm finding strange heartbeat irregularity patterns, doctor."

Dr. Evon was comfortable in this, his element, "George, get an oxygen mask on her at once. I want her breathing monitored closely on a continual basis. Natalie, let's get going with treatments to the burned flesh. Mike, prepare the X-ray. Sophia, begin taking skin and blood samples."

From the ultra sound imagery, Daniel stood up with his eyes wide and reported, "I-I must inform you, Dr. Evon, I have discovered the female creature is pregnant."

"Did you find just one fetus, Daniel?" Dr. Evon asked as he remained professional like a rock.

Dr. McNeil ducked his head down for a moment to take a closer look at the imagery on his screen before he popped his head back up and added, "I have twins here doctor. She is definitely pregnant with twins."

A new report was made by a scientist, "I have found a new strain of DNA which our system deems identifiable."

Dr. Evon marched to the technician's DNA work station and looked over the results. "We have detection of an extra chromosome. Let's run multiple experiments to find out if this DNA is a mutation or compatible with that of a human's. Using similar samples, with care they are not of burned flesh, we need to get to work to find out if our subject can be cloned. If cloning is possible, we need to make immediate preparations for an incubation process. Perhaps it will grow to term to become something inhuman…" Dr. Evon half regretted speaking his mind out loud.

The following information was not confirmed and comes only by the way of word of mouth, but as rumour had it, with top secret testing in the works, multiple other forms of testing were also underway. A host of doctors and scientists were asked to volunteer for a branch project concerning reproductive donations. This was based on mental and physical strengths and only those who passed a series of strict tests were asked. Because of the millions of dollars offered, those who were selected found it difficult to say no. Sophia and Daniel were believed to be amongst those who were asked to be involved in the project. Neither of the two volunteers knew each other for they came from completely separate divisions at the time.

From the male and female reproductive specimens collected from such volunteers, fetuses were grown entirely from within a lab. Though the mothers and fathers to the embryos were under contract to work with such experiments on a professional basis, it was often difficult for the volunteers to not become emotionally involved. The volunteers agreed, in writing, not to ever pursue any emotional attachment to any one from the donor list or the babies which were grown. Created as expendable test subjects, the embryos were exclusively owned by the agency. It was not humane but the focus of science rarely is. This was simply a way for the government to get from point 'A' to point 'B' in the quickest and professional means possible.

Upon a surgical bed, with her limbs tied down using reinforced bonds, the female, unearthly creature remained in a comatose state for months. The babies which were in the womb of the tall burned creature were found to be in a critical and unstable condition. Efforts to save the babies became top priority. Using an ultra sound, the doctors examined the pregnant female alien to see what condition the fetuses were in. A shocking discovery was made when it was realized how one of the twins did not appear to be as healthy as the other. Their first sign was of a slowing heart beat. The challenge of seeing to the recovery of the mother and fetuses was monotonous at times for the whole ordeal seemed to go on and on. Many doctors, nurses and scientists were frustrated with the long hours and grew tired of speculating what it would be like when the mother awoke. Those who tended to the mother the closest, on a daily basis, needed a vacation the most. Unless personnel studied the progress made, it seemed little changed from day to day, still everyone knew the situation had to change one way or the other. With the difficulties associated with patience, no one could tear themselves away from the mysterious project.

Many moments came when the mother's condition worsened and they believed she would slip away in the night, but by morning she was restored miraculously. Though it seemed like a miracle each time this happened, Dr. Evon began to pick up on the trend how the mother seemed to gain in health and strength when she was left alone. He began to set up cameras at night to monitor her at times of her poor health, when the doctors and nurses would leave her for the night. Three cameras were set in place, one to capture simple imagery, the second to capture infra red and the third positioned to film from a thermo-scope.

The doctor was intrigued to discover a strange small dot come into frame each time. This appeared to be nothing more than a common house fly, but it did seem to have some strange interest in the mother according to its flight path. The doctor tried to follow up on this but he later felt he was only wasting his time.

As a matter of fact, what seemed to be a house fly, was indeed a miniature flying robot from the creature's world. When she was left alone, it would come out from hiding and use its limited abilities to help restore the vitals of its master.

Months went by and difficulties arose when spies to the project leaked information about some of the experimentations associated with the project. The moving of operations from place to place became mandatory, as people struggled to keep the project secret and alive. Dr. Evon and Dr. McNeil headed the project and became so wrapped up in it they soon found they did not have anymore to do with their past projects.

Despite all of the set backs along the way, the project always pulled through. Though no one was certain where the money came from, when it was needed it was there.

Unexpectedly, one day, the female creature awoke in a bed in a confidential make shift hospital room. She was able to identify herself by the name of Gastonish. It was as though Gastonish's body instinctively woke itself so she would be coherent for the delivery of her babies. She was strapped to the bed because no one was sure what kind of behaviour the creature would be in when she awoke. Upon the time when the creature awoke, the project leader, Dr. Evon, made contact with her. Gastonish seemed to trust the doctor and speak to him. He used his own methods to kindly get her to talk. She revealed she was a volk and her name was Gastonish, and how she was indeed a being from another planet. (More details in Genation: Book 1, Earth Volk)

This was marked as one of the most extraordinary events to happen to human kind, and like similar documented alien encounters, this too would have to be kept secret from the rest of the world.

Shortly after contact was established, Gastonish alerted everyone to her labour pains. She was taken back to her room where she became extremely hot. Waves of heat radiated from her pregnant belly. She then gave birth to two eggs. Gastonish opened the soft outer shells of the eggs and within each one was a single new born baby. They were still curled up and their bodies were translucent. It was like a sort of physical X-ray but it only lasted a short time after they were born. A closer examination revealed one of the babies had died. The baby had died just before birth and it was still of equal size to its brother.

Gastonish kept the living baby and named him Eddy. According to the operating procedures, Gastonish was not supposed to keep the infant. This rule, however, was bent because of Gastonish's intelligence and co-operation. The project leader, Dr. Evon, had also realized how, to continue with the benefits of Gastonish's co-operation, there would have to be an element of give and take. Gastonish, entrusted to mother her child, provided even greater opportunities for study.

The body of the deceased newborn volk was immediately packed in ice after the delivery and wheeled away to a completely separate and secured medical room.

This room was quite spacious so multiple teams could work near one another to share information. Doctors set to work right away; frantically they ran about as they made preparations for an entirely different project. This other project was conceived of near to the time of Gastonish's first examinations.

The project was named earth-volk and it consisted of transplanting as many organs and fluids of a volk into a number of humans who were of equal age. There was only one problem; they did not expect to have to work with new borns. The doctors made every effort to revive the heart of the volk baby but it was no use. They could not revive it. When the official date and time of the baby's death was given, Sophia looked on and a tear ran down her cheek. Anyone who noticed this tried to ignore it because it was against policy to have any emotional attachment to the project. Nevertheless, Dr. McNeil saw how Sophia was affected and he placed his hand on her shoulder for a moment to give her a little emotional support. He looked at her and pulled the surgical mask down below his mouth to show her, in a brief moment, he really did care. Sophia turned away from him and buried her face in her hands and wept.

A nurse came to Sophia and escorted her out of the room where she was supposed to be left out of the project from that moment on. Sophia was able to talk her way out of being eliminated as she made up a story to explain her emotions. She was the top nurse of her field and an asset to the team so she was given a second and final chance.

"Sir, will we have to bring in the other volk newborn before we can continue?" asked a colleague.

"No, that is not our plan." Dr. McNeil answered. "If we brought in the other volk newborn it would soon be dead as well." He raised his hand and made a wide circular motion for the others to see. Then he pointed to a

14

door at the other end of the room. With that, the room was cleared. Dr. McNeil signaled for a new group of fifty specialists to enter and take over. Dr. McNeil announced "Initiating Phase two." After the doctors came in, the nurses entered, each one of them pushing a cart with a single baby inside.

The specialist divided up into separate groups. As the autopsy of the dead volk baby was performed, grafting surgeries began where they attempted to successfully merge muscle and organs to the cloned human newborns.

The small volk heart which stopped beating was a subject of great interest but despite the attempts the surgeons were unsuccessful at reviving it. Packaged in a zip-lock bag, the small volk heart was placed into a silver case designed to keep the heart frozen.

Somehow, an employee was able to find the case and steel it away. Extra measures were taken with regards to security and the whole project was under intense observation. Throughout the investigation many people lost their jobs. Such people seemed to vanish from the earth. Investigators soon realized retrieving the volk heart was near impossible.

"Are there no more subjects?" Dr. McNeil was referring to cloned newborns. "We have just one other left, sir." A nurse announced. "But it is physically deformed and it is not expected to live."

"Let me see it." The doctor said as he wiped blood from his surgical gloves onto his already blood covered apron. It was bloody from the previous surgeries. A nurse wheeled the baby in and the doctor, Dr. McNeil, lifted the clip board which hung at the side of the trolley. He quickly scanned over the report which detailed the baby's defects. It had miss-figured bones and muscles. Then Dr. McNeil noticed something else which intrigued him about the report. He was personally the father of this baby. Remembering how he felt a kinship with this one, he disobeyed protocol and kept it alive. Protocol clearly stated how any clone, disfigured in anyway must be eliminated. The clever doctor saw a potential where others could not. *A cloned newborn with very little chance of survival would find a second chance through the grace of surgery.* He signed the report and lifted the baby up to check it over. He looked into its eyes and said, "Ah, this one was born without much of its vital organs and muscles but its skeletal form appears to be intact... enough. It will do for our purposes. It will have to do." The doctor said, "Make this one count people - No mistakes!" They went to work on the cloned baby right away. "If the subject is missing a muscle on the right side, replace the left side also." They were busy for hours on end. The hours turned into days and on the eve of the third day, they were finished.

When the surgical chaos was finished, they had five altered clone newborns who survived the brutal surgeries. These five successful newborns were taken away where they were monitored closely, for they needed time to recover. The surgical practitioners needed to find out if the bodies would reject the organs or muscles. Unlike the other newborns, the deformed one, the last one, always seemed to accept whatever it was that was donated and graphed to it. Many speculated how, because the body was deformed, it was instinctively trying harder to survive.

Each of the newborns were unique as one had two volk arms, another had two volk legs, another had a volk head upon its volk body, while another had the torso of a volk with a human heart.

One of the five, had some of the volk muscle implants grow too rapidly for the small human baby. This child did not die, but it did grow up with a severe deformity of the legs.

Still, everyone was always amazed to find the most successful baby was Dr. McNeil's deformed baby. Thanks to the surgeries, all of the deformities were corrected with volk implants. Dr. McNeil decided it was important to name the successful babies. Sophia had suggested once to name their baby Dominic. Dr. McNeil, however, had a clever idea to name him Domin because this would encompass a wider scope of the possibilities for the kind of life this child may one day lead. Domin which was meant to be short for dominion.

One day Dr. McNeil had a meeting with the governing heads of his project. Dr. McNeil tried to explain everything which was already well detailed in his report. "If you need any extra parts for this one," Dr. McNeil was told from his officials, as they made reference to Domin. "Salvage them from the subjects who didn't make it."

Subsequently, Domin did have to under go many other extensive surgeries. It would seem like just when they all thought Domin had gone through all he could, they would put him under the knife again. Dr. McNeil thought the people he worked for were purposely trying to push the surgeries until Domin was dead. Still, Domin amazed everyone as he survived each additional surgery. It was obvious to Dr. McNeil how his officials didn't care if Domin lived or died. Dr. McNeil knew he was not supposed to become emotionally attached but as Domin survived one surgical experiment after the other, he found himself rooting for him like a proud father would. It was a motivation for him to make sure Domin would continue to survive. For this reason, he made it positively clear to everyone how he would be involved in every experiment concerning Domin as he would push to become the project head.

As Domin grew from a baby into a toddler, he was subjected to less and less surgeries until finally they all seemed to end all together. Domin had scars all over his body from the countless muscle and organ transplants. He also had many bandages to cover the more recent surgeries. Dr. McNeil tried to do what he could with laser treatments to make the scars less noticeable but as people were brought in to replace others throughout the project, they would be discouraged to try to point out a previous incision and find it was difficult to locate. They found having scars as a record of what was done was preferred.

Unfortunately for Domin, he started out in life, more less, with the appearance of a human boy. The doctors and scientists were disappointed; they hoped to see some sort of volk traits shine through.

Coincidentally, the volk baby who had survived his birth was named Eddy and he was making quite a name for himself, a name which was quickly vanishing under a growing secrecy of security. No expense was spared to ensure Eddy remained the government's best kept secret.

This volk baby was born with transparent flesh, which soon after, darkened to an opaque greyish baby-blue tone. Hairless and muscled with protruding and exaggerated metacarpals and medi tarsels, Eddy was the object of utmost importance. On its fore-arms shoulders and tops of its feet were light blue caps, or smooth shells. Like its mother, Gastonish, the volk baby's eyes were a deep black. It looked around the room with large wide innocent eyes, penetrating eyes, which appeared to be entirely black. Also, like its mother, it had twin spines, which ran up the entire back to the base of its skull where a line of small bumps traveled up from the back of the head to the fore-head.

It was healthy and strong like an average child of its kind. Humans were busy studying him. The fascination peeked whenever someone predicted of a day to come when man kind would see more of these creatures, when these creatures would visit or even invade the earth.

Many tests were made to compare Domin's development to that of any other human child, but nothing abnormal ever seemed to make the charts. They tested his mind, his senses and motor skills along with his blood. They wanted to find out just how volk they could make a human. Nevertheless, Domin continued to amaze everyone even though many volk traits were not evident right away.

A few years passed before evidence of volk intervention began to take form. Domin began to have nightmares often about monsters attacking and killing him. In his dreams, he was weak and unable to defeat the evil. He rarely had a good nights sleep.

When Domin's dreams were tested by experts in the field of REM sleep, they found their readings inconclusive for the readings were off the chart. If not for the straps which held him he, like his Brothers would not only be restless sleepers, but destructive ones to be sure. It was as though a great storm was brewing in Domin's mind each night, but when Domin was awakened and questioned, he could remember nothing. And so Domin carried on throughout each day like any other child would be expected to, laughing and playing with his brothers, between easily angered temperamental tantrums.

With the accompaniment of many men, the five brothers were escourted throughout a maze of corridors. Before they reached the door to their exercise room, the brothers caught sight of the volk child, Eddy Evon. The window they were looking through was tinted on one side so Eddy could not see the five brothers.

Within a dark room Eddy began running on a treadmill which was hooked up to an alternator. As Eddy ran, a wall of light bulbs began to cycle through from low voltage bulbs to higher voltage bulbs. As Eddy ran the bulbs brightened. As Eddy ran faster, the next set of bulbs illuminated from a soft glow to a bright light.

Dr. McNeil explained what was happening, "As Eddy runs, the treadmill is generating power. Look at how Eddy is concentrating while he exercises. You see, the treadmill is becoming harder and harder to work, but Eddy continues to push his body to run faster despite the resistance."

By the end of the exercise, the room was lit up brighter than a clear summer's day. The Brothers watched as Eddy slowed down and the lights quickly dimmed. Though the Brothers wanted to watch Eddy more as they were fascinated by him, they were carted off to their own exercises. As Domin moved away from the window, he noticed Eddy look up at the window as though he looked right into Domin's eyes.

The large room was packed with countless exercise machines. Hooked to wires and probes, Domin, five years old, frowned at the computers and emotionless scientists. He stood on the conveyor of an exercise treadmill, much like the one Eddy was on, where he was expected to run at some level of efficiency that no other five year old human could. He ran for half an hour while looking at a wall of lights. Domin couldn't seem to even get the smallest and lowest voltage light to do more than wink a little, until he began to cry and finally give up.

They tested his strength with a series of modified weight training machines which where custom to his little size. Then Domin had an assortment of lights shine on his skin to test the effects of his skin to the light. He also had his hearing tested. After the hearing test, Domin's motor skills were tested. Scientists began to paint various colours or chemical compounds on his skin for further experimental possible reactions to the lights.

Following this simple test, a technician approached Domin holding a syringe with a long needle sticking out of it. The child's heart began to race. He decided right then and there he would not accept a needle ever again. The tech squeezed a little of the syringe out and the liquid squirted into the air. Another tech swabbed his arm with rubbing alcohol. As the needle was pointed at him and came ever closer, he began to scream. He then began to punch and kick like a wild person. It took the help of many other technicians to finally hold Domin down long enough to administer the drug.

This annoyed Domin and he glared at the technicians. At the tender age of five, a sound erupted from deep within the child's chest. "Grrrrr..." The look in his eyes was no less of pure distrust and hate for the technicians. This surprised the techs, and they noted the incident as they recorded everything else.

For the next test, Domin was led by the hand around to a chair which looked very much like a dentist's chair, only it had wide straps attached to the arm rests and foot rests. The loose straps were obviously in place to bind the occupant.

Domin took one look at the chair and decided, stubbornly, he was not going to sit in it. He struggled to back away but the men resisted him and continued to force him toward the chair. As Domin became increasingly aggravated, his strength seemed to increase. Five year old Domin successfully overpowered the men.

Pushing one of the technicians, Domin sent him into the wall forcefully. The tech's head made a muffled thump on against the wall before Domin swung around to cripple the other tech's arm and kick him in the shin. When the tech bent forward in pain and almost fell to his knees, Domin lifted and threw the full sized man across the room. One of the techs wrapped his arm around Domin's little neck, while two other men reached out and grabbed hold of Domin, one at each wrist. By pulling his arms in, Domin sent the techs at his wrists colliding into one another before he drove his head back into the face of the tech who had his arm around Domin's neck. All of the men were rolling over as they were gathering up their strength and rising back to their feet.

Domin was so frightened, he ran to the corner of the room where he hunched down into a ball and buried his face into his hands and cried. It was as though his nightmares had become a reality for him. He believed the men would be back soon to kill him for what he had done.

The men whom he feared, however, had other ideas in mind. Dr. McNeil had just walked into the room when Domin had his little temper tantrum and he saw the whole thing. Never before had he ever seen a five year old over power five men. Such an act had some real potential. Though the other technicians did not know it at the time, they had witnessed a pivotal turning point.

Domin sat at a table with his four other Brothers, as he was accustomed to do at meal time. Though the other children at the table were not exactly his biological kin, he was raised to believe they were because they each shared in the same volk implants. Each of the other children had their fair share of scars and bandages, but it was obvious how Domin was the one who underwent the most surgeries.

Seven nurses waited on the children. Domin, of

course, was well proportioned for his bulky muscularity. Though he seemed to brood over everything, he was the most level headed and the one who was considered to be the most likely to succeed in his future.

To his left sat Stroy. Just as Domin's name was a derivative of the word 'Dominion', so Stroy was the short version of 'Destroyer'. He sat in discomfort and pain as a nurse helped him to hold cold packs to his incredibly over sized legs. Not only were the muscles of his legs huge, but so too were the bones. This made the top half of his body seem extremely small compared to his legs. In an unnatural way, Stroy curled his feet into fists as his toes had the ability to do so. His big toes could curl up and around his smaller toes just like a thumb curls over the fingers in a fist. Stroy did this often and said it didn't feel strange, rather it gave him a sense of comfort and security.

Domin did not feel sorry for his brother, regardless of the fact that Stroy would likely be too distracted to eat very much at the table. Stroy was in great pain as he had been on the tread mill breaking his previous record for both speed and endurance. Each of them had other pains and aches as well, like head-aches, healing from surgery pains and of course growing pains.

Next to Stroy sat Narl. His name was shortened from the word 'Snarl' because with all of the countless scars on his face, he always looked like he was snarling. What they had implanted into Narl was not only the brain of a volk but his entire head. Using the skull of the original volk baby, they had managed to implant practically the entire head. Eyes black like a doe and small pointed ears like an elf, though the pinna of his ears were capable of movements, especially the tragus and anti-tragus being muscled, could bend inward and plug his ear much like we are used to putting our fingers in our ears. Other than the occasional massive migraine head-ache, Narl would move in quick jerky motions like a bird or even Eddy the volk. A neck brace was always worn around his neck because his neck was not strong enough to carry such a large head. From the neck brace, three metal rods connected to a metal ring which crowned his head. One rod was on each side of his head and the third was at the back of his head. Multiple metal screws were drilled through the metal crown to hold Narl's head securely in at the center of it. He was quite quiet and loved to observe, but this irritated the technicians. They desperately wanted to know what was going on in the thought process of his mind. He was the only one of the children who was bald which revealed every excruciating scar of his scalp.

Beside Narl was Grud. The name Grud was shortened from the word 'Grudge'. Grud was a lot like Stroy, or so Domin thought, because rather than overly developed legs, Grud had overly developed arms. And like Stroy, the bones in his arms were also volk in origin. Yet for Grud it didn't end there. Skin grafts of thick grey volk skin covered most of his scared arms. The sadistic technicians had also added the original volk fore-arm plates.

Finally, the only other child at the table was Oblit, whose name was short for 'Obliterate'. This one was the strangest of the bunch, because not only was his body grotesquely disproportional, but his mind was beyond normal. The body, or chest and core, was volk but everything else attached to it was human, including his heart. He was a strange scatter brained child and the saddest product of the technicians morbid project. His hair was always messed up and he moved with his twin spined back hunched forward and his human limbs curled inward.

The only child who seemed to always be missing from all of the activities was Eddy. He likely didn't know any of the five Brothers even existed. It was established and reinforced by Dr. Evon how Eddy would be raised exclusively by his mother, Gastonish.

The room had been modified and the overseers of the five Brothers spared no expense as they had each previous year when they celebrated their birthdays. They had a live band who was dressed in teddy bear costumes. Other tables around the room had food prepared on them such as hot dogs, hamburgers, potato chips and ice cream. Camera crews had also taken up multiple stations around the room. They tried to be discreet, but they were not very good at it.

The children could also see the game of; Pin the tail on the Donkey along with a piñata hanging from a string with a mat and a stick under it.

The juvenile music from the teddy bear band was happy and exciting like they were in a circus. The five Brothers looked around the room with wide innocent eyes of youth. Everywhere they looked there seemed to be something interesting to see. If not the people smiling and dancing around, it was the decorations which caught their attention. The music changed and all of the people in the room began to sing. Even the camera crews were singing along;

Happy Birthday to you…
Happy Birthday to you…
Happy Birthday dear Domin, Stroy, Narl, Grud and Oblit…
Happy Birthday to you…

Meanwhile, in another section of the government facility, Gastonish was enjoying some one on one time with her volk son Eddy. Gastonish spoke to Eddy like he was an adult as Eddy replied to her in just such a manner. Gastonish sat cross legged on the floor at a small sized table for children where Eddy sat. They had a plate of cookies and milk as they spoke about money and the important things to focus about in life when the door to their room unlocked and opened. Four technicians came in to take Eddy away for his scheduled tests, but Gastonish was not happy with the technician's timing. Her volk son, was being taken away against Gastonish's will. The whole ordeal of using force to have young Eddy was not going well. Though the doctors just wanted to keep everything on schedule, Gastonish had enough of taking orders from a primate species. Two of the technicians took Eddy out as he screamed for his mother. He reached out to her with yearning eyes. Gastonish wanted her son all the more but the other two technicians raised their tazers to warn her to think twice about any insolence. The technicians wanted Gastonish to back up to the bed where they would apply the bindings, but she shook her head negatively. Eddy was pulled closer to the door but as Gastonish took a step forward she was electrocuted.

Eddy was angered at seeing his mother hurt. Turning on the technicians at either side of him, Eddy moved to attack but before he could, he was tazered in the back.

When Gastonish woke up, she found herself bound to the bed and Eddy had been taken from her. Gastonish's wig was thrown from her head as she thrashed about like someone losing their mind. She was completely alone in the room. It wasn't until Gastonish began to focus her thoughts and settle down, when she began to pose the biggest problem…

Each of the Brothers took their place at the table when

Narl shot a nasty look at Domin with his spooky black volk eyes and said, "Can someone explain why Domin is here? How is he considered one of my Brothers? From one volk Grud has the arms, Stroy has the legs, Oblit has the chest and I have the head. Thus, all of the parts are accounted for so what was left for Domin? The stomach perhaps?" the Brothers tried to contain their laughter as they too shared the same questions.

Domin glared at Narl as he imagined separating Narl's volk head from his human shoulders. The tension was so thick, everyone could feel it. Narl, however, enjoyed it.

Dr. McNeil cleared his throat and spoke to the Brothers, "You know, as humans, each of you were born healthy and strong, but not Domin. We have found that since Domin was born without certain muscles, his body is willing to compromise and fight to attain what is missing. A typical human body has six hundred and fifty muscles. A typical volk body has nineteen hundred and seventy two muscles. We were able, to this point, take some of these extra muscles and surgically implant them with great success. Domin's body has accepted these foreign muscles, but because we were filling in places of his body that lacked muscle, it is not so obvious, in Domin, what we have done. Domin is one of your Brothers, no less as special as each one of you because he is a little bit of each of you. Where each of you are one part of a volk body, the volk body was so complex, Domin has become small parts of the entire body. I'm not sure if that sets him apart from the rest of you somehow, but I do know he will always be your brother. Now enjoy your birthday because as you boys celebrate together it symbolizes, not that you are twins but that you are equal." Dr. McNeil settled the tension when the doors opened to reveal a special birthday surprise the Brothers were ready to party.

They were each turning six years old and when the birthday cake came out, carried by six technicians, they could see five groups of six lit birthday candles on top of it. The cake was massive. It was carried on a large round silver platter. At the bottom of the cake was a huge chocolate chip cookie which measured four feet across. On top of the cookie was an equally large cake. On the cake was a layer of ice cream and on top of that was another layer of cake. It was topped off with another huge chocolate chip cookie. The outside wall of the cake and ice cream was covered with white icing. The whole thing looked like a giant ice cream sandwich.

The six technicians carried the cake over to the five Brothers and they set it down at the center of the table. The flame of the candles flickered before the children. They all looked at it in awe.

Then Narl stood up on his chair and put his hands on his hips. His black volk eyes read the words which were written on the top of the cake's cookie surface.

"Happy Birthday Domin, Stroy, Narl, Grud and Oblit." He read with the voice of an emotionless robot.

Oblit stood up as he filled his lungs full of air and then he blew out the candles. Only he more less sprayed them out as he had his lips pursed too tightly. When he was finished, the other children wiped the spit from their faces only to notice, by some strange miracle, one candle was still lit. At the moment of this realization, all of the other children stood quickly as their chairs toppled back behind them. They filled their lungs with air and blew as hard as they could in competition with one another. Spit was sprayed in all directions and by the end of it the candles were well dowsed out and the top of the cookie cake had a glossy sheen to it.

As the children again, wiped their faces, the technicians looked at one another. They were somewhat confused as to what they were going to do about the cake.

"Oh, no, guys," Dr. McNeil spoke up. "What have you done to the cake?"

The five Brothers looked at the cake, then they looked at one another and a pouty expression came over them like they felt shame and were about to cry. Dr. McNeil was a quick thinker and said, "How would you like to find out who can eat it the fastest?" He asked.

The Brothers looked at one another, then Narl said, "We will need some plates and utensils first."

Then Dr. McNeil smiled deviously and replied, "Oh, no, you are supposed to eat it with your hands behind your backs."

The children looked at the cake and smiled. They all loved to compete with one another. "Ready, set, Go!" Dr. McNeil said.

With that, the children opened their mouths as wide as they could and slammed their faces into the cake. Some of the ladies in the room expressed their disgust of the matter, while the men just cheered them on.

Grud, with his powerful volk arms, began to shovel the cake into his mouth. "No cheating Grud." Dr. McNeil said.

Narl stopped eating and saw Grud was not only cheating, but he was not listening to Dr. McNeil. With his mouth full of food, Narl began to point and grunt to alert an adult to do something about Grud. Glancing up, Grud noticed this and gave Narl a shove with his powerful volk arm. Narl was hurled from the table and then he slid a couple of feet on the floor.

"Grud! That's enough!" Dr. McNeil shouted.

Domin locked his eyes with Grud. "Oh, it is on!" he growled. Domin flew at Grud knocking him to the floor. Domin began to punch Grud in the face violently. Grud used his powerful arms to block the powerful punches, until he finally had enough and slapped Domin off from him. As Domin flew across the room, Stroy jumped out at Domin and kicked him in mid air with a solid fisted foot. Domin was then sent into a new direction where he crash landed into one of the teddy bear musician's drums.

Grud, with his powerful arms shot back up to his feet. He then used his arms to help himself run to the table where Oblit was still eating the birthday cake. Oblit was not phased in the least by the chaos.

Placing his one fore-arm against the cake to hold it back, Grud took hold of the metal platter it was on. He then slid the platter out from under the cake.

The drums were torn apart as little Domin rose up from amidst the band of teddy bears. His eyes burned with indignation before he went to work destroying each musical instrument.

Through sheer will power and volk focus, plus a little help from a sertz, (A guardian robot from her world) Gastonish broke free from the bonds which were holding her to her bed. Tearing her other bonds free, Gastonish quickly leaped from the bed and broke through the locked door. Knocking the guard across the hall, Gastonish bolted from the room with focused anger as she called out to her son, "Eddy! Where are you!" throwing humans to the floor of the hall, Gastonish, with long spindly limbs practically took up the entire width of the corridor. She quick ran down the maze and up a stairwell. She tried to find her son through telepathic means and felt she was on the right path. Like the nose of a bloodhound, her telepathic ability was leading her right to the source of the only other volk she knew. Oh, yes, she could feel the mind of a volk, her son…

Dr. McNeil stormed into the center of the room and

raised his hands. It was as though he could predict there was about to be some devastating outcome if he didn't do something. "Stop it! This madness ends now!" He shouted.

At the authoritative sound of Dr. McNeil's masculine voice, everyone just seemed to freeze. A moment of intense silence passed before a hideously happy clown came bursting into the room. --Honk-Honk-- He honked a little horn and laughed like Goofy. The clown wore a one piece suite which was polka-dotted and seemed to be inflated somehow. His face was white with a red nose, lips and puffy hair. When he walked he took big wide strides as his shoes were three times too large. Two black straps criss-crossed his chest.

He put his hands to his sides and looked around the room. The cake had been torn up and most of it decorated the five Brothers.

"What a big mess!" The clown said in a comical voice. "I don't want to be a party-pooper, but we're gonna have to clean up that cake!" He then reached down at his sides and lifted up two large super soaker water guns which were attached to the straps. "Ha-ha-ha-ha-ha..." the clown laughed and laughed as he shot water at the five Brothers.

Grud, who was still holding the platter, twisted up his body to throw the platter. The clown had targeted him. When Grud unwound himself, he launched the platter at the clown like it was an over-sized frizz-bee. The platter struck the clown and he was thrown backwards. Grud was not happy about this because his intension was to send the platter out at Domin.

The camera crews were busy trying to decide where to point their cameras as everything began to unfold at once.

Just then, the five Brothers could see the party was

over when Dr. McNeil lifted his hand into the air. He shaped his hand to form a gun which was the signal for the technicians to use tazers. Just then, the technicians revealed their stun guns.

One of the technicians shot at Stroy who was standing near the clown but Stroy was too quick for them. He kicked out his legs and jumped away. As he ran he proved to have extraordinary capabilities, but the clown was accidentally hit with the tazer. The sound of a little girl screaming filled the room but it did not come from a little girl, it came from the clown.

Oblit reacted to the sound of the tazer being fired. He ducked down under the table. From there he could see the legs of a technician coming toward him. He then reached up and split the table apart as it was designed to do. Oblit leaped up through the center of the table and right up through the birthday cake. As he bursted out of the top of the cake he shouted "Surprise!" His hands had scooped through the cake as he jumped through. Then with his hands full of cake, he threw it at the oncoming technician.

The teddy bear band began to try to apprehend Domin but Domin surprised the band as he fought them off.

Narl ran up behind Stroy as he used him as a distraction. Once he was close enough to the hanging piñata, he took hold of the wooden stick which lay just under the piñata and then he came up swinging. The piñata bursted apart and candy flew out everywhere.

Some of the technicians had helped the clown back up onto his feet, only this time the clown was not laughing anymore.

One by one as Domin fought off the insinuating teddy bears, he watched as his Brothers were all struck by the tazer fire and apprehended, but not before Narl had taken an opportunity to grab one of the tails from the pin-the-tail-on-the-Donkey game. He snuck up near to the clown and while he was still bent over he pinned the tail on him. The clown jumped up into the air with his hand springing around to the pain in his rear end. "Yeeeee-Owwwwuch!!!"

This was the first time in a long time where Narl smiled, but his smile was short as a tazer zapped him from behind.

Last but not least, Domin was surprised when a teddy bear band member revealed how he too had a tazer and he used it against him.

The camera crews seemed to be well pleased by the party, but they seemed to be the only ones who considered it to be a success.

One of the nurses shouted out loud, "This is even worse than last year!"

At once, the main door to the room exploded as it swung open forcefully enough to damage the wall. In stepped Gastonish with a terrible vengeance in her eyes. Wearing a robe over pyjamas, Gastonish scanned the room craning her bald head slowly around from one person to the next before she settled her eyes on Narl. This was the one she had a telepathic link with, but it was not her son. As she stood there examining the messy room and each of the occupants, she began to figure out exactly what she was looking at. A camera crew was silently recording everything. She could see living volk body parts adhered to living human body parts. It was wrong in her mind, but she had to figure it out. Not much time was needed for her to realize how there would have been only one source of volk to allow for such a nightmare to happen. The sick tamperings of the humans and her other son who died at birth was the only answer.

Only it wasn't good enough for Gastonish to figure out what was happening on her own. She needed to hear about it from a human. Someone was accountable for what was going on and how someone had some explaining to do before that person was going to pay.

Gastonish stepped into the room with a wide stride and back handed the clown who stood before her shaking his wobbly knees like an overwhelmed wreck. Thrown to the teddy bear band, they all fell down like bowling pins.

Without a moments notice, Gastonish had the scruff of Dr. McNeil's shirt in her hand as she lifted him off the floor. "Tell me what is going on here and why I was never notified!"

"I-I…" The doctor tried to speak but not only was he choking, he was scared to death.

Nurse Sophia came running up to Gastonish and gently held her long forearm. Gastonish looked down at Sophia but her eyes were still hardened and striking.

"Please don't hurt him… Please!" Sophia pleaded sympathetically.

"These are my children, who gives you people the right to do this." Gastonish spoke with such emotion, a tear ran down her cheek.

"These are my children too." Sophia spoke with equal passion in her voice as she reached across to Gastonish's powerful arm which still held Dr. McNeil off his feet. "And they are his children as well. We do this for the sake of not only the children's life but for the lives of all man-kind."

Gastonish looked past Sophia to Narl once again as she shot a telepathic thought to him. As Narl received Gastonish's thoughts into his mind, he also received a great deal of pain as Gastonish shifted her telepathy to abstract Narl's memories.

"Ahhh!" The little person shouted as he put the

palms of his hands to the sides of his large volk head and fell to his knees.

Domin ran to Narl as Gastonish ran out of the room screaming in frustration. Dr. McNeil ran after Gastonish but he stopped at the open door and shouted down the hall to the security team, "Seize her and lock her up in her room!"

Domin put his arm around his brother Narl and asked, "What did she do to you? Are you alright?"

"I think… I'm fine…" Narl spoke between heavy breaths, "She told me… she was our mother…"

Chapter 2

A reflection of scars and brutality stared back at Domin as he spent a little quiet time by himself behind a locked door of his bedroom bathroom. Shirtless, he studied his image in the mirror. Slowly and gently, he ran his finger tips over the scars of his young but muscled torso. Domin wondered why he was chosen to be so powerful and then tortured under a surgical knife as his reward.

He hopped right up onto the counter and moved toward the mirror until his fore-head was pushed up against it. He looked himself right in the eyes and frowned. "Who am I?" He puzzled. "What is my purpose? Why do I have to be so different?" As he glared into his own eyes, he began to see something. He could see a fire. It was there right behind his eyes. A fire burned with a rage which was bigger than the facility. It was bigger than the people who oppressed him and his Brothers and who made insane decisions for them. It was bigger than any of his problems.

It was there and it was more real to him than the scars he could touch on his body. The rage... It surged through him. It coursed through his veins like electrical energy, and he liked it.

His body became tense. He tried to tighten every muscle in his body beginning with his finger tips which he formed into fists. Then up his arms to his neck, and then moving down his chest and back to his buttocks and thighs, and all the way down to the tips of his toes.

He pressed his fore-head against the mirror harder and harder, until he finally pulled his head back slightly before thrusting it forward smashing the mirror.

"What was that!" He could here a nurse say from the other side of the bathroom door. Her key was heard being inserted into the door knob, before she entered the bathroom. "Oh, no, Domin. What have you done now?" Domin looked at her like she was crazy. He had a thin trickle of blood running down his face from his forehead. She lifted Domin down from the counter top to the floor and began to wet a face cloth.

Domin looked passed her into the bedroom. There he saw his Brothers in their beds. The room was divided into two by a sheet of transparent plexy. On one side of the room of the transparent divider were two bunk beds and one single bed. Nurses assisted each of them as they prepared for the night. At the head of each of the beds were computerized consoles. From these consoles wires were attached to each of the Brothers to monitor their vitals through out the night. On the other side of the transparent divider was a desk with computerized components on it with a couple of chairs behind and a cot.

Domin could see all of his Brothers sitting up in their beds looking at him. "Wow, cool, Domin." Stroy cheered.

"I was wondering what was taking you so long in there." commented Narl, who always had something to say.

The others laughed and Domin just tried to blow them off. The nurse dabbed the moist cloth on his forehead to sop up the blood. Her name was Sophia. She was particularly kind to each of the Brothers and they respected her for that. It was not easy for a nurse to win the affections of any of them.

"Domin, what has gotten into you?" Her voice was firm but kind, "Now, I don't want to see this kind of behaviour in you again. Is there something bothering you?" She bent down on one knee and looked him in the eyes. Domin had always kept so much bottled up inside. She pulled him to her and hugged him tightly and meaningfully. "You can tell me you know. Just start talking and I will listen."

Domin took a deep breath and looked down at the tiles of the bathroom floor. "You wouldn't understand…" he said as his words trailed off.

"Oh, well, you never know. How about you give me a try? I just might surprise you." Her offer was most enticing. Deep from within, Domin did have a great need to be mothered. He looked over her shoulder to his Brothers who were snickering about him. Sophia noticed this and closed the bathroom door so the two of them could be alone.

"I don't need to tell you about my history." Domin told her, "It is just not easy… being… me…"

"You are right, Domin. I know it is not easy for you or any of your Brothers." A tear strolled down her cheek. "I have felt the pain of each one of you from the moment the five of you came into my life." She hugged his small muscular frame again. As she held Domin, her fingers lightly played over the scars of his back.

"Those scars are only on my skin." Domin explained. He took another deep breath. "I have scars that hurt much more which you can not see."

Another tear fell from Sophia's other eye. "I'm so sorry, Domin. You always have been a very special boy to me you know. You also must know, throughout your life, you will be hurt. Those who you trust the most and who are the closest to you, the ones you love… They will be the ones who will hurt you the most. Don't let it surprise you when people you love let you down. This is the way it is for everyone." Sophia stood up.

Domin was not sure of everything she was trying to

tell him, but he knew there was more to what she was saying than what was said.

She put her hand to the door knob, but before she turned it, she paused and said to him, "You must believe me, Domin… I do feel your pain…"

Domin felt a great sense of gratitude for Sophia. He didn't have a mother. At least no mother he knew of, but she was very motherly to him.

He would try to remember her advice.

The base was loud and the music had a beat which put the body in motion. Within a spacious exercise room which was equipped with a wide assortment of weight training equipment, the Brothers tirelessly worked out. Each of the Brothers were exercising hard on a separate piece of equipment and each one of them had their own personal coach. They worked up a dripping sweat as the coaches drove them hard. It was the job of the coaches to work the Brothers to the point of total exhaustion. The endurance was inhuman, but the Brothers were not aware of how much greater their endurance was. They were told by their coaches to go further and give more effort. But as always, at the end of the day, they were told how great and special they were. Though a lot of time was spent to tell the Brothers they were created to do great things, the Brothers did not really listen to what was said. Later, however, they would come to realize how these moments were meant as confidence builders. It was to provide a sense of positive thinking. Throughout the exercises, the Brothers were attached to a series of wires connecting them to their own computer to monitor the changes in their bodies throughout their routines.

The room was buzzing with activity. There were technicians and camera crews along with some military personnel who had shown up for a work out. At the center of the room Dr. McNeil stood with Dr. Evon as they compared pages from various spread sheets attached to their clip boards. They made comments and checked off items one by one as they strolled around the room visiting each of the Brothers and checking their computers.

Like machines, the Brothers worked the exercise equipment. Exercise was not only a great way for the Brothers to escape their problems but it was also like a drug to them. A robotic like trance was noted on the faces of the Brothers on more than one occasion. One of the camera crew members made a comment once how the Brothers had expressions of wide eyed insanity when they were in training. The more they exercised, the more they felt the need to push their routines further. In these moments, unrealized by any of the technicians, they would sink deeper into their own private place of rage. This was also a primitive place of power, control, self awareness and ultimately invincibility. None of the brilliant scientist understood the full extent of what was happening at the core of each of the Brothers. Nor would any of them speak about it for such transformations were occurring at their core, in their sub-conscious.

Primarily, the living flesh and DNA was dominating the human soul's of the young boys, only, it was happening at such a subtle pace, the changes were masked by the natural changes of their growing young forms. The testosterone levels were increased and far more potent. It was like steroids for them so even the parts of the children's bodies which were human would also respond and grow. Such body parts were; bones, skin and muscles.

When they exercised, they would actually be speeding up these processes. Unfortunately, their young human minds were not so quick to accept and adjust to the volk implants. A chemical imbalance in the brains of humans was a sure side effect. This imbalance was sure to trigger mood swings of violent natures. It was ironic how a creature as sophisticated as a volk could cause humans to become primitive and brutally angry.

The drum beat of the music became heavier. The music, louder and more intense. With this pace the exercises the Brothers were engaged in had also heightened. The equipment was being worked at its peek of potential.

Domin was engaged in lifting a barbell weighing 150 pounds.

Stroy was focused with a determined expression upon his face as he pushed his favourite powerful leg weights of 200 pounds.

Narl was tensed up and in deep concentration while pulling down on the bow flex.

Grud, huffed with persistence and drive, pushing up a maximum weight of 180 pounds with his spectacular volk arms.

Oblit was going crazy on the pedal bike making the difficult tension look easy.

The human veins looked as though they were so thick, they were going to explode. At the peek of their work out, the technicians and camera crews began to take an interest in these veins. The veins of the Brothers became red and the blood could literally be seen pumping through them.

While all of this was going on, Narl's mind was busy. He exercised with his eyes and ears closed. With so much blood pumping through his volk mind, he was able to trigger an extra sensory perception. Volks are capable of this ability but not without a significant amount of focus. Extraordinarily, Narl had achieved a telepathic connection to the minds of his Brothers, though at some basic level. Familiar with this method of the mind, Narl had experienced something very similar when Gastonish telepathically linked with his mind. With this new experience he simply continued his moderate exercise while he observed.

The music took an incredible turn as it changed midway through the high temp beat to a slow and dreary melody.

The Brothers were warned this would happen and they tried to work through the change in music and carry on with their routines, but it was as though someone had taken all of the wind out of their sails. At once, their veins subsided until they could barely be seen.

Just then, Narl tried to make his presence known to his Brothers by speaking to them in their minds. He wanted to give them a message to work harder and to prove music has no bearing on the kind of exercise they do. This message was not received in this way at all.

Each of the Brothers immediately clapped their hands over their ears and screamed out their pain. Like a claw scratching deep gouges into their brains along with a powerful reverberating sound, they each shared the excruciating experience. Narl felt their pain also but only as some sort of telepathic feed back. He too was distracted and released his hold of the bow flex. The bow flex reeds snapped back to their up-right positions.

As instantly as the pain began, it ceased. Everyone decided to take a moment to wind down. Each of the Brothers were given a glass of water. When the water had quenched their thirst and the heavy breathing had subsided, the questions began to start.

"What happened to you guys back there?" asked a coach.

"Ya, what was all of that about?" asked another.

Stroy began to answer. "It was very strange, like someone..."

"Had pushed a knife into your brain?" Narl finished Stroy's sentence.

"Yes, why yes, that was exactly what I was going to say." Stroy commented suspiciously.

"Well, that's not what it felt like to me at all." Domin started, "I felt like someone was trying to..."

"Get inside your head?" Narl answered again.

Domin glared at Narl. "Sure, like a telepath." Domin uncovered the obvious with a cold warning interwoven in the way he spoke.

All attention went to Narl. The camera crews along with the coaches doctors and technicians. "Are you telepathic?" Someone asked.

"Can you tell me what I am thinking right now?" they went on and on.

While Narl was overwhelmed with questions, Dr. McNeil and Dr. Evon were listening to what was being said as they walked around from one computer to the next to see the charts. The computerized charts from each of the exercise stations held a wealth of information. From the results, Dr. McNeil and Dr. Evon were able to find, without a doubt, evidence of Narl's telepathic ability and the effects these very specific brain waves had on the other Brothers.

Amidst the chaos of questions, all of the Brothers began to complain of migraine head-aches.

The doctors huddled together outside from the range of the camera crews and collaborated amongst themselves. "You know of the heat we are under from the higher-ups? Perhaps now is a perfect opportunity for us to consider negotiations with interested foreign nations."

"You mean, use Narl as our back up of persuasion?"

43

asked Dr. Evon as he crossed his arms and eased back into his seat.

"No," Replied Dr. McNeil with a crooked smile. "Not back-up. Come, I think it's time we have a little chat with Narl."

The five Brothers were all strapped into their heavy metal chairs which were bolted to the four inch thick steel plated floor of a large cargo container. The seat belts of the chairs were like the ones used by military single pilot aircrafts. The confinements of the cargo container was poorly lit with a few small battery powered lights.

Strapped into the row of seats were two armed guards who were dressed in black fatigues and loaded to the hilt with weapons. The two guards spoke not a word. They looked identical because of their large helmets.

Narl, telepathically asked his Brothers. "Why can't these responsible people be more specific about where they are sending us? Why do they need guards when they already have our co-operation? And why are we facing the wall when we should be pointed in the direction where we are heading?" The others could not provide answers to Narl's questions because the telepathic process was far too excruciating.

However, Domin leaned in toward Narl rubbing his head and said, "Brother or no brother, if you try to get inside my skull one more time, it'll be the end of you."

Narl could feel the intense anger radiating off Domin, and the others also glared at him with equal fuming tempers.

They could feel the momentum and hear when they were loaded onto a flat-bed transport, then onto a plane. They were relieved when they had finally touched down in a new territory after the long flight. From the plane the container was loaded onto a transport again and driven to a stop where the side of the container was opened and a black curtain covered the wide opening just beyond the thick bars. The Brothers were waited on with refreshments as the entire journey was a full nineteen hours.

The voices of European political heads were heard echoing throughout a large room. Narl could read the minds of the delegates at the private meeting. Through the use of his telepathy, Narl could also see what they could see. Though they spoke in their Russian language, Narl could understand them even better from their thoughts. The mind link helped him to sharpen his skills at the foreign speech. The others had to rely on the translators for understanding.

They had set the container on the far end of the inner warehouse. The meeting was being held in a Soviet military air-force hangar. The Soviet air-force base was located in the northern region of Soviet soil. They too had a secret they kept veiled behind a red curtain.

The voice of an American government negotiator spoke with strong bold words. "Thank you for you hospitable welcome, but there is no need to continue this senseless review of our joint policy act. Let's get down to the real reason we are all meeting here today." He turned away from the microphone for just a moment to clear his throat before he continued. "We are aware you have knowledge of the life forms who dwell within our borders and who are, lawfully, our property. I am speaking of an alien race known as *Volks*. Primarily I am speaking of the mother and child whom we have come to know as Gastonish and Eddy." The hangar was dead silent. The spokes person had everyone's attention, completely. "These creatures, who came from another world of un-Earthly origin, are like no other intelligent creature we have encountered from space. The threat of this species coming to our world to dominate it, is all too real, however so unbelievable as it may seem. As we have made ourselves clear, so many times in the past, we can not risk exposing Eddy or Gastonish to other foreign powers. Our agreement was not to bring them here today..." The negotiator's voice was cut short as the Russians voiced their disappointment and disdain. It was their understanding they would have the opportunity to view the volks in person.

The Russians were so upset, in fact, they had all of the locked doors barricaded and guards were posted at the exits. The Americans were also surrounded with armed Soviet soldiers.

"You, you Americans have violated our agreement! Open the curtains!!!" commanded the Russian consulate, Sergei Laurov. A soldier stepped up to the container and pulled the black curtain down so the curtain tore away from the fasteners which held it to the top rim of the container.

It was then the Brothers were exposed. They sat in their chairs, still buckled in securely. The tension immediately disappeared as all eyes became fixed on the young half-volks.

At the drop of the curtain, Narl could not keep himself from fixing his eyes on the red curtain on the Soviet's side of the hangar.

One of the American government agents leaned in close to Dr. McNeil's ear and whispered something to him. Dr. McNeil stood up and walked to the staircase at the side of the container. He used an electronic key card to unlock the door to the canister. When he entered the canister, he immediately approached Narl. He bent forward and leaned in close to his ear, "Now Narl, you know what to do..." But Narl did not respond to Dr.

McNeil, not in the least. "W-what's wrong with him?" Dr. McNeil directed his question to the Brothers.

"We don't know." answered Grud with a blank expression.

"He has always been a little strange." came an explanation from Stroy.

"A little?" questioned Domin humorously, but Domin noticed Narl's ear pinna tragus and anti-tragus was closed which was a sure sign if he was shutting out the world by plugging his ears, he was locked in telepathically.

"We need him to co-operate with us now!" Dr. McNeil glanced back at Narl with disappointment in his eyes. "You are his Brothers. One of you has got to get through to him. Do whatever you have to, now!" discouraged, Dr. McNeil stood up and stormed out of the container.

"What are these, *things*, supposed to be?" asked Sergei, the Russian delegate as he turned his head slightly and twisting his nose up in disapproval, "They are not volks."

"These are subjects who are apart of a very special scientific experiment." The American negotiator, Willis, took over the conversation. "If we are to be invaded by such powerful creatures as these volks, we will need a way to protect ourselves. Through these five Brothers, we can see how our genetics are not so indifferent from the volks. They differ by only one chromosome. Here, in these Brothers you can see how we as humans can make an unprecedented leap in our own evolution. Witness the success we have found in the grafting together of human and volk flesh."

They waited for just a moment to find what kind of reaction they would have from the Russians. Finally, the answer they had waited for came, "This could very well be some unequivocal hoax. We will need a tissue sample to verify both human and volk are indeed bondable." Sergei cocked a skeptical eye.

From this remark, a European crew of four doctors, dressed in white lab coats and carrying their own case of medical supplies, entered the container hesitantly. Through a time consuming course of procedures, the doctors made their way from one brother to the next until they had seen each one and from each one a physical examination was performed. The scars were checked over for validity and documented as where each incision was made. Finally skin, blood and tissue samples were taken. An American agent met the doctors as they were leaving the container at which time he had given them a packaged folder which contained many experimental results.

It did not take long before the samples were authenticated. The Russian delegate, Sergei Laurov, returned to his podium and spoke into the microphone, "It does not matter to us that you have created these freaks, or how you have living creatures known as volks. You think you have the upper hand, no? But you do not. It is not so special for you to have volks when you see, we too have one of our own." The great red curtain dropped and a huge fully matured volk stood there at a height of twelve feet tall. He was menacing with broad shoulders and decked out in some heavy black armor. Its limbs were laced with many cybernetic implants and prosthetics. Though it marveled the senses, it carried an apparent history of difficulties, failures and pain. But despite the set backs the Russians had certainly experienced success with their volk. It was a powerful and shocking sight to find a living and breathing volk in Russian custody.

The surprise of setting eyes upon the powerful might

of the Soviet cyborg volk seemed to over accentuate its massive muscles. For a moment, it was as though the might of the Soviet cyborg volk filled the entire hangar.

"You thieves!!!" shouted Dr. McNeil as he pointed at the Soviet cyborg volk. "You are the ones who stole our volk heart!" Sure enough, as plain as day, the volk heart, encased in a liquid filled, sphere shaped glass container was embedded in the cyborg chest and thumping away.

Thumpity – thump – thumpity – thump...

Hoses and electrical wires could be seen bound to the heart and channeling all which was required to keep it pumping strong and mature. Though the heart was powerfully active, it was well yoked in place within the jar with a unique harness of stability.

The hangar erupted into a roar of angry voices. Threats and demeaning insults were spat back and forth as each side expressed how they had been victimized by the other.

A petrified expression of concentration seemingly cast in stone was upon the darkened face of the cyborg Russian volk.

When the Russian delegate began his squabbling again, to intimidate the Americans, Domin was the first to realize Narl was not being difficult, rather he was busy, engaged in a telepathic link with the Soviet cyborg volk.

Domin began to whisper his suspicions into his brother's ears. Then he tried to signal Dr. McNeil, but he was too wound up about the stolen volk heart. Domin tried to get the attention of anyone who would pay him some mind. Everyone, however, was transfixed on the opposite side of the hangar... The menacing cyborg volk.

The Americans present were in a state of shock,

unprepared as they did not suspect the Russians of having a volk at all.

A Russian technician came to the podium and began to direct everyone's attention to a mechanical device which was attached to the left half of the volk's head. "We assure you this volk is entirely under our control. With the mind restraint, this volk depends on us to do all of its thinking for it. We are all quite safe and I would advise you to use the same safeguards on, not only your volks, but these strange mock-ups as well." He glared at the five Brothers. Not only did they glare right back at the Russian speaker, but the cyborg volk also turned its eye to look at him as well. No one seemed to notice the small detail of the cyborg volk's eye as it quickly returned its gaze back to the fore-front.

All of the Brothers took an immediate offense to what the Russian speaker said about the mind control device. "How could he make such a blatant suggestion?" asked Stroy malignantly.

"How dare he have the audacity!" Spoke Grud with a dark shadowy dryness in his voice. "Haven't we lost enough? Now we are expected to forfeit our sanity?"

Oblit began to spaz out and fight against his restraints. He paused a moment with his entire body tensed up and pushing against the straps which held him. "Have we not been through enough pain?"

Narl then opened his eyes wide and his mouth even wider as the communication between him and the Soviet cyborg volk finally reached a climax.

The mind controlling device no longer had any affect while Narl was in control of the beast. The Soviet cyborg volk's eye blinked as though awakening from a deep sleep. It then, under Narl's control, turned to the Russian stage of representatives. It move on them and wrapped its' powerful mechanical hands around the structure of the stage, the Russian technician at the microphone began pointing and shouting at one of his counterparts who was at a computer terminal.

Panic filled the hangar when the Soviet cyborg volk began to tear the stage from its footings. There was no doubt the cyborg volk was out of control. Chaos followed as the Russians tried desperately to flee for their lives. They jumped over one another as they struggled to clear out. Their efforts were, however, in vain. There was no time available to react.

The Brothers tried franticly to remove their restraints, but they could not. A few swift Russians were quick to fire some shots at the volk but the shots merely ricocheted off his armor. The American armed forces were not given the order to engage the cyborg volk so they were forced to stand down though they would have had plenty of opportunity to react and target its weak points.

Within a matter of seconds the Soviet cyborg volk had torn the stage free and hurtled it in the direction of the on-looking Americans. At this unexpected action, chaos spread through every inch of the entire hangar.

What happened next was like a living nightmare for the Brothers. The Soviet cyborg volk began to advance on them as it stomped its heavy feet to the concrete floor as it march closer and closer.

More than ever, the Brothers fought against their restraints, all except for Narl of course. Oblit let out a cry of insanity, before he managed to tear himself loose, his great volk chest yearning for the heart of the soviet cyborg volk. Guards were given the signal of authority to shoot at the dangerous advances of the unpredictable cyborg volk. The two armed guards who stood at each end, within the container, began to open up on the Soviet cyborg volk with their assault rifles. Lifting its heavy metal arm to protect its face, the cyborg volk continued its advance. At close range, sparks sprang from the robotic prosthetics of the Soviet cyborg volk's arm as shots rattled off.

When a couple of bullets sparked off the jar of the cyborg's heart, a long thin crack appeared across the glass surface. Oblit flew at the guard firing his rifle snatched from his grasp with a quick fluent motion as he passed by.

Effortlessly, and with no distraction from the bullets, the cyborg volk brushed the bars of the container out of its way. The bars snapped free rapidly. Oblit dropped the rifle to the floor and turned around only to be mesmerized by the beautiful volk heart beating in a golden yellow liquid before him. The Brothers who were still bound to their seats thought they were being attacked. Despite the attempts to thrash their way free the Brothers were unable to free themselves from the seat restraints.

A quick movement of the cyborg volk's arm knocked the unarmed guard to the ground. The other guard turned to aim his weapon to defend his partner. As Narl gave the thought command for the cyborg volk to confiscate the guard's machine gun also, Narl knew he would be too late but Oblit appeared from out of nowhere. Spinning through the air flailing his arms and legs, Oblit slapped the weapon out from the guard's grip and kicked him in the head. The guard fell heavy and limp.

Reaching into the container, the Soviet cyborg volk broke Narl's straps free. Narl snapped out of his hypnotic telepathy and the moment he did so, the Soviet cyborg volk froze in place. The telepathic link was broken. With no further thought or direction, it merely waited for its next command.

"Do not fight him!" Narl told his Brothers. "I control him! You can fight with him!" But the cyborg volk began to back up a step and straighten his stance as it seemed to be thinking for itself. Narl fell back into a seat where he could concentrate. Raising its hand to its head, the cyborg volk lightly touched the mind control device which was mounted to the side of his head. He found his sense of touch was missing as the metal cybernetic fingers clanked and scraped against the housing of the device. A look of sadness washed over the volk's face as it found a sense of not being able to connect to many of its emotions. Its life was no longer its own.

The eye of the cyborg volk grew wide and a sensation of insane frustration, coupled with the will to survive, filled the creature's soul. It scratched at the foreign device attached to its head which both damaged it and caused excruciating pain. Reeling back, the cyborg volk roared like the wild beast everyone saw it to be.

Narl tried very hard to re-establish his telepathic link but the cyborg was no longer co-operating. In fact, the telepathy began to have much the same irritating effect it had on Narl's Brothers.

The cyborg volk began pounding at the container to make the telepathy stop. Domin shook Narl, "Stop this right now!" He told him, "Don't you see, you are making it go mad!"

Narl came out of his mental communication just as Oblit, Stroy and Grud leaped out of the container and attacked the twisted cyborg volk.

Though the Brothers were just children, they were a formidable team for their passion was for the fight. Each of the Brothers, fought with their own unique pattern which exclusively suited their specific ability. Though they were young and in need of the polishing up of their skills, they had a lot of experience already at beating up on each other. Now, however, they had an opportunity to fight as a team and rely on each other's strengths.

The cyborg swung its pinching hand at the Brothers as they flew at him. While Stroy and Grud faced the menace from the front, Oblit snuck around undetected. He pounced onto the volk's back and pulled at wires and thin steel rods which ran up under the volks skin at the base of his skull. The Soviet cyborg volk spun and fell back onto the canister, but before he did so, Oblit had sprang up so high he caught hold of an over-head hangar crane.

Domin and Narl dashed out of the canister as the large volk flattened it as if it were made of tin foil. The cyborg volk was down and it was having a lot of difficulty getting back up.

In the meantime, Domin called to his Brothers to help lift the stage and rescue the people who were trapped inside. Many of the people were injured and in desperate need of immediate medical attention. The main doors of the hangar opened as Soviet military aid was on the scene.

Narl sent a telepathic suggestion to his Brothers. The suggestion was about how wonderful it would be to escape all of this and be free from the control and pain of the Governing forces. The only problem with this suggestion was how it was received in candescent pain. Each of the four Brothers bent forward in unison placing their hands to their heads like a great serge of pain had hit them in the form of a mass migraine headache. Domin put one arm around Narl's shoulders then he slugged him in the nose with his fist. "I told you, brother..." Domin spoke harshly under his breath. "Don't do that..." Then as an after thought, Domin added, "It was a nice thought

54

though." The others smiled at the comment while trying not to be obvious about it and keep it on the low-low.

The Brothers were busy moving pieces of debris from the stage into a pile when the cyborg volk rose up for round two. He tore the canister in half and took a step toward the Brothers. The canister was just a sample of what the soviet cyborg volk had in mind for them. It was also advancing on the wounded as well.

Narl faced the cyborg volk and placed one hand to the side of his head. His mental command caused the cyborg volk to stumble backwards as though it were hit by a powerful weight. The cyborg volk turned to look over its shoulder at the Brothers. It glared with a violent hatred in its eyes. Then, strangely, it focused in on Narl. Without warning, the cyborg volk had leaned forward into a rampaging charge. It ran at the people causing the concrete floor to shake with each pounding foot step.

Stroy ran headlong at the cyborg volk, but the cyborg had only one target, Narl. Sliding across the floor, Stroy moved low and between its legs. When he was right under the cyborg, he kicked out his legs at its ankles. This caused the cyborg to trip and fall forward. It slammed its large metal framed jaw onto the floor. Oblit came from out of the rafters and landed on the volk's back, wondering if the jar of the heart was ruptured. Grud ran out with his massive volk arms raised up over his head, where he drove his fists down with all of his might. He smashed the cyborg's head to the floor just to be certain he would not forget the taste of the concrete.

Surprisingly, the robotic fingers of the cyborg took hold of Grud's leg. He threw him to the far wall. Again, the cyborg rose to his feet, its volk heart beating powerfully within the cracked housing of the jar. It held out its mechanical arms and on the right arm a manie gun popped out. A flame thrower surfaced from his other

55

mechanical arm.

Rapid fire pummeled the Brothers as they quickly fled the hail of powerful bullets from the cyborg's machine gun. Meanwhile, the flame thrower lit up in a spray of liquid fire. Domin was already on the move, he made his way around to the side of the cyborg volk and moved in on him with all of his might. His speed rammed the cyborg so hard he was pushed right off the ground where he was sent through the side wall of the hangar.

The aluminum siding tore open under the soviet cyborg's weight like it was made of paper. Domin had bounced off the robotic monstrosity which did not phase him in the least. He broke out into running. He bolted out through the great torn opening in the side of the hangar. Domin's Brothers followed close behind. At the moment the open air washed over them, they slowed for a moment to take in their surroundings.

It was this moment when the Brothers shared the same sense of freedom even though on either side of them were isles of Soviet military aircrafts. The jet fighters were like a fleet of soldiers standing at attention with their noses pointed upwards professionally and egotistically.

Overhead, a swarm of Sukhoi Su-15 Flagon soviet air assault interceptors circled like vultures.

The Soviet cyborg volk stirred as it rose up from the pavement. Placing its robotic hand to its chest, the soviet cyborg volk found the yellow liquid was leaking out of its heart jar. It lifted its' weapon and began firing rapid rounds of armor piercing ammo at Domin. As Domin ran around the volk, it decided to raise its' other flame throwing arm attachment weapon to target even one of the little expedient Brothers.

Fire bellowed from the flame thrower. Stroy, with his powerful volk legs, had leaped clear over the head of the soviet cyborg volk. He landed next to Domin and scooped him up just as the flame thrower seared at him. Stroy's powerful legs elevated them over the height of the cyborg.

When the cyborg volk looked up to watch Stroy and Domin come back down, the other Brothers worked together to attack the cyborg volk from behind. Stroy and Domin fell like boulders as they came back down to earth, while Narl, Grud and Oblit noticed a Mikoyan Gurevich MiG-23 Soviet "swing wing" aircraft fighter bearing down on them aggressively. The cyborg volk fell forward with Narl, Grud and Oblit pounding and tearing at it from its back. The Brothers moved with the likeness of a wild and hungry pack of wolves.

When the cyborg volk fell forward, he sprawled out over the pavement with his flame thrower blazing across the ground. Stroy and Domin landed in the midst of the flames. Stroy knew only how it was too hot for them on the ground. Immediately, he jumped again while carrying his brother, Domin. The Mikoyan Gurevich MiG-23 began to open fire on its low approach.

Domin noticed a danger when the flames were sprayed near to a refueling station. As he ascended over the shoulder of Stroy, he found it difficult to warn his Brothers. Despite Stroy's shoulder digging into his side, he managed to say; "Get out of here! Its' gonna Blow!!!"

Before they knew it, the Mikoyan Gurevich MiG-23 soviet aircraft came in too fast and too close, as the pilot fought to veer off missing Stroy and Domin as they were in mid leap. They jumped so high, they came right up into the jets' flight path. With some quick thinking, Stroy and Domin successfully grabbed hold of the underside of the jet. Stroy used the strength of his powerful and agile volk feet to secure a grip. The two of them took off with such force, Domin thought his arms were going to be torn off, while Stroy was certain his feet would be severed if not for the volk support.

The cyborg volk began rolling over. Its' flamethrower attachment was obviously damaged and it was not going to be able to stop blowing fire until its' fuel was depleted. Bending forward, the flame showered over the refueling station. Narl, Grud and Oblit looked on with their eyes wide with surprise. They bolted from the area, making tracks as fast as they could. The three Brothers booked past the torn open hole on the side of the hangar. The people inside watched curiously as the Brothers ran past.

Dr. McNeil was the first to realize the emanate danger when the flames rained over the fuel tanker trucks that were parked next to the jet refueling station. The on-lookers ducked back into the hangar and warned the others to get back. The flames spread quickly as they consumed the entire station and set it all ablaze. The cyborg volk was unaware of the dangers around him. He was just trying to rise up to his feet once again.

Narl, Grud and Oblit had run out into an open area of the air strip. Narl shouted to his Brothers, "Hold it!" The others stopped to look at him. They had hopes they were at a safe distance away from the expected explosion. "We will be unsuccessful in our attempt to outrun the fire when it blows!"

Oblit looked around quickly, then without speaking a word he put one finger from each hand into the holes of a man-hole cover which was just under their feet. He lifted, but the metal cover was too heavy. Narl and Grud bent down with their brother and readied themselves to assist. When the lid was lifted enough for the other Brothers to slip their fingers under it, they worked together to lift it up.

The refueling station, along with a number of tanker trucks, ignited into a thermal explosion. The magnitude of destructive light and burning bits of materials had such force behind it, the explosion threw many of the aligned MiG-25, "Foxbat" jet fighters out across the air field.

The soviet cyborg volk was also caught up in the explosion which sounded like a final benevolent roar of life from the mouth of the beast.

Fire and chemical gas threatened to devour everyone and everything, but the initial bright flash of the explosion was quickly replaced with a thick black plume of black ash. Oxygen followed in with a salty breeze from the ocean.

Narl, Grud and Oblit slid the man-hole cover to the side and emerged from the drainage pipes. It served as a formidable retreat. When they climbed out, they met the burned corps of the soviet cyborg volk. Its' chest had been blown open, the jar had been shattered and the odour of burned, sizzling flesh hung heavily in the air. Within the cavity of the cyborg volk's chest, still strapped to the harness was the charred remains of the lifeless volk heart.

An eerie calmness existed over the entire base. But they knew it was just the calm before the storm. The Sukhoi Su-15 Flagon interceptors circling over head were careful not to fly too low as there could be more explosions to follow.

Narl pointed to one of the "Flogger" jets and the others quickly saw how Domin and Stroy were hanging from the belly of it. Many other jets were obviously informed of the stow-a-ways and followed close behind in a 'V' formation. Narl, Grud and Oblit watched as Domin and Stroy held onto the Mikoyan Gurevich MiG-23. The close knit fleet traveled over head and headed out over the ocean. As the fleet began to circle, Domin and Stroy let go of the jet and dropped into the waves off shore.

Oblit and Grud began to run toward them to rescue them from drowning, but Narl shouted. "No! Not that way! The soviets will surely cut us down if they catch us running all the way to the ocean."

"We can not just sit here." Came Grud with a dark coolness to the tone of his voice which masked the frustration and panic he felt.

"This way, Brothers." replied Narl as he disappeared back into the drainage system. The large underground drain led them straight to the ocean. The three of them could be heard breathing and splashing as they ran as fast as they could to get to the end of the pipe.

When they finally reached the end of the pipe, they were met with bars which blocked the entrance of the drainage system. Grud pushed his way past his Brothers and grabbed a hold of the bars. His enormous volk arms expanded as his muscles tightened under the thick grey skin. He jerked forward, before he pulled back. With his volk muscles taut, dark red veins pumped blood over the surface of his grey skin. He worked the bars with twisting and turning until they gave way under the pressure. The concrete cracked and broke as the bars were quickly miss-shapened. Then with an attitude of boredom, Grud pushed the bars aside and they crumpled in on themselves.

The three Brothers, wounded, climbed out of the pipe and moved swiftly across the beach to the low tide. Domin and Stroy were not far away and they could see them swimming to shore. Narl, Grud and Oblit ran into the ocean.

When all of the Brothers met, they were in ocean shallow enough they could all stand up. "Are you injured?" Narl quickly asked Domin and Stroy.

"We are fine." Domin answered as Stroy coughed out sea water. "Look, Brothers, we have done it. This is our golden opportunity. Let's get out of here and be free of these scientists once and for all."

There was a long silence as the Brothers considered Domin's proposal. They looked around at the beauty of the ocean. It was not so dissimilar from the pictures they had seen of a tropical paradise.

"I'm with Domin." Grud said with agreement, "We absolutely must get out of here. We all know the next thing we will lose is our minds if we stay."

"We need to get moving right away." Stroy added.

"Hold it!" Narl announced clearly. "Being free is easier said than done." Narl told them. "Where would we go?" He asked. No one had an answer. "We are in Russian waters. Do you propose to swim away? And if we go back to land how sure can you be we can find a safe place where we will not be found? No, we will be hunted and killed."

"Look, Narl, you are a smart guy, but if we go back willingly, they will kill us." Grud warned them. "I will have to stick with Domin on this one."

"How can you be so sure they will kill us? I suspect not only will the Americans protect us, but they will commend us for returning to them willfully and we will build a trust which has not been established yet. It will be through this trust and willful co-operation where we will guarantee no mind control devices will be necessary." explained Narl persuasively.

Grud did not need a second to think about the situation. For him everything was quite clear. "Narl, that is your opinion. I have my own opinion, and I am getting out of here." Grud eyed his Brothers. "Who's with me?" He stood back. The sea water lapped against his chest as his other Brothers looked at him. He expected the others with the exception of Narl perhaps, to join him right away and he was surprised when this did not happen. "What is it? You all need more time to think about this?" No one spoke a word but much was being said. "Hey, this our freedom. Our long awaited and well deserved freedom. What difference does it make if we are in America or Russia. Freedom for us will always be the same, because, face it. We *are* freaks. It is our destiny to be treated as freaks no matter where we are."

"And it is to that fact where I would like to point out the Americans have given us a place to call home. I am not disagreeing with anything you say, Grud, but perhaps this isn't the perfect timing for our great escape."

"Whatever!" Grud was openly discouraged. "Don't you know we are wasting time talking about this? We need to act." Pounding the water's surface and pointing, Grud continued to argue. "Right now they are regrouping and organizing. It won't be long before they start looking for us..." Grud let out a breath of disappointment. "Do whatever you want. I'm out'a here."

Grud turned to swim away, but Domin reached out and grabbed him by the shoulder. "We are Brothers." He said forcefully. "And we can't afford to split up. Just look up" He said and they all looked skyward. "Those air-crafts are not just circling because they have nothing better to do. They are keeping tabs on us. They will follow us no matter where we want to go, and they will take us before we have an opportunity to meet land... Come on. We need to heed, Narl's suggestions. He has not steered us wrong in the past."

Grud put his hands to his face and kneaded his fore-head like he had a head-ache. "Alright then, what are we going to do next?"

"We go back to the underground pipes and get back

to the Americans as quickly as possible." Narl instructed.

Though returning to the Americans was not a simple task, a speedy call for military reinforcements was made. The Soviets lost the opportunity to capture the Brothers so they tried to blame the Americans for the costly loss at the air field and their secret weapon, the Soviet cyborg volk. Before the Brothers returned to American soil, a fair compensation for damages had to be worked out in a peaceful manner with the Soviets. Within military circles, aggressive tactics were on the verge of being deployed, but Government heads did not want to call attention to the secret meeting. With the names of those involved with the covert affiliation, it would raise too many questions where the leaking of top secret subjects related to volks would be too risky.

The Americans, along with the Brothers, were granted diplomatic immunity before they boarded a plane to take them home. The Brothers were hailed the heroes and they knew it as they each walked out from a small bus to the stairs of the passenger plane. With a confidence and strut in their step, the Brothers, in shades climbed the stairs to the plane knowing they had proven themselves valuable and how they were quite safe under the protection of American forces.

Narl in particular was proud to once again be correct in his decision making, for everything was happening just as he predicted.

Changes were evident after the return to America. The Brothers had been moved to a new military installation which was far more secure. It was located in a remote area of Alaska. Though the constant testing of the Brothers hadn't changed too much, the training they did was far more controlled by the military. Each of the

Brothers had risen through the military ranks quite steadily. Besides having the advantage of volk strengths, the Brothers were part of an elite task force of soldiers who had such refined skills, they were virtually unbeatable.

The elite soldiers prided themselves in the details of their missions. They would study their enemies and the lay outs of their strongholds. They devised mission formulations and carried out their operations exactly as predicted. Their simplest solutions being, not only the quickest but the most effective.

This elite military division of six men in Alaska, were chosen to join the Brothers in a series of difficult training exercises with the expectation of the Brothers to not only acquire equal skill, but to surpass their instructors. The program extremely belittled the recruits as a system of control using humility.

One of the elite instructors was an expert in archery and other silent weapons. Another was a master in the ninja arts. A third was an explosives and demolitions expert. A fourth opened the minds of the Brothers to unique and strenuous survival techniques along with the hidden strengths of the human body; mind over matter. The fifth was a munitions expert who trained the Brothers how to drive tanks, fly helicopters and jet air planes. A wide assortment of military vehicles, missile launchers and other weapons of the like were under study.

The sixth elite soldier was not only the strangest of the bunch but the most dangerous and unpredictable. Though he walked and talked like a man, once he began to train, it was as though he took on the personification of an animal. All of his fighting styles and techniques were derived of the animal kingdom. Many times, if it were not himself giving an example of how to defeat a wild beast with his bare hands, it was one of the Brothers. All of the

Brothers had been injured in some way during their time with him.

As the Brothers grew into teenagers, each of them experienced the same struggles with anger and rage. Due to the conflict of volk and human transplants they found the challenge of controlling their anger becoming increasingly difficult with age. Their military instructors tried to use these emotions to push their pupils harder. They were taught their anger was the source to power which would always overthrow their adversaries.

Dr. McNeil was always impressed whenever he would walk in on the Brothers practicing before a training exercise. In a group they would shadow box with countless punches at incredible speeds. Their bodies moved with an inhuman fluent speed. Rolls, tucks and a variety of effective kicks, they were very impressive. They knew, in a fight, it was not good enough to be centered with control, balance and discipline. They also had to master their speed and power. Much of their training had to do with molding and shaping their minds as fighters. It was through this and other self managing skills where they were able to hone their abilities without letting their rage get the best of them.

The structure of the training was well organized, but the Brothers still had a long way to go before they were truly in control. It was always the same. They all trained very well together, but they would all fall at once with the same Achilles heal. Rage was their greatest set-back.

The military, along with specialty scientists, were unaware of the dangerous potential they were dealing with. The exercises were a perfect way for the Brothers to sink deeper into their own fiery rage. They would go momentarily mental as they lost control, for the more they gave to feed their rage, the more their rage would demand more from them. It was consuming them.

Narl was the first one who pointed out the dangers to the consequences associated with the level of inhuman and intensive training method used. He tried to explain the conditioning of their sub-conscious and preached to his Brothers to resist the rage. "By resisting the rage within, we are resisting our own insanity. Find the line and don't cross it." Narl warned.

Though none of the Brothers were very good at talking about their own feelings, they all agreed it was too late for Oblit. It would seem rather humorous to most of the Brothers who didn't understand the full nature of what was going on, unlike the most recent incident where Oblit had seemed to go entirely insane. Within Oblit's large torso was a simple human heart and the demand put on his heart was serious enough where he had to be put on a strict schedule of meds. While in training, Oblit began destroying an indoor obstacle course where he lost all sense of completing the exercise as he was instructed. At the center of the exercise Oblit began destroying the wooden structures and the gas pipes which blew gusts of flames. The instructors tazered Oblit and they had also shot him with tranquilizers, but not before he had severely burned his arm and the left side of his face.

Since the incident, Oblit was not living in the same bunk house as the others. The Brothers felt bad for Oblit and they could sympathize with what had happened to him because it could very well happen to anyone of them as well. Narl sat with his remaining Brothers and tried to share with them some of the thoughts he was able to receive from the instructors. The Brothers had found it tolerable to link with Narl's mind as long as it was important enough and brief. They could learn from their instructor's experiences and assimilate their skills with ease. In this way they were able to match and often exceed their teacher's ability.

All of the Brothers cared for one another deeply and the telepathy orchestrated by Narl only proved it.

Again the Brothers were woken up early in the morning and taken to a remote area in Alaska. They were driven to a white dome, where inside, another senseless obstacle course awaited them. The six elite soldiers stood in single file and at attention. Next to them, the Brothers also stood at attention.

Looking across to the other side of the dome, they could see Oblit. His arms and legs were bound out straight, like a star formation, and he was within a metal barred cage. The cage was built as a double cage, one next to the other. Oblit was in one cage while the second cage was empty. Within the cage Oblit was roaring and yelling in a fit of rage. He was foaming at the mouth and he looked malnourished. A guard who was posted at the cage door was instructed to enter the cage and gag Oblit.

Though it was quieter after he was gagged, the Brothers did not feel better about what they had seen. A drill instructor came out to inspect the line before he explained to everyone what he expected of them as they maneuvered the course. As always, the course was designed to allow the trainee to exercise all of the skills they developed. They were expected to shoot arrows, fire weapons, balance along high wires and fight against martial artists and wild animals alike.

When the drill instructor had finished explaining all of these things, he added, "All of you are expected to pass this obstacle course with no problems since it is not designed with any more difficulty than you are all accustomed to. Once you have all completed the course and navigated to the flag area at the other end, we will release your brother, Oblit. With regret, we are informing you now upon the moment Oblit fails any aspect of the course, he will be immediately terminated."

The mouths of Domin, Grud and Stroy literally dropped open and their eyes widened. "Does Dr. McNeil know about this?" Domin shouted out.

"Silence!" The drill sergeant shot back. "You will learn your place, Domin. You are soldiers now! You and your Brothers." He said, half mocking them. "All I ask is for you all to complete the course. Is that not fair for you girls?"

"It is fair, Drill sergeant!" Narl shouted.

Domin, Stroy and Grud looked at Narl without turning their heads. They remained standing at attention while inside, they were digging deep into a fresh supply of anger. Their bodies tightened as veins popped out over their fore-heads.

A foreign thought poked into their minds. Grud, Stroy and Domin winced as they were suddenly aware of Narl's plan to assist Oblit telepathically through the obstacle course. It would not be easy, but it maybe the only way for the Brothers to protect Oblit.

First, Domin went through the course, followed by Grud, then Stroy and finally, Narl. The guard at Oblit's caged was ordered to release Oblit. He walked up a platform, into the empty cage next to Oblit. The guard locked the cage door behind him by punching a code into the electronic pad lock. A separate pad lock was mounted next to him and he punched a different code into it. Oblit's cage door had unlocked and swung open. He then bent down and pulled two pins from the floor which released Oblit's ankles. Then the guard pulled two pins from over his head and Oblit's wrists were freed.

Oblit tore the gag from his mouth and sprung from the cage. He roared horrendously. He turned on the guard. Anger burned in his eyes. He leapt to the cage as though he was about to tear it apart. The rifles of the military were cocked from either side of the dome. Guards flooded into the dome and took aim at Oblit.

Oblit did not take his eyes off the guard as he growled low and ominous. The guard could not keep himself from shaking. Sweat began to bead upon his forehead.

The eyes of Oblit suddenly relaxed and he slowly climbed down from the cage. He took a couple of steps back and put his hands to his head. He looked around the dome as Narl spoke to his mind. Oblit had a sense of direction and purpose.

He turned to the obstacle course. He looked across to the far end where he could see his Brothers. Narl spoke to Oblit's mind. *"We can see you, Oblit. We are here on the other side. You can join us here where it is safe. I will be with you through the obstacle course. Just stay with me. I need your co-operation. We can do this together."*

With that said, Narl tried to keep his brother calm as he entered the course and stepped up to the first challenge. The course was timed, whereby it had to be completed under a certain time frame or else the trainee would be disqualified.

In Oblit's case, he would be dead.

The first obstacle was a series of stalls. Each of the stalls had a different weapon. The weapons were silent weapons. There were compound bows, javelins, throwing stars and darts. Each of the Brothers had been well trained with each one of the weapons. Narl assisted Oblit to choose one of the stalls at random. The stall he entered had a javelin within it. Oblit took the javelin in hand and bounced it in his hand for a moment to find the center. He fixed his legs into a stable stance as he sized up the target which was 500 meters away. With his eyes locked onto the target, Oblit ran forward like lightning and lunged the javelin into the air with every human muscle of his limbs and every volk muscle of his torso. The javelin soared through the air like a missile. The shot was a bull's eye targeted through a shadowy form of a man. Oblit hit the target dead center.

The Brother's cheered, but Oblit did not acknowledge them at all. Rather, he bent forward and put his hand to his head as the pain of Narl's telepathy began to take its tole.

Everyone was worried for Oblit's condition, until Oblit straightened up and took a deep breath. He bit back the pain and continued on. The next obstacle was the ninja challenge.

Walking out onto a bamboo floor with an empty red carpet stretched over the center of it, Oblit knew to march right out to the center of it. There he stood and waited. A narrow door slid open to the far left and one to the far right. Men came running out from the doors who were dressed in black ninja attire complete with masks and each one carried nun-chucks.

They swarmed Oblit for a moment and Oblit just stood like a statue in wait of the first strike. Finally, one of the ninjas from furthest away came dashing in toward Oblit. He used the other ninjas as leverage to jump high over the heads of the others. Spinning a nun-chuck in each hand the leaping ninja accomplished a front flip and came in at Oblit to both surprise and distract him as the others also advanced their attack.

Oblit not only snapped to life but he took on an entirely different character. He let go of his logical mind and relished in the wild monstrous side of his alter-ego. The ninja, who was coming in at Oblit from the air was twirling his nun-chucks at either side with the intent to crush Oblit's skull. With a crazy roar, he grabbed the ninja out of the air by his leg and used him to beat the other surrounding ninjas senselessly. No one was able to come near enough to Oblit to land even one blow.

Wildly, Oblit thrashed at the surrounding crowd with violent, striking blows. As the ninjas tried to gain a foot hold on the situation, Oblit was already busy building a pile of broken bodies. One speedy little ninja was able to knock off a shot to Oblit's muscled volk back with his nun-chuck.

Oblit turned to the little ninja; his eyes were wide with rage. Spinning at the ninjas with flailing arms Oblit was the bomb who sent the group of ninjas sprawling through the air. Swinging his arms again, Oblit bull dosed through another group of ninjas who were trying to regroup and they too went flying as well. Very few ninjas were left standing.

Still moving with incredible speed, Oblit created a pile of fallen ninjas before he climbed the holding a pair of nun-chucks twirling in each hand. He glared at the remaining ninjas and spoke with the sound of death in his deep chested voice, "Come..." The look in Oblit's eyes was enough to leave traumatic scars in the minds of the ninjas for the rest of their lives. They dropped their nun-chucks and fled through the still open doors at the right and left of the obstacle chamber.

Oblit, dropped his nun-chucks as one of the ninjas at the bottom of the pile groaned in pain. Oblit stepped down from atop the mound of bodies, where he stepped on the groaning ninja's head pushing his face into the red mat. It was enough to silence him.

Oblit meandered on to the next challenge. Narl gave Oblit some quick instructions and reminded him how he did not have a lot of time left. Oblit opened the door to an empty floor of rubble. With the shaking sound of an earthquake, the floor began to rise up with cables and construct itself into a three story concrete building. This

71

next room was designed to assimilate explosions within a building structure. Because the building was designed for training purposes, the building was able to dismantle and reconstruct itself after each exercise.

Oblit was familiar with it and knew to dart inside of the lowest floor. As he moved quickly through the maze of walls, explosives began to detonate. The idea of the exercise was to stay ahead of the explosions and keep a clear head in a panic situation.

Narl assisted Oblit as to where to go and Narl shared Oblit's experience as his human heart jumped with each explosion. There were no stair wells in the building, because the idea was not to climb to the next level, rather, when the explosions went off, the next level would come down around him.

Oblit made it to the first safe zone. A large hole was cut out of the ceiling above him which led to the next level up. The bottom level collapsed all around him and before he knew it he was in the second level as it came crashing down. Oblit was once again on the move running to stay ahead of the explosions within the maze of the second level.

One explosive went off near to his heel and the force of the explosion was enough to trip him up. He rolled forward but bounced back up and running. The explosions were able to come much closer to him now and the ceiling was about to come down. He continued running using both his hands and feet like an animal. Oblit's mind seemed to light up with hostility. The problem of mounting anger in conjunction with the telepathy was becoming more than he could handle. He moved like a brutish beast on all fours, but the technique was enough for him to successfully make the needed distance.

With a heavy crash the second level came down,

surrounding him. Despite the heavy dust and burned smell of the explosives, Oblit pushed on. With a roar of madness, he could feel the powerful strength of the hunter leave him. He ran with extraordinary speed, but as Oblit did so, he began to have the perception of everything moving in slow motion. Even the sounds of the explosions faded off into the distance, however the sounds of his heavy breathing and the thumping of his heart became even louder than ever. A heat surged throughout Oblit's body from his head to his feet. Then came sweat which seemed to pour from his skin. Oblit felt as though his head was beginning to expand like a balloon, his chest contracted inwards as his vision became spotted with darkness.

"I'm losing him." Narl spoke quietly as he fought to keep focused.

Domin could see Oblit emerge from the third and final level of the explosives test. When he heard Narl speak, he noticed Oblit collapse.

He still had three more challenges left of the obstacle course. The survival challenge of mind over matter, the munitions challenge of target practice with large caliber fire arms and the animal challenge. In this final challenge he would have to fight a trained tiger with the skill and technique of a tiger.

There was only one problem, Oblit wasn't getting up. Domin slapped Narl across the face, "You are not helping him! You are killing him!" Domin ran out to Oblit with Grud and Stroy following close behind. They climbed up the cage of the tiger and ran across the roof. They then leaped over the munitions course.

At a side long glance, Domin could see a sharp shooter lining up a shot from high up inside the dome. *"No, they couldn't kill him now."* Domin puzzled.

"There was still plenty of time left for Oblit to complete the obstacle course."

Stroy, with his powerful volk legs was able to jump twice as far as Domin and Grud. This put him right at Oblit's side well before Domin and Grud. As Stroy knelt down next to his sleeping brother, a quiet bullet slapped Oblit on the side of his head. The impact of the bullet caused Oblit's entire body to convulse just once.

Stroy wasn't sure what had just happened as he examined the bullet hole at the side of Oblit's head for a second. When the reality hit him that his brother was dead, he threw his head back and roared.

Domin and Grud had dived into the freezing cold pool of the survival challenge in a desperate attempt to get to Stroy and Oblit. They swam the challenge like they had never swum it before. Grud was the first one out of the pool because he had the advantage of his powerful volk arms.

Grud and Domin, with freezing cold water pouring off them, examined the bullet hole which took the life of Oblit. They stood up along with Stroy and fixed their eyes on the sharp shooter who was situated in the suspension frame work of the dome. They were about to go after him when tranquilizer darts came whistling in. The Brothers were hit with the tranquilizers and then it was over.

Chapter 3

Before the Brothers had time to mourn the passing of their beloved brother, Oblit, they were forced to under go unscheduled surgeries. No choice was given to the Brothers. They were the property of the government and they hated it. The volk parts of Oblit's body were surgically added into the bodies of the remaining living Brothers. Domin sustained the most attention as Oblit's volk chest and back was exemplified in him primarily.

Over hearing Dr. McNeil speaking to Dr. Evon as Domin was becoming more conscious after his surgeries, he heard Dr. McNeil explaining how he had added some part from the volk brain to Domin's nero nervous system. This was to assist Domin where his original human mind was deficient.

Stroy received additional pelvic assistance as Grud received additional volk chest muscles to strengthen his arms. Neck muscles and tendons were added to Narl so he would no longer need to wear a neck and head support brace. It took weeks for each of the Brothers to recuperate from the operations. They were shown a video recording of Oblit's burial. They had to miss out on it because the surgeries were very complicated and there was no way any of them would have the strength to attend.

The Brothers were furious about the entire situation. They all wished they had made the decision to escape when they were in Russia.

When the technicians were aware of just how upset the Brothers were, they called on the project manager. Dr. McNeil came to visit the bed ridden Brothers and he asked, "Why do you grieve? It is because of your unique bodies how Oblit has an opportunity to live on." The Brothers were not sure what Dr. McNeil was talking about, until he continued. "Oblit's flesh is still alive thanks to the four of you. He is alive within each one of you. He must be very grateful that most of his body did not have to be in that casket. Rather his body is in this room and it remains alive, and all of the thanks belongs to the four of you, his Brothers."

"We want to have a funeral of our own when we are well enough to do so." Domin demanded with no respect intended for Dr. McNeil.

The doctor nodded his head, "I will grant you your request, if it is truly what you want, but like I said, he is not dead. Personally, I do not believe a funeral is necessary. It is like denying the gift we have given you."

"A gift?" Narl asked with disgust. "How is it a gift when you murder our brother, force your freakish surgeries upon us and twist it all into believing we will thank you for it?"

Domin tried to rise up out of his bed, "I hate you…"

The other Brothers equally shared in Domin's hatred and despair. They pulled at their bed straps which held their wrists and ankles to the frames of their beds. As weak as they were, they revealed a display of violence and of vengeance for the blood of their brother. "If I could, I would tear your throat out." Grud told Dr. McNeil. After Grud spoke his threat, he looked away as though he were looking out into deep space. What Grud was actually experiencing was a telepathic suggestion from Narl. What he told Grud, along with the others, was to not utter another word. Vengeance would be theirs, but it would come at an opportune moment, very soon.

Dr. McNeil shrugged his shoulders and fixed his tie, "Is that supposed to surprise me? All you guys are so much alike. You hate the world, so predictable. Why

77

don't you try singing a different tune for once." he walked around the room lifting the charts which hung at the ends of their beds. Dr. McNeil scribbled something on each of the charts, "I am recommending you all to attend an anger management course once a week. I know the gentleman who will lead the sessions. He is good." He smiled and tried to suppress a chuckle. Looking up from the charts, he glanced at each one of the Brothers. "He's real good." He then, promptly left the room through the white double doors.

Within the coming hours, Domin and his Brothers had grew stronger in strength and fought against their bonds to be free. They spat cruel remarks to the doctors, telling them they were their captors and they would soon pay for holding them against their will. They became louder and louder until they were no longer making any sense and just roared like shackled beasts.

While the Brothers had their little temper tantrum, Narl was reflecting on how much sense his Brothers were making. Through all the tests and surgeries, Narl reasoned how much they were treated like dirt before he spoke. Unlike his Brothers, Narl was more level headed. "Why aren't you experimenting on the positive effects of treating us well? No, you insist on doing everything backwards! We are treated with less than favorable methods. It is not natural yet you make notes as though our negative feed back is natural, but it is just a response to the way you treat us like your lab rats!" Thick dark veins branched out over Narl's cranium.

The doctors huddled together to quietly discuss the incident. The doctors really hadn't considered the effects their experiments might have, and they didn't realize they were treating the Brothers in a demeaning fashion.

The doctors called Dr. McNeil to the room to have a

chat with the Brothers. Soon after, Dr. McNeil walked into the room with Dr. Evon. They listened to the Brothers as they explained how they felt mistreated, before Dr. Evon made a solemn vow, "I assure you all, we will do our very best to make specialized accommodations for not only you Brothers, but for Eddy and his mother, Gastonish, as well."

Though the Brothers had many questions on the matter and demanded further explanation, the doctors were not at liberty to discuss what was meant by specialized accomodations.

While Dr. McNeil opened a brief case, Dr. Evon addressed the Brothers, "Please, be patient. Dr. McNeil has something the heads of military affairs wishes to present to you, but before we continue I must ask you to place your right hands over your hearts and repeat after me; "On this day I pledge my life." The Brothers repeated the words together. "To stand and fight for freedom and justice following any and all given orders I receive." The Brothers repeated this sentence of the oath as well. "I will never quit as long as life surges through my veins. For the sake of our nation and our nation's capital we will prevail."

Domin sat back expecting the doctors to just blow more empty winded promises or to change the subject altogether.

Opening four small black cases, the Brothers could see within each case was a single golden medal. Dr. McNeil explained what the medals were and why the Brothers deserved them. "It is for your great strength and endurance, the completion of difficult tasks, training, surgeries and countless tests we have run. The Government wishes to recognize your sacrifice by awarding each of you one of these medals." Lifting out the first medal, the Brothers were in a state of awe. A bright shiny gold medallion suspended from a black ribbon with a single vertical purple stripe to the left with a golden clip at the top. Moving from one Brother to the next, Dr. McNeil clipped the small bright medal to their shirts. "You are officially part of the government's list of elite military property. You four have been designated a team code name; the Blackguards. Sworn to guard and protect the innocent. To you Brothers, the Blackguards, we applaud you and commend you."

Dr. McNeil stepped back to Dr. Evon's side and they clapped and cheered for the Brothers, as did the nursing staff. The Brothers were very proud if not for the recognition alone.

Domin lifted his medal and read the engraving which encircled a logo of a grizzly bear's claw, "The Blackguard - Elite Protector of America."

Later when the moment of praise passed and the Brothers were alone again, Stroy asked, "We have all been very bitter about the government and its military, but now we have these medals. Does this change how we feel about everything?"

Sitting in their room with a stack of twelve pizza boxes on the table, the Brothers ate and drank pop. "No it certainly does not." Narl came storming into the conversation. "This does not make up for anything and it will certainly not bring Oblit back." Narl threw his half eaten slice of pizza on his plate, disgusted.

"I have to agree with Narl on this one." Domin opened a pizza box and stacked three pieces upon one another before flipping a forth piece on top. He could barely fit his mouth around it but when he did he bit off more than he could chew.

Without speaking, the Brothers began to fill their mouths. While they were all chewing and not speaking a word, Narl tilted his head to the side ever so slightly as he invaded his Brother's minds.

On a sub-conscious level through telepathic communication the Blackguards were building a rage of one mind. As they brooded with unease for the loss of their brother, Narl could not hide how he felt responsible for Oblit's death. As the others tried to share their opinions of how Narl should not feel responsible at all, Narl pushed forward with a warning. *"Brothers, we all share a deep desire to draw strength from our anger. I believe it is a side effect of our human bodies rejecting any kind of linkage to volk flesh."* Narl began to share the final moments of Oblit's life. Narl was able to depict the experience of death in great detail, for he was telepathically linked to Oblit when he died. *"Our anger has the potential to be our greatest ally or our greatest foe. To Oblit, his anger was a death trap."* He shared how Oblit lost control to the point of no return. It was difficult to know if it was the bullet which killed Oblit, or if even before the bullet struck, he may have already been dead.

"Dr. McNeil is not our friend." Narl added. *"He is just saying what he needs too to gain our co-operation or more to the point, to keep us under his control. As long as we give them what they want we remain as test subjects with the same worth as lab rats."*

"And if we don't co-operate?" Grud asked as he cracked his volk knuckles.

"No doubt, we would share in the fate of, Oblit." Narl swiftly answered telepathically.

"Possible, of course, if we don't co-operate, we would be forced to have mind control devices attached to our heads." Domin reminded them.

This final comment left them to brood all the more. The Brothers loathed the idea of such nightmarish devices.

Narl explained to them how he does not want to be connected to any emotions any longer. For now on he would dedicate the rest of his life to logic. His Brothers admired and understood him completely. They agreed with him and made the decision to follow logic as well.

When Dr. McNeil and the other nursing staff returned to the Brothers, they found them to be far more silent than usual. The Brothers needed to formulate a plan, but for the moment they were biding their time.

As anger escalated between the Blackguards, Narl had his hands full in his attempts to calm his Brothers down. He had to remind them of the plan, and how if one of them went rogue, it would jeopardize everything. Within the telepathic linkage of thought, they would say, *"Enough is enough. We have had it with this place. We will tolerate it no longer. The moment we are trusted with a little freedom, we will escape."*

While enroute to delve into a study session with colleagues on the limited physicalities of the Brothers, Dr. McNeil was approached by a shady group of military personnel. The four soldiers looked like very tough mercenaries with cut off sleeves and dark green head bands. "Dr. McNeil? We represent the government's secret service division. On behalf of the military we are ordered to escort the Blackguards to a secret location for military training. You are to take us to the Blackguards where at such time they will fall under our protection."

Dr. McNeil was taken off guard at the encounter. "Um, first of all, the Blackguards don't need protection from you, and second, if the Blackguards are going to be drafted into military service, it won't be by you."

A second soldier dressed to fight but not in military fatigues, "You misunderstand our intent, sir. We are not here to draft the Blackguards, we will only test their level of fighting skills and then they will be returned to you. Here is the official notice and it comes straight from the minister of defence. You can have it verified but I think you know the real thing when you see it." The soldier smirked and Dr. McNeil was about to let it go without having it verified, but once he made a call on his cell phone, he knew for certain he had to let the Brothers go.

Under cover, the Blackguards were taken to a restricted and illegal fighting arena in China. There they found themselves sitting on a bench at the edge of what looked like a boxing arena, only it had no ropes to keep the fighters inside.

Hooded and in robes, the Blackguards sat patiently as the rules were announced. "If you use weapons you are disqualified. If you step off the platform, you are immediately disqualified. If you surrender by saying, "I surrender," you are disqualified and if you die you are disqualified, otherwise anything goes."

Only the most dangerous men and women of the planet come to this place. It was the only significance of bringing the Blackguards here so they could be tested fairly.

Each of the Brothers were very small compared to the seasoned fighters they had to contend with. Grud went at the largest man who was not only strong but rather obese. Other challengers who fought the obese man were not able to hurt him when they punched him. His strategy was simple, he would just stand in the ring and let his opponent wear themselves out trying to punch him before he strangled them. He was undefeated and when he took a look at Grud, though Grud had large muscled arms, he was still a child in most people's eyes.

The bell rang and the fight was to begin. The obese man took his position at the center of the ring as he always had. Grud came at him and slugged him in the stomach. The obese man lurched forward as he hadn't expected to be hit so hard. Grud whaled on the Obese man's head before chasing him off the stage which disqualified him.

Stroy was up next and he challenged a woman who had a zombie look in her eyes. She was tall and skinny and she moved like her bones were made of rubber. The bell rang and Stroy came at her pounding his feet on the stage with every step. Stroy grabbed the woman but she bent around him and ended up behind him. She hit Stroy's head and knocked him to the bloodstained floor. As she moved in to pounce on Stroy's back, Stroy flipped over and grabbed her with his volk feet. Stroy's toes were like fingers and his big toe was like a thumb, by the way it could curl up over his other toes when they curled into fists. With one foot, Stroy caught the limber lady and with his other foot his slugged her in the face. With the limber lady dazed, Stroy tossed her into the air above him. When she fell down, Stroy kicked her with both legs and she was launched into the rafters.

Domin was the next to enter the ring. He was more evenly matched than Grud and Stroy as Domin's adversary was a highly trained ninja nut who fought like a man who was out of his mind with madness. From the moment the bell rang, Domin used caution and blocked many of his opponent's attacks. Domin saw an opportunity to take a shot and did so, but he found he only caused the crazy man to stand erect as though in shock with his eyes wide and bugged out. Suddenly, the crazy man went ballistic as he screamed and threw his arms around. He scratched at Domin's head and almost tore his ear off. Domin backed away with his hand to the side of his head. He knew something was terribly wrong when blood poured down into his hand. Blood red veins branched out over Domin's body and throbbed before Domin roared and charged in at the crazy man.

The crowd was not sure who was the craziest as Domin did not allow for the crazy man to fight back. Domin was all over the crazy man with strike after strike. Domin so violently beat the crazy man, he killed him in the middle of the ring.

At that point, the Blackguards were escorted back to America and into the safe custody of Dr. McNeil. Narl felt cheated by the whole ordeal as he wanted to prove his skill at driving his opponent insane. The military were content knowing Narl had a brilliant volk mind and they didn't want to risk it.

The doctors began to take note of the peculiar change in the Brothers. The Brothers did not seem to be so edgy, where they used to get upset so easily. According to the computer's brain wave pattern charts, there has been an increase in stress and anxiety. But their behavioural changes are quite the opposite.

"What is causing them to suppress their emotions?" Dr. McNeil wondered as he reviewed the charts.

Even stranger, were the, off-the-chart, readings of Narl's brain wave patterns. Though the readings were off the chart, experts had found the patterns, on a lesser scale, were relative to someone who was in a conversation. The fact how he was sitting still at the time the readings were taken suggested Narl was the organic radio controller who was sending and receiving info telepathically.

As a result of all the improvements which were noted on all levels of the Blackguard's charts, many top people from other divisions began to show more interest. A specialist entered Dr. McNeil's dark office to deliver a folder of progress charts. With use of a video player, Dr. McNeil was busy watching and taking notes from video footage of the Brothers exercising. "Dr. McNeil, I have the recent term charts you have requested."

"Ah, thank you Colton. Would you have a situation over-view for me as well from what you have already seen?" Without taking his eyes off the images depicted on the screen, Dr. McNeil seemed to sink further into his chair.

"Yes, sir, the Brothers seem to be far more focused than ever. There are other changes as well. From the results of their anger management course, they appear to be in control of their anger." Colton could see he wasn't gaining any interest from Dr. McNeil as he too became captivated by watching the Brothers exercising on various equipment and challenging unnatural weights.

Dr. McNeil was puzzled at the information, he surely expected otherwise. Colton continued, "Other improvements have been noted in their health, their attitude to exercise, heightened intelligence and flawless military skills. Strange, however, how each of them improve at the same pace."

"Perhaps it is not so strange." Dr. McNeil said as the footage began to focus in on Domin, "They all had some huge eye openers; one from their experience in Russia and the other, the death of their brother. They've been reminded of their own mortality." He stroked his chin with his fingers and thumb as he thought about the Brothers. Domin was running on the treadmill and pushing with all his might. The lights on the panel lit up with higher voltage lights as the treadmill became harder and harder to keep going. Domin pushed even harder and the lights became just as bright as he had seen Eddy Evon do in the past. Domin's veins branched out over his body and he began to roar as he pushed past his limits before the lights exploded with an overcharge. "Maybe they are growing up. I couldn't be more pleased with the results." The video ended and Dr. McNeil pushed away from the desk to look at Colton.

"Really, sir, you do not seem very pleased. Lately, you appear to have a lot on your mind." Colton observed stretching out his neck as though his collar was uncomfortably tight.

"That's true." He rubbed his face with his hands and took a deep breath like he was recalling his stress. "I have heard a rumour, our reports of the Blackguard's improvements have caught the attention of the military. Apparently, the improvements are just what they have been waiting for." Dr. McNeil looked past Colton to the closed office door behind him, before he continued. "I half expect armed forces to come marching through that door with a certified order to take the Blackguards from us."

The next day, the Blackguards were taken out to an ice cavern which was a huge chasm of melting ice forms. Much of the inner cave had fallen in which left many large pieces of ice smashed to the floor all around the chasm.

The three armored transport personnel carriers opened up and many decorated military soldiers came out with the Blackguards. The Blackguards, along with the other soldiers, stood in an inspection line. The wind blew with a bite in it as it washed snow over them. They waited obediently for Sergeant Jefferies to begin. Dr. McNeil accompanied the sergeant. "Well you boys think you are the best because you managed to pull off some fancy maneuvers in the field which raised some eye brows. I am not so easy to impress. Say hello to special agent Dr. McNeil and his crew of soldiers who are the real deal." The young soldiers looked at the Blackguards. They tried not to show their surprise at their appearance.

The Blackguards appearance was much less clean cut. They had developed an edge and a character to their fighting style. Clad in armor, over their grey cover-alls. Each of the Brothers had an identity to protect and they did so by wearing hoods and ninja masks. They had an obvious body mass to their toned physics. The cover-alls could not disguise how the Blackguard's fitness and structure was from years of excessively disciplined training. All were inwardly intimidated by their solid, powerful, superhuman bodies.

"Dr. McNeil, would you like to introduce your team?" The sergeant passed off the spot light.

"Absolutely, sergeant Jefferies." Dr. McNeil turned to speak to the soldiers. "As you can see, each of the four Blackguards have their names displayed on their chests." Dr. McNeil went from one of the Brothers to the next, "This is Narl." Narl's masked head was the largest. "Grud" who had impossibly huge arms, "Stroy" He said as he put his hand to Stroy's shoulder. Stroy could not hide his massive legs. "And this is, Domin." A slight smile revealed where Dr. McNeil might have had a keen likeness for Domin. "You will all be divided up into four groups and each of the Blackguards will lead each of your groups."

"We are here to expand on your methods for search and destroy tactics." Sergeant Jefferies said, "The four of your groups will use paint ball guns. At each of the four corners of the cave you will find a station. We have Red station, Blue station, Yellow station and Orange station." As Sergeant Jefferies gave the instructions of the training exercise to the Blackguards, other military helpers were handing out packs of paint balls and paint ball guns. "You will sound the buzzer when you reach your station. The door of your station will lock at the moment you press the buzzer so be sure everyone is inside or your team will be disqualified. When the last team sounds the buzzer, the other three doors will unlock and the session will begin. Your mission objective is to eliminate all of the other teams and lay siege to their station. If you are hit you are out and you must return to the armored personnel transport. The team who wins will be determined by special agent Dr. McNeil and myself. We will take into account the number of kills, versus the number of stations which are taken over. One hint of advice to you all, listen to your team leader. It could mean the difference between your team's success or failure. Any questions?"

Narl looked up at the ceiling of the ice cavern. For a second or two there was complete silence, then Narl could contain himself no longer, "Are you sure this is a safe location for this exercise?" He asked hesitantly.

"We have had our seismic personnel out here all day. It should be very safe. If you people don't like it then do your job efficiently and swiftly, then we will all get back to the base all the sooner." Sergeant Jefferies answered.

"Yes, sir." Narl replied with a stiff salute.

"Each of you will know what team you are on by the colour of the pack you have been given. Now put on the back-packs and head out with your team leader to you stations... You heard me people now go, go, go! This is no picnic for you ladies. As far as your concerned, this is war!"

The teams immediately split up and headed out. As they hiked through the large field of ice, it was clear why the cave was the location of choice. For one thing it was out from the wind chill and there were many places to hide or find cover.

The soldiers found it difficult to keep up with their team leader. They were always well in the lead with so much more endurance. Each of the Blackguards made it to the stations quite quickly. There they waited for the other young soldiers to join them.

The stations were small wooden houses built on stilts with high pitched metal roofs shrouded in thick layers of ice. Inside each of the stations was a bright red button mounted to the opposite wall from the entrance. To the left was a blank wall with a circle marked on it. Within the circle were two other circles like a targeting grid. Above the targeting grid was the instructions, "Mark your team's colour here." While each of the Blackguards waited for their other team members to show up, they loaded their paintball guns and fired off one shot at the center of the bull's eye. Each of the Blackguards then began fastening thin ropes to the feather ends of their arrows.

The Blackguards waited for every last team member to enter the station before they hit the buzzer. When the final buzzer sounded, the exercise began. The doors to the stations were unlocked and opened before them. The soldiers moved to exit each station.

"Go nowhere." instructed each of the Blackguards. They each had similar strategies from their training. Arrows were shot out in various directions from the stations. The compound bows and powerful arms sent arrows which burrowed deep into the ice. The lines of rope were strung for various purposes. The Blackguards began to split their team members with tactical plans. Some of the teams slid out into the field of broken ice boulders along trolleys connected to the tight ropes. While other team members swung out on the ropes. As the team members moved out, they shot at the moving targets of their oppositions.

Each of the ropes led the soldiers out to specific destinations. Some soldiers were positioned at the top of slippery ice slides. Everyone started out moving very fast, but no one was as fast as the Blackguards. Many of the shots taken at the Blackguards were deflected by chunks of ice which the Blackguards would use to intercept the paint balls hurled through the air. Soldiers began to fall like crazy as the Blackguards opened up on them with their paintballs.

Each of the Blackguards were equally matched except for one. Narl had a unique advantage over his Brothers. Domin, Grud and Stroy clued in on what Narl was up to immediately. They expected such a move from the beginning.

Narl used his telepathy to peek into the strategies of his Brothers throughout the course of the exercise. He had instructed a choice few of his team members to make their way through the ice to the opposing stations. He knew his Brothers had left one team member behind to guard their station. While Narl, remained in high places within the cave, he was able to watch his team members and guide them through by shooting a paintball out ahead of each of his choice members. These paintballs Narl shot were to not only mark the way for his people to follow, but from time to time he would protect them by shooting opposing coloured soldiers.

Unfortunately, Narl was able to know of his Brother's strategies but they had no way of knowing what *Narl* was up to.

Domin swung out to an icy peek where he paused to observe the pattern of the skirmish below. He looked for clues as to what his Brothers were up to. Paintballs flew at him from below and he was forced to leap to another tower of ice.

Finally, Domin could see Narl's team was moving in on the stations at one time. Narl dropped down from above and hit Grud and Stroy with sucker shots from behind.

While Narl laughed at them, they boiled within with tempered rage.

Domin roared like a beast. Narl shot his head around and looked at Domin with a devious grin. Then Domin was flicked in the head with a threatening telepathic suggestion.

That was it. Domin warned his brother countless times in the past not to use his telepathy on him. As far as he was concerned, the exercise was over, now it was personal.

Narl's team members shot those who were left behind to defend their stations, before they hit the bull's eyes within the stations to claim them their own.

Domin slid down the icy tower, then he rammed into it with his shoulder. The tower of ice cracked under the stress, before it began to teeter over. With the massive structure crashing down, Domin hoped he caught Narl under the tower of ice. But it did not surprise Domin to learn Narl could see it coming and rolled out of the way.

Narl popped up from behind an icy boulder unexpectedly. He shot three shots from his automatic paintball gun. Domin was able to flip himself to the right and dodge the shots. Domin lunged at Narl and wrapped his hands around his neck.

A horn sounded from the stations. Narl's team had won. Narl struggled under the might of Domin. Then he manipulated his face to grin at Domin. Domin looked into Narl's eyes. He wanted to see his brother realize who exactly he was dealing with, but Narl used his telepathy.

As terribly uncomfortable as it was for Domin to experience, he was forced, with a control not his own, to release his hands from Narl's throat and begin choking himself with his own hands.

Domin rose up as he gasped for air, before he fell to the icy ground on his back. His back pack was squashed and the spare paintballs inside blew at once. Narl rose up over Domin and rubbed his neck as he stared his brother down with his telepathic control.

Noticing the conflict, Stroy and Grud came flying in to intercede for Domin. They tackled Narl to the ground and Domin was immediately released. Throwing his black mask to the floor, Domin spat blood before his coughing turned to a growl of blind rage, but the distracting voice of Sergeant Jefferies came booming and echoing throughout the cave from loud speakers. "That is it, people! I am sorry to have to cut this little exercise short, but we have an unexpected guest here and he says it is urgent for him to speak with the Blackguards. Fall in people. Do it, now!"

The four Blackguards stood up. Narl sneered at each one of them bitterly. Anger gleamed from his black beady eyes but they were professional soldiers before they were Brothers so they managed to leave one another alone as they began walking back to the cave's entrance.

Within the armored personnel transport, Sergeant Jefferies and Dr. McNeil were intently observing what was happening in the cave via the countless cameras previously placed throughout.

The side door of the transport slid open, and a decorated General came inside.

"General on deck!" Sergeant Jefferies alerted as he stood up straight and saluted. Dr. McNeil also stood up straight and mimicked the sergeant.

"At ease, gentlemen." spoke the General from the confidence he built into himself as a result of his years of experience and service.

"Is there a problem, sir?" asked sergeant Jefferies with a slight twitch of intimidation.

"That depends on how you choose to look at it." replied the General before he continued. "I have a military operation which has gone sour. I also have the clearance to draft the "Blackguards."" The General ended his words as he scowled at Dr. McNeil.

These were the dreaded words Dr. McNeil did not want to hear. "The Blackguards?" Dr. McNeil repeated with intimidation. Despite his best efforts to come across calm and collect, he could not keep a small bead of sweat from trickling down his fore head. "Though I would like to help you with your problem, I assure you the Brothers are not ready for war. They are still just children."

"They have training and skill which surpasses our best men. I want them, and you are ordered to comply." The General answered with a grave coldness.

Though it seemed impossible, Dr. McNeil could not just let the military steal away the project he'd poured so much of himself into. "I understand, General." He responded with a salute and a click of his heals.

The General pinched the thin gold frames of his mirror tinted sunglasses to adjust them at the bridge of his nose. "General *Graham*…" The General added quickly to fully introduce himself.

"General Graham, sir, if I may. The Brothers are my life's work. If it is decided for them to go out into a true combat situation, what are the chances they will return in one piece?" Dr. McNeil asked with authentic concern quivering in his voice. He then realized this may be the last moment he may ever see the Brothers ever again.

"I'm not going to sugar coat anything for you, Doctor. The truth is war is brutal and ugly. It can no more differentiate between a young rookie soldier or one of your Hell born super soldiers. Your morbid looking freaks of science are very impressive in a scuffle, but I don't believe they can win an entire war for us. However, we have a situation elsewhere in the world, and I need your boys to give us the edge. We need the upper hand, desperately." He looked at the Doctor with a frankness in the way he stretched half his mouth back somewhat like a smile. "You asked my opinion, Doctor. If they join us in battle, I am confident you will see them again..." The General lowered his tinted sunglasses to look Dr. McNeil right in the eyes. "if not as heroes, in body bags."

At those words, Dr. McNeil's face went pasty white. The General could see how the news was affecting him, though he could not understand how a person could form a bond with the Blackguards. From the General's limited knowledge of them, they were just angry little lab experiments. General Graham continued his message as he described the battle situation and how it required the Blackguard's involvement.

"Seven of our brightest young recruits have been captured by Taliban terrorists while we were engaged in a fire fight within the Afghanistan city of Kabul. The battle was started over a possible apostasy. We had managed to plant tracers on some of the Taliban prisoners we set free during a prisoner exchange procedure. Though the siege has revealed the hidden Taliban stronghold, we are unable to simply destroy it. For one thing, a series of intricate tunnels run throughout the dry rugged mountains in the province of Ghazni. Most of these tunnels are naturally formed and go on for miles. They have not captured only American troops. They are also holding 23 South Korean Christians.

"I have also been trying to draft another similar person who is like your Blackguards. His name is Eddy Evon. He is a volk who is located in "D" section at the moment, if I remember correctly. This little fellow is so classified, the entire project is locked down tighter than a nuclear submarine."

"You can forget about putting Eddy out on the front line. I know Dr. Evon, he is not only very stubborn, but he has a tremendous amount of pull to insure he gets what he wants. And you can expect the same difficulties if you try to get your hands on the Brothers." Dr. McNeil's attempt to intimidate the General proved to be most unwise.

"Oh? And you expect me to believe you can put up the same kind of muscle to defend the Blackguards as Dr. Evon?" General Graham was obviously toying with Dr. McNeil.

Breaking from his stiff stance, the doctor turned to the General sympathetically, with the idea to meet with the General's compassion, providing he had any. Dr. McNeil was not interested in playing any further games. He did his best not to break down before General Graham, "The Brothers are my life." Dr. McNeil told him though he knew inevitably he would lose. The General reached for the inside pocket of his dark green military jacket. An impressive collection of medals and stripes of rank reflected in the fluorescent light. The General handed Dr. McNeil a sealed document. When Dr. McNeil opened the document, he found an order signed by people who had overridden his authority.

Dr. McNeil sniffed and wiped his eyes as he collected himself before he added, "If you take the Brothers from me then I will be a man out of a job. Please authorize my request to join you to observe the Brothers' performance in battle."

General Graham stroked his chin and eyed Dr. McNeil in a suspicious manner. Finally, he said, "We can arrange something to accommodate you." answered the General with an awkward grin.

The night before the mission, the air borne infantry, who would accompany the young Blackguards, visited them at their home. They tried to party with them though alcohol and other intoxications were forbidden. They told dirty jokes and listened to loud music and before the night was through they gave the Blackguards their own facial tattoos. Each of them looked like they were wearing Indian war paint. Domin received a simple black shadow design around his eyes. The others had more intricate markings over their fore heads and cheeks.

Domin reached up to the bandages covering his new surgical wounds. He tore off the bandages to reveal the stitches underneath. "Let's do this..." He stated from a desire to put his training to use in a real combat situation.

Narl also reached up to his new bandages and tore them off. Then Grud and Stroy followed suit as they too began pulling off their bandages.

To their surprise each of the Brothers found tattoo designs on their shoulders of a planet and eagle with the words, "Property of the U.S.A." Each of them were branded with four small numbers under the tattoo, Grud's number was 2003, Narl's number was 2004, Stroy's number was 2005, Oblit's number would have been 2006 and Domin's number was 2007.

Under the instruction of the military, the Blackguards suited up into new custom designed specialized armor. They were quickly led into the transport which drove them to an Alaskan air-force base.

The wind blew hard over the icy run way. Never the less, the transport aircraft, with the Blackguards securely strapped in, blazed its way through the strengths of nature's icy breath. Within the craft, the Blackguards were briefed on the current situation. With the Blackguards was a group of airborne infantry. *'At last,'* thought the Blackguards, *'We are on a real military mission.'*

Phase one of the rescue operation required a specialized Hawkbat stealth helicopter to fly to the vicinity of twelve thousand miles from the target in Iraq. Across the plains beyond a steep mountain range lay a gas pipe line. The pipe line was void of any gas as the project was still in the process of being assembled.

The Hawkbat deployed a programmed target lock on missile MX9114. The missile isn't particularly big, but it packs a real messy punch. Through the late night hour, the missile moved low over the eastern coast. Avoiding radar detection, as it moved up onto the shore the missile raised it's altitude to climb over a mountain. Zig-zagging through the valley on the other side, leaving a trail of exhaust, the missile began to move over the plains where it picked up speed. Always keeping low to avoid detection, the missile moved into a thick evening fog which blanketed the landscape until finally it hit its programmed target destination. The empty pipeline exploded into a mess of destruction with fire and crumpled metal strewn about at a radius of one hundred and fifty meters.

Elsewhere, as the Blackguards journeyed near to the same pipe line, but a different location of it, they traveled within a swift air charter jet. Looking at one another, the Brothers marveled at one another's military armored battle fatigues. Each of the boys wore dark grey uniforms, but their armor and weapons were customary and chosen to fit their specific talents and military strengths.

Narl wore a full face mask and helmet. His tinted visor made him seem very mysterious. He mainly carried grenades which were electronically activated with proximity movement sensitive clay more mines. Black gloves, knee and elbow pads were worn for protection with a double bladed knife in each boot as he carried two light weight stealth M-1911A auto pistols.

Grud wore articulate armor sheathing around his powerful volk arms. From the armor of his arms he could fire small missiles and rounds of ammunition. He also had a strap of darts around each thigh with a samurai sword at each hip.

Stroy was mostly protected with armor over his upper body. Smaller sections of armor protected his muscled volk legs, but they could not be over protected without becoming a nuisance. Strapped over each shoulder were mini M-60 machine guns loaded to the hilt with ammunition.

Domin never felt comfortable relying on automated guns. He carried a compound bow and a sheath of arrows. His belt was loaded with throwing stars and drug tipped darts. He wore armor over his chest and upper back with shoulder plating which made him look huge like a football player who ate a football player. He also wore gauntlets which had short spikes at the elbows. Other armored plating covered his thighs and boots.

Each of the Blackguards also wore a black back pack which was stuffed with other supplies they would need.

The pilot's voice, raspy over the intercom, announced, "The target zone is on approach in T-minus thirty seconds. Prep for departure." The moment the broadcast was made, all of the soldiers, with the company of the Blackguards, stood up.

The worksite where the gas pipeline project ended was not only incomplete, but under construction. The project was on schedule with an encampment of employees and equipment, only all was abandoned as everyone was required at the site of the explosion.

The stealth jet equipped with vertical take-off and landing quickly descended near the construction camp of the pipeline where the rear bay doors opened. The Blackguards quickly departed from the back-up of soldiers as they drove out of the jet and down the ramp, each one of them riding silent black electric powered motor cycles. Through the darkness of night the Blackguards wore night vision goggles, but they were of no use within the surrounding thick fog.

Riding out from the landing zone the four traveled from the rocky lined clearing and up onto a road which was made along the stretch where the pipeline would soon be. Domin rode out in the lead using a sophisticated GPS built into his wrist gauntlet to help him stay in the center of the road.

The fog was so thick, everyone was getting wet and the Blackguards had to rely on their other senses because they were riding blind. The dirt road was crude covered with big jagged rocks and pot holes. Built straight at a slight grade for the pipeline, the road was traveled with the sound of a swarm of bees. Soon the Blackguards quickly entered the work camp at the mouth of the unfinished pipeline.

Stopping just outside the open pipeline, the four Blackguards found the worksite to be very desolate indeed. Abandoned like a ghost town, all of the trucks and many of the tools were called away to the area of the explosion along with all of the personnel.

The Brothers shared a sense of the mission being more of a game than a serious military operation. They were dressed like ninja assassins and they loved it.

Grud leaped off his cycle and jumped into the mouth of the pipeline. When all of the Blackguards had stepped off their cycles, Domin began tossing each of the cycles up six feet to Grud, who caught each cycle and set them inside the pipe. Next, the Blackguards climbed into the pipe. Stroy was the last to join the others. It was at this time when they found the camp's cook had stayed behind.

Approaching on foot, from out of the thick dark fog, the Iraqi cook asked timidly for the Blackguards to identify themselves in his Iranian language. Narl spread his arms wide and backed up protecting his Brothers into the veiling darkness of the pipe behind them.

Using the Iranian speech, Narl answered the cook, "We have orders to go inside the pipe to assist with repairs."

Though the cook thought he might have seen a short young person with an unusually large helmet, he was set at ease with the reply. As the cook said good-bye, he heard a strange buzzing echo growing feint from the pipe as the Blackguards sped off into the distance on route to their next destination.

Using a GPS built into his gauntlet, Domin began to slow down. The three others following Domin slowed their cycles with him. According to the GPS reading, the Blackguards had reached their next target location. They dismounted from their cycles as Stroy initiated a cutting torch to begin cutting through the thick hide of the pipe.

101

After cutting a hole through the pipe large enough for them to fit through, they escaped the pipe and headed down a steep hillside which was covered with olive trees. Besides the cover of both the trees and nightfall, the fog was still very thick.

Only a short distance down the slope, the Blackguards came to another above ground pipeline, only this was a pressurized water main and the Taliban had conveniently ruptured the pipe some time ago, creating a flow of water to their base of operations. Free clean water ran down the mountain and no one would dare challenge what the Taliban claimed.

A wide river of water ran through 20 acres of the olive trees which aided in concealing any sounds the Blackguards made. Rumbling and sloshing down the steep grade and through the water, the Blackguards found themselves at the edge of a lake. Each of the Blackguards had a black self-inflatable raft in their possession and they used these rafts to float out onto the lake.

It was, for the Blackguards, like waking to a dream with countless small waterfalls running down and out from between the olive trees. Not a sound was made or heard. The fog wasn't quite so thick upon the surface of the lake and the Brothers noticed how the lake was filling with water but the water level wasn't rising. As they paddled down the lake, they found a lazy current was adding to their speed. At the end of the long narrow lake they came to a bottle neck where the water dropped off to a rapid river.

The Blackguards followed the powerful windy river to a lower pool where, at the edge of the rocky embankment was a small pump house, equipped with a filter system. This was what the Blackguards were searching for because it meant they were just above the Taliban base.

Domin, Grud and Stroy stretched their black ninja masks over their heads. They embellished the animal symbol of claws on their foreheads in honor of their mystic martial arts instructors. With admiration for their duty and for one another, they all shared in a sense of invincibility which came naturally with the confidence of their youth.

The mission began with the silent transport jet whistling in from the east hemisphere. The Blackguards climbed down the mountain side near the Afghan terrorist stronghold which was built deep into the mountain at its base. Where the rock of the mountain met the flat sands of the desert, two outcroppings of sun baked stone reached out to the desert at either side of the base in a horseshoe like formation which resembled a dried up harbor. The powerful spot lights scanned the remote area just outside of the Taliban base, which was the most probable access to the base. Where the flat and desolate desert met the heel of an abrasive and rocky mountain range, spotlights oscillated to and fro stretching out long fingers from the searchlights probing the dark fog for the possible threat of movements. After each of the Blackguards repelled two hundred and forty meters down the cliffs to strategic positions, they waited just out of sight before reacting to a telepathic signal from Narl. Like setting up pieces to win a game of chess, the Blackguards reacted to the telepathy and leaped out at once using the element of surprise to its fullest as they descended a swift doom upon the unsuspecting guards.

The fog came alive with silent strikes, taking down each of the posted guards one by one before they were able to sound an alarm. Domin used his compound bow, Stroy threw his ninja stars with accuracy, Grud cast needle sharp poison tipped darts and Narl projected telepathic suggestions for soldiers to willfully jump from the great height of the outer wall. At the base of the mountain and dug in deep through an intricate web of tunnels was the fortified base of the Taliban.

The sun was beginning to bring light to the distant horizon. Powerful spot lights came to life at posts along the second wall which stretched out multiple beams moving about and lighting up the inner area in search of would be attackers. The defences of the inner area lit up brighter than mid-day. With lightning speed, the Blackguards whirled ninja stars at the source of the lights. At once, all of the spotlights blew out. Speedily the Blackguards secured the entire surveillance perimeter along the walkway of the second great protective wall.

With the use of their training, the Blackguards moved in on the Taliban compound like wraiths, the four Brothers made their way deep into the Afghan stronghold. With their night vision goggles fitted over their eyes, the Blackguards moved quickly through the shadows. Narl did not have night vision goggles because his ability to see in the dark was built into his helmet. With a touch of a button at the side of his visor, Narl's sight lit up in green.

Chapter 4

Domin was the first to realize the Afghan stronghold was built into an old mining site of tunnels and shafts. These caverns were built deep into the steep rocky mountainside. With great skill, the Blackguards used silent weapons to destroy mini surveillance cameras, but they failed to find and destroy them all before detection. Machine guns fired and the Blackguards were surprised when they found themselves in the violent reality of war. They accomplished taking out all lights and hostile terrorists swiftly.

There was no time for the Blackguards to be distracted from their mission. The explosions and gun fire had alerted the entire terrorist stronghold. Through fire and wicked flame, the Blackguards just kept coming with unstoppable swiftness. With deadly acrobatic skill they delved deeper and deeper into the complex establishment. Like indestructible entities, the Blackguards moved. Deep within the bowels of the mine shafts, bullet heads and shell casings rained down from above and ricocheting off their armor.

For a time, the terrorists thought they had the upper hand. However, though the Blackguards were few, they were able to give such punishment right back to the terrorists with their own arsenal of weaponry. Narl quickly reloaded his guns as he drained them as though he had an endless supply. Grud unloaded his rapid fire wrist chain gun. Stroy was a specialist at using structural damage against his enemies, and if Domin wasn't implementing his silent weapons, he relied on his animalistic fighting techniques. Their rage fueled their power.

Busting their way into the large main banquet hall, they climbed walls and leaped from trestle to trestle as they pressed their attack. Narl tossed proximity grenade explosives which had a five second delay before they were armed. Well behind the Blackguards the explosions threatened to bury them alive as they detonated any followers.

With wild warrior ninja skill, the Blackguards set off smoke bombs to disorient the terrorist as they moved about undetected. Traveling quickly, the enemy had trouble tracking their intruders. Fear preceded the Blackguards, the deep tunnels were rank with it. Narl understood the translation of what the terrorists were saying through their radio connections. *"We detect multiple subjects. They're in the South Eastern corridor, sub level- J."* words were spoken with heavy breaths over the com.

After breaking out of the main hall they found themselves in the next chamber which had many pens. The pens contained; camels, horses, goats, a donkey and a large in ground water pit. The animals made noise in response to the commotion. Throughout the deep caverns, remains of old and broken down machinery from the days of the miners were abandoned. As Taliban soldiers ran about in a frantic effort to prepare themselves, dust had no time to settle. The Blackguards were not interested in randomly destroying everything. Their focus was to destroy the Taliban terrorists, find and capture the leader and free the prisoners.

They pushed their way through to the weapons hold. Breaking down the old wooden door, they found a huge assortment of weapons cache along with a ground to air missile launcher stationed at the center of the chamber.

It was no less like the Blackguards had shaken the bee hive when out came all of the bees. Above the dazed

Taliban soldiers, they could barely see the movement of the Blackguards as they leaped and swung like circus acrobats in the rafters The Taliban soldiers couldn't see them in the dark but the soldiers could certainly hear the activity. With a high-five, Domin and Grud slapped their hands together in mid swing. Stroy and Narl also gave each other a high-five while in mid leap from one structural beam to another.

When the soldiers gathered for a run at the weapons cache, Narl took action to thwart their plan. With a gunshot to a barrel of a black, tar-like substance, the barrel blew apart and instantly burned emitting a thick black smoke. The Blackguards immediately fastened gas masks over their faceless ninja masks.

The chamber of the weapons cache was within a small room. Many terrorist soldiers turned from the smoke to fight the Blackguards with knives and hand guns.

One of the Taliban soldiers dived into the pen with the donkey. Still high up in the support beams, Grud saw this and broke off a piece of rock from the ceiling. The soldier lifted his head cautiously as he tried to target the shadows above. While the soldier was scanning the rafters for signs of the intruders, Grud gave a quick flick to his volk wrist as he threw the jagged stone and hit the donkey square in its rear.

"Hee-Haw!!!" bellowed the shaken donkey as it kicked and bucked the soldier in his buttocks, launching him over the rails and into the pool of water.

These terrorists were not ready to fight. They were off balance and did not have time to take hold of their assault rifles, because they were woken out of bed and most of their weapons were secure under the guard of the Blackguards.

Narl was able to read the humans with ease. He

could predict the human's next move not only from their body movements and eyes, but by their very thoughts. From reading the minds of the enemy, Narl could tip off his Brothers before they were attacked so they were not caught unaware.

Riding along zip-lines, Domin, Narl and Grud used the thick smoke filled room to their advantage as they came together, back to back at the center of the chamber. Stroy swung out on a nylon rope by the strength and grip of his feet before he executed a perfect back flip and landed amongst his Brothers. Pounding heavily on the wooden floor, Stroy with his powerful volk legs, stood up straight as the old floor creaked.

Brandishing nun-chucks from their back packs, the Blackguards began twirling them in fluent simultaneous motions. The sound, like a helicopter in the room as the nun-chucks beat at the air with a dangerous warning of dread. This strategy, the Blackguards called, "Invincibility."

The Taliban began to build in confidence as their number improved. Many of the soldiers were very young. As the surrounding Taliban soldiers observed the Blackguards, they began to realize they were not invincible, rather these were children who were defeating them. Surrounding the Blackguards, the Taliban soldiers began to cautiously squeeze in. One soldier fired a shot from his pistol which glanced off Narl's nun-chuck in mid swing. Narl did not like this and as the Blackguards reacted with a swift attack, Narl began penetrating the soldiers minds with hopelessness and fear to dwindle their confidence.

The brawl was on. Grud used his powerful volk arms to send many soldiers flying with each stroke of his nun-chucking. Stroy was impressive using a combination of kicks from his powerful volk legs along with skillful nun-chuck maneuvers. Domin and Narl were equally impressive with ground shaking, earth quaking technique and power.

Before the Taliban soldiers could ready themselves, they were quickly struck down with eye popping, heart pounding amazement.

Just one level below, a group of Elite Taliban looked to the ceiling as they tried to follow the sounds of the nasty scuffle overhead. The Taliban leader, Omar al-Gaddafi, crouched down behind a table, turned over on end. Guarded by his closest and trusted bodyguards and his second in command, Abdelhakim al Bashaaga, they waited, dreading the moment when they too would have to face the intruders.

The leader of the Taliban, Omar al-Gaddafi was thin and old and did not look to be in good health, he donned a long grey beard and a turban. His loose clothes were cleaner than the others with a leather strap of pockets slung from his left shoulder to his right hip. He also wore a belt around his waist loaded with bullets and a side arm at each hip. In the eyes of Omar was a devious wisdom from a lifetime of battlefront experience and sneaky tactics. Surely, he was one who could not be trusted.

At his side stood Omar's peculiar and mysterious second in command, Abdelhakim al Bashaaga, dressed entirely in black wearing a black turban with a gold badge of authority at the front and a black veil of fabric covering his entire face with holes cut out for his eyes to see. He too had a beard and appeared very dangerous. At his chest he wore a criss-cross belt of M16 bullets.

Trying to remain quiet, the bodyguards were vigilant as they prepared to protect their Taliban leader. The wood creaked and thumped as dust fell from between the cracks of the ceiling. Some bodyguards stationed at the base of the winding stair well, signaled for Omar and Abdelhakim to remain hidden. The ceiling gave way at the center of the chamber to the great weight of the brawl above. Everyone from upstairs fell down stairs. Omar, the Taliban leader, could not believe his eyes as he beheld the sight of the muscled Blackguards emerging from the dust for the first time.

Gunfire lit up the dark and dusty compartment, as the bodyguards did not spare their ammunition. The armor clad Blackguards pushed off the broken beams and lumber before pressing their attack. With quick actions, the Blackguards disarmed the bodyguards by hurtling heavy pieces from the broken support beams at them. After knocking the guards to the floor the Blackguards were quick to capture them, all but one who remained hidden behind a stack of barrels. The Taliban leader, Omar, and his second in command Abdelhakim, surrendered with their arms stretched high as they stood up from behind the overturned table.

Stroy and Domin moved around behind the Omar and Abdelhakim and bound their wrists with heavy duty zap strap bonds. Domin was satisfied to see the Taliban high command captured. He and his Brothers were successfully pulling off the mission according to their instructions. Finally, the Blackguards would have due respect for who they were and their abilities. Domin saw how the eyes of the Taliban leader, Omar, were wide and glazed over as though he was in a trans. Glancing back at Narl, Domin noticed he was up to his old tricks again. Narl was staring at the Taliban leader and it was obvious he was inside his head.

"Find out where the prisoners are." Domin told Narl as he shook his shoulder. Domin wasn't sure if Narl, fixated, could even hear him.

Within the mind of the Taliban leader, Narl was

amazed to find how devious a web the leader's mind was. Here, Narl found a hard life for this individual and a deep resentment for anything American. Nevertheless, his goal was not to destroy the Blackguards for he knew the rise to power must be obtained through leverage. The Taliban leader wanted to capture the Blackguards above all else and use them as bargaining chips to blackmail the Americans and secure his position as leader. The Taliban leader had a futile plan to lure the Blackguards into a back room, which was a cell, and lock them inside.

Narl enjoyed a battle of wits and through his ego he always looked for an opportunity to prove his intellectual power. "The prisoners are in that back room." Narl pointed to a door for his Brothers to enter. "Isn't that right?" He asked the Taliban leader though fully aware it was a trap.

"I'll remain behind to keep the prisoners secure." Grud said as he slammed his great fist into his wide palm with a dusty cloud.

"I insist you come with us," Narl told Grud with a commanding tone in his voice. "These prisoners are secure and we may need your assistance."

Grud looked at Domin then Stroy before he huffed and shrugged his heavy set shoulders, "Yeah, whatever."

Narl was aware of the trap set for them but despite the danger, he figured they had the potential to find themselves in a superior position over their captives. The Blackguards were just about to enter the back room when Domin stopped everyone and turned back to face Narl once again. "I have a bad feeling here, remind me what we are doing?"

"Do not worry, Brothers," Narl smiled with confidence to reassure his Brothers, "We have allowed ourselves to be captured. Do not resist the Taliban, rather, let them believe they have the upper hand." Narl explained like he knew something they didn't.

"I don't like it!" Taking a step out of the cell Domin protested.

"Oh, and you believe you can come up with a better plan?" Narl challenged Domin pushing his chest against him.

"It's too risky, you bubble headed nut-job." Domin insult didn't seem to bother Narl as he was certain he was leading them into a trap.

"Yeah, we had them right where we wanted them. This battle would be over now if you hadn't botched it up." Grud added in agreement with Domin.

"You may be right, but we don't want to just win the battle. We want to win the war." Narl stated optimistically.

"I hope you have a plan you want to fill us in on." Stroy added as he and his Brothers looked back at Omar and Abdelhakim. The Taliban leaders were still standing side by side with their hands bound behind them. Satisfied, the young Brothers turned back to their group talk.

"Didn't it feel great?" Narl told them, "We totally dominated these weaklings. Among humans, we are Gods. Our time will come, Brothers. Our time will come when we will have the opportunity to do what an army of human American soldiers cannot and win this war. Then we will be proclaimed the heroes. This cell will not be the end of us." Narl smiled a most devious smile. "Now, lets go. Get inside and I'll fill you in on the details."

But the Blackguards would not go into the cell. Domin pushed at Narl with his chest so hard, Narl had to steady himself or fall backwards. "Narl, if you want information from these guys, just take it. We don't surrender."

Stroy had Domin's back as he added, "What's wrong with accomplishing the mission and capturing Omar so he can be interrogated later. Everyone knows you'd be the best to head that operation."

While the Blackguards were talking, Abdelhakim nudged Omar with his elbow and nodded his head for Omar to look past Narl. When Omar looked, he saw one of their bodyguards in the darkness peeking out from behind the stack of barrels where he hid.

Omar spoke in a clear firm voice and said, "Abu." With no fear of anyone else hearing him. The eyes of the Blackguards turned to look at Omar and his eyes seemed fixed on something in the distance of the room. Without warning, Narl was brutally struck at the back of his head knocking him unconscious. The bodyguard, Abu quickly put a knife to the belligerent Narl's throat.

The Blackguard's were surprised at the sheer size of Abu for he was the biggest Taliban they had ever seen. Abu's clothing was well worn and the front was opened wide exposing the impressive muscles of his hairy chest. He had a long black beard and long black hair growing down over his shoulders with a dirty head band.

Abu began shouting at the Blackguards, while threatening to cut Narl's throat. Though the Blackguards could not understand a word Abu said, it was clear they were ordered to surrender or else Narl would be killed.

The Blackguard's hesitated for a moment, before they placed their weapons on the ground. Domin hesitated a second longer than Stroy and Grud as he wasn't sure if Narl's loss would be so bad, however, seeing his Brothers relinquish their weapons and the recent suggestion Narl made to surrender, he followed suit.

Fathi Belhaj, one of the arrested bodyguards stepped

near to Abu and turned his back to him. Abu used his knife to cut Fathi's bonds. Fathi immediately went around to their leaders, Omar and Abdelhakim and released them from their bonds as well.

Omar and Abdelhakim began shouting orders in a panic as the bodyguards were released and began clubbing the Blackguards, Domin, Stroy and Grud. The Blackguards, still just children, realized with regret that their military training did not teach how to be effective prisoners. However, because of the frequent surgeries, the Brothers had to endure throughout their young lives, they had developed a great thresh-hold for pain. The Taliban were impressed with how much punishment they could endure.

When the flogging was at an end and the Brothers could hardly move, the bodyguards stripped them of their armor and weapons before they went to each of them, one by one and removed their ninja masks. They were horrified by the faces of each of the Brothers, but they were no different from scared faces of children, but when they removed Narl's helmet, they were mystified. Narl wore the face of a volk with a head shaped unproportional with haunting black eye. So curious was the face of Narl, the Taliban had to pause in a moment of silence to take it all in.

Though none of the Taliban was ready to discover such a sight, Omar broke the silence with level headed leadership. "First I must punish all of my soldiers who have failed to protect our fortress, then I want to find out what these things are." Omar pondered his curiosity with Abdelhakim as he poked Grud's volk arm with the barrel of his pistol.

Abdlehakim peered at the Blackguards from the eye holes of the black veil covering his face. He was not sure what these warriors were, "This one with the large head, looks like an alien from another planet."

"Perhaps they are all from another planet," Omar stroked his beard as he wondered what strange history came with the young soldiers who accompanied his presence. "It looks like human children in possession of parts from a creature we do not know... The alien flesh gives them great strength."

Through the eye holes of the veil hiding his face, Abdelhakim looked away from the Blackguards and then to Omar, "We have connections who can find out for us what this special American group is and if they are worth anything to anyone."

All four Blackguards were tossed into a cell with the other prisoners. Bleeding and bruised, the Brothers only wore their boxers as they moaned and rolled around on the stone floor in pain. The seven young soldiers did not let the other South Korean prisoners go near the new comers of the cell for they were not sure if the Blackguards were dangerous. To the eyes of the insufferable prisoners, the Blackguards looked like hideous freaks, creatures snarling with elusive movements and considered extremely dangerous.

The Taliban leader, Omar al-Gaddafi, along with the assistance of his second in command Abdelhakim al Bashaaga, made contact with Afghan government officials whom they controlled. From their sources they were able to crack top secret military files where they learned of the half volk Brothers who were code named the Blackguards.

When the Taliban leader realized the significance of capturing the Blackguards, he began to conspire with his military intelligence to come up with options how to get the most from the world for the price of their captives.

When contact was made, through a video feed, to not only the Americans but the entire world, Omar al-Gaddafi demanded one billion dollars from the American tax payers as well as the release of many Taliban captives by midnight or else he would have not only the Blackguards put to death, but the seven American troops and all of the 23 South Korean Christians.

He ordered his soldiers to first sedate then bound and gag the Blackguards before taking them, along with the other prisoners, to a separate tunneled out section under the Taliban stronghold. There a video camera stood upon a tripod. The Blackguards were forced to kneel down shoulder to shoulder with the other prisoners shackled to a long rusty chain behind.

Thick, heavy support beams were gathered and assembled into shapes of huge standing 'X's. Each one of the prisoners, including the Blackguards, was blind folded. Additionally, the Blackguards wore burlap sacks over their heads. Soon after all was in order, the terrorists began to work the camera so Omar could show the world they had over thrown the military's top soldiers.

Dr. McNeil arrived at a make shift base camp far from the Taliban stronghold. Within a tent, Dr. McNeil found General Graham near a computer console. A technician was stationed at the computer and a second military officer was stationed at the radio communications post.

The General was barking orders at a Sergeant before the Sergeant saluted the General with a click of his heals, turned and marched off. When the General noticed Dr. McNeil, he waved for him to approach. "I have bad news for you, Dr. McNeil."

The doctor paused in his tracks. "W-what is it?..." He feared the worst. However bad the news maybe, he did not wish to beat around the bush. He wanted to know straight up. "Were there any casualties during the Brother's mission?"

"A video message is in progress. Therein, we are dealing with ransom demands from the terrorists. They proved the Blackguards have been captured alive." The General spoke with disappointment in his tone.

Dr. McNeil was also surprised by the news and as he looked upon the video footage he was shocked. At first he could only see the prisoners with three dirty half naked little people on their knees with their hands bound behind their backs and burlap sacks covering their heads. A closer look revealed the surgical scars and then he noticed the bulging muscles of Grud's shoulders, then Domin's chest.

"Where is the fourth Brother?" The doctor asked hastily.

"There is one laying down beside them." The General answered robotically.

"Beside them? Why is one of them laying down? You said they are all alive!" Dr. McNeil was sweating and frustrated.

Omar stepped into frame and removed the burlap sack from each one of the Blackguards. Dr. McNeil identified each of the Brothers who were gagged and bound before he too shared in the General's disappointment.

Omar bent down to the body lying on the floor and removed the burlap sack from his head revealing Narl with his eyes closed.

The face of Narl on a broad band television network was disturbing to say the least. It was the first time the world would see the face of a volk. Omar began to speak, then a separate female voice was heard, from the news broadcast, translating what Omar was saying, "As you

118

can see, these hostages have been punished and beaten, but how interesting it is to see their wounds healing so quickly." Pondering this for a moment, Omar looked at the camera as his face hardened with a stern sense of business. "Here's what we are going to do. If our demands are not met, we are going to begin cutting these things up into pieces, then we are going to build the creature you have robbed body parts from. After that, you can watch as the other prisoners of our possession perish one by one."

Dr. McNeil shook his head, "No, General. I can't accept the Brothers being defeated this way." The General looked at Dr. McNeil and squinted his eyes in skepticism. Dr. McNeil explained further, "After all of the work put into these Brothers, I can't believe this is how it will end for them. If I know the Brothers, and I think I have a pretty good handle on how they think, they're up to something." Dr. McNeil hoped his uncertainty was masked by his confidence successfully.

The General huffed, before adding, "In any case, we will soon know for sure, Dr. McNeil. No compliance to the terrorist's ransom demands will be met. If the Blackguards have no plan, we will soon witness their death."

"Why won't there be any negotiations?" Dr. McNeil was grasping at whatever he could, while knowing he had no time and no power to help the Brothers.

"Our experts know, if we give in to these immoral crooks, they will kill the Blackguards anyway. Nothing will stop them from trying to do that now." The General looked at Dr. McNeil and for a moment, a hint of compassion glinted in the General's eyes, "But I hope you are right, and the Blackguards know what they are doing... I really do."

Foggy dreamlike images began to appear within the blindfolded thoughts of the Blackguards. Unsure of where the images were coming from, it soon became clear, Narl was waking up.

He was about to react to the severe pain of his body, but the Brothers quickly filled Narl in on what had been taking place while he was knocked out and they told him to stay perfectly still.

Four 'X' shaped crucifixion crosses were erected with thick heavy posts and each of the young Blackguards were shackled with old rusty iron bonds to their outstretched arms and legs.

The female voice continued to translate Omar's words as he walk behind the Blackguards. "It was difficult for us to figure out how we would proceed with dismembering these foolish young soldiers. Would we take the arms and legs first?" Omar put his hands on Grud and Stroy's head. Fear gripped the boys, before Omar let go and slapped Narl's cheeks to wake him. He removed Narl's blind fold again and inspected his closed eyes carefully. "Perhaps the head should come off first." Narl would have winced at these words but he had read Omar's mind and knew what was coming next, "But we found it would be the torso that would have to come first." Omar yanked the blind fold from Domin's head as Abdelhakim pulled a long sharp sword from its sleeve. Domin's eyes were wide as the strong lights burned for the cameras.

"Time is running out and we have heard no answer from the Americans. It would be a shame to have to kill so many. Perhaps that is what you want. I had no idea the Americans could have such cold hearts. No matter, you shall soon find as we take off a limb from this one. We will replace the limb from one of these others. We will keep doing this until we have completed the entire puzzle. As you all likely know, the head will be attached last. We figured this would be the most excruciating method for this crude operation, and it is because of this method we are excited to get on with it." Omar raised his hand and Abdelhakim, with both hands holding the hilt of his sword, lifted it high over his head like an executioner of the dark ages.

In that instance, Domin wondered if Narl was pleased it was him who would be the first to perish. He wondered if Narl knew he stalled when Abu held a knife to his throat.

Omar spoke the seconds as the midnight deadline for the American's response drew near. "Five, Four, Three, Two, One..." Omar's hand remained in the air past the time of the deadline as he listened carefully for a response on the radio, but there was nothing.

Domin's veins began branch out over the surface of his muscles. As the blood vessels thickened, pulsating with dark red blood, Grud and Story coupled Domin with the panic roar of a caged beast as the three Blackguards fought for their lives against the shackles which bound them.

Abdelhakim was growing anxious with his arms holding his sword to the rock ceiling. Omar shook his head in disappointment and finally dropped his hand which was the signal for Abdelhakim to start chopping.

Narl lifted his head and opened his eyes wide and stabbed Abdelhakim's mind with a fear he never thought possible. Abdelhakim was so shaken he fell backwards.

Not only did the camera man get a jolt of telepathic fear but the same sense of fear was conveyed through the volume of anyone watching the video feed. Incidentally, the camera man was stricken with such fear he accidentally kicked over the tri-pod and the Camera crash

121

upon the stony floor. All video feed was gone as a result of the impact and the camera was so damaged it could not be used further.

The video feed flickered and went to static. Due to the chaos, Dr. McNeil and the General were not sure if the prisoners or the Blackguards were alive any longer. General Graham, however, had made up his mind. "The rescue mission is a complete failure."

"Should we move to the next phase, sir, and send in our sky striker attack force?" asked Sergeant Harmes with a sense of urgency in his voice.

No one wanted to dispute the General's decision for besides his undisputed rank of authority, he was known as a hard shrewd man. Dr. McNeil could not control himself with so much riding on the mission. It was not just about the Brothers, it was about his entire future. "We don't know if the mission is a complete failure for sure, sir! We must wait for confirmation before our next assault." The General paused for a moment as he contemplated whether or not to scrub the mission entirely and blow the entire Taliban facility sky high. It was obvious to him how Dr. McNeil did not agree, but he could not have his own people questioning his authority.

General Graham took Dr. McNeil by the arm and directed him out of the control tent. He whispered, strong and forcefully when he said, "You must know, no one really cares about these creatures you have created, Dr. McNeil. The Blackguards are expendable." Dr. McNeil's eyes were wide as he listened to the General, "The government has Eddy Evon, a true and unaltered volk. That is all the officials are focused on."

The words came as a shock to Dr. McNeil, though he was not sure why. He always knew this was true.

Domin broke free from his shackles, before Grud also tore the iron from its wooden foundations by the strength of his volk arms. Stroy kicked his volk legs out and the shackles snapped. Domin swung around and quickly freed Grud's legs and Stroy's arms with a merciless yank at the old rusty chains.

Domin, dodging bullets, veered left then right making his way closer to Omar. An array of bullets sprayed toward Domin, as rage and power pumped through his veins while he used a couple of the Taliban guards for shields. One bullet struck Domin's shoulder and he knew they would all have to reacquire their armor and weapons as soon as possible.

With a great roar, Domin dropped the minced guards and hurtled a barrel at the soldiers firing at him.

In the midst of a small window of time, Domin made his way to Narl where he expected no less than an instant answer to his question. "Where did they take our armor and weapons? We need to get it all back!"

Narl closed his eyes as he swiftly scanned Omar's mind for the answer. Upon opening his eyes, Narl pulled Domin close and said, "Our things are not far. Follow me!"

Narl signaled the other Brothers to follow as they quickly ducked down an adjacent corridor. The Blackguards broke through a door which led them into the Omar's private chamber. There on the floor was all of the armor and weapons belonging to the Blackguards.

Vivaciously, the Brothers helped one another as they nimbly dressed and snapped their armor and weapons in place.

Domin could hear the shouts and footsteps of the approaching Taliban soldiers. Together, the Blackguards raced out the door of Omar's chamber to meet the soldiers. As the Taliban reacted with gunfire, the rage of the Blackguards was fueled all the more. A fire was shared as it burned in their eyes, where they had a strong belief this enemy was already defeated. Domin was the first to charge into the squad of Taliban soldiers with his fast swinging samurai swords glinting in the light of their gunfire.

When the Taliban soldiers had either fallen in the gun fight or fled, the Blackguards approached the seven American soldiers who were shackled.

"You guys American?" asked one of the soldiers who was malnourished and had been beaten.

Grud stepped closest to the soldier, "Yeah, we have come to free you and the other prisoners." Breaking the chains by stretching them apart, Grud managed to calm the nerves of the prisoners a little, though his presence was unsettling.

The American soldier continued, "We weren't sure who's side you were on. No one has seen any of you before."

When the prisoners were freed from their chains, the multitude ran through the caverns together with Narl at the lead with a torch in hand. He led them all up through the levels of the deep base. The Blackguards protected the prisoners as they killed many Taliban. Around each new bend of the dark caverns the group ran into more Taliban combatants, but they were no match for the quick, precise skill of the Blackguards. As the group ran throughout the maze of tunnels, climbing higher through the catacombs, the Blackguards were helpful keeping the prisoners together as many of them needed to be carried or else they'd be left behind. Everyone put their faith in Narl as they trusted him to lead them though the caverns or they would all surely be lost.

The group boarded an electrical elevator cage whereby the push of a button wound a cable and winch to take them up to ground level. Seven groups of five had to take the elevator before everyone could be together at the top. Domin went with the first group to the top where he had to stock and assault the unsuspecting Taliban within the spacious vehicle garage port. When the area was secured and everyone was accounted for from the lower levels, Domin led the group to a specific military vehicle. What Domin showed everyone was a stolen armored American troop transport carrier. It had plenty of room to seat everyone. While the Blackguards and the seven American troops were tending to the comfort of the 23 South Korean Christians, Domin took the wheel of the trop transport and started it up.

They drove fast throughout the windy tunnels as they implemented their escape plan. Narl sat next to Domin to assist him in driving through the tunnels without getting lost.

Moments later, Domin brought the troop transport through to the tall inner gates. Smashing through the inner defence wall then through the next outer defence wall, they headed out across the sandy desert plains.

"When will we see some support from our allies?" Grud asked from the back of the transport. The Blackguards were surprised by the amount of time that went by with no contact from the U.S. Armies. They suspected they were merely watching the show. "If they won't help us, then let's show them we'll complete our mission with or without their help." Domin shouted amidst the growling engine of the old personnel carrier.

"It looks like our support has come at last!" stated Narl as he pointed out the windshield to the sky. There the Blackguards saw a stealth air force jet flying out of the clouds toward them before it deployed a nuclear warhead. The missile coiled through the sky above trailing smoke. A long plume of dust was stirred up in the wake of the armored personnel carrier as well, as the missile narrowly passed over them and moved beyond where it hit the Taliban stronghold.

Domin suspected a strong resulting shock wave from the nuclear blast so he shouted, "Get your heads down!" When the missile disappeared down the throat of the Taliban strong hold, a second later fire exploded from every fissure and lifted the entire surface structure of the mountain. When it settled, the mountain shrank due to the collapsing tunnels and crumbling rock. The shock blast kicked the rear end of the armored personnel carrier into the air before it crashed its nose down into the sand.

During all of this, the military held back at a safe distance.

Dr. McNeil and General Graham could see everything from their satellite eyes in the skies. The armored personnel carrier was seen as it emerged from the Taliban stronghold. Dr. McNeil believed with all his heart, the Brothers had freed the prisoners. Each and every prisoner would be accounted for. General Graham extended his hand to Dr. McNeil and Dr. McNeil shook the General's hand as they smiled, though each of them were celebrating two very different ideas of the mission's victory.

"I'm sorry for your loss Dr. McNeil. The Blackguards were most impressive indeed." said General Graham from his tight smile of teeth.

"Thank you, sir. But I was just curious, if by some 'miracle' we find the Brothers do come through for us in

126

the end and save the prisoners, what would be done for them and their heroism?"

"Come now, Dr. McNeil, you don't know when to quit, do you?" The General let out a breath as though the doctor was just wasting his time. "Well, we did have plans for a hero's celebration in their honor. Why what did you expect?"

"Well sir, I was hoping I would have the opportunity to renew custody of the Brothers, I mean the Blackguards, and continue with my project along side Dr. Evon." Dr. McNeil added, though doubtful he would ever have control over the Brothers the way he had in the past.

General Graham cocked an eyebrow at Dr. McNeil suspiciously before he turned to address the other people in the tent, "It is with deep remorse and regret that we had to lose such exceptional soldiers as well as the twenty three South Korean Christians, but we are victorious in destroying one of the Taliban's main operations outpost." Reaching into a cooler, General Graham lifted out a bottle of champagne. He twisted the end and popped the cork out. "The days after this mission will be part of a safer world!" The General's words were followed with a roar of cheers. He poured the bottle into many wine glasses which had just been set out. Everyone in the tent took a glass and lifted it. After they drank General Graham turned back to Dr. McNeil and said, "I would sign them over to you, McNeil, only they no longer exist. I am sorry, but you will just have to get over it." He lifted his own glass with the others again and shouted, "Here, here!"

Silence and darkness filled the compartment of the armored personnel carrier. It was as though God had struck the vehicle with an enormous fly swatter and all within were stunned. Small movements gave way to moans and coughing as the occupants returned to the living.

Everyone was in an uncomfortable heap as all were forced forward when the vehicle nose dived.

"Ow! My arms are pinched." Someone said.

"Get your foot out of my eye." Spoke another as everyone tried to untangle themselves from each other.

"You okay?" Narl asked Domin as he gently reached his hand out.

"I'm fine." Domin answered, shaking off the affects of the incident.

"Wise of you to tell everyone to get down before the blast. You may very well have saved everyone's life by doing so." Narl added thoughtfully.

Domin tried to start the vehicle but the engine would not turn over. When everyone was standing up in the back, Domin rose up from the driver's seat and joined them. Narl sensed Domin was giving him a cold shoulder.

"We have to get out of this tin can." Domin said before he grabbed hold of the latch of the door.

"Step away from that door right now!" Narl commanded.

"I've just about had enough of you…" Domin began before Narl cut him short.

"Radio active fall out is everywhere outside, you open that door and we will all be contaminated." Narl explained with a deathly warning in his eye.

"What do you suggest we do? Wait for American troops to come and save us?" Domin mocked.

"Yeah, I've had it with American troops…" Grud stepped closer to Domin. "We could have used their help and they nearly blew us all up."

"Right, they won't be helping us." Stroy stated as he tilted his head causing his neck to make an eerie cracking sound. "They did nothing to help us in negotiations and they probably think we are dead right now."

"We need to get everybody outside!" Domin spoke forcefully. "If the Americans see the prisoners are alive, they will come and we will all be sent to the scrubbers to be decontaminated of radio activity."

Narl ran at Domin and tried to push him away from the door. When Narl found Domin too strong to move, he grabbed at the door latch, "I'm sorry! I can't let you open that door. You'll kill us!"

"Hey, fathead, I am corporal Johnny Smyth of the second regiment, get your butt away from that door, boy. I'm pulling rank from here out." came the sudden command from the young corporal.

Domin leaned in at Narl and said, "He's talking to you, fathead."

Narl frowned at Domin as he let his hands slide off the latch before he unexpectedly charged at the corporal and head butted him. The corporal flew back to the wall of the transport behind him. Everyone gave Narl a perturbed look.

"Don't call me 'boy.'" Narl ignored everyone except for Domin as he turned back to Domin and said, "Now, get away from that door, or do you wish to try to out rank me as well?" Narl put his hand to his temple to threaten telepathic control.

Each one was tired from all of the fighting. They were very dirty and out of breath. Domin was darkened by the black smoke of burnt gun powder, "Our mission would have been a complete success, but you suggested we should let ourselves be captured and we almost lost our lives! Just shut up Narl. No one wants to hear another word from you." At the sound of Domin's powerful voice of reason, Narl let his hands hang down at his sides as he seemed to freeze in place and look carefully at each one

129

of his Brothers in bewilderment.

What Narl saw was how his Brothers were going to betray him. They were all going to team up on him in their reports, as will all of the others also. In their reports they will explain how Narl was about to send them all to their deaths. He could see clearly how his Brothers would get all of the credit for the entire mission and Narl would end up in a cell.

Narl's lips curled and his eyes became darker and full of anger and hate. "You did this on purpose!" Narl accused as he pointed at his Brothers with his finger. "It was probably your idea too wasn't it, Domin." He gave Domin a look of death.

"What are you talking about?" Domin said looking down on Narl, "We couldn't have escaped the tunnels without you." Pulling the latch and opening the door Domin began to help everyone out one at a time.

The smell of ozone from outside hit Narl's sense of smell and he seemed to just snap. "Do Not Patronize Me!!!" Narl put his hand to the temples of his head and blasted his Brothers with an aggressive wave of telepathy like nothing he had ever done to them before. Narl was so upset by his Brothers, he hoped to discredit them by causing them to fight the American soldiers who were organized behind him.

Under the influence of Narl's mind, the Blackguards; Domin, Stroy and Grud charged at the unsuspecting platoon of seven men. They fought the soldiers by slapping them around. The soldiers were in no condition to fight yet they did attempt to put their military training to use. The Blackguards fought against the mind control and though they did hurt the soldiers, they tried to go easy on them. The fight was not fair in the least, but Narl had no desire to stop until he saw the seven soldiers dead. This would discredit his Brothers so he could take the credit for the mission.

Everyone in the tent was celebrating when Dr. McNeil caught everyone's attention and showed them what he was looking at on the satellite imagery. There in the monitor the people, including General Graham, saw all four of the Blackguards come out of the broken armored personnel carrier. From the grainy view of the monitor, the ambiance of the silence changed, but when the Blackguards began to attack American troops, General Graham sprayed champagne from his lips in surprise. Dr. McNeil thought he saw the General's eyes turn red when he looked at him. General Graham did not react well when he saw the Blackguards turn on the American troops who were victims of imprisonment and torture. The General's temper was like a second nuclear blast when he shouted at Dr. McNeil. "What kind of freaks are these?! Doctor, you have created monsters!" Dr. McNeil stammered as he tried to explain, "Now, Dr. McNeil, you are unemployed!" The General hastily grabbed the communications com and ordered, "You have a new target. Send in everything to the target location for clean-up and terminate the Blackguards, now!"

One of the South Korean Christians threw a rock at Narl and pegged him square in the fore-head. Domin, Grud and Stroy found themselves standing over the wounded soldiers like bullies, but when the telepathy subsided, due to the rock, the Brothers charged at Narl swiftly. They were so upset with Narl, they wanted to kill him. Narl quickly gathered himself as he took a step back and touched his hand to the temple of his head with a smile of confidence. Just before they were going to pulverize Narl, the Brothers were again under his telepathic control. Narl toyed with his Brothers as he laughed and made them fight one another.

Meanwhile, Helicopters, transport vehicles and tanks quickly approached from the distance to follow their orders to destroy the Blackguards. Narl shifted his black eyes to the offensive convoy and with a simple command of thought, he sent his Brothers off and running to meet their attackers. Narl had such a lust for battle and blood he could not stay behind to watch his Brothers engage the enemy. He too raced to fight the American soldiers, all the while keeping his Brothers under his control.

Jumping, rolling and running with incredible speed, the Blackguards were able to evade bullets zipping by and explosions which lifted sand and rock with angry bursts of fire.

Narl gave his Brothers enough of a choice they were able to fight for themselves, as long as they fought the American soldiers. Domin resorted to his favourite battle tactic which was to turn his enemy's weapons against themselves. He jumped onto a tank to draw the fire power of the other military vehicles. When he was targeted and before he was struck, he darted over the front of the tank and leaped away as the tank was decimated behind him. Stroy, Grud and Narl also entered the fray as the military brigade came to an immediate halt.

Like ghosts, the Blackguards would pop up and appear for a split second to unleash a quick but powerful attack before they disappeared again. The military was just too slow for the ninja trained half volks.

Many soldiers lost their lives as the Blackguards began to disable and kill one military vehicle after the other. The worst mistake the soldiers made was to open their doors to come out and defeat the Blackguards, because the Blackguards would enter the vehicles and destroy the occupants in a blink of an eye.

One soldier within a transport vehicle grabbed a grenade and activated it. Narl quickly entered the transport and killed the platoon, but the soldier dropped his grenade and it went off too soon for Narl. He couldn't close the tragus of his ears soon enough. The blast shook Narl so much he lost his telepathic mind control link along with his hearing.

When Domin, Grud and Stroy were free from Narl's control, they immediately turned on him. They knew just where to find Narl because their minds were linked. The Brothers entered Narl's transport to attack him. The side of Narl's body was burned and blackened. As Narl struggled to rise up, Domin came in at him swiftly and punched Narl in the face. Domin felt no remorse for Narl any longer. Falling flat on his back, Narl quickly recovered, though his thoughts rattled in his skull, he used his telepathic ability to control Grud and Stroy to defend him. The rage within each one of the Blackguards rose to a level considered dangerously too high.

The military had been cut down to a pathetic wounded few. The word was give over the broad band radios how the next plan of attack would come shortly when the air force deployed sting ray missiles over the battle ground. The intent was to destroy the Blackguards for good. Those who were fortunate enough to still have the ability to move did what they could to flee the scene.

Though the punches from Grud and the incredible kicks from Stroy were almost too much punishment for him to handle, Domin did a real good job at returning the abuse. Blood pumped through the dark red branches of veins over the skins of the Blackguards. Narl was deaf to the sounds of fists pounding on flesh and the heavy

133

breathing and grunts, yet he inspired the fight with his mind just the same. The inside of the transport was a very confined area for a fight, to say the least, but Domin took Stroy in a head lock and rammed him into the bulkhead.

Stroy fell to the metal floor, supported by his hands and knees, he screamed until there was no more air left in his lungs. Countless veins appeared and grew like webs over his skin. He seemed to continue to try to scream for a moment though no sound was coming out. The throbbing veins seemed to quiver under his stress as there was very little of his original skin tone left for all the veins. Finally, Stroy collapsed and just laid still.

Grud sought vengeance and came at Domin, but Domin gave him an upper cut to the chin knocking his head into the ceiling.

Grud was dazed for a second, before he had a look in his eyes, the likes Domin had never seen before. Insane fear and rage transfigured his face to the point where he became an unrecognizable wild beast. A shadow of pure hate formed around Grud's eyes. The veins of his head and around his face were pumping with dark red blood. Grud let out a scream of agony and pain. He put his hands to his head and dropped to his knees. His face became flushed as though he were delirious with fatigue. His breath grew still then he fell to the floor limp, next to Stroy.

Domin turned on Narl. He was deeply grieved at Narl, but as angry as he was, he did not want Narl to die. Domin experienced an immediate hit of telepathic energy punch into his mind as he began to feel the stress and anxiety from a memory Narl had of Oblit's death. Realizing how Narl was using this memory to drive the Blackguards to the brink of insanity and death, Domin decided to confront his telepathic brother. At a glance over his shoulder, Domin was sure Grud and Stroy were still conscious enough to watch from their delirious states. "Narl, I told you before, *'Brother or no brother, if you try to get inside my skull one more time, it'll be the end of you.'*"

Domin reached out to the metal conduit which ran along the inner wall of the transport. He saw his veins slither out along his fore-arm to his hand. Tearing a conduit free from the inner wall of the transport, Domin lifted it over his head to destroy Narl once and for all. Narl hit him with a terrible magnified telepathic wave which sent pain throughout Domin's entire body. Domin dropped the metal pipe and collapsed to the floor. The pain contorted his body into a misshapen form. Narl sat up and continued to tighten Domin's arms and legs into some kind of torturous pretzel form.

Then the most mysterious thing began to happen. Domin, through sheer will power, began to fight against Narl's telepathic strength and influence. He began to untwist his body. Domin believed, some volk parts existed more randomly within him than his Brothers. He believed some part of his brain was volk, be it some small part to do with his nervous system. Domin's eyes were focused with an anger he had never felt before. A growl began to rise from deep within his chest as one hand came down onto the floor then the other. He straightened his legs then he began to rise up.

Narl began to panic as he found he was losing control. Stroy and Grud could not believe their eyes for they knew, to fight Narl's telepathy would mean Domin would have to endure a phenomenal amount of pain. Domin took hold of the metal conduit once again as he rose up. The tip of the pipe slid along the floor as, limping Domin approached Narl.

Domin began to roar insanely as he thrashed and pummeled Narl with the heavy metal pipe. Narl's head was opened up and Domin quickly felt his control of his mind return. It was finished.

Narl was dead and Domin had killed him. He thought such a feat would cause him to slip into a great sense of depression, but the exhilaration of the moment and the end to Domin's pain had actually felt very rewarding to him. Domin didn't truly know how much he disliked Narl until he was dead.

Domin turned to his only remaining brothers, Stroy and Grud. The face of Domin was a mess of dirt, ash and the splatter of Narl's blood. Stroy and Grud saw the intensity in Domin's eyes. Though their blank faces didn't show it, they feared for their own lives. Domin marched right past them, he had a strange sense something was amiss outside.

"Come, we have to get out of here." Despite Domin's words, his Brothers did not move.

Domin poked his head out of the transport and noticed the American forces had pulled out. All that could be seen from the fleeing military vehicles was a dust trail. Domin's suspicions were unsettling. He sniffed at the air and listened to the silence. The military was not sending any back-up by land. Far off to the horizon, however, Domin caught sight of a single aircraft bearing down on them.

"Oh, not again…" breathed Domin, with discontent and dismay.

He jumped right out of the transport and looked around to assess his surroundings. There to his dismay, he found himself in the midst of a war torn waist land. There was no time left to prepare. In less than a minute the fighter jet would have him targeted and it would all be over.

Letting out a slow breath of thought, before Domin darted back into the military transport. He raced past

136

Stroy and Grud, who hadn't left their seats, as he veered toward the driver's seat. The decorated transport navigator, though dead, was still strapped into position. With his heavy armor and large physic, Domin would not be able to fit between the seat and the controls. Domin took hold of the driver's seat and tore it out from the floor, cadaver and all.

The force and strength Domin had to exude was far more than he could physically handle. The volk muscles of his arm had tightened so powerfully, the human bone snapped under the volk strength.

"AAAHHHGGG!!!" Domin roared in absolute pain. "Damn these frail human bones!" Though the pain was excruciating, he was trained to work through it.

He knew what had happened for he had seen his Brothers end up with fractures and torn ligaments where human frailties met solid volk robustness.

He turned the key and the motor roared to life. Domin punched it into gear and dropped his heavy foot onto the throttle.

Dr. McNeil observed the monitor's satellite footage displaying images in real time. Certain something was wrong, Dr. McNeil thought it was most peculiar for the Brothers to be inside the transport for so long with no activity. "What are they doing in there?" The doctor could see smoke from a possible explosion within. Dr. McNeil glanced over his shoulder at General Graham. The General was engaged in something at another monitor. He held an ear phone with a small attached mic to his ear. "Fox one you are cleared to engage. Make it a two strike target elimination. Go in, take out the personnel transport then circle around and decimate the area in a one hundred foot radius."

"That's a go on a two strike elimination." answered

back the pilot of the jet fighter, "First target, the personnel carrier and second target the area of the personnel carrier. Sidewinder missiles at the ready, sir."

"No General!" Dr. McNeil protested, "The Brothers are still down there! Let me send my men in there. They can defuse this entire problem and bring the Brothers in and don't forget the captured leaders inside."

"That is a negative, McNeil. You will control yourself this instant or be court marshaled. This is a military situation. One more outburst like that and I will have you arrested!"

Dr. McNeil immediately backed off, but he gave the General a look of urgency for him to do something. When General Graham saw how Dr. McNeil would co-operate, he told him, "My orders are to leave no retrievable remains of the Brothers if they went rogue."

Dr. McNeil was just about to say something when the first officer reported, "We have movement General."

Everyone crowded in around the monitor. The transport lurched forward. As it headed out of the mass of wasted military vehicles, it headed straight for a broken down tank two miles away. The tank bellowed black smoke from its port hatch. The transport broad sided the tank and both vehicles lurched away from the high speed impact. The collision was harsh and it kind of insinuated there were other unseen problems going on in side the transport.

Dr. McNeil couldn't tolerate any more. He felt terrible. Guilt poked at him with the thoughts of not doing enough to help the Brothers, the Brothers who were more like sons to him. As Dr. McNeil's mind stirred, helplessness ensnared him. He left the control tent to get some air. Remembering he was still carrying his cell phone in his pocket, Dr. McNeil quickly began punching up phone numbers of anyone whom might even remotely help him in some way. Poking his head back into the tent from time to time, he could see the jet fighter quickly moving in for his targeted assault. Dr. McNeil made a couple frantic calls on his cell phone in a desperate last minute attempt to stop what he feared would soon happen. He let his phone slip from his hand and fall to the ground as he accepted he was just too late to do anything any longer. He watched helplessly, from a distance, as the missile was fired and the transport of the Brothers was vaporized.

The jet fighter veered off and immediately circled back to target the area around the smoking ruin. A surge of light filled the monitor's screen. The occupants of the tent cheered for a moment, but seeing the General was not sharing in the elation of the moment, all voices simmered quickly and everyone was down to work again.

General Graham stayed to look over a few results which were reported, he turned on his heels abruptly and stormed out of the tent. He did not stop at all to make eye contact with Dr. McNeil. Still feeling terrible, Dr. McNeil decided he needed to take a walk to clear his mind.

The moon in the sky gave quite a bit of light to the encampment. Never had a star lit sky seemed so clear as it was that night. Soldiers moved around Dr. McNeil with purpose when he noticed a transport in the distance. It was unloading exhausted American foot soldiers. Among the soldiers were the seven American soldiers who had been rescued. Each one of them had obviously experienced the worst beating of their lives. Dr. McNeil jogged near to the transport and tried to see some of the people who were the last ones to have been near the Blackguards in action.

All of the 23 South Korean Christians had also been saved along with the soldiers. When the soldiers came out, they were asked many questions. One of the roughed up American soldiers began to speak, "I had never seen anything like it, ever. These super soldiers showed up. They did some amazing things, but for some reason, they attacked us." The escapee was difficult to identify for the layers of dirt and ash on his face. "I think the one with the fathead made them do it... Otherwise why would they fight us? Why save us, then beat us up? I-I just don't understand."

"I'm sorry, sir, but the super soldiers were killed in action." answered a female soldier reporter.

"What? No way! These guys were professionals." Quivered the voice of the beaten soldier, "They were, like, invincible, you know?"

"I am sorry to be the one to tell you this but from our understanding, they were caught up in the friendly fire of an air strike." The reporter explained further.

"Well, sounds terrible, *if it is true*, but I wouldn't doubt it if these soldiers were able to find some way out. The way they would fight, they were like, --*like magic*." No one responded to the soldier's statement because by the look in his eyes he was dead serious.

Dr. McNeil knew exactly what the soldier meant. He knew his sons. They were indeed, like magic.

He turned away and began to walk back in the direction of the control tent. As Dr. McNeil walked he began to consider the possibilities how the Brothers may have escaped the 'no win situation.'

Once back at the control tent, he found his cell phone, right where he dropped it. He went inside the tent and asked to view footage of the final air strike. Sure enough, the military transport was destroyed, but there was something odd about the prior collision it had with the burned out tank.

He watched the footage over and over. Finally, Dr. McNeil left the tent in a quiet and peculiar fashion.

Outside the tent he began to make many more calls. He organized his men to do a little investigation of their own.

Dr. McNeil led his team directly to the smoking tank near the chard ground of the missile strike zone. This was the last place of significance the American army would consider. Sure enough, just as Dr. McNeil had suspected. The three Brothers; Grud, Stroy and Domin were lain near to the tank. They had obviously jumped free from the transport at the time of the collision.

Somehow, Dr. McNeil was not surprised Narl was not with them. The Brothers were burned, wounded and unconscious. The team under Dr. McNeil's authority had recovered the bodies of the Brothers and made preparations to return home to North America.

With the help of Dr. Evon, Dr. McNeil had the opportunity to reinstate his project of the volk Brothers. Unfortunately, Stroy and Grud didn't make it. Though their hearts were still beating, their minds had undergone such stress where the affects were permanent. Stroy and Grud were brain dead. Their minds had finally, fully succumbed to the affects of their own extreme anger. Just as Oblit could not deal with his anger, so Stroy and Grud had also met with the same outcome. It was Dr. McNeil's diagnostic how anger was brought on as a chemical imbalance of the brain due to the incompatible fusion of volk to human flesh.

Dr. McNeil began to scribble into his project journal and added this entry. *"Why Domin always seems to have the capacity to deal with the fusion where all others fail, I can not guess. I, therefore, will complete my work and take all I can from Grud and Stroy and put it all into Domin."* So much sacrificed for the project's sake, it left Dr. McNeil feeling very little for himself and his career. Domin would now be Dr. McNeil's last hope. If he lost

141

Domin, everything would be lost, not only the last Blackguard, but his own flesh and blood, his son.

Again, under the knife of surgery, Domin was Dr. McNeil's prize project. There were a few moments where Dr. McNeil regretted what he was doing. It was not his intent to ruin a person's life. *"But for the sake of science,"* he would tell himself, *"it has to be done."*

Dr. McNeil looked down at the broken unconscious body of Domin, his son, laying on the surgical table. "I hope, for both our sakes son, this is the last time you have to have a surgery like this."

One of the younger doctors in the room asked, "Do we have to use Domin for this procedure?"

Without skipping a beat, Dr. McNeil answered, "Domin is not only the perfect age, but he is one of the very few who's body will accept the volk transplants in the early stages of growth. Both the host body and the transplanted organ must be able to grow still so they will bond. As far as the age of these muscles and the body of the patient, we don't have much time left. To implant them into someone else will be even more difficult with mature people and volk parts because they would no longer be able to grow and amalgamate together. Unless you have someone waiting outside, who is just as eligible, we will have to use Domin."

The bodies of two of Domin's deceased Brothers were laying on beds side by side. Dr. McNeil looked at the bodies and thumbed through the pages of notes for all he wanted to do for this particular project. He knew he would be at it for hours. *'This will be the toughest surgery yet.'* Dr. McNeil thought.

What is left of the Brothers; Stroy and Grud was graphted into Domin's body. During the long and rigorous forty eight hour procedure, Dr. McNeil met with

142

the most unexpected surgical set backs of his career. For one thing, Domin, Stroy and Grud were so wound up by their anger, they were not aware of the bullet wounds they received.

Domin, alone had twenty six bullet wounds in various places. Many of the muscles and organs Dr. McNeil wanted to transplant were damaged from the recent battle. If he decided to use some of these parts, there would be extra healing time required.

Tired and fatigued, Dr. McNeil sat back in a chair next to a computer monitor. The other technicians and doctors had gone home. The doctor watched as Domin's strong *human* heart began to beat and cause the little lines of the graph to bounce up and down with each pumping rhythm.

'*The surgery was a success.*' He thought as he let out a long breath. He felt good though he was tired. His satisfaction came in knowing he was a father who had saved his son's life. Domin was now fully proportioned with equal implants of muscle and organs throughout his body. They had also added titanium metal rods to his skeleton in multiple places to strengthen his structure under certain foreseeable punishments Domin would no doubt put himself through. The rods were designed to adjust to further growth of the young man.

Dr. McNeil remembered it was his sperm sample which created Domin in the first place. "Domin, my son. What doesn't kill you will only make you stronger." He whispered to Domin's ear.

Though the surgery and bodily fusion acceptance was achieved, Dr. McNeil was still faced with challenges of how to dispose of unwanted volk flesh and to keep the entire second stage of his project secret from General Graham and the rest of the military.

Moments and days after the final surgery, Domin would scream out in agony, as the pain he felt was an unbearable torture. Pleading for the doctors to make the pain stop, Dr. McNeil replied, "We have given you our strongest pain relief medication but it makes very little difference. Your body is somehow unaffected by drugs."

Domin recovered day by day, the pain was so intense he asked Dr. McNeil to just terminate him. Of course, Dr. McNeil could never do such a thing, but as the days passed, Domin's pain became increasingly tolerable.

With the accomplishments of being able to walk again and eat whole foods, Dr. McNeil notice how Domin became very detached from the regular responsibilities of his life.

Inwardly, Domin was experiencing a great sense of depression for the loss of the only family he ever knew, his Brothers.

Domin's loss hurt him to his core because he felt responsible for each of his Brothers' deaths. Furthermore, because Domin had acquired his brother's volk body parts he felt an added weight of shame's burden.

Standing in front of a tall mirror, Domin untied his hospital gown and let it drop to the floor. Wearing only his boxer shorts, Domin's fingers touched the healing wounds of the bullet holes. For now his wounds from battle and his cuts from surgery were easy to distinguish, but in time, he knew, the scars would become hard to differentiate from battle wounds and scars of surgery.

As Domin examined himself at the mirror, he began to boil with a new sense of anger. Shutting his eyes tight, Domin felt the pain would go away, but it was the opposite reaction which proved true. Tightening his muscles throughout his body and clenching his teeth, Domin felt a heat move through his blood. A gentle hand touched Domin's shoulder with a soft female voice calling Domin's name.

When Domin opened his eyes, he looked at the image of himself again through the mirror. Nurse Sophia was next to Domin, trying to calm him as the blood pumping through his veins slowly eased away. It was then Domin realized he was on the verge of losing it and tearing the entire facility apart. Nurse Sophia was not aware of the fire she had just put out with kindness. She was there to comfort Domin when no one else could.

Nurse Sophia was so kind and gentle with Domin, careful not to agitate him. Together, they discovered Domin's new strengths with his brawny volk arms of Grud and mighty volk legs of Stroy.

Waking up at nights in cold sweats, Domin remembered his dreams in detail as they were always the same, they were of his ghosts of the past. His dreams usually started out with dreams of Narl, then he would also see his other Brothers who would back him up.

Domin thought he was going crazy as he began to see his Brothers while he was awake. Dr. McNeil gave Domin some medication but as always it wouldn't work, so he resorted to some wholesome fatherly advice. One night Dr. McNeil and nurse Sophia stayed up all night with Domin and tried to explain away the dreams. Domin needed the talk for he needed to confront his feelings. From the entire night, Domin came away from it all with a single piece of wisdom spoken from Dr. McNeil which made all the difference, "Domin, if one of your other Brothers survived and you were a ghost in the room with him, would you not want to give comfort to the one left behind who carried the burden of guilt? I know you would. You loved and respected your Brothers. Each of you knew you were put on this planet because you were to accomplish great things, incredible things. Try to carry your Brothers around, for now on, like you would the law, in your heart. I am reminded of biblical scripture from James 4:11; *Brothers, do not slander one another. Anyone who speaks against his brother or judges him speaks against the law and judges it. When you judge the law, you are not keeping it, but sitting in judgment on it.*"

Dr. McNeil was invited to speak to Dr. Evon about Domin's situation. Dr. Evon suggested Domin be sent to the top secret Knolix Island. There he would be with his last remaining brother, Eddy Evon, who was 100% volk. Domin would also be given the opportunity to go to school and perhaps make a friend or two.

Dr. McNeil asked if he too could accompany Domin to the Knolix Island, and his wish was granted.

Chapter 5

Upon the time when Domin was aboard a small ship, an idea had been proposed to have wild animals roam freely on the Island. Selected wild animals were delivered in cages and crates, two by two. There were five ships in all on this particular expedition. Each one of the ships looked like fishing boats and they all had the same destination; the Knolix Island. The animals were selected; one male and one female, such was reminiscent of Noah's Ark.

They carried a very specific assortment of animals to balance a very eco-friendly circle of life. A specific assortment of plant life was selected to attract a variety of birds. The animal inhabitants had to complete a cycle through nature's method of predator and prey. For this purpose, hundreds of species were chosen.

For most of the journey, Domin was not interested in anything to do with the Island described by Dr. McNeil, but when they could see it far off to the horizon, his curiosity grew. The ship's captain was gracious enough to lend his binoculars to Domin and he took great interest, at that point, to focus in on whatever he could of the mysterious Island. By the time the ship was preparing to dock, Domin was very excited to get off the ship.

The ships traveled in at the Island side by side. Each of the captains pushed the bows of their boats right up onto the soft white sands of the Knolix shores. The specific ship to which Domin was a passenger of docked at the sandy beach last. Immediately, men began to prepare to unload the cargo.

A long mechanical crane extended its boom out from the deck of each boat. They would reach into their cargo holds with large hooks at the end of two inch thick cables. One by one, cages and crates were unloaded to the beach. Within each of the containers was an animal who would soon become acquainted with its' new home.

With his black toque pulled down tight over his head, Domin watched all of the activity at Dr. McNeil' side. "Isn't there something I can do to help?" Domin asked as he studied the activity around him.

"No, Domin, I told you. These men must carry out their assignments. You are not supposed to get involved in any way at all." Dr. McNeil answered rather frustrated. He seemed to be rather preoccupied by all of the hustle and bustle going on around them. Domin was just trying to bide his time, waiting for his turn to be escorted off the boat.

Domin wore a black shirt with a brown vest and dark green pants. At his feet was a large duffle bag which had all the belongings he owned.

As a cage was being lifted out of the cargo hold a metallic snap was heard reverberating like a chime. All attention of the crew, aboard the vessel, was focused on the cage being elevated by the crane.

Domin ran forward and looked into the cargo hold. The cage was ten feet off the floor and the creature inside was angry and thrashing about. Domin could not be sure what kind of creature it was, only it had sharp teeth which glistened as it reflected light and its' fur was a light rusty color of brown. The way it growled sent chills up everyone's' spines. As it charged at the bars, the weight was tearing the top away from the cage.

The structure of the cage lost all integrity and fell to the floor. The bars clattered apart around the furry creature.

"Look out!" Someone from below deck shouted. "It's free! Run! RUN!!!" the crew members who were in the hold scattered in panic as they fled for their lives.

"No! Noooooooooooooo!" A voice of a victim trailed off as the creature roared and thrashed as it attacked.

"It's got Johnny, we gotta get out'a here!" came another voice.

Domin could not stand the sounds of such mayhem another second. Before anyone knew what was happening, Domin leaped into the hold. He landed on the floor surrounded by the light beam of the sun. Beyond the beam of light, it was difficult to see anything. Domin could hear the feet of the crew members shuffling in the dark. He could also hear the breathing of the men and the thumping of their hearts in their chests.

Then the distinct guttural growl came again like a warning specifically to Domin. Locating where the sound was coming from, and with it Domin heard another sound. A curious sound of something wet being torn. It wasn't until he heard the sound of teeth gnawing on bone when he realized it was the creature feasting on poor Johnny still.

"Over here, guys. I'm at the door." Spoke one of the crew in an audible whisper. More shuffling was heard as the men tried to make their escape.

Domin backed away into the shadows and waited. Dr. McNeil shouted into the hold, "Domin, are you ok?.. Domin, answer me! Where are you?" Before long one of the men came out from where he was hiding and ran through the beam of light to cross the cargo area to the door. The creature reacted to the sudden movement and came charging out at the man. The creature shook all over as it roared and moved with extraordinary speed. Before the creature was able to get its' claws into the crewman, Domin charged into the side of the hairy creature and knocked it down. The creature grunted in a confused manner. The crewman was laying on the floor screaming, but Domin lifted him up and threw him at the open door.

Domin turned his attention on the beast and roared like he had never roared before. His entire being was on fire with the ultimate power of anger. The creature's eyes did not leave Domin as it cautiously moved around him. It was sizing him up. As it moved into the beam of light, Domin could see it was a bear, but not just any old bear. When it reared up onto its' hind legs at its, full height of ten feet, the vicious grizzly bear was all kinds of angry.

Domin took a step toward the grizzly to intimidate it. It wasn't until he did so that for once, fear had snuffed out his fire of anger and confidence. The look in the grizzly bear's eyes, so wild and inhuman, he would take this image with him to the grave, *'but not today.'*

Without warning, the grizzly's claw came swooping in at Domin and scored three deep scratches into his cheek with a single swipe.

Domin was thrown from his footing and rolled into a crate of two bobcats. The crate crumbled under his weight and the two cats darted away into the darkness between the other crates. Domin moved and began to rise up with blood pouring out from his cheek. He turned to face the grizzly just as it decided to make a charge at him. Domin moved quickly to deflect the bear but not before getting an upper cut in on it as it moved past. The grizzly was able to stop its forward momentum without crashing into more crates as Domin had.

The grizzly spun at Domin roaring as it wildly attacked. Domin fought back at the bear and was able to get a good jab in at its' ribcage. Domin's confidence level began to rise. The two of them were at a stand-off.

Domin began to reflect on his training. He remembered his Brothers and the sense of invincibility he had with them. He remembered the extensive drills. They were trained as ninjas. They were ultimate fighters, but most of all, they were trained to fight with the skills of animals.

At the moment when Domin was looking his adversary right in the eyes, he took on the ferociousness of a grizzly bear. In Domin's mind he was no longer fighting the grizzly, for he himself was a grizzly. This was a coliseum where two grizzly bears were going at it toe to toe.

The bear moved on its' paws, and so also did Domin. The grizzly snorted its contempt. So also did Domin. Finally, the grizzly bounded at Domin and rose up at him with a loud sounding roar. Domin also rose up and his roar was reminiscent of the grizzly's. They locked their arms around the back of each other's neck. The grizzly tried to work it wide jowls around Domin's neck but Domin pulled his head back quickly before the bear's mouth snapped shut. He then moved his head in at the bear and bit down on its' ear. The grizzly roared in pain and swung its' head up and back. Domin was lifted right off the floor and was tossed across the cargo area behind the grizzly.

The grizzly moaned in pain as it turned on Domin. Blood dripped from the grizzly's head. Domin rose up from the broken crates. His mouth was covered in blood... The grizzly's blood. Then he spat out the grizzly's ear onto the floor.

Domin rose up like a grizzly and roared again with his lower lip hanging loosely. The grizzly thrashed its head from side to side in frustration, then it ran at Domin to finish him. Domin also had enough of this. He too charged at the grizzly. Domin leaped into the air to get the drop on his enemy, but the grizzly rose up also. It caught Domin out of the air and slammed his body down

152

to the floor. Domin was underneath the great king of the wild.

The grizzly's mouth quickly came down and surrounded Domin's face. As he felt the sharp teeth grating over his scalp, he reached up and took hold of the bottom jaw with one hand, then he grabbed its' upper snout. Domin was not about to let the grizzly bite down onto his head.

The grizzly was surprised by Domins' great strength, and like wise Domin was amazed at the powerful jaws of the great bear. Then Domin let the grizzly know just what he was dealing with. Domin stretched the mouth of the bear open. The bear tried to back up but Domin was too strong. The grizzly began to panic as the pain of its' open jaw became more than it could bare. The claws of the grizzly began to scratch at Domin's chest. Domin realized he would have to end this immediately. A tearing cracking sound came from the grizzly's gaping mouth followed by a series of popping sounds of cartilage and ligaments. Then Domin roared into the grizzly's open mouth as he broke the bear's jaw completely. A pathetic air filled scream came from the bear. It was the kind of sound a bear rarely, if ever, made.

Domin was so outraged by the pain the grizzly inflicted on him he began punching the wounded animal. The bones of the grizzly's chest were heard cracking with each thunderous strike. Domin rose up high into the air with his fists combined together before he heavily drove his fists down on the bear's head.

Domin did this thunderous action again and again despite the people who came into the hold to calm him. It was uncertain if Domin would turn his anger on the people. Domin's cheek still bled dark red blood, but it was not as fatal as the puncture wounds of his chest. Though Domin did not know it, his lungs were slowly filling up with blood.

Dr. McNeil put his hand on Domins' shoulder and spun him around. "That's enough now, son." The doctor spoke with a kindness that calmed Domin quickly.

The look in Domin's dark tattooed eyes was almost enough to inflict pain. Dr. McNeil thought Domin might snap and attack him, but instead Domin coughed up some blood and passed out at his feet.

Domin awoke in a hospital bed. The interior of the hospital room was very spacious and clean. The walls, floor and ceiling were white. The medical staff wore white and the room was sectioned by curtains hanging from rods suspended from the ceiling.

A door opened at one far end of the medical room as a patient was leaving. At each end of the room were upper and lower cabinets. Domin was not certain if he was still on the Island. Technical medical machines beeped. One was to monitor his heart rate with a continuous paper graph automatically feeding through the machine.

Dr. McNeil leaned over Domin as he patted a small damp cloth on his fore head. "You won't die on me, Domin, you know why? Cause unlike your brothers, you're a survivor."

Domin's chest was covered over with a cast. A large white bandage covered his cheek with a little bit of red ooze seeping through it.

"You have just recovered from a surgery. Just look at you. Here we go again, right? One hundred and sixty stitches to your chest alone, plus eighteen to the deep scratches to your face. But what does a few extra scars mean to you? You have more scar tissue over your body than you have of smooth untouched skin. By giving me a reason to put you back on the surgical table, I was able to

154

add a little more volk to you from my supply. At this moment, you are perfect, or as perfect as we could hope. Your chest will not only have the muscles of a volk, but the tough skin of a volk as well. Only, I have one other minor mishap to inform you about. All of the energy you used to fight the grizzly bear, the injuries you've recieved and to pump fluids through your volk muscles became too much for your human heart to handle. In short, you died on my operating table. All we could do was put a rush on a new heart for you, but there were no hearts compatible to your blood type. We looked into a pig's heart and found we could use a heart that's a little bigger and stronger for you. Nurse Sophia mentioned how the bear was a part of the pig family and compatible with humans, and thanks to you, a bear's heart was readily available, so from this moment forth, you will have the power and heart of a grizzly bear."

Domin just laid there in his bed staring forward into nothingness as though his mind was focused on images from his memory. Dr. McNeil sat with him patiently.

"M-Dr. McNeil?" Domin spoke with tired, slurred words. His wounded cheek was swollen to twice its' size. "I hate my life." He told him.

Dr. McNeil's heart sank. He felt like he would be blamed for all he put the Brothers' through sooner or later. Never before had the Brothers blamed Dr. McNeil for anything, rather they had always looked up to him as the leader no matter how hard he pushed. The hardest part for the doctor was explaining how everything was a requirement of the work he had to do. Dr. McNeil wasn't supposed to get involved emotionally, but he truly did care for them all. He thought they knew.

"It's my fault." Domin began to cry in self pity, "I killed them. My Brothers. I killed them all."

This was very unexpected to Dr. McNeil. He could

not have imagined how Domin was carrying around such a burden of guilt. "Why do you keep on bringing me back to life and caring for me? I deserve punishment. I deserve to die."

"No, Domin. You are mistaken. There are a lot of people who must share the blame for your brothers' deaths. Anyone who had a position of responsibility, along with your brothers, are to blame. Me and my staff made you who you are today. The government got their dirty fingers into all of you. I mean, I'm sure you could find an angle to blame the volks as well, but I'll tell you, when you were born, you were a cripple. Thanks to surgeries and volks you are not only better, you have superhuman capabilities. I knew earlier on, you had the greatest life expectance of the Brothers. You were brought into this world with misfortune but look at you now. Now, you are the greatest warrior. Never forget, Domin. You are the greatest warrior there ever was or ever will be. It was destiny that brought you to this point. You and your brothers were an unstoppable force when you all worked together. The moment your brothers decided to quit on the team, everything failed."

"Nurse Sophia once told me how everyone I care about would betray me. Looks like she was right."

"Nurse Sophia? That name rings a bell, who is she?"

"My nurse from the Alaska base." Domin clarified.

Dr. McNeil remembered her now. How odd it was Domin spoke of her for she was his biological mother.

"It is time for me to bury my past. I don't want to go back. I need to start over with a clean slate. I want it to start here, on this Knolix Island. A new name and a whole new identity."

"Well what?" Dr. McNeil smiled as he was delighted to entertain Domin's feelings. "You want to blend in with other humans and be called mike or something?"

"Not exactly. I know I am not like everyone else. I just need something other than, Domin, something I can use to drive a stake into the ground and say from this day onward, I am a new person. Perhaps the name of the Island would do. Knolix."

Dr. McNeil thought about Domin's request for a moment, then he said, "You single handedly defeated a grizzly bear. I for one will call you, Grizz."

Domin shot a look at Dr. McNeil like he was a genius, "Grizz? Yes, this will do." Grizz answered.

"Well, this couldn't be a more appropriate moment. I have something for you. A gift really." Dr. McNeil reached into his jacket pocket and pulled out a long leather string. What dangled at the center of it was a tooth from the grizzly bear who was killed aboard the ship.

Dr. McNeil tied it around Grizz's neck. Grizz took the tooth and held it up, pulling at length on the leather string to see it. Grizz chuckled, and placed his hand over his chest as he winced at the pain. Smiling, he looked up at Dr. McNeil, "I am, Grizz." He said with an affirmed acknowledgement.

"Yes, you are Grizz, but you are registered here on this Island as Domin, so while you are here, you will have to be Domin for a little while longer." explained Dr. McNeil.

"Then I will leave, tonight." Grizz answered as though he had just made his decision. He tried positioned himself to hop off the bed.

"Are you kidding? Just look at yourself, you are a mess. You need to recover. I still need you, and besides, you are so young. You have a whole life time ahead of you to fulfill your destiny." He held his hand out to Grizz. "You must stay."

Pain surged through Grizz's body like a lightning

bolt and he winced. Dr. McNeil offered his hand to Grizz and Grizz took the Doctor's hand before they shook, "I'll stay." He smiled in his coy but playful way, "For now."

Dr. McNeil removed Grizz's bandages and cleaned his wounds. He then reapplied new dressings and filled out his chart. In his observation he found Grizz's wounds had healed up quite a bit in a short period of time. "Increased immune system still seems functional." observed Dr. McNeil.

"My thought exactly." Grizz replied as he rose up to get out of bed.

"Whoa, now just where do you think you are going?" Dr. McNeil asked with his arms poised to support Grizz should he suddenly lose balance.

"I am well now, Doctor. Thank you, and good-bye." Grizz stood up and took hold of a pair of crutches leaning near by. He placed a crutch under each of his arms and began to hobble his way to the door. Grizz left the hospital on crutches though many of the hospital staff protested against his decision. The crutches bowed under Grizz's great weight. No one could stop him no matter how hard they tried. Grizz just simply ignored them as he slowly continued to the door. He made his way outside where he found himself in the middle of the little Knolix Island town of Scamp.

The town was situated in a tight crevice. The outside of the hospital was old and run down but the interior was new and clean. A sign above the creaky looking door read Hospital. The entire complex seemed to be built into the side of a cliff. Grizz returned inside the hospital. "What's going on here?" He spoke loudly. He didn't care who heard him, he spoke to Dr. McNeil. Grizz went straight to the back of the room using his crutches. "Oh, this door looks interesting." Grizz pointed out. "Does it go deeper into the Island?" He joked. He was met with some very odd but blank faces. "Oh? So its' true, is it? That explains the digital key pad next to it."

"Are you finished playing around?" came Dr. McNeil, "It is just the freezer."

"The freezer? I want you to open this freezer. What will I find in here? Frozen volk embryos?" Silence followed for no one was sure how to answer Grizz. Grizz was certain the silence could only mean one thing. "Oh, I am on a roll. Now, open it or I will tear this door from its' hinges."

Dr. McNeil slid his hand into his pocket, before he paused to look up at Grizz.

"Don't make me do something we will all regret." Grizz warned with a squint of his eyes.

Dr. McNeil took his hand out of his pocket when he revealed he was holding a pass card. He slid it through the card slot and entered a quick code on the key pad. A green light came on and a click was sounded as the locks released. The door opened and behold, it was truly just a freezer full of medical supplies and extra blood. There was nothing out of the ordinary.

"You have your staff well trained. I don't recognize any of them yet they don't seem to be uncomfortable in my presence." Grizz observed as an attempt to keep from looking too stupid.

"They have all studied up well on our past records and the detailed files of who you are." answered Dr. McNeil.

"Well I'm sure the other residence of the Island don't know my file. They will surely freak out the first time they see me… Well, let's just get this over with."

Grizz marched outside again, right into the middle of the dirt road. He stood there breathing with the cool steam of his breath puffing from his mouth and nose. He was expecting his presence to start a panic amongst the

Island folks. To his surprise the people hardly paid him any mind at all. Domin was very puzzled by this. He approached a young lady and said, "Hey, don't you find me scary?"

"Well, you're no more scary than, Eddy Evon seemed when I first met him." She answered most assuredly.

Grizz then approached a burly man. Rising up before him Grizz lifted his arms out to his sides and then curled them in to show off his muscular biceps. "Buddy, you never seen anything like this before, have ya?" Grizz winced his face under the pain of his new tight stitches.

"Um, actually, I think I've seen bigger arms on Eddy Evon."

"Eh, I don't believe you." Grizz told him. The reactions of the people of the Island were so strange to him. "Just tell me where Eddy is. I want to see him."

The man raised his eyebrows for a moment and pointed across the town. "He should be at the old mill."

Grizz was used to getting a reaction from people which was more anxious. It frustrated him he did not strike the same kind of fear into the people as he was used to.

Without a thank you, Grizz turned from the man and hobbled off down the road with his crutches in the direction the man was pointing. There in the distance, Grizz could barely see the old shell of a building. That must be the old mill.

Grizz figured he could just stay on course to where the man had pointed and he would eventually find himself at the old mill, but when the road veered off, Grizz decided he would keep going right through the thick forest. He found the forest to be part evergreen trees and part jungle. It was a strange Island and as he made his way through the thicket, he realized the Island was far bigger than his first impression of it.

His pathless journey led him to a cliff's edge and at the bottom of the gorge was a river. The river wound its way down the mountain side steeply. The river was much like a long cascading waterfall only the water pooled in several places as it made its way down. He looked up the mountain and to his surprise he found the old mill. It had an old water wheel which didn't turn because water wasn't pouring over it. Beyond the old mill, Grizz saw the tall cone like shape of the great mountain of the Island. The sound of the river thundered and echoed, but in the midst of it he thought he could hear the voices of people talking. Grizz shook his head. He must have been hearing things.

Then he heard another shout, much clearer this time and it came from the old mill. Grizz turned to hike up the cliff's edge when the ground under his feet gave way. Grizz fell to the river. His crutches clattered and broke around him as he tumbled over the boulders. Momentum threatened to take him down the mountain to the ocean, but Grizz braced himself and he slid to a stop.

When he had stabilized himself, he let his anger get the better of him. He lifted up a small piece of wood which was all that was left of his crutches. He threw it away and growled as he put his pain behind him and marched right up the steep river bed. As his rage was heated, he ignored the freezing cold water pouring over him. Working his powerful fingers in and over one rock after the other, he climbed up to the old mill.

Grizz made his way up, and under the tall support beams made of old timber logs which were grey and dried with age. Continuing even higher, Grizz made his way up high enough to peek through an opening between the old wooden slats of the wall. There he saw Eddy Evon confronting a group of four young soldiers. They seemed to be upset with whatever Eddy was doing there.

Eventually, Eddy said something to the men which caused them to get into their military jeep and drive away. Grizz distinctly heard Eddy say something about a weather experiment. Eddy then marched into the old mill and began moving heavy equipment around. He had many strange looking devices Grizz could not recognize. *"What is he doing?"* Grizz wondered. He watched as Eddy twisted metal in his bare hands to create what he needed. It was as though metal was like clay in his powerful volk hands. Some metal was too thick for him to mold so he would toss it into a pile of metal scraps. Then he used what looked like a wrist watch which shone a blue light over the metal. This caused the metal scraps to rise into the air, mold together then take a perfect shape of what he needed it to be. Then Eddy went back to lifting and positioning heavy objects again. While Grizz was under the floor, the floor boards would bow and creak under Eddy's great weight. Dust and grit sprinkled over Grizz's face with each step Eddy took. Grizz worried if the old construction of the mill would fail and Eddy would come crashing through any moment.

While Grizz was spying, a little red ember of light flew out through the crack in the wall and flew around Grizz's head like an annoying flying insect. Grizz swatted at it, but it evaded his efforts and flew away. Grizz thought it was very strange but considered it was just a rare tropical glow bug. *"The Island is probably full of them."* He thought.

Grizz turned his attention back to Eddy who was busy working hard and fast. Before long Eddy had constructed something very large and complicated, but Grizz did not care at all what it was. For a moment, Eddy stopped working and turned to face Grizz. Grizz thought he was well concealed. He ducked down immediately. He thought he had been made for sure, but when he heard sounds like Eddy had returned to his project, Grizz decided to take another look. When he was certain Eddy did not know of his presence, he began to come up with plans to prank, Eddy. Grizz wanted to humiliate Eddy into believing the old mill was haunted.

Grizz climbed up under the mill and began to thump on the floor boards. The sounds he made were like heavy footsteps coming closer to Eddy. {Thump - Thump - Thump!} Grizz could hear Eddy stop working for a moment, but Eddy did not call out or ask who was there. Grizz decided to add to his haunting by adding a chilling moan with the sounds of creaking wood. Eddy still did not call out or reveal any sign of fear, rather he set to work once again only he had also quickened his pace.

Grizz tried to shake the old structure and roll rocks down to the steep river, but Grizz stopped toying with Eddy when he noticed water become diverted down a long trough where it began running over the old water wheel. To his amazement, the old water wheel began to turn. Inside, Grizz could see the water wheel was charging some kind of alternator. Eddy flipped a large switch and energy current began to travel up between two power poles.

Within the old mill Grizz could see a great cloud forming from steam coming out of the machine. Eddy stood back from his controls to marvel at his great creation. He smiled as the cloud began to darken and swirl amongst the rafters. Lightning shot out of the cloud with a deafening thunder clap. The lightning curved as it shot through the room before it struck an old pick ax hanging on the wall. Eddy tried to turn the device off by hitting the main power switch. It was too late. The cloud had matured into a storm cloud of gale force winds. Not only did the dark active cloud fill the old mill, it also surrounded and swirled around the roof outside as it grew.

Grizz looked away for just a moment when the bright flash of lightning hit, but when he turned back, he was surprised to find Eddy standing at the wall glaring through the crack at him.

"Identify yourself!" Eddy shouted his demand at Grizz.

The volk's hand punched through the wall and grabbed a hold of Grizz's vest collar. Grizz spun around as he dropped down under the old mill. When he spun he managed to slip right out of his jacket. He could hear Eddy smashing through the wall above him. Instinctively, Grizz kicked out the three large timber supports of the old mill and the whole thing began to teeter toward the river below. Grizz heard the footsteps of Eddy stomp toward the door. He must have commenced a great leap, because it was not long before the old mill did indeed roll over the rocks as it dissolved and was lost to the water of the steep river.

At the sound of helicopter routers, Grizz and Eddy fled the site. Eddy headed down an old dirt road, while Grizz blazed a trail of his own down through the thick forest to the beach.

Grizz needed time to think. Though Grizz felt a keen sense of relation toward Eddy Evon, he refused to dishonour the memories of his Brothers, by trying to understand the volk. Eddy was something of an enigma to be sure. He was a pure blooded volk. This was something Grizz would never be. How could he compete with him? To Grizz, Eddy was everything he wanted to be, along with nothing he wanted to be. The experience of being so close to the volk was unlike anything he had experienced before. Grizz was not through trying to figure out the volk but one thing was sure, he despised Eddy.

Grizz was out all night long. He could not sleep at all. His soul was constantly being tormented by not only pictures in his mind from his past, but emotions as well. Seeing Eddy Evon was like seeing all of his Brothers again. And in a way, Eddy was his brother as well. The emotions were like heavy weight wrestlers and they were smothering him.

With an insatiable need to be free of his mental unrest, Grizz began to run up the side of the single steep Knolix Island mountain. He ran up using both his hands and feet with only the moonlight and gravity to guide him. Finally he reached the top and he struggled to control his gasping breaths. He fell to his hands and knees, but as he let fatigue over take him, he collapsed to the ground.

Later, when Grizz had regained his strength, he sat upon the peek of the Knolix Island and gazed out at the horizon as rifts of rolling clouds filled with the new light of an early morning sunrise. As the sun approached the horizon, the clouds became a wild fiery red amongst softer purples. The striking colours faded to a gentle softness.

Golden clouds lined with luminescent silvers were reflected in the calm ocean. Light yellow behind mostly pink, manifested throughout the clouds surrounded within the light blue of the low sky. Such new fresh colours reminded Grizz of a newborn baby; innocence, love and peace.

The light of the sun winked open over the horizon and stretched out beams of light like outstretched arms. Lifting off from the horizon, the sun carried with it an emotion. *'Why can't every morning be woken in such a manner as this?'* Grizz wondered.

Never before had he ever witnessed an experience of

165

nature like this. Of all the loss he had experienced, the disappointments and frustrations, Grizz saw a disconnection between his opinions of the world, due to circumstances, and how the world actually was.

From a distance, everything appeared perfect, but it was not perfect. Still, in this moment, and with great effort, Grizz found it in himself to renew his outlook. Just as the sun would still rise despite his personal afflictions, Grizz set his mind to the like wise of positive thinking. Each day must start fresh and new.

The sun was his coach. So strong and stubborn in its decision to rise and give light to each day, Grizz would be equally stubborn to be positive for the day.

It was rare for him to have a meaningful nostalgic moment, but from time to time, when he was by himself, he would be fortunate enough to touch upon opportunities of tranquility and peace.

Grizz was not the only person responding to the early morning sunrise. Dr. McNeil was also out for a walk along the beach. He was relaxing with his thoughts in the moment. He loved the smell of the ocean in the morning, the way the breeze filtered through his long hair and the feel of the fine sand between his toes.

As he casually walked along, he noticed a strange sight far off to the distance, near some large volcanic stones. The image of a person laying on the sand. He took his hands out of his pockets and began to jog along the sea shore. As he neared the person on the beach he found his nightmare become a reality to the point where it became evidently clear to him. It was Grizz, and he did not appear to be breathing. Dr. McNeil ran to him as fast as he could and rolled him over onto his back. He checked his air way, then his pulse. Both of which were strong. The Doctor took a deep breath and then sighed a relief. He then slapped Grizz to wake him.

The slap certainly did the trick because Grizz shot his hand out at Dr. McNeil and grabbed him by the throat. Grizz was immediately on his feet and he released Dr. McNeil as soon as he recognized him.

Dr. McNeil coughed with his one hand rubbing his neck and the other hand helping to support his weight on the sand. After a few good breaths of fresh air, Dr. McNeil asked, "Grizz? What is the matter with you? I find you on a beach where you then try to kill me?"

"Don't act so shocked about that. I was sleeping and you slapped me. You're lucky I didn't change your name to breakfast. You would be toast, of course." Grizz replied as he ran his fingers though his thick dark hair. The Doctor was clearly not in the mood for Grizz's dark sense of humour. "Speaking of breakfast, I'm hungry. Where can we get something to eat?"

Dr. McNeil just looked at him for a moment like Grizz was crazy. He was offended by Grizz at first but as he looked into Grizz's eyes, he could see there was no intent to be offensive. He smiled and Grizz reciprocated. Grizz helped the doctor to his feet and the two of them walked up the dirt road to the town in the crevas.

The two stepped into a small café where Dr. McNeil ordered a coffee and Grizz, as always, ordered three full breakfasts. He had many pancakes, eggs and bacon. Dr. McNeil reached across the table and asked, "Are you going to eat all of that toast?" As he lifted the toast off Grizz's plate, Grizz slapped his hand and the toast fell back to his plate.

"Hey, what did I say to you about toast." Grizz grumbled as he went back to stuffing his face with the food. He glanced up at the Doctor from time to time, before he tossed Dr. McNeil a piece of toast like he was tossing scraps to a dog.

Dr. McNeil chuckled and raised his eye brows. "Typical Domin, will you ever change?"

After they enjoyed a breakfast together, Dr. McNeil took Grizz to a large old home that looked like a hotel. There Grizz was enlisted as a tenant and introduced to some young boys. The room was very small and not very well kept. Though the boys had their own bunk to sleep in, Grizz had the impression they would get into each other's things. Grizz was told these boys would be his room mates. Dr. McNeil introduced Grizz to the boys. "This is your new roommate and his name is, Domin. Domin this is Nathan, Tommy, Justin, and Hal"

"Yeh, it is interesting to meet you." Grizz said as he held out his hand for one of them to step forward and shake it. The four boys looked at him but none of them stepped forward to shake his hand right away. As the moment quickly became stale and awkward, Grizz began to lower his hand. Just then, Hal stepped forward and took Grizz's powerful hand in faith that he would not be hurt.

"Domin, eh? Is that supposed to be short for something?" asked Hal as he put his best fake smile on.

"Dominic?" Nathan offered a likely answer.

"Domination!" answered Grizz, in a thunderous base-like tone from his chest. "But my friends just call me, Grizz."

Dr. McNeil felt comfortable at Grizz's choice to use the word friend with the boys. "Well, I have a lot of things to see to, so I'll leave you young men to get settled." Dr. McNeil smiled and quickly shuffled his way out the door. From outside the small room Dr. McNeil's voice was heard, "I will have your stuff sent up to your room, Grizz."

"Seems a little cramped in here." Justin said. All eyes turned to him and Justin did not like it at all. He quickly grabbed his rugby ball which was not far from him. "Rugby anyone?" Justin stuttered a little with a nervous voice. "We can talk and play while Grizz waits for his stuff to be delivered."

The boys talked very well together as they tossed the ball to one another. The game put them all at ease and allowed them to open up comfortably. As they passed the ball to one another, Grizz asked his roommates why they are on the Island. Nathan was the first to reply when he said, "Now you have to understand, I can't go into any details of any kind but basically I'm here for safe keeping."

"Safe keeping?" Grizz repeated, "So am I. Can you tell me why they want you for safe keeping, Nathan?"

"Well, I harbour a formula in my mind." Nathan answered vaguely.

"Tell me your formula!" Grizz pressed him.

"That's impossible, Grizz. It would spell his death. You know we have only two choices. Live here on the Island and protect our secrets or die." Justin reminded everyone.

"You all know why I am here, right?" Grizz asked them.

The others stopped tossing the ball for a moment and looked at one another. They shook their heads as they agreed none of them knew Grizz's story, "No, we don't know anything about you at all." Tommy answered for them all.

Grizz let out a breath and shook his head, "Well, just one look at me I would say it is obvious. I was born human but as an infant I had many alien parts grafted into my body. It was for this project, I was born."

"Oh, kind'a like me I suppose." answered Tommy, who was an average looking young man. "I was born on another planet in the star cluster of, Zeta Recticuli."

169

Justin had been passed the ball and he kept it in his possession as he just looked at Tommy. For a moment, everyone just stared but when they could contain themselves no longer, they all burst into laughter.

"Ha, ha, good one, Tommy, you're an alien. Ya, right." replied Nathan in disbelief.

"I'm not an alien, but I was born on a planet which was not earth." When everyone could see the seriousness in Tommy's eyes, they became deathly quiet.

Justin passed the ball to Grizz and Grizz passed the ball back to Justin. "And your story, Justin?"

Justin caught the ball before he looked down at it and answered, "My parents were powerful in the arts of witch craft. They are dead now but I am expected to be equally as powerful. The specialists of this Island don't seem to get it but if I am expected to be anything like my parents, I will need some training." Justin shot the ball back at Grizz.

"And you, Hal?" Grizz asked with another toss of the ball.

Hal caught the ball and looked at it for a moment in concentration. He seemed reluctant to join the conversation and answer. "My father has a contract with the Island officials to harvest and manufacture trees into building materials. He begged and pleaded for my mother, my brother Burl and myself to come out here with him and he finally was granted his wish so we could still be a family together." Hal was embarrassed, he didn't have a real good reason for being on the Island. Because he wasn't special like the others he wasn't sure if they would still accept him in their little click.

"Are you hiding the truth from us?" Justin asked with a skeptical eye.

"No, I swear. My father is organizing the logging project and he has a lot of workers who will be joining them. You must have noticed the activity, not to mention the equipment. If you don't believe me, I can prove it to you. No problem."

"Forget it!" Grizz told Hal though he seemed to be speaking to everyone else. "He's not lying."

Hal had as little choice as anyone else for being at the Island and none of them were certain what their fate would eventually be.

"Well, that settles it, I guess." Grizz told the boys, "We're all going to die now." He looked at each one of them and there was a strong sense of Grizz's true intentions which revealed a strong bond and deeper understanding had developed for one another because they shared. Grizz laughed and the boys also laughed with him. "Listen, no matter how much people try to control you or own you, you belong to no one. This Island has no hold on me."

Playing pass was fine for a little while. The early morning sunrise had truly set the stage for the rest of Grizz's day. He was having a very good day. Then Grizz waved a group of five other young boys over. He told them, if they wanted to play against them as five on five he would give them his necklace with the bear's tooth if they could win. The game went very well for Grizz's team. He would get Tommy, Justin, Nathan and Hal to pass the ball to him and then he would charge through the other boys to the other end of the field.

The other team threw their hands in the air and accused Grizz of cheating. They said, because Grizz was so big, he was too rough and not very fun. This only made Grizz angry, but Hal suggested a new strategy. Grizz would be the first to have the ball. Then he would pass it to Tommy, Nathan, Justin or Hal depending on how open they were. When the ball was caught, Grizz came charging in and cleared a path for his new friends.

171

The opposing team finally did quit after this.

Tommy made a suggestion, "Why don't we join a rugby tournament."

"I don't know, what if Grizz really hurt one of the other players?" Nathan turned slightly to Grizz, "No offense, but you do play kind'a rough."

"It's just who I am. I cannot change. I always win. An eye for an eye. A tooth for a tooth, but in my case, if you poke me in the eye, you lose your eye. If you knock one of my teeth loose, you won't have any teeth at all."

"An eye for an eye, Grizz?" Hal questioned him. Grizz was rather curious as to how someone could question such popular wisdom.

"Of course." Grizz replied.

"Interesting, I was taught to love my enemies." Hal carefully watched the expression of Grizz's scared face.

"Love my enemies?" Grizz gave Hal a look like he was a creature from Venus. "There is no satisfaction in giving love for a betrayal or something even worse than a betrayal."

"Friend, I know how you operate. There is nothing special about it. Everyone, I'm sure, thinks like you or at one time thought like you. *Kill or be killed.* Right?" Hal waved his hand in the air and looked away. "Over rated." Came Hal's comment.

"So what is it you were taught?" Grizz asked as he crossed his large arms and cocked his eye at him. "Surrender to your enemy?"

"He has a good question, Hal." came Tommy.

"I have faith in God. God reigns supreme. It is not my right to inflict pain or to seek revenge, rather I am supposed to love my enemy and pray for those who prosecute me. Reply to insults with compliments. Say something positive to lift the mood and distract evil. If revenge is needed, my Father in Heaven will take action

172

in a time of his choosing. Domin, you need to practice love. You have a lot of darkness and hate inside of you and you give these negative thoughts and feelings too much attention. The greatest way for you to practice love and positive thinking is to think about those you hate the most and find it in your heart to love and forgive without expecting to be forgiven or to receive an apology."

"Hal really knows his stuff, eh Grizz?" asked Nathan.

But Grizz didn't miss a beat, "How can a person think like this when he is in the situation of being faced with hateful opposition? Perhaps you can fill your mind with flowers and pixie dust, but that won't make everything ok."

With wide eyes, Nathan, Justin and Tommy were bewildered by Grizz's comment and looked back at Hal for his response.

"No, Domin," Hal spoke confidently, "When you are trapped the Lord will provide a way out, until it is your time to die. I believe the Lord will reveal to me an escape route, but if it is his will to empower me it will be done so, in His way and at His time. It was David who defeated Goliath after all. He did not surrender to him."

"Nice theory, but in my experience what you say could not possibly work." stated Grizz strongly.

"There is only one way to know for sure. We must put it to a test. Now because this is a test, we need to understand that we are acting out our aggression, if in fact it is aggression we want to use. The rules are; no one is going to get hurt, right?"

"Just as a Mexican likes a little spice in his taco, I like a little pain in my fight."

"This is not a fight, Domin. One rule, no pain, get it?"

"Got it." Grizz agreed.

"Good! Ok now, Grizz, you begin. I want you to start a scene by being the aggressor." Hal advised.

"What should I say?" Grizz questioned.

"I don't know, try something mean." Hal answered.

"Like what?"

"Are you trying to tell me you haven't done this before?" Hal waved his hands to clear his thoughts. "Tell me I'm a low down snake in the grass and it's about time you cleaned my clock."

Grizz smiled as though he would finally have a little fun. Stepping forward, Grizz pointed his finger at Hal, then his face changed completely, "You are a low down snake in the grass!" He spoke with such forcefulness, Hal momentarily lost his concentration. Grizz leaned forward to get his face right up close to Hal's and continued with his voice deeper in his chest to roll out a devious whisper. "And its' about time I cleaned your clock."

Hal swallowed hard and tried his best to just brush it off, "Well, clearly you *have* done this before."

Grizz grabbed Hal by the scruff of his shirt and lifted him to an adjacent wall. "What are you going to do about it?"

Hal remained calm, "First of all, you don't want to do this."

"Enough talk, now you die!" came Grizz as he was bringing the act to an end.

"But if you kill me, friend, you will miss out on all of the good things I had planned for us."

"Good things like what?" Grizz asked.

"Well..." Hal thought for a second, "Don't think of us as enemies, Grizz. We should be more like close friends, or even better, we should be like brothers."

"Yes, think of us as four of your brothers." Tommy added as he gently put his hands on Grizz's shoulder. No one wanted anyone to get hurt over a game and Grizz seemed to be taking the game just a little too far.

For a moment, Grizz could actually see the boys manifest into his Brothers; Tommy and Nathan were like Stroy and Grud. Justin turned into Oblit and Hal looked like Narl. Grizz shook his head then turned away to let out a breath as he blinked his eyes hard. The experience had upset Grizz.

"You win Hal, you all win." Grizz said as he turned to walk away.

"I thought you said, '*you* always win?'" asked Justin.

Grizz did not stop walking, but he did speak clearly when he said, "Not this time, *Brother...*" The way Grizz's voice cracked made his words seem sad.

Though Hal was able to make his point he couldn't help but to wonder what it was he had said to cause such a strong reaction from Domin, and would this moment be the beginning of something else?

Grizz had done his best to ignore his roommates for the rest of the day. He had little flash backs to the recent days when he and his brothers shared their lives together. Good memories were mixed with tragic ones. When Grizz would catch sight of one of his roommates, his memories would start all over again involuntarily.

Grizz tried to sit down in the dorm's cafeteria by himself, but it was not long until Hal came and sat next to him. He slid his tray over to touch Grizz's tray. He wanted to get his attention, but Grizz just ignored him and continued to slurp up his soup.

"Hey, pal, I hope I didn't say something to upset you." Hal said, "It was just an exercise." Still he had no reaction from Grizz. "Was it when I mentioned brothers?" That did it. Grizz stopped eating and just sat glaring at his food. Hal knew now how certainly there was something about Grizz's past that upset him. "Did

175

you have a brother? Perhaps more than one? Would you like to talk about it?"

Abruptly, Grizz stood up from the table. He gave a look, so intense, as he glared into Hal's soul, Hal felt his thumping heart actually skip a beat. A growl rumbled from Grizz's chest as the right side of his upper lip quivered. The sound filled the cafeteria and everyone stopped eating in response to the sound like a large diesel engine block, minus a muffler. Grizz left the table along with his food and did not make eye contact with Hal after that. Hal watched as Grizz left the cafeteria. He sat back and chewed on a piece of toast while he thought about Grizz.

"What happened?" asked Tommy, with Nathan and Justin who were not far behind him.

"Nothing happened. I can't get through to him." Then a thought came to Hal. If he wanted answers, he knew just the man to call, Dr. McNeil.

Grizz walked into the bathroom and approached the urinal. He unzipped for business and began a moment of relief just as a group of young people entered the bathroom as well. "Hello Domin, or should I say, Grizz." Came Hal with so much friendliness Grizz was about to pop. The boys were just a little too chummy for his liking. "I just spoke to Dr. McNeil on the phone and he had a lot to tell me. I now know about your brothers, but there are many other things I would have liked to know that he said he wasn't allowed to tell me. I, personally don't know why you wanted to keep your brothers a secret from me. It's not that big of a deal, is it? I have a big brother, his name is Burl. See? Like I said, 'no big deal.'"

"Can't I have a moment to myself?" Grizz spoke in a frustrated and threatening tone. "Get out…"

176

"Hey, we are not here to give you a hard time. We are just trying to knock down any walls between us so we can get along better. We are roommates and we might be roommates for a very long time. Let's make the most out of our time."

Grizz finished his business, zipped up and flushed. He was ready to trash the entire bathroom and all of his roommates with it, but as he stood washing his hands and looking at the senseless wall paper, he realized the entire situation was senseless. It would all pass shortly, all he needed to do was ignore the whole thing.

Finally the boys gave up tying to talk to Grizz. Grizz walked out of the dormitory and continued walking. He enjoyed the nature and being alone with it. Everything was so much simpler when he was alone.

On his own, Grizz walked for hours. Strolling along the shore of the Island, Grizz figured he walked clear to the other side of it when he realized he would have to begin his journey back if he was going to be back in time for supper. Only, he did not want to go back. Why should he? He was happy right where he was.

As Grizz looked out at the beautiful spectacle of nature before him, with the endless ocean and wondrous colours of the distant sky, he found a small Island not far from the shore. Spontaneously, Grizz bounded into the ocean with a splash equivalent to a cannonball and swam out to the small land mass. When he climbed up onto the rock face, Grizz walked through a small cluster of trees and found a miniature private beach area on the other side. Using a few logs and a lot of stones Grizz was able to dig out a small cavern and use the material for his walls and roof.

So Grizz decided he would live in this place for the time being because it pleased him.

Within his little make shift home, Grizz had built a

fire. He was able to construct the trap out of mere branches from the little amount of trees that grew there. Grizz pulled in a trap from just off the shore of his little Island. In the trap was a lobster. He roasted the lobster over his little interior camp fire. As darkness began to set in around him, the ocean began to grow in its' own turmoil. Waves began to kick up a heavy spray of water which poured down into Grizz's new home. The soft glow of the fire abruptly went out as the water doused the flames. Just as Grizz began to climb out of his little fort he was bathed in light and water. The water was from the ocean and he expected that, but the light came from above and it was very bright. The wind was powerful but a rhythmic thumping was heard within it. Grizz quickly realized a military helicopter was hovering over him. A loud voice came from a speaker.

"Domin, do not be alarmed we are sending down a rescue harness to you. Put it on and we will take you back to your home."

For a moment, Grizz wanted to run for it, but he was wet and cold and the helicopter was not his enemy. By accepting the harness he knew he would soon be warm and dry sleeping in a room with his roommates again.

"Rise and shine, Grizz." Came the chipper morning voice of Hal. "What happened to you last night. You didn't get in until late."

"Don't worry about it." Grizz flatly answered.

"I hope you weren't upset with me for something I said." Hal added.

"I said don't worry about…" Grizz paused. He could see that the problem was not Hal but himself, "Listen, buddy, I am not angry with you. I just have a lot of things to work out for myself. You need to give me my space and I will come around when I feel like it."

178

"Very well, my friend. That's good enough for me." Hal replied with a bright smile.

From that moment, Grizz found his roommates to be tolerable to be around.

One day, Grizz was playing rugby with two teams of young men. They decided to have a game on the beach where a ferry was scheduled to dock later in the day to unload some new faces of people who were to become added to the population of the Knolix Island. The sun was high in the sky and the day was warm but the wind carried an unusual chill. The signs of fall brought whispers of winter. In the meantime, the game was on. There was nothing like living for the moment, and the young men would agree, though no one would say it, but to be playing sports bare chested was a great way to win the attention of a possible beautiful young lady who might step off the ferry.

Both teams were equally matched. On one team Grizz played front and center and on the other team Eddy Evon had him at a face off. From experience, Grizz knew Eddy was next to impossible to go up against. The volk was stronger, faster and seemed to be able to read his thoughts to counter every move he made, but Grizz loved a challenge. He was tired of playing against humans who were unable to keep up with his own endurance. When Grizz went up against Eddy, he felt like a human who had to go up against his equal. Grizz inspire his team mates to push themselves harder. Even in the way of financial gain they were challenged as they would often place bets between Eddy and Grizz to see who would out shine the other.

"You think you can out smart me? Think again, Domin." Eddy, spoke hypnotically.

Here again Grizz wondered, *'How does he do that?'* Eddy and Grizz rarely had a lengthy conversation with one another. Grizz was not ashamed to let Eddy know how much he despised him. Most of the reasons Grizz didn't like Eddy were because he was envious of him. Grizz felt belittled by him and Eddy seemed to know his thoughts before he even spoke them. Grizz was certain, just as his brother Narl was able to telepathically read minds, so to could Eddy. This made Eddy potentially, very dangerous. There were just too many things Grizz had seen and interpreted in Eddy as being the same thought process as Narl.

When the two faced off, Grizz found he could have two scenarios he would try just before the beginning of the next period. As long as Grizz would keep his mind clear and make his decisions on the fly, he found his chances increased at outsmarting Eddy.

As the ferry was moving in at the dock, Grizz decided to bank left when he had been thinking about banking to the right. He slipped past Eddy and plucked the ball out of the sky. Cradling the ball in his arm, Grizz ran through the opposing players with his other palm out ahead of him. He could feel Eddy coming up behind him. The volk was predictable that way. With an incredible leap, Grizz flew over a wall of opposition players and tucked his legs up bringing them clear from Eddy's wide arms closing in around them. Grizz rolled out on the sand, then a pile-up of players were stack on top of him. Grizz was capable of knocking them all off but after many previous games he had learned to honor the rules. Likewise, Eddy would not join in on the pile up of players because inevitably someone would get hurt.

The game moved into recess as the people stepped off the ferry. The boys on the beach couldn't help but to stop and get a good long look at who was getting off. All of the new comers seemed to be regular looking people, except for one. A young lady with long blond hair stepped off the ferry and onto the dock. She held one small bag, like a cross between a back pack and a purse.

She walked to the edge of the dock and studied the activity on the beach. Military officers patrolled with some on foot and others on motor cycles or jeeps. Then she noticed the young boys who were standing together looking at her, or rather gawking at her. She smiled brightly and waved. No one was sure if she knew how her presence had captivated everyone, but after she waved and everyone on the beach waved back, the boys felt quite ridiculous when they caught each other doing so, she must have had a pretty good idea.

Some of the young men made some dirty comments about the new girl, but Grizz just kept to himself. He could see Eddy mirroring him in almost the exact same way. Would this girl be a prize to compete for between them? Grizz was determined not to let that happen.

Grizz had to go to the bathroom so he followed the trail up a steep and wooded path. Near the beach were a couple of pit toilets which could be accessed from both the beach and the road to the ferry dock. Grizz tried to do his business as fast as he could. The door flew open as Grizz was pulling up his shorts. There he stood, speechless before the wide eyes of the new beautiful blond girl who had just stepped off the ferry.

"Eep!" Came a strange reaction from her.

Grizz made a slight motion forward as the door slammed shut in his face. Grizz tumbled back onto the toilet seat. He was annoyed as he arose and hit the door to open it, only at times Grizz didn't know his own strength. The door shattered and blew apart. He looked up the trail and saw the girl running in fear for her life.

"Oh no, what have I done?" Grizz contemplated. For

a moment he considered just letting her go. It would be for the best since chasing her would likely not end well. Grizz looked down at his feet and saw the girl's purse next to a bright yellow tropical flower with red tipped pedals. Such a flower was rare, especially for the Knolix Island. Grizz plucked up the flower and the purse and darted off into the jungle.

The young girl recognized where she was and knew it was just a little further to the road that would lead to a home which was prepared for her and her parents. She slowed to a walk. She was out of breath as she frequently glanced behind her to see if the scary looking Grizz monster was behind her. She still had to relieve herself and she was surprised she hadn't already peed her pants. The path she was on led her between two tall stone walls. This gave her a sense of claustrophobia. A distant sound of something large crashing through the jungle, with the grunt of a deep voice, gave her chills up her spine. She looked left, right and up at the top edges of the stones. She began to jog and found herself on a flatter path where she could see into the jungle on either side of the trail as she walked around the bend in the trail she came to the road. She could see the people of the ferry boarding a military tram to take them to the town.

Finally, she had a sense of safety, but she still really needed to go and tinkle. She didn't think she could hold herself for the trip to town. Glancing around, she decided she would quickly find a secluded area off the tail where she could relieve herself.

The young lady cautiously ventured into the jungle, all the while, she half expected the scary monster-man to appear. All she knew was she would feel much better after she did her business and boarded the tram. Deciding she was far enough off the trail and in a position where she could finally go in private, she hunched down and made a contribution to nature.

The bushes near her began to rustle. As she stood up pulling up her pants, the scary man reappeared. The young girl let out a horrific scream. Grizz held out the purse and flower as he winced through the ear piercing scream. The girl's scream seemed to go on forever. Grizz set the purse and flower down at her feet and disappeared into the jungle.

A short time later, the military came to Grizz's dorm room and asked him about what had happened. Grizz was not happy with the girl at all but gave a formal statement and was later told to meet with the girl and her parents. It was an awkward situation to say the least. Dr. McNeil introduced Grizz as Domin, as he was known on the Island. Then the doctor introduced the girl as Sally Coppler. Grizz was given an opportunity to explain his side of the story. When she realized Grizz was not a person to be feared, she was able to rest easier. Grizz felt better after he met Sally the second time. Grizz even liked her a little though she continued to show subtle signs of unease around him. Both Grizz and sally agreed not to mention the incident to anyone but rather to call it a misunderstanding to a bad first impression and pretend it never happened.

Photos of Eddy Evon and his mother, Gastonish, were brought into the meeting and shown to Sally and her parents. It was standard procedure where Island officials extended an elaborate explanation of the primary Island residents to all new comers. Grizz was escorted out but he still heard the doctor explain, "Eddy and his mother were not dangerous either and during your stay here on this Island, you are expected to treat our special residents with the same respect you would show anyone else because the Knolix Island is a community and..." The door to the room closed and Grizz could hear no more.

183

Later in the same week, Mr. Dalton made a fool of Grizz in front of the whole class with a lesson about bullying. At recess, Grizz was laughed at out in the schoolyard.

A boy named Jeremy felt cocky after he observed Grizz receive a pep talk about bullying. He'd been picked on by Grizz many times in the past and thought Grizz was getting the point not to trouble people anymore. Only, Jeremy wanted to be sure Grizz knew exactly how much he bothered him and how Eddy would protect kids whom he hassled. "Domin, you are a big dweeb! We all know you are scared of Eddy."

"Shut up Jeremy, you don't know what you're talking about." Grizz tried to put a cork in the situation. Everyone has a bad day.

"We are not blind. We see how you leave kids alone when Eddy is around." Little Jeremy had no fear, no respect.

With the intention to give a customary lesson in respect Grizz lifted his fists into the air and brought them down upon the student desktop. "SHUT UP!" Grizz shouted. The desk was destroyed. Grizz tossed it to the side and glared at Jeremy. "You're going to wish you had never said that."

Jeremy became pasty white before he bolted out of the classroom and down the front steps. Grizz exploded from the main double doors and leaped the distance over the steps to the ground. Tumbling a little, Grizz rolled to his feet and continued his pursuit.

Dashing around the corner of the schoolhouse growling at the children in a threatening manner, Grizz almost ran right into Eddy Evon who had Jeremy cowering behind him. Grizz ignored Eddy as he continued to charge for Jeremy. Grizz's clothes fluttered ferociously with each threatening tread under foot at attack speed. As Grizz moved in, diving for the kill, Eddy grabbed him and lifted him up by his shirt. Grizz clawed and ripped at Eddy's sleeve.

While Eddy held Grizz in the air, he turned to Jeremy and asked, "What did you do to make Domin so angry?" Jeremy had fallen to the dirt and seemed to be in a state of fear stricken shock.

A young punk rock-like little girl tattle tailed on Grizz explaining what was said leading up to the chase.

"Is this true?" Eddy asked, but before he could get another word in, Grizz ripped off Eddy's sleeve and started clawing at his arm. Eddy shook Grizz to distract him. Grizz found it difficult to scratch through Eddy's thick grey volk skin, but he finally managed to gouge his fingers in enough to draw a little thick dark scarlet blood.

Grizz kicked Eddy in the face at the same instant. Ripping at his own shirt and Grizz fell from Eddy's grip.

Not only did Grizz land on his feet, but he bounced back toward Eddy. The impact of Grizz's combined weight and strength surprisingly pushed Eddy to the ground. Like a cat, Grizz again pounced on top of Eddy while he was down. Eddy tried to defend himself. Eddy took Grizz by his hair and yanked him off, but Grizz came at Eddy again ruthlessly, jabbing a fist out to strike Eddy, Eddy grabbed Grizz's arm and used his momentum against him. Eddy lifted Grizz up and sent him flying into a bush. Grizz crawled out from under the bush with burning eyes of vengeance, with a low and sinister growl. Eddy found Grizz's primitive rage entertaining somehow and bellowed out a deep menacing roar of his own.

With incredible speed, Grizz ducked back into the bush and disappeared into the woods.

The military of the Island began to conduct

themselves in an anxious manner as though their time was running out. They demanded more tests to be done on Grizz to challenge the thresh hold of his strength and endurance. They dressed Grizz in heavy bulletproof armament. Grizz trained with the military's most promising soldiers. Such men were specialists; the best of the Best. Clearly favored over the human soldiers, Grizz the Blackguard was honored as a true warrior. Because of his lightning quick reflexes, and his focused and cunning mind, no one volunteered to challenge him after a few short examples of his ability. The military officials were looking for a soldier like Grizz. Though they could not have Eddy Evon, they could, in fact, have Grizz. None of the human soldiers measured up. It was made quite clear the hero, with whom the people liked in Grizz, was the promise of tomorrows' soldier.

According to the pages of charts about Grizz and Eddy Evon, It was clear how Grizz started out with physical and mental abilities like any other human child at his age between three years of age to six, but as time went on the graphs revealed how Grizz became above average in human standards. Nevertheless, he had a long way to go before he would be at a level to compete with a volk.

After Grizz had completed a six hour physical offensive routine, he sat exhausted and he could hear the doctors and military technicians speaking low in such a way as to not let Grizz hear them, only Grizz heard them anyway as they said, "Training and exercise is one thing but for Domin to fight as a soldier is quite another."

"But if you really want him to prove himself, why don't you have him challenge somebody his own size. Let's get Domin to fight against a volk."

"You mean, Eddy Evon? No way!"

"We can submit it as advice in writing, but I won't

186

have any part of such a project without the proper approval."

"No, no. I'm not talking about Eddy Evon. I'm talking about the other volks."

"Huh? But they are not ready. In fact, I'm not sure how you've even heard about them. The whole project has a long way to go before the incubations can begin."

"What about our prototype." A long pause followed. "I've seen it, look…" The military tech pulled out a card from a zipped pocket on his arm. "You see? I have majestic clearance."

The doctor quickly took the card from the soldier and closely examined it. "This card is a fake! Where did you get it."

The soldier snatched the card back, "Relax! We are on the same team aren't we?" He stuffed the card back into the pocket and zipped it up again. "Besides, look at my rank. I should'a had the clearance a long time ago. What are you going to do about it?" The soldier lifted his rifle to the doctor's chest and gave him a judgemental eye.

"Well, what a ridiculous question, you know I won't do anything. No matter what you know, the prototype would not be a good idea. What would you prove? What if Domin killed the prototype or if the prototype killed Domin? Then what? It would just be a loss and an unnecessary waste."

Letting his rifle drop down and hang loosely in his grip, the soldier responded, "Well, there you have it. The project is a bust. Even if we could advance human kind, the volk species will always rein superior."

'Could it be?' Grizz wondered, *'Somewhere on the Island there is a volk whom he and Eddy have not met yet.'*

187

Grizz spent a lot of time working on a mountain bike which he had made some special modifications to. The wheels were triple wide as he had attached three well treaded tires together. The frame was extended with shock absorbers added from the graveyard of cars next to Big Wheel's auto wrecking. He carried mostly old beat up military vehicles, but every so often a broken civilian car would be sent in.

Grizz saw an old red VW bug get shipped in. It appeared to have been some sort of dune buggy at one time perhaps.

At Big Wheels Auto Wrecking, Grizz found the new set of shock absorbing springs he needed off the Volkswagon. He let the owner of the yard, whose name was Big Wheels, know he was taking the rear shocks. Grizz put his weight on the pedals of his bike and rocks flew out from the rear tire. Grizz would imagine adding a motor to his bike, but he knew the greatest power came from the strength in his legs. When Grizz wanted to travel at great speeds, he would push himself further and whatever power he desired was there for him.

The tires of Grizz's bike would skid out from under him as he pumped his pedals with amazing force. Dry dirt and small rocks were spat out behind him as he applied more power than needed. He raced up a steep road and caught some air as he recklessly came bounding over the peek. For a moment Grizz lifted his bike over his head, before he replaced it under himself again before he landed. As he came around the rising corner of the road, Grizz looked off through the distance of trees. He imagined seeing the volk prototype he heard about. He wasn't sure what was meant by a prototype. *'Could it mean the volk who was mentioned appears differently somehow?'* Grizz couldn't be sure.

Grizz picked up speed through a straight of way as

his legs pumped the pedals like a motor screaming at maximum overdrive.

Grizz came bounding around a tight corner kicking up a huge plume of dust behind him when he came nose to nose with a massive volk. It was Eddy Evon. Grizz tried to turn away as Eddy also tried to move out of the way, but the collision was inevitable.

The silence that came with a motorless vehicle coupled with Grizz's great speed was a sure recipe for disaster.

The volk shot his hands out in front of himself to glance the bike off to one side. The maneuver was almost successful but Grizz inadvertently went toppling head over heals. The two youngsters found themselves rather dazed and sitting on opposite sides of the road. Neither of them had a snappy come back, where in most other situations they would. This incident was just something they hadn't expected to happen. Grizz huffed and a ball cloud of dust came out of his nose.

Eddy Evon shook his head and began to chuckle. "What in the world was that? How fast were you going?"

"I was looking for someone." Grizz answered as he slapped dust off his arms.

"Well, it seems there is no problem with your transportation, except you were going a little too fast." Eddy corrected him.

Usually Grizz despised being corrected by the likes of Eddy, but with this particular situation he didn't seem to worry about it, "Are you aware you are not the only volk on this Island?"

"Are you suggesting you are a volk?" Eddy asked with a speculative look in his eye.

'Did he know? Wasn't it obvious enough? If anyone else was to ask Grizz if he were a volk he would have told them he certainly was, but to have a perfectly unaltered

189

volk ask him if he was a volk... If he had to ask then the answer was already pretty clear.' Grizz leaned forward and stood up as he also lifted his bike upright. "That's not what I was talking about." Grizz answered. "I heard there is at least one other volk on the Island and it is called a *prototype*."

Eddy just looked at Grizz for a moment as though he was looking for something in Grizz's face which would reveal the hoax. Eddy was actually trying to read Grizz's mind, but he hadn't mastered that skill yet. Still there was nothing to believe Grizz was lying. Grizz's allegation didn't make much sense to Eddy because he had traveled all over the Island through the eyes of his sertz many times and he has never encountered any signs of another volk of any kind, nor had he found some hidden home either.

"A prototype volk you say? What else can you tell me about it? What is its age? Is it a male or a female? Where did you hear about it?" Eddy asked persistently.

"I don't know much about it. All I know is what I heard from a doctor speaking to a soldier." Grizz told him openly.

"So this volk is able to stay one step ahead of everyone else to keep from being spotted? It sounds like a Bigfoot story to me."

"It's not just a story." Grizz quickly became frustrated with Eddy.

"Why should I believe you aren't just pulling another one of your pranks." Eddy replied with a smirk.

"Yeah, sure it was just a prank, ha, ha." Grizz was not pleased with Eddy's comment, he inspected his bike and found the front tire was bent. With his bare hands, Grizz bent the front tires back so they were somewhat straight again. "You know Eddy, you're not as perfect as you would like everyone to believe."

"That is not a bad repair job, Domin." Eddy complimented. "Who are you, and what was it that brought you to this Island?"

"Wouldn't you like to know..." Grizz hopped onto his bike and glanced back at Eddy. He snorted, before he brought his weight down on the bike pedals as he pulled back on the handle bars. Dirt flew out in Eddy's direction as he rear tire spun, but as the wheel gained traction with the road, he was again speeding on his way down the road.

Eddy watched as Domin rode away. *'Domin's bike sure is cool!'* Eddy thought. He then shifted his gaze to the tall pyramid shape of the Knolix Island and wondered, *'What secrets do you hold?'*

Chapter 6

One day Grizz was out on the Island running which is something he enjoyed to do to reap the rewards of freedom, living on the Island. He was letting his hair grow out and he liked the way it made him feel as the wind caught it and threw it about. One of the other things he liked about the Island was the landscape, with multiple levels and steepness. He could run as fast as he wanted through the jungle forest and then leap from the edge of a steep plateau. He used the existing trees and the structure of the land to ease his descent. Once on the solid ground again he bolted off running.

While he was exercising for pleasure, he heard the sound of a small voice that seemed to chirp a couple of times. Grizz stopped in his tracks to listen. He heard the sound again only more definite. He moved quickly in the direction of the sound and it led him to a blond girl who was sitting on an old concrete bridge which had ivy creeping all over it. The girl was crying with her head down and her knees tucked up to her fore head. At the far end of the bridge, tied with leather straps were two horses. One horse was jet black but the other horse was brown with a white spot on its nose.

As usual, Grizz came charging out of the bushes and thundered his way to a stop on the path which led to the bridge. Sally lifted her head as the horses reeled back. Securely tied, the horses were not going anywhere. Sally's eyes were puffy and irritated with tears running down her cheeks.

She was both annoyed and frightened as she screamed horrifically. No one could hear her but the horses tried all the more to be free.

"Shut up!" Grizz told her sternly.

Recognizing it was Domin, Sally *did* stop screaming, but she was still very annoyed. Sally jumped up to calm the horses, "Go away!" She told Grizz as she stroked the noses of the horses which seemed to relax them instantly.

"What's going on?" Grizz pressed her.

"Nothing, I just want to be alone." she was perturbed as though Grizz was the very last person she wanted to open herself up to.

Grizz felt a sense of enlightenment and a desired to share. "No, really, is it your parents? Are you in trouble? What?" But Grizz was becoming too nosey for her liking.

"If you don't leave, I'll scream!" she told him.

Grizz believed Sally, "We've been through this before, haven't we?" Grizz reminded her. "More times than I care to remember... Maybe I can help you. I have been through a lot you know." Grizz spoke softly and humorously, "I have attended anger management courses." He lifted his eyebrows a couple of times.

"Is that supposed to surprise me?" Sally retorted with a giggle as she tried to wipe away her tears. She didn't know Domin could be funny.

"No seriously now, just listen," Grizz was about to try to make a difference in Sally's life. "In those courses, I was taught, each of us were born for a specific purpose in life. I had to learn this for myself and it was not easy. Believe me." Grizz stole a moment to look at Sally to be sure he had her attention before he continued, "Sometimes we need to step out of ourselves for a moment to see the bigger picture and how we fit into it. It is not until we begin to realize where we are in life, is exactly where we were intended to be all along. That is when we begin to find out a specific way in which we belong and have a purpose. There is a value to you and to what you contribute. When you can see it and you can live it, everything else becomes easy."

"Well, I can't live anything because I can't see it. I don't get it! I am not worthy of being valued, Domin. You have no idea what I've been through, what I've seen or what I've done. I haven't been sent to this stupid Island for no reason, you know!!!" Sally broke down and wept some more.

Grizz let her cry for a few minutes then he said softly, "You think you've experienced anything worse than I have?" Grizz's eyes told everything, all of the pain, the struggles and the hurt he tried to oppress deep down inside. "I know I'm not the nicest person in the world, but there are reasons for why I do the things I do. It is all a part of who I am, and I like it. The difference between you and me is you would like to be somebody you're not."

Grizz struck a chord with his final remark. Sally stood up and brushed her jeans off, before she replied, "Fine!" Grizz jerked back defensively. He thought she was about to attack him. "The reason I am here is because I broke up with a boy who I was about to make my boyfriend."

"What kid were you about to date?" Domin asked.

Sally didn't want to mention the name, Eddy Evon. Grizz sniffed at the air. "What is that smell I detect? Is it food?" Grizz could smell the food Sally had packed and intended for her date with Eddy Evon before he blew her off.

Pulling open the pack, Sally began to remove some of the items. She had two large, foot long, subway sandwiches. Next she pulled out a box of crackers with a container of cheese spread then two bottles of purified water.

Grizz looked at this and began to lick his chops.

194

"Are you planning on letting all that go to waste?" Grizz drooled with hunger in his voice.

"No, of course not." Sally handed a sub to Grizz. With a quick stroke, Grizz tore the sub in half so he was holding a six inch sub in each hand. Biting into one sub after the other, Grizz tried to speak, "Mmmph, these subs are great! Did you make them?"

"Yes, I did." Sally was proud to offer for she knew what she used to make the subs.

Sally used chicken breasts, cheese, bacon, lettuce, tomatoes, onions, avocado, mushrooms, egg and a special recipe of sweet sauce and mayonnaise in each of the subs.

Unwrapping the second sub, Sally nibbled off a small bite as she was amazed at how much Grizz could eat with each bite.

"Wow this is sooo good. You sure your almost boyfriend won't mind?" Grizz continued to speak with his mouth full. It was clear to Sally, nothing could stop Grizz from eating. Cracking open one of the bottles of water, Grizz threw his head back and chugged it all at once. After wiping his mouth on his sleeve, Grizz looked at Sally and belched with a smile on his face. He looked at Sally, then he eyed her sandwich. "I hope our little talk has made you feel better." He told her as he looked back down at Sally's sub.

Sally left Grizz with the rest of her food including her subway sandwich. "Yeah, I feel so much better."

Grizz tried not to look entirely insensitive as he was getting ready to take a fresh bite. "I hope you can patch things up between you and whoever it is you fancy." By this time Grizz had completely ignored her as his only goal in life seemed to be how he would eat everything.

Sally could see nothing good was going to come of her confession so she tried to end the entire scene. Untying the horses she said, "Its not important anymore, but what is important is I get home now, it's getting late, but thank you Domin for being so nice to me. You're a true friend and I'll never forget you. Take care of yourself." Quickly making tracks, Sally took off but Grizz remained sitting on the bridge stuffing Sally's food in his mouth.

Within the class of the Knolix schoolhouse, Grizz and only one other student, a young boy named Jeremy of ten years old, were in before the bell with Mr. Dalton. Grizz was trying to make an official complaint about Eddy, the volk. "There is something that's just not right about, *Eddy Evon*. He is too good to be true, can't you see that?" Grizz wanted to convince Mr. Dalton that Eddy was the real bully of the school, but Mr. Dalton chuckled,

"Domin, you are making a big deal about nothing. Despite Eddy being my top student, he won't be with us, for a while, I suspect. He has accepted a job with the new logging company. Now, Eddy's always been a good kid. I can't imagine he will ever get himself into trouble. Eddy's a real smart cookie, if anyone is going to be disciplined..."

Mr. Dalton just glared at Grizz to imply *he* was most likely to find himself in detention yet again, before Eddy, but Grizz just shot an angry look right back at the teacher until he lowered his eyes and retaliated.

"Now, if you'll excuse me, I have some photos I would like to prepare before I share them with the class." Mr. Dalton stood up from his seat and went to the back room. He closed the door behind himself.

Grizz was fuming. He glared at the door Mr. Dalton had closed. *'It just isn't fair! Eddy gets away with everything and I keep getting in trouble for nothing.'* It was like Grizz was trying to light the door on fire with his gaze. The teacher was just on the other side of it. What was there to stop him from going in there and beating a lesson into the teacher? *'No, there has to be another way.'* Grizz thought. *'Hmmm, Eddy is gone? Maybe forever? Cool, this means I am the top dog, the big Chief and Eddy's nowhere to stand in my way. Now, maybe I can have a little fun around here.'* Grizz stretched his neck to looked over Mr. Dalton's desktop and saw a lone thumb tack on it. The tack was somewhat out of place. Then an idea came to him. In the spur of the moment, Grizz quickly left his desk and approached the teacher's desk where he placed the tack on Mr. Dalton's chair.

'That'll fix him.' Grizz decided, but when he turned around sharply, he saw Jeremy, whom he had been chasing earlier. Grizz smashed his fists down on Jeremy's desk top as his stare seemed to burn holes through the boy. The desk cracked and creaked under his immense pressure. Grizz grabbed the small boy by the scruff of his neck. With Grizz's face bunched up and tight with rage, he spoke roughly. "You will say nothing about what you've seen." Jeremy clasped his hands around Grizz's wrist. He could feel Grizz's great strength. Grizz picked up Jeremy's eraser and squeezed it in his hands, mincing it in his fingers. The eraser was crushed to pulp and sprinkled onto Jeremy's desktop. "Get the point?" Grizz was finished terrorizing the boy so he shuffled his way back to his desk.

The schoolbell rang as it was shaken by a student. The students came stampeading into the classroom as fast as they could to take their places at their desks. Mr. Dalton entered the class and the students sat silent and attentive. Grizz eyed the other students from his desk but he said not a word.

Mr. Dalton studied his classroom of students for a moment before he focused on Grizz. He noticed some tension in the room as Jeremy seemed somewhat

197

frazzled, "Hey, Jeremy, is Domin messing with you?" Mr. Dalton questioned the boy.

Grizz shot a look at Jeremy with his eyes, without turning his head.

Jeremy could not conceal his fear. He shook his head with tears running down his cheeks. "N-no." Jeremy answered with a shaky voice.

"You see? No problem." Grizz lifted the palms of his hands comically.

"Right." Mr. Dalton replied sarcastically as he walked down the isle of desks, "Jeremy is always scared to death after you pal around with him." Mr. Dalton passed by Grizz's desk before he turned around and looked down on Grizz from behind.

Grizz did not turn around to look at Mr. Dalton. "This ends now, Domin." Mr. Dalton told Grizz sternly. "I'm sick of this kind of behaviour."

Grizz just ignored him. With a wave of his hand, Mr. Dalton grew a wide smile on his face before addressing the class. "Hey, guys and gals, I can't wait to show you these pictures of a trip I made recently to Hawaii. It was a real doozey."

Everyone in the class rolled their eyes and sighed. They had experienced the boredom of Mr. Dalton's stories in the past. Even the ones which were, "Real doozeys."

The school teacher gave the hand full of pictures to a student who sat in the front row on the left side of the class. "Now, look at them, then pass them back so everyone can have an opportunity to see them. And for heaven's sake, please try to keep from smudging them with finger prints."

"Yes, Mr. Dalton." The class responded in unison.

He went over to his desk like he was about to sit down.

Grizz sat up in his seat as he expected the show to begin any minute. He could imagine the sharp point of the tack just gleaming away reflectively at the center of the teacher's seat.

Jeremy put up his hand. "Oh, oh, Mr. Dalton."

Mr. Dalton paused, he turned to give his attention to Jeremy. Grizz also turned to face Jeremy, but Jeremy could feel Grizz was threatening to end his life at once if not for his blood thirsty gaze alone.

"Yes Jeremy? Did you have something you would like to share?" asked the teacher respectfully as he took another step closer to his desk.

Jeremy turned to look at Grizz with fear twitching in his eyes. After swallowing hard with a dry throat, Jeremy looked back at Mr. Dalton. "Yes, sir." Grizz was about to launch from his seat and pounce on the poor little guy. Jeremy could sense Grizz was about to attack him, "My father grew up in Hawaii." cleverly Jeremy twisted his statement.

"Oh, is that so?" Mr. Dalton moved away from the desk.

Grizz tightened his fists under his desk as he was so close to having Mr. Dalton sit down on the tack.

Mr. Dalton found this to be his cue to begin his long story of a trip which no one else seemed to care about. He paced back and forth using many hand gestures as he tried to explain every detail of his experience to Hawaii.

"Oh, come on!" Grizz thought as he stewed in frustration, *"Doesn't this guy ever sit down?"*

The stack of about thirty photos came to Grizz and he thumbed through them in a matter of a few seconds before he quickly passed them on. Grizz stirred in his plastic chair biting his nails. He was not able to sit comfortably. The uncertainty of how the next few minutes would play out was really getting to him.

Finally, everyone had seen the photos and Mr. Dalton took a step toward the student to collect the photos.

Grizz shot out of his chair and shouted, "Don't worry about it Mr. Dalton!" He quickly stepped over to the student with the photos, "I'll collect them for you." When he took the pictures from the student he snatched them rudely with a strange grin on his anxious face. "You just sit down sir and take it easy."

Mr. Dalton just watched Grizz for a moment as he tried to figure him out. "What are you up to, Domin."

Grizz approached Mr. Dalton, "Wha, me? I'm just trying to help" He handed the photos to the teacher very nicely, next Grizz pushed Mr. Dalton's shoulder with his fist, just a little. "Just go take those over to your desk and put them away."

Mr. Dalton reached back and let the photos flop to the desk top. He kept a suspicious eye on Grizz as he swung back around to sit at his desk.

Grizz stretched out at his desk. He had his hands behind his head and he stretched his legs out as far as he could, "Oh ya, this is the life. I just love this plastic chair. So comfortable." As Grizz leaned back on his chair, Mr. Dalton took a step back. Then another step. He was backing up to his chair when the back of Grizz's chair snapped. Grizz fell backwards and smacked his head on the desk of the student behind him.

The class laughed, but Grizz did not find it very funny. Not one bit. He rolled forward and rubbed his sore head.

Mr. Dalton was closer than ever to sitting on the tack. Now he was coming over to Grizz to check on him and see if he was okay. The frustration and anxiety coupled with the pain of bumping his head and the humility of the students laughing at him had pushed him too far.

Grizz looked up at Mr. Dalton and said, "No, don't come over here." Mr. Dalton stopped at Grizz's request. Adding to his first comment, Grizz became louder as he said, "Can't you just sit down!!!" Grizz brought his fists down on the desk top so powerfully the desk split in two.

Grizz relaxed back into his seat and became strangely silent. The other children were no less shaken up by Grizz's out burst. Everyone did their own part to keep from getting worked up, but Grizz had the potential of being a very dangerous student.

"I hope that is the end of your mellow dramatic entertainment." Mr. Dalton said when it appeared Grizz had settled down.

"Ya, ya. No worries, pops." Grizz disrespectfully replied. The remark was followed with the laughter of his schoolmates.

"Pops?" Questioned Mr. Dalton, the class grew silent immediately. "Very well then, thanks to Domin, you will all now have a pop quiz." He went to his desk and took a pile of papers and began to hand them out.

Many students sighed and grumbled about the inconvenience of having to do a quiz. "Quit'yer gripe'n!" Grizz shot back at the other students. "We were gonna have to do the quiz no matter what, anyway."

"Don't be so sure, Domin." The teacher returned with his quick response.

Everyone settled into the test and the class became very quiet. Mr. Dalton paced up and down the isles of desks. He was like a cop searching for a student who was breaking the law by cheating somehow.

Finally, Mr. Dalton walked back to his desk. Grizz looked up from his test paper. Jeremy gasped, he looked at Grizz with wide eyes. Grizz looked back at him and broke his pencil. Mr. Dalton responded to the snap of the pencil's wood. The teacher's rear was just above the chair. He stood for a moment, just scanning the class. Then the teacher teetered backwards and sat down.

'Oh revenge was sweet.' Grizz thought, only something wasn't right. Grizz couldn't believe it. Not only did the teacher sit down but he sat right on the tack, hard. Only, there was no scream like there should have been. In fact, Mr. Dalton was sitting at his desk comfortably. He began to mark pages of materials from the other day.

Grizz looked over at Jeremy and Jeremy wore a stunned expression on his face. He too was expecting a very different reaction.

"How could this be?" Grizz wondered.

For the remainder of the lesson, Grizz tried to figure out what had happened. He hadn't noticed the teacher removing the tack from his seat earlier. Nor did Grizz see Mr. Dalton acknowledge anything on his chair at all.

It wasn't until Mr. Dalton arose from his desk and turned his back to the class to write on the chalkboard when Grizz could see the silver head of the thumb tack. What Mr. Dalton wrote was a deadline date for each student to have their science fair project completed. He wanted all science project descriptions handed in by the end of the school day. Meanwhile, all Grizz could think about was the shiny head of the thumb tack which was stuck to the center of the teacher's rear end. Somehow, the sharp point of the tack had gone right up between the teacher's cheeks. The tack remained in place with Mr. Dalton completely oblivious to the entire thing.

Grizz could not contain himself. He bursted out with laughter. Just before Mr. Dalton turned around to face Grizz, Jeremy noticed where the tack was as well. Only Jeremy was very serious about the whole ordeal. He was not about to laugh about it.

"What is the meaning of this, Domin." Mr. Dalton spoke strongly.

Grizz tried to suppress his laughter, but he only caused other students in the class to giggle as well.

Jeremy's hand shot up into the air. Mr. Dalton turned to Jeremy, "Well?"

Grizz snapped out of his giddy mood and growled at Jeremy like a rabid dog which caused the boy to hesitate. Then Billy blurted, "Domin put a thumb tack on your seat Mr. Dalton. You sat on it and now it is stuck to your pants."

Mr. Dalton's eyes grew wide. "Uh?" he responded before backing up to the door.

On the other side of the door, Mr. Dalton pulled out the thumb tack. The teacher bit his lip and shook his head. When he returned to the class everyone was very attentive to what he had to say next. "You may not know this Domin, but you are a role model to the rest of the students of this school. When you do something as foolish as this for your own selfish kicks, you give the impression this kind of behavior may be tolerated, *but I assure you it is not.* You are hereby suspended from school for two weeks and I think this punishment is entirely necessary and appropriate to send a strong message to the other students. Do you realize how bad this situation could have gotten? I could have ended up in the hospital. Now gather your things and get going. I will be in touch with Dr. McNeil shortly."

The muscles of Grizz's entire body went tight and he could not remove the scowl from his face. He stood up from his desk and fought within to keep his cool. He stepped out into the isle and turned from the teacher. Grizz saw the students were watching him intently, as were his roommates. As Grizz began to take a few steps his eyes met with Sally Coppler. A look of fright was in her eyes before she turned away and looked down at her books. Grizz marched past them all to the main doors of the school.

Usually, Grizz finds a way to blame his problems on other people, but this time he knew it was all his fault. *'Why do I do these things?'* He wondered. Grizz walked out of the schoolhouse. He carried his books down the stairs to his bike. He looked down at his bicycle chained to the' flag pole. Turning Grizz looked back at the glowing window of the school. He was an outcast, there was nothing he could do about that. He let out a breath and felt as though he was beaten by Eddy all over again.

Big news preceded Eddy Evon before he did return back to school. Hal who was one of the young boys Grizz shared his room with, died during a tragic accident on the job with the loggers. Eddy wasn't gone long for shortly after the time of the accident, Eddy came back to class regularly. With him was a rumour he was responsible for Hal's death. Grizz would have immediately noticed the change in Eddy and poked at him about it but Grizz was suspended. Still, Grizz heard how Eddy was more of a quiet person who kept to himself a lot. Eddy's depression gave way to suspicion as people wondered if there was any truth to the rumours that Eddy killed Hal, but conclusive evidence from a polygraph revealed Eddy to be innocent. So much speculation was tossed back and forth it was anyone's guess as to what really happened.

One morning, Grizz arose early and rode his bike throughout the roads of the Island. Riding through the little dark town of Scamp which was strangely tucked into a rocky fold of the Island, Grizz was reminded of all the ways Eddy Evon had tried to make the pitiful Island a better place for the people to live, only despite the young volk's efforts, everyone still wanted to leave. A prison, no matter how it is decorated, is still just a prison. Grizz made his way to the schoolhouse where he felt real good deep within. In fact, Grizz felt better than he had felt in a long time. He was no longer a student at the school but Grizz wore this with a sense of pride and freedom because he never felt he could fit into such places for very long anyway. When Grizz rode into the schoolyard, his old schoolmates waved to him and some pointed as they had many other mornings when he had brought his bike to school. Grizz was the first student to own a bike and use it as a means of getting to school. He had started a trend where other classmates followed suit and did the same. It was only after Grizz made a bicycle that others could have bicycles brought to the Knolix Island.

The attention Grizz thought he was receiving changed in a single moment, for as Grizz was riding through the school parking lot, Eddy Evon came riding in behind him driving a red supped up volkswagon, dune buggy car which he obviously picked up at Big Wheel's.

All of the kids gathered around, they all wanted to see Eddy's new car. Eddy was, once again, the most popular kid in the school. It was just too easy for him. Grizz knew he would never be seen on his bike again from that moment on. All of the good feelings left Grizz as he went to a very dark place inside, where jealousy and bitterness crept in to smother his soul. Grizz complained, *it wasn't fair*. Grizz felt he deserved more. To be suspended from school only made him seem worse and made Eddy seem better. Still, Grizz was physically more powerful than the other children of the school, except, perhaps, for Eddy Evon, but this was never proven. Grizz began to despise the human side of himself as he was continually reminded how a volk was superior and humans were inferior.

As Grizz watched the students gather around Eddy and his stupid looking car, Grizz dismounted from his bicycle seat. He let his bike slip from his hand and clatter to the ground. Grizz felt like an invisible ghost as no one seemed to see him at all. The bike died when it fell that day and Grizz took off as his Island adventure continued, on foot.

From where Grizz stood, he could see out to the horizon but the beautiful colours were gone. With the choppy waves lapping the shore at high tide, Grizz studied the silhouette of a huge aircraft carrier anchored about ten miles off shore. The sky was dark and covered with endless cloud. A cool breeze moved over his face like a draped sash of cold silk was being pulled over him, and there in the wind he noticed a lone snowflake which was a prisoner to the throws of the wind. The snow flake moved wildly through the air with such speed and freedom of unpredictable reflex that somehow it spoke to his soul. He understood something about himself as he watched this. Just as the snow flake was entirely unattached to the effects of the world around it so to Grizz would be unaffected.

With a decision made internally, Grizz let go of his school books. Life for Domin had been extremely hard. What was the point. Was he to live his entire life this way? As Grizz, Domin decided to take charge of his own future. He was no longer a lab rat. So much negativity had been pumped through his veins, but with a new subconscious decision, Grizz confirmed a decree to burn positive self-change through his blood.

Grizz began to run up the road and he felt great. He was looking for some way he could burn the excess energy which over populated his veins. He decided to leave the road and head straight up the steep mountain of the Knolix Island. As he looked ahead to see the peak of the great mountain, Grizz saw how a low cloud only let him see half of the mountain's great height.

Pushing forward Grizz found the Island to be more challenging than he thought it would be. Though the mountain was very steep, he did not stop. He would have to exhaust all of his strength first because this was a contest for Grizz as he challenged the Knolix Island itself. He used his hands to grab at the tree trunks as his feet tended to slip in the moist incline. Pushing on up the mountain the air became thinner, quickly but Grizz paid no mind to it. The temperature also grew colder as Grizz climbed, but he was expelling so much energy he barely noticed the changes. He moved right up into the cloud where visibility became a challenge and he liked it even though it began to snow.

The volk implants of Grizz's thighs were exceedingly generous with the power and stamina they provided, but as he worked his way up, further into the clouds, he began to feel the volk muscles begin to burn. *'Oh, what I would give for a cup of water right now!'* Grizz wished.

Grizz soon realized the burning feeling in his muscles was not just a hard workout for his muscles, but pain from the potential of over working his body. The pain became too unbearable for him and Grizz began to wonder why he was even climbing the mountain anymore. It was just some stupid idea to prove something to himself. It wasn't going to contribute to any significant change for him. Pounding his feet up the steep side of the mountain as Grizz neared the top of the mountain, he stepped out onto the less steep road. Slowing down quickly on the dirt road, which Grizz had been crossing multiple times as he made his own stubborn path right up the mountain's face. The overwhelming pain caused

Grizz to collapse on the road where Grizz laid on his back and let his large chest rise and fall as it needed to. Like the thunder of a drummer pounding on his chest, Grizz felt his grizzly heart pounding within.

Hearing a faint and strange sound which was a type of electronic humming, Grizz opened his eyes and realized it was not a sound just in his ears. Propping himself up on his elbows, Grizz looked around. The strange sound came from above him but because of the cloud around Grizz, he was not able to see the source of the sound.

Grizz rolled over and began to climb again only much slower this time because his body was screaming at him to rest. Strangely, the rock and trees stopped at a berm of curved high density steel. Finally, Grizz climbed right up out from the cloud where he saw the top of the Knolix Island appeared to look more like the top of a strange flower shaped skyscraper. The top of the mountain was open with metal panels positioned in an open mode.

An apache military helicopter thumped the air with its rotor blades as it rose up out of the steel Mountain peak. The giant black dragon fly looking aircraft turned, and for a moment, Grizz thought he had been spotted. The helicopter moved away and skirted over the layer of cloud beneath it.

The sound of the electrical hum began to grow and then the great panels of the mountain's peak began to close in. Grizz felt a renewed sense of adrenaline coursing through him. He quickly shook off the fatigue from just a moment before. He leaped to the nearest slow moving panel and climbed up onto it. He peeked down into the throat of the mountain and saw three soldiers standing together upon an empty helicopter pad. Along the outskirts of the helicopter pad, Grizz noticed a bulky machine which drove on tracks. Grizz was no longer thinking about what he was going to do next, for he had no plan anyway. Grizz responded in a spontaneous type of auto pilot.

Leaping over the closing panels into the inner area, Grizz pounced on top of one of the soldiers. The rifle of the soldier flew up as the soldier was pounded down. The other two soldiers were entirely taken off guard as a cigarette dropped out of one soldier's surprised and gaping mouth. The rifle which was tossed into the air, fell down right into the arms of young Grizz.

Grizz quickly turned the rifle on the two soldiers and said, "Don't even think about it! Now, drop your weapons and get your hands up! Come on, get them up there!" The pain in Grizz's legs caused him to wobble his knees and have trouble standing. With his sheer will power, Grizz managed to keep his cool and not fall down. He was convincing enough, the soldiers let their rifles clatter to the floor as they put their hands up and surrendered. "Alright, you two will take me to the *prototype volk.*"

Turning his attention from the soldiers, Grizz examined the bulky machine which wheeled upon the tracks. Turning the machine around Grizz found the machine was a complicated wheel chair. Sitting in the chair was a young dazed volk strapped to the mechanical chair. The volk appeared to be half of Eddy Evon's age.

"So, you must be the prototype..." Grizz studied the creature and all of the human technology built right into its flesh. One key detail was all too familiar to Grizz when he examined the device attached to the side of the prototype volk's head; mind control. Instantly, Grizz was reminded of the Russians' attempt to create a cyborg-volk. Grizz talked to the prototype volk though it did not seem to have consciousness. All the while, Grizz kept his

209

rifle trained on the disarmed soldiers. "You look just like Eddy, only younger. This is what Eddy used to look like before I met him." Grizz figured.

The soldiers acted like Grizz was speaking a foreign language. Grizz realized the soldiers were not certain what he was talking about. Taking a step closer to the soldiers Grizz thrusted his fists out and smoked them right across in their faces with one blow. The soldiers dropped to the ground. Grizz hoped he hadn't hurt them too seriously, but one thing was certain, the soldiers were not going to be getting up any time soon.

A door slid open behind the mechanical chair. The prototype became activated and its eyes open. Surprised, Grizz jumped back when he saw this. Then the mechanical chair of the prototype volk sped away from Grizz in reverse where it entered the open door. Grizz ran after the prototype volk but the sliding door closed too quickly and he was cut-off.

A voice spoke over the intercom and Grizz knew he was being watched. "All units, landing pad one has been compromised. All units head to upper levels and use extreme caution."

Grizz looked around at the area he was in and realized there were some small black bulbs near to the top of the rim. He knew these were cameras and he would not be alone for long. Grizz used one of the soldier's rifles and shot at the cameras and each one of them shattered to pieces. The panels had finally closed up above Grizz and he was trapped.

Darkness enveloped Grizz for only a few seconds before the fluorescent lights flickered on. He began to search the pockets of the downed soldiers. There he found each one of the soldiers had a personal pass cards with a bar code and magnetic strip on the back side of it. Grizz immediately took one of the cards and went to one of the six identical doors surrounding him. He plugged the card into the slot next to the door which had a red light on it. The light turned green and Grizz smiled. The door made a sound like the locks were disengaging, then the green light turned red and the sound of the door relocking was heard.

Grizz roared and began to pound on the thick metal door with his fists ferociously. The impacts began to jar the door from its moorings but it was not about to open for him. Grizz went back to the soldiers and searched them. There, he found they had a strange style of pocket explosive, like a grenade. Grizz activated one and tossed it to a door and covered his ears. The explosion was intense but it was also not enough to open the door. Grizz tried two explosives at one time and the explosion was far more effective but the door still remained.

"These things are useless." Grizz took all of the explosives that were left and piled them at the foot of the door. Chuckling, Grizz was about to activate the explosives, but before he did a door slid open behind him. The sound of an alarm had been sounded and within the door was a corridor with red rotating lights hanging from the ceiling every thirty feet.

"Oh? Well, that's no fun." Grizz stuffed some of the explosives in his pockets and slung two of the rifles over one shoulder while he cradled the third one. Cautiously, Grizz entered the door.

As Grizz found there were not many people in the inner maze of corridors, he decided stealth was likely not going to do him any good. Hustling down the corridor as fast as he could, Grizz came to the open doors of an elevator. Hitting a button marked 'Sea level one' the doors immediately closed and he began to descend. Unexpectedly, someone had stopped the elevator to get on. When the doors opened, Grizz came face to face with a technician of the inner secret Island. Reaching out quickly, Grizz took hold of the technician by his white lab coat pulled him into the elevator with him. After resuming his descent to 'Sea level one' Grizz focused on taming his new pet. Forcefully, Grizz roughed up the technician and threw him over his shoulder. Looking for ways to not hurt anyone, Grizz came to a door at the bottom of the stairs where he forced the technician to establish dominance. When the elevator stopped the doors wouldn't open without proper clearance. The technician was forced to use his access card and open the elevator door.

Grizz came lumbering out of the door and right into the middle of a computerized monitor control room. With the technician held in a headlock, Grizz examined his surroundings. All of the people froze in place as they all just stared at Grizz in disbelief of his presence. The room was decorated with lots of silver trimmings and white interior. Within the spacious room were open levels which linked to smaller glassed in offices. The series of stairs and cat walks made the room seem busier than it was.

A quick discharge of ammunition into the air grabbed the attention of everyone in the room, then Grizz shouted. "No body move or I will kill the book worm here!" Grizz pushed the young technician against a computer desk. The youngster began to grovel and in his snively way, he said, "Please don't kill me. Oh, please, I have so much to live for..." Grizz quickly cut the technician off, but not before deciding this was one useless and pathetic life form.

"Shut up!!! No one has to die, just give me what I want, and what I want is information." Grizz put the barrel of the rifle to the scared technician's fore head. "One of you should be able to find a file on me, now pull the file and read it to me."

Soon a male voice came from an upper inner level, perhaps the person in charge. "We do not appear to have a file of you on record."

Grizz pointed his weapon in the General direction of the technician who spoke and he released a quick round. Purposely, he missed, "Don't give me any of that! Now, do it or you'll be mopping up Mr. piddle pants in five seconds."

"No, please, I beg you, don't kill…" The technician who was with Grizz began to cry when Grizz cut him off again.

"I said, shut up!!!" Grizz nudged the technician's forehead, "Now, where is my file!!!"

"I have it!" Someone shouted. It was a female technician. "I can bring it to you after I print it out."

"Negative, I have a computer right here. Send the file to this computer… NOW!!!" The rifle fired a shot and everyone in the room jumped at Grizz's powerful demand. Everyone was surprised Grizz hadn't killed his hostage. That is, everyone was surprised but Grizz. He had purposely shot over his hostages' head because he knew it would be the most effective way to get the technicians to give him what he wanted right away.

The monitor flickered and then it was there. "Read it, book worm." The technician tried to read the computer screen but he began to blubber as he cried. Grizz pressed the barrel of the rifle to the man's head. It was as though he had pressed a button because the man began to read like a robot.

"You were born on May, 29th 2002. You were created in a lab which was a secret location at the time, in Vancouver. Your bio-logical parents are doctor Daniel McNeil and assistant Sophia Delgado."

When Grizz heard who his parents are, he was

surprised that he knew them. Memories hit him of how each of them did parent him through his life. They must have known. Grizz wondered how strong the connection was between him and his parents because they were *still* here with him on the Knolix Island. Having knowledge of his real parents did not explain away the secrecy. Grizz was certainly not from a *normal* family. His own parents signed the release forms which gave him up to the nightmarish experimentation, experiments that were pushed so close to impossible it was a miracle he wasn't dead. Not only did Grizz's parents set him up for a life of pain, they performed the risky operations as well. The whole thing was so unbelievable it couldn't be true, but it was true. This, before Grizz, was the bizarre truth to his weird life.

The technician continued with the report, "Abnormalities were revealed early on in the stages of your development as a fetus. Your parents saw to it that every available living child be used for volk surgical grafting. A twin brother of Eddy Evon, who was born dead, was used for all of the grafting procedures. Any of the babies who successfully accepted the volk transplants were considered *'Brothers'* not only to one another but to Eddy Evon as well. Upon your birth from the incubator, you were examined and found to have missing bones and various other tissue abnormalities. In breach of procedure policy, you were selected by your parents to be a subject of testing. Documentation was signed by your parents which would not leave anyone of the research team liable for your possible death. Statistics showed you were of very high risk of not surviving the intense surgical procedures."

"Only five brothers survived to grow to adolescence. Of the five Brothers, you were the only one to survive."

Seeing a tab on the monitor marked 'Photos,' Grizz

pushed his hostage away and the nervous man went sprawling onto the floor. Grizz could not be distracted from his attention on the screen. Images came up in the hundreds and Grizz saw exactly what was involved in the surgeries. He saw many failed surgeries where others were cut open for, 'the project,' as they were so fond of calling it. He saw his own Brothers as they underwent the knife of the grafting processes.

Grizz began to breathe heavily. A temperature began to rise within him. "No, this is over. All of this has to end." His eyes narrowed in a focused seriousness "I will end it right now!" Grizz's rising temperature manifested into the inevitable of blind insane rage. Grizz went to work as he destroyed the computer on the desk beginning with the monitor. The computer sparked as it was torn to bits and the small pieces flew across the room. The technicians stood back in fear of what Grizz was going to do next.

He was about to turn his rage on the people when a voice broke out on the intercom. "Domin, refrain from any further action as the authorities of the Island are on their way to you."

"To arrest me? Come now, do I look that stupid to you? Now that I have stumbled onto your little secret under dwelling here, your soldiers will shoot first and ask... Oh, sure, they're just gonna shoot to kill. Forgive me if I am going to fight for my life. Get ready, cause when I go I intend to take as many of you with me as I can!"

"No one wants to hurt you Domin, you have to believe me! We can work something out here. Just don't stop talking to me."

"What? You trying to distract me? Who are you anyway! I don't want to talk to *you*! I want you to send Dr. McNeil and Sophia Delgado. Yes, those are the only people I will talk to. You better send them soon as well before you begin to lose technicians." Domin intended to be true to his words, he jumped up to the second level where he grabbed onto the supports of the platform and hoisted himself up. He approached the crowd of technical workers. They crowded in close to one another as Grizz had them trapped. Stepping forward slowly with his hands tense and clawed, Domin was like the spider moving in on the flies.

Beginning to speak, knowing the intercom would pick up on his words, Grizz said, "You just don't learn, do you! I warned you again and again what I'd do if you continued to push me, and what do you do? You just don't stop! You take and you take! No one takes responsibility when they're wrong, but today justice has come! Today is the day I take everything back!"

ROAR!!!

"Grizz, leave those people alone. I am here, Grizz, it is me, Dr. McNeil." Grizz recognized the slight Irish accent which Dr. McNeil tried so hard to mask.

At the words of his father, Grizz quickly settled down and tried to compose himself, "You better get in here fast, dad. We have something I need to talk to you about. Oh, and we might as well make this a family meeting so you best bring *mom* with you too." Grizz said with the power of malice in his voice.

The elevator door slid open and an army of military soldiers took positions on the other side. They were unmoving and ready for their next orders with their weapons trained on Grizz.

Grizz turned to them and smiled. "This is a stupid move you idiots." Grizz was ready to fight and die if need be, but he did not see how it was necessary. If they had been following things on the monitors it would be quite clear Grizz just wanted answers, not bloodshed. "Come on then, let's do this." Grizz said, he raised a rifle in each hand and knew he had to stand his ground with the technicians grouped behind him.

Dr. McNeil came running out of the door right in front of the soldiers. Behind him, Sophia followed. The doctor was waving his hands with his arms spread out wide, "Easy Grizz, don't do anything, we are here. Both of us and we want to talk to you, son."

"Domin, we are not the enemy!" Sophia added, she then signaled for the soldiers to crowd back into the elevator. Turning back to the open elevator door call button, Sophia touched the button and the elevator doors slid shut. The soldiers were immediately cut off.

Grizz jumped off the catwalk of the upper level and pounded his feet on the floor. He let the weapons fall to the floor as he walked near to his parents. "You knew, didn't you? You knew this whole time you were my parents and you said nothing to me. Why?"

"I was not aware Sophia was the other donor. Everything was handled with extreme secrecy." Dr. McNeil answered.

"I don't believe you. Now that I think back to what you both have said to me and how you said it, I am convinced you knew everything the whole time. Even Narl knew for crying out loud. I feel like I was made the fool in all of this!" Grizz focused in on his father, "How much did they pay you, *daddy*?"

"Easy son, you don't want to say something you'll regret here." The doctor tried to calm Grizz.

"You two volunteered for the conceptual experiment without considering the consequences to an innocent life, my life!" Grizz studied their reaction. Neither of them were prepared for him. He was expecting some kind of emotional retribution, like love and sympathy. Grizz found neither. He didn't know how starved he was for it until that moment. To Grizz's disappointment he found his parents to be like robots. Grizz felt like they just continued to treat him like a test subject and not at all like their son. His idea of a family was apparently not going to be found in the likes of the three of them. "You don't even really know each other do you?" Grizz observed.

Dr. McNeil explained, "It was part of our agreement from the beginning. Keeping everything a secret from you was necessary, don't you see? You would never have been as special as you are if we hadn't done what we did. You were born with an under developed body. Look at you. You are stronger and more powerful than any other human. You're perfect and we had the opportunity to admire you on so many different levels as we intently studied every facet of your being. You couldn't know the truth or it would have distracted you from the focus you needed. You should thank us for the information we with held from you."

From Sophia's stone cold expression, Grizz noticed a tear begin to roll from the corner of her eye.

"I was conceived in a lab, under a microscope, in a little Petri dish?"

Dr. McNeil continued to explain further, "You are unique, Grizz, for you see, I tried to graph an extra chromosome into your very DNA. This was known by no one and the technique had the virtue of never being done before." He took a step closer to Grizz and placed his hand on his shoulder as he said, "You were the one who was the least likely to survive, yet all of the other, so called *"normal"* test subjects, had perished from our experimentation while your body had accepted far more implants than we thought possible."

Grizz seemed to melt at his father's touch. Sophia approached him and put her arm around him, "I was with you from the time you were born, though I wasn't allowed to get too close. Your father was with you as well. You doubt our love for you? There is nothing easy about this situation, but this is our situation and we don't have a lot of options here. We can only make the best of it. Please believe me when I say, it kills me inside to see what our government has done to you, but you, my son, I am so proud of you for your strength. I love you and I always will."

"I am proud of you as well son, and I love you too." The family folded in together to what became their first embrace.

Grizz was speechless. He was so happy for the opportunity to bond with his parents. It wasn't something he had ever prayed for or even thought possible, but the gift of family was his in that moment.

The moment, however, was far too brief for Grizz as Dr. McNeil inserted a needle into Grizz's shoulder and injected a harmless knockout solution.

Grizz jumped up and tried to take the needle out but before he knew it, he lost consciousness. *'How was it?'* He wondered, *'At such a tender moment he was again betrayed by his parents?'*

Dr. McNeil received word that General Graham would be coming to the Island in the next few hours and it would not be a favorable visit in the least. *'I should never have mentioned I tried to graph an extra chromosome into Grizz's DNA. I am going to be fired for sure... Or maybe, even worse.'* He put his hand to his throat with the thought.

General Graham certainly knew of Domin from the surveillance recordings and the reports from the Island's officials. Dr. McNeil could clearly hear the General's voice speaking to him in his thoughts, demanding to have Domin. "I will take him by force if you choose not to co-operate with us, McNeil."

Dr. McNeil quickly organized a plane trip aboard a private falcon 10 passenger jet for Domin and many other boys whom he was aware played rugby with him. Every period the navy scheduled certain ocean vessels from battleships to submarines to cruise near to the Knolix Island. It was just dumb luck an aircraft carrier was near to the Island at that particular moment. He had to have everyone board a ferry from the Island to take the others to the aircraft carrier. The General was arriving by helicopter and the Falcon 10 still hadn't lifted off. It would not be long before the General would have the entire Island searched. First, the General organized the Island troops to locate and contain Eddy Evon. The Falcon 10 was taking off from an aircraft carrier, when the General, aboard his helicopter, flipped through some photos on his Blackberry. He stopped at an image of Eddy Evon. Giving Eddy Evon an odd stare, the General knew, no matter how much he would like to have authority over the volk, he knew it would not be granted.

Dr. McNeil had the boys aboard the Falcon 10 and they were well on their way before General Graham suspected they were escaping. The Falcon 10 raced down the runway of the aircraft carrier before it lifted off. To Dr. McNeil, lift off felt like a giant hand reached down and scooped them up.

When General Graham found out Domin was included with the rugby team who had left the Island, he was furious. Orders were given to deploy an air force squadron to escort the Falcon 10 back to the Island. Air traffic control had difficulty organizing a squadron as quickly as the General demanded. General Graham prioritized the mission simply because Domin was not permitted to leave the Knolix Island under any circumstances. Such a mistake was not supposed to happen and there would be serious reprocautions for it. As a secondary precaution, the General boarded the helicopter once more and had it take him to the aircraft carrier where he would have hands on control. He spoke to Island officials and the captain of the aircraft carrier who gave the clearance to let the Falcon 10 take off in the first place. Everyone told General Graham the Falcon 10 was on a scheduled flight to a rugby tournament and it was scheduled also, to return that very same day. All of this came with the proper approval documents signed and delivered by Dr. McNeil himself.

The General was suspicious of Dr. McNeil's intentions. After changing into a fighter pilot's uniform, General Graham boarded an F-35 Joint Strike Fighter jet which was one of five to go out ahead of the Falcon 10 where he landed and waited. At the Liberty town airport of the mainland General Graham went directly to the air traffic controller and watched carefully as they tracked the Falcon 10.

When he saw the Falcon 10 change course and plot a new heading to land at an adjacent airport from the one it was scheduled for, General Graham's temperature rose. With his face red, he contacted the air force with the use of a phone from the tower.

"This is General Graham, I have tacion clearance blue 5A. I need Sharp squadron twelve in the air to follow a target marked vector 44 west mark 85 North, heading North, North East. Relay message to Captain, Tyrel; Attempt contact, if contact is affirmed give orders to have the aircraft land at the nearest port. If he experiences any resistance at all, he has the clearance to destroy target at his discretion."

"Message received and orders are being carried out

221

now, sir. Please await verification, Sir."

Years of training was written over the lines which chiseled General Graham's features. He did not smile, but his eyes were calculating and tight as the presence of his professionalism seemed to penetrate the entire air traffic tower.

Aboard the Falcon 10, Grizz awoke slowly from the drug Dr. McNeil had given him. Grizz tried hard to open his weary eyes. He was surprised to find himself in an airplane and even more surprised to find his father, Dr. McNeil sitting in the seat next to him.

One seat ahead of Grizz was a very young punk girl from the Island. She was hanging over the head rest of the seat and singing to Dr. McNeil. Her eyes move back and forth from the doctor to Grizz then back again and again as she sang. She was dressed like a little punk rocker. Her hair was black but half of it was shaven short while the other side was a series of fourteen inch long liberty spikes which were coloured green at the end.

The little punk girl sang;

Moon-light,
Aura so bright.
Dark forebodings
In the shadow of the night.
Can't hide from the Spector
Can you hear the guardian's whisper?
At the end of it all,
Will you still love me,
For who I am?
At the end of it all,
Will you still love me,
For who I am?

Don't you remember me, Don't you remember me…
I'll wait for you on the other side
Don't remember me…
I'll see you on the other side,
Don't wait for me…
I'll love you on the other side.
Don't remember me, Don't remember me, Don't
remember me…

Grizz moaned, looking at the ceiling and the girl vanished to her side of the seat. "Where in the world are we?" Grizz asked with his throat groggier and deeper than usual. "Oh, yeah, I remember now. You, my own father, drugged me. You have betrayed me for the last time." Grizz tried to lift his arms but he found he had no strength in them at all. "I'll have my revenge, later, when I get my strength back."

"No, Grizz, you will not hurt me or your mother. We are trying to protect you now. You are in great danger. It is important for you to know who your real friends are. Though you may not believe it, I am family, and you can trust me." Dr. McNeil began to explain how Grizz was safe on the Island. There they had a frequency umbrella which masked any signals that anyone was trying to pick up on from a satellite. Since they left the Island, it was possible for other, non-friendly agencies of the world to locate Grizz and go after him. "Of course, no one can find you unless they know to look for you."

Grizz snorted as he tried to reason, but his mind still seemed sloshy and heavy with cement, "Bring'em on…" he replied fearlessly.

The little girl popped her head up, back over the seat and laughed, "Oh, is he awake enough to talk to me?" she asked, she obviously found Grizz to be incredibly fascinating. Grizz opened his droopy eyes and looked at her. The first thing he noticed was her black spiked hair which was colored green mostly at the sharp ends.

"Who are you?" Grizz slurred his deep voice.

"I am Kiki Vixen. Dr. McNeil said you like to be called, Grizz? That totally rocks!" she told him with a big grin on her face. "We shared our class together. You always kind'a kept to yourself so I'm sure you don't remember me."

"Kid, we left Halloween back in October." Grizz told her as he did remember who she was. Kiki used to freak Grizz out because she would stare at him so much.

"You should talk." she had more than attitude, Kiki had a rare kind of edge and it was something other than childlike.

Grizz made a comical surprised look at Dr. McNeil, and the doctor could not hide a chuckle.

Kiki began to talk about the music she liked to listen to and began to get into a lot of detail about random metal punk band members. Grizz was not paying any attention to her at all. First, Grizz made circular motions with his neck as he felt his strength returning quickly. Grizz looked around the plane to see the faces of the other passengers. He recognized each one of them. As the others made eye contact with Grizz they would say, "Hi, Grizz." he saw Chuckles who was invited along to cook for them.

"Hello, Grizz" came a greeting from the rugby team of course.

Grizz found he was seated half way down the aisle in a modified window seat. It was modified to accommodate his irregularly heavy build. Out through the window, Grizz could see the wing of the plane. "Not much of a view…" Grizz grumbled.

The other passengers of the aircraft were residents of the Knolix Island. They were truly a remarkable people

224

for there was not one of them who treated Grizz like he was any different than they were. As Grizz reflected on this, he just settled back into his seat and let himself pretend for a moment he was just like everyone else. He closed his eyes and relaxed, letting go of his strength and honed skills as the airplane jostled and bounced with minor wind turbulences. The background sounds of the people talking became as dry and senseless as the wall paper design back at the dormitory bathroom. Grizz turned his head and looked out the small side window. He watched as the plane cut through the clouds.

Grizz could see multiple jet air planes emerge from the cloud. They were six F-35 Joint Strike Fighter jets. He turned to look at his father. The Doctor had his neck craned to look past Grizz out the window. Oddly, one of the pilots signaled Dr. McNeil to join them in the cock pit. Dr. McNeil stood up from his seat as though Grizz no longer existed. He walked to the cock pit door where he went inside and closed the door behind himself. *'This is not good...'* Grizz thought as he turned his head back slowly to the view of the fighter jets. The other passengers of the plane also realized there were jets outside. It was then Grizz realized their plane was surrounded.

The plane suddenly lurched into a steep climb. The, "Fasten Your Seatbelt" sign began to flash. Dr. McNeil came out of the cock pit and hurried back to his seat where he quickly buckled up. *'No, this isn't good at all...'*

The Falcon 10 lurched left, then abruptly it lurched to the right. One of the jets eased in behind the Falcon 10 and targeted its' right wing engine. A hail of bright ammunition came over and under the wing until a shot quickly landed its' mark on the engine. Fire blew out of it, followed by thick black smoke. From Grizz's seat he could see the whole thing. There was no time to react. The passengers yelped as they each took startled breaths. The impacts rumbled through the hull of the craft like thunder. This was followed by the clatter of seatbelt buckles locking together. A second volley of ammunition came and started the other engine blazing in a second explosion. The passengers were all silent now as they braced themselves and prayed.

Grizz did not buckle up though he knew he should. He no longer felt like everyone else anymore. The engines of the plane did not provide any further thrust. The Falcon 10 silently glided and Grizz could see the F-35 Joint Strike Fighter jets veer off like a flock of birds. The plane slowly began to drop its nose.

Grizz ripped at his seat belt until he tore it off. Grizz shot out of his seat and clumsily muscled his way down the isle to the cock pit. He was thrown around the plane a little from all of the turbulence, but he dug his fingers into the seats determined to reach the pilots. With his powerful arms and legs, Grizz worked against the ever pressing momentum of the craft. When he had finally made it to the door of the cockpit, the plane had pitched its rear end straight up and the momentum of the nose dive grew ever stronger.

The plane exploded unexpectedly. No doubt caused from some effect of the engine damage. Grizz forced the door open to find the pilots trying to correct their trajectory in desperation. They began to drop their altitude toward some snowy, jagged mountains. "The fuel leek has ignited!!!" Shouted one of the two pilots through his clenched teeth.

As the Falcon 10 quickly descended, the pilot searched for some place to put the plane down where it would receive the least amount of damage. They were headed straight for the base of a huge mountain with a steep smooth face. The pilots hardly batted an eye at Grizz. Desperation of survival kicked into overdrive within Grizz. The affects of the drugs no longer held him in a drowsy state. Grizz saw the pilots trying to pull back on the controls. Grizz stepped forward and put one foot on the dash of the plane as he wrenched the sticks back. The landing gear was already down and the nose of the plane quickly came up. This changed their direction.

The plane climbed up the side of the mountain, just skimming over the jagged rock and snow. As they climbed the plane came closer and closer to the mountain. "We're not going to make it!" Shouted one of the pilots as he covered his head with his arms.

The belly of the air plane began to scrape along the smooth rocky cliff's. They were slowing fast but they held on for every bit of distance they could climb. Finally, when the plane was making a terrible sound of metal grating against the rock, the pilots could see they were at the top of the mountain. The nose of the plane poked up and over the peek where it tilted forward and miraculously the entire plane came to rest.

Grizz let out a breath and turned to look at all of the passengers. They were white knuckled with shocked expressions on their faces. Grizz spoke to them, "I think we can all breath now." Grizz looked at Dr. McNeil and the Doctor smiled back at him. He was very proud of his son. At those magical words of comfort, the passengers seemed to sigh at once with peaceful smiles, content to be alive. Grizz took one step toward them, but this simple action came with the most dire consequences.

Whether due to the howling winds or other force of destiny, it would forever more be Grizz's opinion that his shift in weight caused the entire plane to move. Grizz's eyes bugged out as he braced himself.

"Buckle up! Buckle up! Buckle up!" Grizz

instructed everyone impatiently.

The rear of the plane tilted back down over the cliff and they could feel the sound of metal scraping as the Falcon 10 slid off the sheer rock. Grizz wanted to run back to his seat and strap back in, but there was no time. With the sudden pitch of the plane, the people knew what was coming next.

Grizz toppled back against the pilot's controls. White knuckled, blood pumped through his veins as Grizz gripped a viselike hold on the navigation console's supports. There he hunkered down as low as he could and stabilize himself between the two seats. As Grizz looked on at the terrified faces of the other passengers, his eyes settled on the little girl, Kiki. Her eyes were so young and innocent despite her Halloween punk costume. It sickened Grizz to wonder if the last thing he would see in his life would be the death of this child.

For Kiki, the moment seemed to slow and movement became surreal and distorted. The sound around her had vanished as though their sudden reverse velocity had left all noise behind at the top of the mountain.

The passengers in the back seats wailed and screamed in fear. If this were a rock video she would have thought it was cool, but something from deep inside her had awakened and she was aware of the impending doom that held them. She was utterly scared and her soul trembled.

The plane rolled and tumbled as it fell down the mountain. The wings snapped off and the tail separated. With ear splitting thunder and unceasing rolling and pounding, it was clear, going down the mountain was one hundred times worse than going up.

228

The plane finally slid to a sudden stop. Everything was silent and dark. Taking took a moment just to breathe, Grizz soon heard the sound of someone cough. This was his first sign someone besides himself was alive. Opening his eyes slowly, Grizz looked around.

"Is anyone there?" Grizz called out. All he could see at first were dim shadows. "Can anyone hear me?" Grizz waited but he heard no response. *'Everything is dead silent...'* Grizz thought, *'How many are dead?'* A moment later, the rustlings of the survivors stirred. Along the crushed ceiling were the rows of seats and many passengers hung from them as they were still safely locked into their seat belts. One by one the people who were free from their seats began to get up. They were all in a state of disoriented shock.

Not sure if he was fine or just in denial, Grizz did not feel as though he was in the same daze as the others. Besides a nasty cut on his arm, Grizz had been well protected where he had braced himself like a piece of the air plane's iron frame work.

Setting to work helping the people, Grizz found many of the passengers were not severely hurt, rather they just needed simple attention. A leg needed to be free from where it was pinned, but most just needed to be carried because they were too weary to walk. As Grizz helped those who were closest to him first, he found these were not just random faces on a flight, he knew each one of them. These were Grizz's family and they were in the weakest state he'd ever seen them, yet at the same time, Grizz realized how the strength of humans *was* a marvel indeed. Grizz was proud to find humans were just as strong and resilient as a volk to survive such a plane crash as this.

The two pilots were dead, but as Grizz helped the

wounded he began to find no further rise in the number of casualties. One by one the passengers were pulled from what was left of the battered aircraft. Grizz took each one out into the sharp, cold wind passing over them. Grizz tried to see into the distance of the blizzard to get an idea of their surroundings. As near as he could tell, the plane had settled into a flat plain or self near to the bottom of the mountain.

Re-entering the broken vessel, Grizz found the two pilots slumped in their chairs, dead. Trying to avoid finding his father's body, Grizz carried out the limp body out of the scruffy large man. The elderly man was not Dr. McNeil but Chuckles Billadoe. Grizz found himself irritated because his father was still not accounted for. Chuckles was not dead, but he was barely conscious.

On the Knolix Island, Chuckles Billadoe was a cook, and a very talented cook at that. Once, Grizz entered Chuckle's 'Billadoe Bistro' and Chuckles asked Grizz if he was a hunger man. Grizz told him, "After I eat all your food and the wall of this dump, you can decide for yourself."

"I won't argue with that, trust me, I believe you." Chuckles thought back to an encounter he had once with Eddy Evon where they competed to see who could eat the most. Now the generous and entertaining cook was barely clinging to life.

Grizz tried to keep Chuckles coherent, "Stay with us Chuckles. You'll be just fine. All I have to do is get you off this mountain, then I'll find you some help."

"Save the others, Grizz. I am not strong enough to go on." Chuckles smiled before he drew in a breath and looked off into space. Grizz reminded of such a moment when he could practically see the ghost of Chuckles leave his body. He seen this before in the death of each one of his Brothers.

230

The others looked on as Grizz buried Chuckle's body in the snow. Kneeling beside the snowy grave, Grizz not only reflected on his own life but the connections he had with so many of the island's residence. A chill shook Grizz from his rest and he rose to his feet.

As the sting of the mountain's breath blew over Grizz, he found his titanium metal bone supports were like having his skeleton and flesh frozen from the inside. It was not just cold, it was painfully cold. He felt like his body was in danger as the pain escalated.

Grizz staggered back inside the remains of the aircraft and collapsed onto the floor. This surprised many of the people because to them Grizz was the strongest of them all. A moan began to rise forth from Grizz soon to become a loud whaling. The people stood back in fear of him, but one person placed their hand upon Grizz's back. Though Grizz appreciated the gesture, he did not stop crying out as the pain was so intense.

He could hear a voice from the person who touched him and the voice was organizing the others. Soon Grizz had many people around him and they closed in on him and held him next to their bodies. The warmth of the people caused Grizz's pain to subside. Soon after, Grizz was no longer making any sounds. Listening to the plans being made, Grizz recognized the voice of his father, Dr. McNeil. He rubbed his hands together and breathed into them. A cloud of steam arose, and Grizz stood up once again. The two pilots and Chuckles died, but an astounding number were spared with minor wounds.

It was obvious a fire would have to be made, so Grizz quickly tore the seats from the ceiling and made a pile on a crumpled sheet from the fuselage. It made no sense to him to try to build a fire on the snow. He followed his nose to a small pool of jet fuel. Using a twisted piece of metal, Grizz gathered some of the fuel and threw it over the pile of upholstered passenger seats.

"Alright, who's got a light?" shaking off some snow from his broad shoulders, Grizz could feel the pain of the cold chewing into him again. The others stood huddled within the remnant of the broken shell of the plane. They stared back at Grizz with blank faces. Clearly, no one had a lighter on them. "All I need is a spark people, then we will begin to get a little warm." A great gust of wind blew over them and Grizz's body involuntarily tightened up. "Oh, come on!!!"

Grizz marched over to the wreckage like he was going to hurt someone. The crowd opened up and Billy came forth holding the small body of a child. Grizz stopped. "No... Oh, please God... no..." But when Grizz recognized the girl, it was Kiki Vixen. Gently, Grizz took her in his arms and held her close. Her body was still warm.

Just as Grizz wept over her, she began to stir. "Oh... Oooohhhh..." she looked up at Grizz. While Kiki was still in Grizz's arms she had never felt so safe, she asked him. "You will save us, won't you, Grizz?"

"For you, little one, I will try. All I need right now is a light." Grizz told her as softly as his gruff voice could.

"Oh, a light?" Kiki spoke as she pulled out a cigarette and then tried to light it with a very small lighter.

Grizz couldn't believe it. He put Kiki down as she began flicking at the lighter in an attempt to get a flame in the snow and wind. Grizz plucked both, the cigarette and the lighter out of her hands. He crushed the cigarette in one hand and walked away from Kiki to the pile of seats. Punching his hand into the heart of the upholstered pile, Grizz gave a flick of the lighter and flames leaped up all around. Grizz spun around and handed the lighter

232

back to Kiki. He turned again and held the palms of his hands out at the bon fire to absorb the heat.

"Let's get warm everyone." Grizz announced as people were coming out to the fire. Dr. McNeil stood next to Grizz as they gazed at the great flames. Dr. McNeil was proud of his son, but Grizz was not ready to refer to the doctor as his dad. "Dr. McNeil? It's time for us to get to work."

They checked their inventory to see what kind of resources they had. With his father's help they device away to evacuate everyone from the crash site and get off the mountain.

Using the liners from within the walls as curtains Grizz was able to seal off two sides of a tubular section from the plane's hull. To keep from freezing, Grizz had to constantly go back to the fire which expelled a black toxic smoke. Unfortunately, there was not a lot of time. The fire was not built to last so Grizz had to work fast. The enemy for Grizz was the cold temperatures. Grizz wanted to do what was necessary to get moving right away and he wouldn't have had it any other way. The idea was to make a capsule that could move over the snow like a sled. With this they would have transportation.

The people were instructed to stay warm and remain inside the tubular plane section as Grizz worked on it. They agreed, "Grizz made a small hut for us. He will save us all."

Tommy tried to encourage Grizz when he said, "Thank you Grizz, if you weren't here with us, we would all be dead by now."

"We can't be sure of anything right now, I need to get out of here and I am taking all of you with me." Grizz told Tommy as if no one had a choice.

The day was growing dark. With everyone inside the

transport sled Grizz marched out in front where he had cables laying in wait upon the snow. The cables were found hanging out of the broken frontal landing wheels. The crumpled fuselage with the fire raging upon it was tied to Grizz's cables so he had the fire near him as he began to pull the transport sled over the surface of the snow.

Through the cold, snowy laced windstorm and fog, Grizz pulled the tent covered sled. He seemed to know where he was going and the others were satisfied with that. Choosing a direction down the slope and away from the mountain side, Grizz actually had no idea where he was headed, and he could not even see his own feet through the snow and fog as he continued onward. Despite the thick snow, Grizz was working very hard to keep moving and pull his friends upon the sled. He was breathing heavily and he would cough with each breath he took inward because the snowflakes were like feathers in his throat. The fire died down to a glow and the heat was quickly being taxed to the point of giving little comfort.

The slope seemed to go on forever without increasing its' pitch. The cold and pain invaded Grizz and grew stronger as it quickly over took him. He moved slower and slower until Grizz could pull no further. Collapsing into the snow, Grizz could no longer feel his arms or legs because they were so cold. Hearing Kiki begin to cry frustrated Grizz and angered him, but he could no longer contend with his frozen flesh. Grizz did not want to let Kiki down, nor did he want to let anyone else down. "No! The end will not come for me and my friends like this!"

Numb from the intense cold, Grizz did not care about himself any longer. Not knowing where the energy came from within, Grizz's veins began to throb and grow.

The thick, dark half-volk blood pumped through his veins visibly. Willing himself to rise up again, Grizz pushed through the deep snow. When they came to the crest of a hill, Grizz, in some kind of robot like trance, pushed his way through the deep snow to the back of the transport sled. Pulling the seam of the curtain liners from where they were fastened Grizz opened up the transport. The people inside were astonished and frightened to see Grizz. They wondered why Grizz had to stop and open up their protective wall.

Grizz explained, "If I push you now, this whole sled will be sent down a very steep slope. I don't know if this is going to save us or kill us, but I cannot keep on pulling you all through the snow." His lips were frozen so his words were slurred. Though the survivors may not have understood what Grizz was saying, they were too cold to argue with him. Grizz put his weight into the sled and it began to tilt over the steep hillside. Just as the sled began to move by its' own momentum, Grizz grabbed onto it and pulled himself aboard. They all kept their heads down as the sled picked up speed. Blind faith was all the occupants had to cling to. Frighteningly similar to the plane crash was the experience of moving tobogganing down the mountain at high speed. The sled moved out from under the storm cloud as Grizz poked his head out of the tent to see where they were headed.

When he realized they were headed for disaster, Grizz shouted, "Brace yourselves!" Grizz quickly took hold of Kiki and gestured for everyone to bail out the back of the sled. Grizz shouted to the others, "Let's go! Let's go, come on!!!" He tucked Kiki into his shirt so she was near Grizz's chest as he dove out the back. Rolling to a stop in the snow Grizz looked on as the other passengers spilled out the back as well. Time ran out quickly as the sled was quickly lost over the steep edge.

Dr. McNeil was the last one who had jumped out of the sled. As the doctor stood up from the snow, he realized just how very close he slid to the edge. Looking over the crest of snow, Dr. McNeil could see dark distant shapes far below of a valley filled with trees. It was not easy for the doctor to see anything through the pressing darkness. A crack appeared in the snow at his feet. The doctor took a few steps backing away from the crack. Envisioning a phenomenal thickness of snow hanging over the vertical drop, he told the others, "Be sure to keep as far away from the edge as possible." After Dr. McNeil said this, the sound of the sled crashing to the bottom of the cliff echoed upward and filled the valley. The others obeyed Dr. McNeils' advice and moved away from the ledge.

"Now what are we supposed to do?" Justin complained. "I have freezing snow in my clothes."

"We're all going to die." from a perspective of fear and hopelessness, Nathan spoke.

The moment grew very quiet as the group watched Grizz turn and slowly head back up the slope. When Grizz had rolled out of the sled, Kiki had been torn from Grizz's shirt. Plucking the young girl out of the snow, Grizz held her close. She coughed and smiled up at him, then she kissed him gently on his cheek. So grateful was Kiki, now, once again, Grizz saved her life. Kiki was not the only one to believe, as long as Grizz was with them, they would survive. Soon Grizz returned to the others carrying Kiki in his arms. Each of Grizz's steps sunk knee deep in the snow. Dr. McNeil noticed Grizz was quivering from the cold.

Turning to Dr. McNeil, Grizz said, "There was no rugby tournament, was there, Dr. McNeil?" Dr. McNeil's face went white and the stunned look in his eyes revealed the truth. "All of this was just a ploy to get us off the

Island because General Graham was about to ruin your career, right? Well, I know the truth and I know this whole situation is all your fault!"

The group looked at Dr. McNeil surprised before Grizz dropped forward into the snow, "I… am… sorry…" Grizz told them. Kiki climbed up out of the snow before Grizz could fall on top of her.

Dr. McNeil lept through the snow to Grizz where he checked Grizz's pulse and realized his skin was extremely cold he also noticed Grizz's lips were turning blue. The doctor knew, if Grizz didn't warm up shortly, Grizz would die. Everyone felt a great debt of gratitude to Grizz for bringing them down the mountain from the crash, though they were still not sure who to blame for the plane crash in the first place.

Ultimately the cold situation was like the judge dictating what would soon become their final demise. As difficult as the circumstances were, Dr. McNeil knew he had to prioritize. The others depended on Dr. McNeil's leadership and he was positive they would cleverly think their way through without losing any more lives. Before the situation became survival of the fittest, Dr. McNeil turned to the others and said. "Grizz is still alive… Listen, I know we have been through a lot, but we cannot quit now. We will get out of this, but we need to fight for our lives. This means working together. Whenever possible, people, tighten the muscles of your body rhythmically to assist your limbs with blood flow. Use whatever you can to make a snow cave for the night. We should have enough material to line the bottom of the cave so we can stay close through the night, exchanging body heat. In the morning we will have to re-assess our situation."

The group looked at the snow as they built up the courage to dig into it, but a rumble from high in the mountain caught the people's attention, then a glow of flashing lights lit up a section of the low lying storm cloud.

A black Su-37 Terminator Soviet Acrobatic jet fighter slipped out from under the pillowy ceiling. This Su-37 displayed obvious damage from a prior dogfight.

The cloud opened for a second time as a United States air force hypersonic spy plane was hot on the tail of the Soviet Su-37. The aggressive U.S. Aircraft was white in colour and was referred to as the Aurora, SR-71 Blackbird. This baby was capable of mach six which was like one mile per second. Equipped with vertical take-off and landing, the American intelligence agency saw fit to deploy this top-secret spy plane, which was sleeker in comparison to the Soviet Su-37 Terminator.

From the time the two jets dropped down out of the storm cloud, the survivors on the mountain were mesmerized by their presence. In pursuit of the black Su-37 Terminator, the Aurora SR-71 fired two missiles. Weaving through the sky braiding smoke trails behind, the missiles met their target at the hind quarter of the black Su-37 Terminator jet and it exploded in a blaze of brilliant fire and smoking shrapnel.

Everyone standing in the snow watched as the nose of the black jet went down over the high ridge like a black smoldering comet spewing fire from what was left of the frontal hull. The white Aurora SR-71 blackbird jet swooped in low over the party of survivors as they jumped up and down waving their arms to be rescued. In the wake of the Aurora's great speed, the group was pushed down in to the snow. *'Were we spotted?'* Dr. McNeil wondered. *'Perhaps Grizz will survive this ordeal after all...'* But the situation quickly grew sour as the white Aurora SR-71 disappeared into the distance.

"This does not surprise me." Dr. McNeil told the

others. "Grizz is being tracked and because he is out in the open a competition of war is in progress. Other nations of the world will fight now and Grizz is the prize." Despair washed over each one as silence returned with the distant whistle of the cold wind. Each one felt so meek, tiny and insignificant next to the powerful forces around them.

A strange crackly hush was heard behind the group and it came from high over the snowy ridge. The nose of the black jet jumped over the berm throwing snow out ahead of it. The front end of the black jet tumbled and broke as it raced down the steep slope toward them. There was nowhere to run. Everyone just huddled together in terror, but the broken jet did not crash over them, rather it dug itself into the deep powdery snow shelf and came to a dead stop at their feet. The hot smoking ruins of the black jet hissed and sizzled before them.

"Come on! Help me pull Grizz close to the jet!" Dr. McNeil called out, "He needs to be heated from the remaining cryogenic fuel of the ruins."

It took every living person and every last ounce of strength they could gather to drag the body of Grizz near to the heat of the wreckage.

Grizz opened his eyes in response to the heat. Through his pain he found renewed strength to and approach the black broken hull. The windshield canopy of the cockpit was missing and the pilot's remains were severely burned within.

Grizz shivered, as he imagined the metal bone implants throughout his body to be made of ice adhered to his bones and lodged under his flesh because that was how intense the pain was. There did not seem to be anything he could do to keep warm. Grizz tried to climb up onto the wreckage of the Soviet Su-37 Terminator's burned and crumpled hull. Being how the metal of the hull had cooled, the others followed. Getting closer to whatever heat still came off the acrobatic jet fighter was all the group could do to fight the relentless chill. Through his aggravation, a thought came to Grizz, *'I'm sure Eddy could handle this better than me... Oh, what I'd give to switch places with him now.'* Grizz had thoughts of Eddy, which reminded him of home. Home reminded Grizz of being snuggled up, safe and sound in the warmth of his soft bed.

The wind blew in at them as the dusk turned into night. A faint glow came out from under the remains of the jet as the engine core continued to burn. Though the survivors huddled together on top of the wreckage next to the plume of black smoke, they could not keep warm. The wind penetrated their clothes and chilled them to their bones.

With frost covering hair and skin pale and unhealthy, no one cared any longer if the enemy were to find them. They hoped to be captured so they could be warm again. In a cell they imagined they would eat and get some due rest.

Each one began to lose consciousness and pass out from the cold. Grizz felt the effects of the frigid cold mountain overtaking him as well, once again. It was such a terrible experience for him, he preferred to die so his torment would come to an end.

Chapter 7

On the verge of passing out, Grizz looked up and saw the heavens open up with a great light. The sound of thunder shook the group and their surroundings. It was the Aurora SR-71 Blackbird as it slowly descended from above creating a turmoil of wind. Thick snow swept cloud and sharp shards of abrasive ice cut at any exposed skin. The craft landed and a crew of humans dressed in grey astronaut styled uniforms, came out from a belly cargo ramp and took each one of them inside. The aircraft lifted off in the same manner as its arrival, straight up. They began to thrust forward, gradually accelerating to the point of attaining hypersonic speed.

The interior of the craft was of a rough design of metal framework. The aircraft slowed quickly and descended vertically where the cargo belly ramp doors opened again. Grizz and the others were mysteriously dragged out of the aircraft and onto the white sandy beach of some small remote tropical Island.

Grizz was dropped onto the sand where he nearly smacked his head against the base of a palm tree. He landed on top of a cocoa nut so he pushed it away with his stiff cold arms. The cocoa nut rolled near to some other fallen cocoa nuts. Mid-morning, the hot tropical sun beat down on them all. Grizz could only watch as the snow on his blue, frozen fingers melted away. The beads of water evaporated in the sunlight and the colour slowly returned to his hand. Grizz could see the others laying out on the beach thawing out as well. *'Is this paradise? Are we dead?'* Grizz wondered.

The three crew members, still dressed in astronaut attire, went back into the aircraft. There they undressed.

When they returned, they wore grey light weight pants and sleeveless shirts, but they were obviously military. Two high ranking male officers and one female communications officer. The only person from the cold group who was of any interest to these soldiers was Grizz. One of the male officers kneeled down next to Grizz and opened a black bag. Handing a stethoscope to the blond female officer, she began checking Grizz's heart rate and other vitals. Moans began to come from the others as they thawed out and awoke.

When the captors spoke, they sounded like they had European accents. "Quickly, now. We were not supposed to take everyone, only the experimental subject of the secret Island. That is the one, the big ugly one, kill the rest."

'We can't be dead.' Grizz answered his own question. *'Otherwise these soldiers wouldn't be trying to kill us.'* Lifting his head slightly, Grizz looked off into the distance to get an idea of their surroundings. They were not back at the Knolix Island and if there were other people living on this unidentified tropical Island, they were nowhere to be seen. Grizz noticed, for the moment, they were unaccompanied by any Island residents.

In a cold fashion, the military captors marched across the sand of the beautiful beach. The distinct sound of small hand guns being cocked awakened Grizz to the realization there was no time left to think. The captors stood over the frozen bodies laying on beach. In an execution fashion they were ready to kill at point blank range with no concern of who might be watching.

Grizz let himself go into a defensive autopilot mode. Taking hold of a coconut, Grizz beamed one of the male soldiers in the head. This distracted the other two long enough for Grizz to charge out over the sand like a beast, all the while drawing strength and life from the heat of the burning tropical sun. Stretching forward with all his weight behind, Grizz drove his fist into the other male soldier's stomach before he could draw his weapon. The soldier hunched forward as Grizz crouched down low, spinning with his arms tucked in close to his chest. Springing upward, Grizz thrust his fist up under the soldier's chin for a lethal upper cut. The soldier's body stretched as he rose into the air, but the soldier's ascension was disrupted when Grizz's half frozen body remembered it's training and kicked out his leg from behind sending the soldier flailing into the crystal blue sea.

The final foot soldier was the female communications officer. She seemed to be in a state of disbelief to see her commanding officers defeated so quickly. Defensively, she lifted her hand gun. The fear which gripped her caused the gun to shake in her hand. Grizz kicked a cocoa nut at her as she turned her head away, firing the gun. The bullet blew the cocoa nut in half and the milk sprayed back at her.

When the female communications officer turned her head back to look at Grizz, she was surprised to find his face almost touching hers. Before she could get off another shot, Grizz had swiped her gun from her grasp with one hand while he threw her effortlessly one hundred meters off shore into the ocean with his other hand.

The pilot began to fire up the engines of the Aurora. Grizz gathered the hand guns from the two wounded male soldiers before he boarded the Aurora up the cargo ramp. The pilot of the vertical take-off war plane began to lift off from the beach. As the ramp began to close, Grizz moved into the aircraft as it rose up pushing sand over the still cold bodies.

At a running pace, Grizz made his way to the access

cock pit port of the vessel. The access man door was closed and locked, but Grizz used one of the guns and shot out the latch. Kicking open the door, Grizz growled the words, "Surprise!"

Targeting the intricate controls of countless lights, dials, switches and buttons, Grizz unloaded the clips from each of the weapons. He dropped the weapons and plucked two fresh guns from his pockets and in turn he fired them at the windshield.

With an incredible leap, Grizz seemed to fly over the dash where he exploded through the glass. Fearlessly, Grizz kicked off from the air craft and caught hold of a nearby peek of a palm tree. He had to work around the great leaves, but after Grizz established a firm hold of the tree, he turned and watched as the air craft plummeted into the sea, where it hissed and bubbled. Before long, the aurora sunk under the clear water's surface.

The thawing survivors on the beach were all sitting up watching the magnificent Aurora SR-71 Blackbird sink. When the frozen survivors had awaken from the heat and commotion, Kiki pointed to the top of the palm tree and shouted, "Look! Up there! Its' Grizz!!!"

Grizz slid down the stalk of the palm tree. The group gathered themselves as they all stood to their feet. Together, they ventured into the tropical Island.

They found, not far from the beach was a road. They walked down the road for twenty minutes and hadn't seen even one vehicle drive past them. The road led them to a little Teeki beach bar. The area was kind of busy with the locals enjoying themselves. The group were so relieved to find civilization. The dark skinned locals appeared to be enjoying each other's company on the wide deck overlooking the beach. Not far from the Teeki beach bar were some beach side houses and huts.

Dr. McNeil and the others went to the bar and began

to ask questions. They wanted to know the name of the Island or if they had a telephone. Unfortunately, the locals of the Island did not speak a word of English and they were all very uncomfortable with Grizz's presence. The initial staring finally subsided as the people could see they were not there looking for trouble. As long as Grizz was with his white friends no one made any trouble for them.

Dr. McNeil searched the pockets of his pants and pulled out his old worn wallet. A look of relief washed over the doctor's face as he let out a sigh. First, Dr. McNeil ordered a round of water and a full pitcher, then he added a platter of their pineapple bar-B-Q chicken for everyone. No one would forget how good that chicken tasted.

With no basis of communication, Dr. McNeil began to speak to the others, "You people must know you are all fugitives, now. It would not be wise to turn yourselves in or go back to the Knolix Island. If you choose to leave us now, that would be fine. This Island would likely be a risky place to try to start a new life because this is where they will begin their search. You will stand out like a sore thumb since you will be counted amongst the few white people who live here." He looked out at the beach, then to the horizon before he continued, "I have a confession to make…"

The others were dead silent with their full attention on the doctor. "Spit it out, now!" Grizz told him.

Dr. McNeil hesitated before he said, "Grizz has a holming chip on him and I need to remove and destroy it."

Everyone was shocked at the news, "What's the problem here, doc? Is this a matter of life and death here or what?"

"Grizz we were rushed off the Knolix Island and I

haven't got the proper tools I need for the extraction."

"Where is it?" Grizz asked.

"The holming chip is embedded in one of your wisdom teeth."

Immediately, Grizz began marching around the beach bar as he searched for something he could use to get at the chip. He marched in behind the bar itself and looked through the shelves under the main counter but he found nothing. He proceeded out of the bar with the bar tender shouting at him. Grizz was about to tear some of the vehicles apart in the parkade, but he stopped and looked at the large deck. He approached it and took a peek underneath it. There he found some old rusty motors, a few tires and next to the tires was an old tool box. He opened the tool box and found a rusty hammer, and pliers. Grizz took the pliers and tried to open them. They were very stiff, but he managed to work them loose.

Grizz returned to the others at the bar. "Just point to the tooth." Grizz told his father.

Dr. McNeil chuckled, "You can't just pull out a wisdom tooth with a pair of pliers."

"I'm not going to keep asking this. Now, which one is it!" Grizz was seriously out of patience.

"Very well, son. Open up."

Grizz opened his mouth wide and the doctor took the pliers and inspected the teeth. "Ah, yes, here it is. Practically impossible to locate, but I was the one who put it there so that sort of took the mystery out of it." The doctor tapped the pliers on the tooth.

Grizz closed his mouth and gave a disappointed look to Dr. McNeil. The doctor thought Grizz was about to discipline him but Grizz just asked, "Is it the furthest one back?" He took the pliers from his father.

"Yes, that's right." The doctor answered.

Grizz turned his back on the others and shoved the

pliers into his mouth. The spectacle started a stir amongst the people right away, for everyone had their eyes trained on Grizz from the moment he entered the bar.

As he yanked and pulled on the pliers, people voiced their disapproval and moved back. A crunching sound was heard. Tears ran from the corners of Grizz's eyes. He relaxed, then he pulled hard again. Blood trickled out his mouth and down his chin. A chilling, shrill of a scream came from Grizz as he negotiated with the pain. Next, a cracking sound was heard, then a fleshy tear before the tooth came out.

Grizz gave the tooth and the pliers to Dr. McNeil, "I don't want to hear you tell me that was the wrong tooth, understand?" Grizz said before he spat out some blood onto the table top and played with the vacant place where his tooth used to be with his tongue.

Picking up the broken tooth, Dr. McNeil cracked it open and found the little black holming device within before he commented, "Yeah, that's it."

Grizz picked up the rusty hammer, lifting it to smash the holming device, Dr. McNeil quickly stopped his arm, "No, it still functions!" The doctor exclaimed.

"You sure? I broke the tooth, besides, I want to be sure it is destroyed, right?" Grizz asked with a slight tilt of his head.

Dr. McNeil shook his head. "The holming device was created to be very durable. If you were to be blown up, like in a bomb blast, let's say, the holming device was designed to withstand such force. This way your death could be confirmed in a battle situation. You'd also be surprised how much information it can hold. Let's leave it here, so this is where everyone will come looking for you. All we need to do is get as far away from here as possible."

Grizz removed his necklace with the bear tooth

hanging from it and left it on the table next to the holming device and a few drops of his blood.

Grizz and the rest of the group took to the road. It was not easy to keep running. Everyone was exhausted and there didn't seem to be any presence of a threat hard on their heals. The Island seemed to be sparsely populated because for the five miles they walked, only three vehicles passed them by.

They made their way to a town where they found a beachside hotel. The hotel was called the Swahilli Cabaret and it appeared to be a popular vacationer's haven with a casino on the main floor and a lively beachside bamboo bar. The group immediately headed straight to the music and multitude of people where they tried to blend in with many of the other white vacationers. The music was fun and uplifting. It was a spectacular party with dancing and the smell of food cooking on many bar-B-Qs.

The group, with Grizz, didn't exactly seem to fit in with the other happy vacationers. They slowly moved through the thick crowd in single file to the tables. Grizz quickly sat down at an already occupied table of six. The people took one look at Grizz and quickly but quietly vacated. They had left so quickly, they left their drinks behind. Grizz and his father hadn't a second thought of claiming the drinks for their own. The others were again thirsty and hungry after the five mile walk, they began to eat and drink what was left. Grizz held his pinna colatta up as his father clinked the edge of his glass to it.

"Cheers!" Dr. McNeil said with a crooked half smile and a gleeful eye.

Grizz snorted a quick chuckle as he took a mental snapshot of the moment. While they rested they talked about their plans of where they would go next and what the best method would be for their next course of action.

Grizz decided everyone would have to split up very soon. He felt he was their greatest threat because even without the holming device, Grizz would attract authorities and danger. Basically, Grizz commanded the others to leave right away and he was so strict and adamant about it the others quickly left the table.

"Dr. McNeil..." Grizz called, "Would you care to remain here with me a moment longer?"

Dr. McNeil was standing, but he looked around to make sure there was no noticeable immediate threat. "Sure, son, I'll stay with you as long as you need." Though he agreed, just being near Grizz was dangerous, Dr. McNeil also knew, Grizz was his best chance for protection. There was no better body guard.

For a moment, Grizz and the doctor just sat with a strange awkwardness between them. Dr. McNeil was able to pick up on how Grizz needed him to be fatherly, so he said, "Grizz, the future is ours to create. Now that you and I are free from the Knolix Island, we are in a place of transition. Through my life I have found it is in ties like this when we need to be very careful about what direction we want to be heading. So tell me what is it you would like for your life?"

"I... I would like something I have never had before... World domination." Grizz answered truthfully. "Dominate or be dominated. That is the rule and I know how to play the game."

Dr. McNeil laughed, but when he noticed Grizz was not laughing as well, he quickly put a lid on it, "Oh, oh, you're serious. I... I thought you were joking." the doctor spoke sheepishly.

A smile spread across Grizz's face. "I was..." he answered. "Before I dominate the world, I would like to have a real family."

"A real family, Grizz? But you have had a real

family all your life. When your brothers were with us, I was your father and your nurse mothered you who really was your mother."

"You crazy? None of it was real!" Grizz slammed his fist down hard upon the table top. Heads turned at the sudden heavy thump. "I want a normal life. Where is my childhood where I live in a house with my mom and dad?"

"Now hold on just a second here. You need to realize you were given the best life you could imagine. You were born with so many imperfections, but thanks to the situations, you find yourself here."

"Wha, here in danger?" Grizz asked harshly.

"Danger? This is just a moment. You and I will get through it like we have gotten through everything else. You started out meeker than meek, but you have become the strongest man in the world."

"Are you forgetting, Eddy?" Grizz reminded his father.

"He is not a man." Dr. McNeil and Grizz just stared at one another for a moment. "What do you want?" The Doctor asked again. "What if I told you I was planning on dating your mother, Sophia, when we get out of this."

A great weight seemed to lift from Grizz when his father said this. Grizz felt he finally had the father of his dreams and he was the most unlikely person yet at the same time he felt it was the most obvious choice for it couldn't possibly be any other. On the other hand, if the doctor was lying to him, he was brilliantly mad because he figured out exactly what it was Grizz wanted.

Grizz decided not to go too deep with anything spoken by his father. He would believe whatever he wanted to believe and at the moment Grizz wanted to believe Dr. McNeil was telling the truth. The two enjoyed the time they spent with one another.

Grizz laughed and knocked the drink back. He stopped smiling and said, "You know, dad, I'm not sure if you already know this but most of the time I feel like I am always standing in the shadow of a great anger. Nothing I do seems to ever free me from this nightmare."

"I am sorry, son. You may not ever be free from that." Dr. McNeil told him.

Grizz did not want to hear this particular answer, but he understood. The doctor was not all powerful but at times he could be very honest. Grizz loved and respected his father, he always had. The two men stood up from the table. Side by side, as father and son, Grizz and Dr. McNeil, breezed out of the party like atmosphere. As they ventured down the street, they kept their eyes open for any police or military activity. They found the citizens of the tropical Island were all black and they made their living primarily as farmers or by catering to vacationers. As Grizz and Dr. McNeil walked past the different shops of the town's main street they could see how the natives liked to sell their goods through their fishing, tropical farming, bamboo, little monkeys, colourful birds and white snakes.

Multiple footsteps came running from behind them. Grizz and Dr. McNeil spun around with haste. They were ready to fight, but it was their own group.

"What is this?" Grizz asked cautiously. "You guys were supposed to split up. What're you all doing here together again?"

Justin spoke but he could barely get his words out fast enough, "They're here. Soldiers from all over the world, we have the Chinese army, the Italian army, the Danish army, Americans, Germans, Russians, you name it they are all here. What should we do?"

Not only were there a multitude of military forces coagulating around them, they were also not hesitant to begin opening fire upon one another. The rapid fire of weapons was heard, and the party was over.

The group followed Grizz into the jungle where they kept low and watched as the military forces arrived in droves. Helicopters and armored personnel boats unloaded troops on the white sandy beaches.

With the surrounding tropical vegetation coupled with all of the soldiers about, Grizz felt like he had taken a leap into the past and found himself in the middle of the Vietnam war.

Grizz wanted the others to go their own way desperately but they were out of time. As the soldiers from around the world arrived in force and fought desperately for the custody of the subject, Grizz, who was, "in the open." There were efforts made to search for Grizz and also to evac the citizens of the tropical Island.

As difficult as it would be to stay alive, Grizz was equally challenged with the responsibility to save his companions who had already come so far with him. A new objective was perceived for them as Grizz led them out of the jungle and back to the main street of the town. The group found themselves running down the side walk of people who were also running in panic. Grizz knew, in the next few moments he would be discovered because of his unusually large size. He had to get out of the open quickly and as he saw a tank drive onto the street in the distance from the beach, they headed into the door of the nearest store. The people who ran the store were at the window trying to see what all of the commotion was. Grizz glared at the store owners as the others ran in behind him. With a grunt, Grizz pointed at the door. The owners didn't need to speak the same language to understand Grizz. They ran out of the store and headed up the street with everyone else.

Looking around the the surroundings of the room,

the group found they were in a dirty little thrift store which sold mostly shoes.

"No, no, no…" Grizz thought. The enemies were closing in around them and they had nowhere to go. "I need transport… Not shoes!!! I need a plane or a boat." Grizz recalled the boats transporting citizens.

Grizz's mad scientist father suggested, "Why don't we use some of this vanishing cream?"

Everyone looked at the doctor like he was nuts Grizz also rolled his eyes but suddenly he understood what his father was trying to say. Grizz began rummaging through the tins of shoe polish. He quickly opened the tins on the counter one by one.

"This isn't vanishing cream." Kiki told Grizz, "It's shoe polish."

Grizz told the others, "Help each other and be very careful to cover all exposed skin evenly. You are all citizens of this Island now. You will keep your heads down and spread yourselves thin amongst the others boarding the boats. You need to go wherever they are sending the Island civilians. It will likely be some neighboring Island." Grizz could see the fear and uncertainty in their eyes. "Now don't worry, they are looking for fair skinned people." The group even went as far as to put on some of the clothes from the store. Kiki found a pair of scissors from behind the sales counter. She cut her hair so she looked kind of like a boy. No green colour was left, only a dark brown in her hair.

With the pressing sounds of gun fire outside the others understood and did not argue. "Be careful how the shoe polish is applied." Grizz told them, "A mistake will mean the death sentence."

Dr. McNeil said, "Listen, No gunfire. Something has changed."

Everyone gathered at the dirty front window. "The

254

leaders of the nations must be talking." Grizz figured.

They noticed some strange order and organization was taking place out the window, "Look down the street how the Russians march alongside the Americans." McNeil observed.

"Obviously, it's a tense situation for them. Look how they seem to squirm with their new awkward orders." Grizz pointed out.

"Do you think they found the tooth and holming device?" Kiki questioned.

"Yes, and I hope General Graham wears the bear tooth necklace, because I intend to hang him by it." Grizz threatened with angry eyes.

"Easy son." Dr. McNeil, spoke like a true father, "Look at you, in your prime. I'm sure you'll get the opportunity to deliver what you were created for."

"What's that?" Grizz asked under his breath.

"Give them hell, son." Dr. McNeil answered.

Grizz smiled with a side long glance.

"Oh, ya!" Kiki responded with a smile of her own. "Cool!" But as Kiki looked at Grizz she realized he did not add any shoe polish to himself. "What about you, Grizz?" Kiki asked with concern, "Aren't you going to use any shoe polish?"

The others took notice upon Kiki's question.

"Look at my size. It would make little difference. This is where we all must part, and I mean it, this time. I cannot go with you, besides, I am the decoy now, so no one will suspect you. I will have their attention."

When everyone was getting ready to head out the front door, Kiki noticed Dr. McNeil whisper something in Grizz's ear. The doctor also wrote his private cell phone number on Grizz's tattoo with his ballpoint pen. The phone number looked like it was part of the tattoo. Soon, everyone left the thrift store at once and dispersed. They hustled across the street to the beach where people were being organized to board the boats. Grizz watched from the window as they blended into the crowds of black people easily. Soldiers swarmed the streets behind them.

Within the crowd on the beach, Kiki found herself next to Dr. McNeil. She asked him, "What was it you whispered to Grizz?"

"Oh, I just said one word to him, 'Surrender.'"

Kiki was horrified by this. She turned to look back at the Island thrift store as the doctor disappeared amongst the crowd. Tears filled her eyes as she watched Grizz step out of the front door with his arms raised up high.

All of the military stopped in their tracks at the sight of Grizz. No one expected to find him surrendering so easily. An American soldier was the first to approach Grizz to arrest him, but as he stepped close enough to touch Grizz, the soldier was shot in the head by a Russian. All hell seemed to open up on the street as the combined forces of soldiers suddenly turned on one another firing their weapons. Soldiers dropped by the dozen with each passing second. Grizz thought he was going to be shot, but it was just as his father suspected. The soldiers would kill one another before they would risk killing Grizz for Grizz was the prize.

The living and the wounded soldiers cleared out of the street as fast as they could to take cover. A brave Russian soldier decided to play the hero as he approached Grizz. Grizz held his wrists out to the Russian. He thought, *'Go ahead, try your luck.'* but the Russian soldier was quickly assassinated by a Chinese soldier before he could get close enough to lock his shackles to Grizz's wrists. Gun fire and explosions followed once again as the Chinese retaliated to avenge their fallen comrade. While Grizz remained still, the gunfire slowly subsided.

Spontaneously, Grizz decided to go for a stroll down the street unhurt. He watched as the boats of Island citizens moved out to sea. Grizz said *'good bye'* to his father in his grizzly heart. As long as Grizz was out in the open, and did not attempt to flee, he was unharmed for he was the trophy to whomever was the last army standing. A twisted game of life and death would decide who was the strongest and they all wanted to win.

Grizz bid his time and waited for the last and strongest army to remain. Hours had went by with many deaths. It was like a strange game of chess as the soldiers would go to arrest Grizz only to find a new sniper to drag out the ordeal.

Finally, a very young German trooper was not only able to get close enough to shackle Grizz, but he was about to tightened one of the cuffs to his own left wrist. Before the trooper could, Grizz surprised the youth. With a quick snap of his arms, Grizz took the rifle from the unsuspecting soldier and spun him around. Smacking the German soldier on the back of his head, Grizz established dominance and used the soldier as a shield. The silver shackle dangled from Grizz's wrist.

There was no fear in the young German's eyes but Grizz was about to put fear in him. Knowing how to read the situation, Grizz didn't make it easy for the young German trooper to fasten the second restraint. Grizz knew, if he was bound and no one took a shot at him, it would all be over and he would then be the prisoner of the last remaining army.

Grizz triggered the rapid fire assault rifle as he reach up to the soldier's chest from behind. He plucked a grenade from the weapons harness from which he wore across his shoulders. Activating the grenade and never letting the pressure off the rifle's trigger, Grizz tossed the grenade a mere five feet from him.

When the grenade went off, the explosion knocked the young German soldier senseless, but Grizz had appeared to have disappeared entirely. The remaining German soldiers began to conduct an extensive search of the area, but Grizz was nowhere to be found.

On the other side of the small mysterious tropical Island, Grizz ran down the beach and dived into the ocean. He had been running, non-stop, from the commotion which was still in progress on the opposite side of the Island. He swam out to a small fishing boat anchored off shore. The sole fisherman of the boat watched Grizz as he swam toward him. As the fisherman was trying to open an oyster with his pocket knife, he had an undeniable, uneasy feeling at the sight of Grizz, even at his great distance. Instinctively, the fisherman kicked the switch of his electrical winch. The cable of his anchor began to reel in. The power and speed Grizz had was more than impressive, it was threatening. Before the black fisherman could start the engine of his boat, Grizz was climbing up onto the deck. Before the fisherman knew it, he was a captive and his local fishing boat was high jacked.

None of the remaining citizens reported anything suspicious, though there was so much commotion, the telephone lines of the Island were over-run with complaints. This only contributed to the chaos and disorganization. To Grizz's advantage, there were no leads to follow.

Grizz took his time trying to communicate with the fisherman though he didn't know a word of his language. The trip was long and most of it was taken with Grizz's threatening message to the poor unsuspecting fisherman.

Within the time of the journey over the sea, Grizz watched carefully for pursuing boats, and he tried desperately to keep warm despite the intensity of the sun.

The metal supports of Grizz's bones were stubbornly not warming up quickly with the rest of his body. Grizz's message to the fisherman was, he would return to kill him and his whole family if he spoke a word of him being on his boat to anyone. The native Island fisherman was so scared of Grizz he did exactly what he said.

"I want you to run this tub, full throttle." Grizz told him, "Get me to North America as fast as you can... I hate the smell of fish..."

In the time of seven hours the fisherman completed his mission and had taken Grizz the distance to North America.

After eating a meal of lobster and shark which was prepared for him by the fisherman, Grizz was ready to leave. The day was over and the dark veil of the night had closed in around them like someone had drawn the curtains of the sky. The fisherman and Grizz looked out toward the distant lights of the great Metro city of the coastal mainland. Grizz approached the fisherman and gave him his shackles as though it were some sort of strange gift. The fisherman wondered if it was some sort of warning. Again, the black fisherman vowed he would not speak a word of his encounter with Grizz.

While they were still a great distance of five miles from the shore, Grizz told the fisherman to go back before he dived over the edge and swam to the mainland.

Grizz rose up out of the cold water of the ocean. His mind was buzzing with madness as Grizz shook off some of the water, telling himself, "I've had it with the cold."

Not sure how to deal with the pain that came with his uncomfortable chill, Grizz took the pain as a rude hand dealt to him from God.

Heat was the only priceless commodity Grizz knew and he felt if he didn't have it right now, he would die. In an attempt to escape his troubles, Grizz began to run.

He ran right up the steepness before him with no regard as to where it would lead him. He found he was under a great four lane suspension bridge. Crossing over a dark field of train tracks and cluttered storage of box cars. Silently and swiftly he flew between them until he found himself in the light of a freight train engine heading toward him. With the likeness of a bouncing ball, Grizz stepped from one wall of the surrounding trains and kicked off to another box car across the lane. Climbing higher and higher until Grizz found himself standing on top of the freight train.

Grizz would have taken a moment to look around at his surroundings if he was interested in where he was, but he felt the air of heat flow up and swallow him. It was perfect. Grizz jumped down to the running board which led to the engineer's cab of the locomotive.

The engineer was with a companion and when they saw Grizz entering their cab, they reacted in fear. The shaken engineers worst nightmare was upon them. They screamed and one of them pulled the line that hung from the ceiling which activated the powerful whistle.

Not ready for the sudden blast of sound Grizz reared back with his hands to his ears as he roared his displeasure. The engineer was more frightened than Grizz as he didn't let off the God forsaken whistle.

Escaping the long and continuous scream from the train whistle, Grizz jumped free, and it was like he flew from the train. Hopping from one car to the next, Grizz left the annoying sound of the train whistling far behind him. From the roof of the last car, Grizz lept a generous distance which also cleared the top of a barbed chain linked fence.

Grizz continued up a steep grade of cement. The cement was a large part of the bridge foundation. Climbing, Grizz pumped his way up under the great highway bridge overhead. As he came closer to the top he could hear the voices of people. Were they shouting down at him? He wasn't sure, but he just continued to motor his way upward. When he arrived to a leveled area he found himself amongst many homeless people. They all gawked at Grizz silently with their eyes wide as they had never seen the likes of such a menacing and dangerous man. Grizz just looked at them breathing heavily before the people came alive with terrified screams.

"Shut up!!!" Grizz shouted back.

He was not about to run out on them because he found at the center of the crowd was a metal barrel lit up with flames to keep everyone warm. Grizz approached the barrel and bent over the heat with his arms stretched out around the flames like he was going to hug it.

As Grizz stood with no concern for the rest of the world around him, one of the homeless men felt the spirit of heroism to protect his friends. The fingers of the homeless man played over the grip he handled over his baseball bat. While Grizz seemed to sink into a trance of pleasure and rest, absorbing the sweet heat of the beautiful trash can, the brave homeless man snuck up behind Grizz. The baseball bat was wound back with all the confidence of a professional baseball player.

No time was wasted as the momentum was released into action with all the strength of the man backing it up. The bat came to an immediate halt as it rested against its target. From the clenched teeth and closed eyes, the homeless man relaxed to see the results of his home run, but to his surprise the baseball bat had found its' rest in the palm of the large stranger.

Grizz moved in on the man. With his nose touching the nose of the homeless man, Grizz said, "Obviously, you are more capable than this life you have chosen for yourself." Grizz sniffed at the man, "Get a bath! Get a life!"

Grizz spoke so powerfully to the man, the man fell backwards to the ground. Grizz found himself standing alone next to the flame of the trash can holding the baseball bat. Grizz motioned the bat as he held his arm outstretched. The homeless man curled up with his arms covering his head. The poor man was certain he was about to be beaten to death, but Grizz just threw the bat with incredible force out to the field of trains.

He could hear the sound of the police sirens amongst the traffic above. Grizz figured he would go up and take a look at what was going on. *'Why not.'* Because Grizz had just arrived at Metro city, he couldn't believe the police were already after him. The authorities didn't know anything about him.

As Grizz walked up the steep trail which wove between the trees, he could see the red and blue lights of the patrol car in the distance of highway traffic. Looking around as the headlights of the heavy traffic passed by, Grizz neared the bridge of congested vehicles where he observed a thinner bridge. What came zooming along its thin tracks was a sky tram. Grizz had never seen the busy sights and sounds of a big city before. The light speckled tall buildings and neon colours left Grizz somewhat mesmerized. The experience gave him a new respect for the world and the humans who created it.

Before Grizz knew it, he was standing too close to the traffic. Straining to see the faces of the drivers as they passed him by, Grizz's presence began to start a commotion. The traffic slowed down to look at him and some vehicles even squealed their tires as the congestion on the road came too soon. The first thing people would notice was Grizz's great size, but when he moved, the passer-bys noticed the inhuman bulky muscular build. As people could see Grizz more clearly they reacted with surprise, fear and panic.

The traffic was already disrupted by the commotion of the patrol car's flashing lights, but the presence of Grizz caused a large traffic jam.

Grizz could hear the sound of panicked screams and voices coming from the direction of the patrol car's lights.

"There he is! That's him!!!" A voice shouted with many of the homeless people pointing in Grizz's direction. Grizz squinted his eyes to see what the big deal was.

From the flashing red and blue lights an image of a man approached him. "Hey, you! Let me see some I.D." It was the police officer.

"I don't have the time." Grizz told him as he turned to walk away.

The officer took a new stance and Grizz knew the officer's revolver was drawn on him. "Hold it, buddy." The officer reacted to Grizz's massive build when he was close enough to see him in the red and blue lights. "Put your hands on your head."

Grizz stopped. He really didn't feel like entertaining the police officer with anything, but for the moment he would let the situation play itself out. Grizz lifted his thick arms and placed his hands on the back of his head. Ominously, in the dim flashing lights of the patrol car and the traffic, Grizz turned and stepped toward the police officer. The officer was in total awe as he had never seen a person like Grizz before. It wasn't Grizz's size that caused the officer's heart to race, but the intensity and anger burning in Grizz's eyes.

Grizz noticed the officer's fear immediately, and he knew he had the upper hand, but he continued to make it unclear whether or not the officer was somehow in control. Grizz walked right past the officer and approached the patrol car. The homeless people saw Grizz coming and that was their cue to get moving in some other direction. The crowd quickly broke up and dispersed. Grizz shook his head with a low chuckle as he saw the people running away.

"Hey, hey, Stop! I didn't tell you to keep walking." The officer was stammering when he talked.

Grizz was totally at ease. He stopped beside the patrol car. The officer saw where Grizz was so he said, "I want you to put your hands on the car! Get your legs back and spread'em!"

Grizz was slightly proud of the skinny little police officer for having the nerve to continue ordering him around. The cop's voice had changed though. There was more authority, confidence and less respect. Grizz didn't like it. Not one bit.

With a side long glance, Grizz knew the police officer was coming up behind him. "Who exactly do you think you are?" The officer asked.

"I am, Grizz!!!" the answer came powerfully and deep. Slamming his hands down on the patrol car, the metal of it crumpled as Grizz's fingers dug in. Establishing a firm grip, Grizz lurched his shoulders back and hoisted the car up. Lifting the patrol car up high over his head, Grizz saw the traffic freeze completely, as did the stunned police officer. Grizz turned with the police car held up over his head. As the shadow of the police officer's impending doom covered over him, the officer fell backwards and squirmed to try and make some distance between him and the car before it flattened him. Grizz shouted down at the police officer, "This world is mine!!!" before he forced the car down and drove it to the ground with a thunderous crash. "You want to stop me? Who do you think you are?" Grizz turned to the drivers who were just sitting in their cars gawking at him, and he roared.

Grizz began to jog down the road and none of the other vehicles followed after him. The police officer tried to swallow his heart which was beating out of his chest as he did nothing more than watch Grizz disappear into the lights of the big city.

Chapter 8

With feet pounding the city streets and the variety of neon city lights streaking past, Grizz came barreling through an intersection causing confusion amongst the drivers and pedestrians. Drawing a lot of attention to himself, Grizz made a hard left turn. His feet sliding along the pavement as his momentum carried him from his traction. For a moment, as he leaned forward, his knee scuffed along the road like a break before he regained control of the corner and set out upon his new course heading.

Behind him, Grizz had three police cars hard on his heals. Lights and sirens were punching and cheering in his wake. It was not long before Grizz came to traffic grid lock on a four lane one way main street. When Grizz leaped into the air, he did not slow down at all and in some kind of magical way he seemed to bounce up onto the hoods and roofs of the vehicles as though gravity had no hold on him. There, Grizz began to hop from one vehicle to the next as he made a lot of distance between him and the aggravated police officers.

Three blocks down the road, Grizz leaped from a delorian roof top and soared through the air where he landed in front of the main doors of a theater. The people who were standing in the line ups waiting to get into see the night's feature were awestruck at the presence of Grizz. He did not seem to be interested in the people, rather, Grizz wiped his arms and examined the water in the palm of his hand. He was still wet and cold. Grizz blamed his wet clothes for slowing him down and hindering his ability to escape the authorities.

Though Grizz was also hungry, he knew he had to

accomplish one thing at a time. First, he had to find some dry clothes. Systematically, Grizz examined the stores which were all still open at the late hour of the night. He was not familiar with any of them. Despite the yelling and heckling of the angry drivers who weren't pleased about Grizz stomping on their vehicles, he saw a display window in front of a JC Penny department mall. The store was still open so he darted across the street and slipped in through the inviting front doors.

Screams accompanied Grizz when he charged in and immediately caught the attention of the store personnel and the other shoppers. Making his way throughout the men's wear section, Grizz searched to find something he could wear in his size, but there was nothing. He tossed many cloths around as he emptied the racks quickly. Many people were chasing him through the store, but the mess only grew at a quickened rate of speed as he frantically looked through the stock. Grizz grabbed a couple pairs of grey spandex jump suits because they were found under a sign which read one size fits all.

"That's enough, pal. You're trapped and you have a lot to pay for." Sure enough a large group of people including the store's managers and security stood before Grizz. They blocked his path to exit the store.

Removing his wet shirt and pants, the people of the store saw the viciously powerful muscles and countless scars. A government tattoo stretched over his bulging biceps. Grizz seemed to have the onlookers in a trance as he never looked away from them while he slowly and ominously dressed in the grey spandex.

Once Grizz was fully dressed, he glared at the people, growling a low warning. They could see not only how dangerous he was but how they made a big mistake believing they could handle him. Charging at the crowd with his head lowered, Grizz rammed right through the crowd of people like a mad bull.

The golden framed glass doors exploded right off their hinges as they spun and cut into the traffic outside. Grizz, the source of chaos, left the department store in search of something to eat.

Not far from the department store, Grizz walked into a twenty four seven convenience store. Marching past young kids who were smoking with mohawks and stunned expressions, Grizz paid them no mind. Not many people occupied the little store. The only other customers were some punks like the ones who hung together, out front. The young wayward gothic folk could not speak a word, much less look away as Grizz came into the light of the convenience store. The look in Grizz's eyes spoke clearly to the punks. *'This guy is pure trouble.'* Never before had the punks seen a man with such an unusually large muscular build.

They too were very unusual, for the punks were twin brothers. Roach wore thin triangular sunglasses which stuck out sharply about three inches too far at each side of his face. His skin was entirely painted black. The long thin head of Roach was topped with a tall bushy fluorescent green Mohawk. A grainy silver and copper gauntlet is worn on his right wrist which looked like a cockroach with a single green light that softly faded on and off.

The other punk was named Rat and he did not resemble his twin brother Roach at all. Rat wore a mysterious long black trench coat. One single medallion hung loosely and low from a long silver necklace. Rat's long bangs hang out over his face like a visor but the majority of it was a short cut. A distinct feature of Rat was his large nose with a duck bill-like upper lip, this gave him the nick name, Rat. Dark eye shadow haunted his gaze. The face of rat was always smirking and gave a sense of untrustworthiness. With his pants covering over his tall boots and raised heels, Rat tried to discreetly hide behind a randomly chosen magazine. The twins watched Grizz from the time he stepped into the store.

The doors opened and a sound chirped to alert the employee at the till of a customer. Over the low soothing music the only other thing to be heard was the sound of Grizz's heavy footsteps. Rat and Roach couldn't believe Grizz looked so great and yet he would ruin it all by choosing to wear his tacky pair of grey spandex. The tight clothing would be embarrassing to most people, but Grizz was happy just not being cold and wet anymore. He had no reputation to protect. It was as though the grey spandex were painted onto his body and it exposed every rippling muscle leaving little to nothing to the imagination.

When Grizz came walking into the store, everyone stopped breathing. Grizz went to the front counter and asked, "Could you get me something to eat?" The employee behind the counter seemed to be in a daze as he shakily put a wiener in a bun and held it out to Grizz.

Before the store employee knew he was speaking his mind out loud, he said, "Your big... I m-mean buff..." Awkwardly the young man tried to smile.

Grizz tore open a bag of potato chips and ate a handful from it.

"You're going to pay for those, right?" The thin young man at the cash register asked. He brought the hotdog closer to his chest. Grizz gave him a disturbing eye. The young man became flushed in the face, "I-I don't see any pockets on your, well, yourself."

Grizz reached out over the counter and grabbed the hotdog out of the employee's hand. With one quick motion Grizz stuffed it all in his mouth, bun and all.

Grizz seemed to have a slight problem swallowing, so he took a step near to the fridge where he took a jug of chocolate milk, twisted the cap off then began to chug it all down.

The store employee was still waiting for Grizz to give him an answer.

Grizz wiped his mouth with his sleeve, and told him, "I have no money!"

The employee slid his hand behind the counter where he secretly pressed a panic button automatically tripping the silent alarm which called the police to the robbery. The employee then added his frustrated comment, "Come on, man. You can't just take stuff like that!"

"Yes, I can!" Grizz corrected him. "I need it, so I take it!" Grizz laid it out for him with the other speechless punks still looking on.

"Don't you have a conscious?" The cashier asked nervously.

"Right now, I only have an appetite." Grizz answered as he grabbed a handful of pepperoni sticks and chewed at them.

"Perhaps you can write me an IOU or something because I am sure one way or another, you *will* pay for what you take." The cashier looked over at the punks, Rat and roach, who were in his store and he winked at them. The two punk twins caught the hint. They knew the police were on their way.

The guy at the till was too confident for one thing and he sneered a smile like the situation was taken care of when he made his last comment. The punks approached Grizz and spoke to him saying, "Hey man, you need food, dude? We have lots O' food... All yo can eat! My name's Rat and this here be mi twin brother Roach."

"Our food is free!!!" The second punk, Roach, spoke

with a high squeaky shout.

"Hey! I can't let you guys take him out of here yet." No one paid any attention to what the cashier was saying, "In fact, you guys need to stay here as well."

The punks were not so foolish, they had to get out of the store right away, but the twins were set on taking Grizz with them. "Let's go big guy, yo gott'a leave with us right now, kat." finished Rat.

As they stepped out from the glass doors of the convenience store, they could hear the distant sounds of police sirens approaching. In response to the sound of the nearing authorities, the twin punks led Grizz to their old and mysterious black van before they sped away.

Inside the van, Grizz found a third punk in the driver's seat. Grizz sat between the two punk brothers on the rear bench seat. So large was Grizz, the punk twins had little room between Grizz and the walls of the van. Grizz turned to Roach and said, "Don't get too close to me, and don't touch me!" Grizz warned before he swivelled around uncomfortably to squint his eyes at Rat. "Don't even look at me!" Like high school kids crammed into tight lockers, Roach and Rat tried to look away from Grizz at the floor and the ceiling and whistle.

Roach, the more courageous of the twins decided to question Grizz. "Or what?!" Roach asked with his strange squeaky helium voice.

"Or you die!!!" Grizz told him as he leaned into him so their noses were almost touching. Grizz relayed a very real personification of being undeniably dangerous and unpredictable.

"I likey diss one!" Announced the punk at the wheel with a frog-like voice. His name was Jakebrake and he was a dirty grease monkey who hated women because he had his heart broken by the love of his life. His contempt ran deep because of the unfathomable betrayal of trust involved. Jakebrake had given up on life and turned to other shattered spirits who were a reflection of himself, the punks. Jakebrake's sad eyes were always enwreathed in a red haze.

Grizz was taken to the secret punk hang out, always with Rat on one side and Roach on the other. From the van, they went into an old warehouse, but the gatherers of creepy night life were not so much inside as they were underneath. The thumping and buzzing of the punk rock noise seemed to vibrate from the walls. Down a flight of wide stairs, Grizz was brought into a whole new world where he found the constant booming and screaming of loud music for one endless party.

Grizz was led through the crowd of punked bodies. Grizz looked at all of the punks who had liberty spiked hair of different colours and said, "What do you guys have to do to make your hair stand up like that, lick wall sockets?"

Rat snorted and sneered at Grizz's humor but he did not smile.

At the center of the large warehouse space was a circular bar with about four punks tending to the needs of their thirsty members. At the back of the room, a door was removed from its hinges and Grizz could see a kitchen on the other side. To the far left, a punk rock band was busy tearing it loose on a stage. What the punks called music, Grizz called senseless noise. An area between the dining tables and the bar had a series of four pool tables lined up. The place was busy with costumed youth competing to be the number one freak with every inch of the popular hangout being used somehow.

Roach and Rat led Grizz to a large table booth where the leader of the punks sat. "Yo gott'a check diss guy out,

XD. He'd just robbed a corner twenty four seven while Roach and me just stood watch'n." explained Rat with a strong sense he was being intimidated by the punk leader.

"Nice hide-out…" Grizz told the punk leader.

The punk leader just shook his head. He had a tattoo of a spider web over half of his face, bald with a thin bar running from ear to ear and across his eyes. The thin bar was a sci-fi shaped pair of sunglasses.

"How do you know diss guy ain't a badge?" the punk leader asked with disappointment though he never, for a moment, took his eyes off Grizz. His voice was deep and scratchy but not as deep as Grizz's voice.

"A cop?" Rat repeated surprised, "Trust me, look at them scars on his face. He's got scares all over his body. Besides, he's massive, man! Have yo eve'a seen a cop who looked like diss dude before, XD?"

"Yo quite sure O yourself, Rat. Fine, we can accept diss dude, but if yo ever bring an outsider to me like diss again, I'll skin yo where yo stand!" The punk leader stood up and leaned over the table to shake Grizz's hand. Grizz did not move. He just stood like a monument of power all his own.

The punk leader just smirked and lowered his eyes for a moment before he withdrew his hand. "Welcome to our little party, I don't believe we've met before. My people call me XD3. I'm the Governor here." XD3 crossed his big arms as the others laughed, "Diss is no hide-out, it's our lair. We are the Bleeding Heart Punks, and these are some O my friends," XD3 motioned his hand to a thin young man at his left who wore a high cut black leather jacket. His black hair was flattened to his head and combed back and resembled a plastic cap. His sleeves were rolled up. Several silver studs lined the outer seam of his pants and his boots had eight inch lifts with strange knobs protruding from behind the tall shins. "Diss

273

be Darkade. Might not look it, but yo couldn't ask fo a more loyal friend. He's solid with good bones."

Darkade looked down at XD3, peering from the darkness of his hood, then back to Grizz without changing his expression in the least.

Darkade's complexion was like that of the living dead. Grizz wondered if the man's face was purposely altered to look like a Zombie or if it was simply some well-crafted make-up. He was a young man with a partially grown goatee.

Also at the table was a lady who looked like a dog that had been beaten her entire life. "Diss is Enemi, a close friend O mine fo many years." Grizz had the sense she was a product of her own making. Likely, she would continuously find herself attracted to people who were cruel and hurtful.

Next to her was another woman who was introduced as Poison, "She's very quiet, not shy... a silent killer." added XD3 with a whisper. When Grizz looked at her, she sent chills up and down his spine, which he was not used to experiencing, especially from a woman. Poison lowered her dark sun glasses and there was just something very spooky about her eyes even in the dimly lit room.

Next to Poison was a small man, of rough features with a presence about him of danger and hate to hide the pain which ran so deep within him.

"Meet Scorpin-X, he's tough and the piro loves to make things explode. He's not alone there, but he almost likes it a little too much, if yo take my meaning." Scorpin-X flipped his zippo lighter open and sneered at Grizz while biting on a toothpick before he snapped the lid of his lighter closed again.

"Diss be Fang," XD3 introduced. "A rouge who once worked fo the militants, a militant who refused to help brave men and women after they'd served, like Fang, who risked everything to defend our country."

"And at last, diss be, Vamporess." She gave Grizz a half smile and waved her long eyelashes at him in a long slow wink. Vamporess's hair was jet black and very short except for her long unkempt Mohawk, she had white skin, black lipstick and eyeliner with dark tight clothing. Vamporess pulled off the look of death like a pro, she owned it.

With a snap of his fingers, XD3 called over someone to serve him, "Bring an extra few chairs fo Rat, Roach and our new guest."

"Right away, XD!" The young punk responded without hesitancy. Quickly chairs were provided and everyone was sitting down at the table in the booth.

"I am, a Blackguard." Grizz told them.

"So what exactly *is* a, *Blackguard*?" XD3 asked leaning over his drink to peer at Grizz expecting an answer.

"We are a highly trained chosen few from a secret underground establishment of a secret underground establishment. There is no way you would have heard about us." Grizz told him as though he was privy to secrets not even the esteemed XD3 could have.

This answer was not acceptable for XD3 so he pressed for more. "Don't underestimate us. We're not just some ally way pack of stray cats, try me. Give me a name and I'll verify yer claim fo myself."

Grizz just stared at XD3 for a moment before he answered him by saying, "Knolix."

XD3 just looked at Grizz sceptically before he smiled and leaned back relaxing into his seat.

Rat leaned in close to XD3 and covered his mouth with the back of his hand as to not be heard, "Oh, XD, I might'a forgot ta mention it but, I promised diss

Blackguard free food. All he could eat."

XD3 rolled his eyes and sat back. He lifted his arm high to get someone's attention through the small window to the kitchen. "Bring us the table sized party tray!" XD3 called out.

Almost immediately, a crew of loyal punks from the kitchen came out and cleared their table. They took the dirty dishes back to the kitchen and then quickly returned with a huge tray the size of their table top. When the tray was set on the table, those sitting at the table were amazed at the incredible spread of food; a shrimp cocktail fountain, dripping with hot seafood sauce, was the main focal point at the center of the table. Four fire torches surrounded it. Red hot lobsters were stacked with hot melted butter bowls. A mountain of fried chicken was stacked on a platter. Buckets of hot gravy were nearby and available for a bargain discount price. Two inch thick steaks which were larger than the plates they were served on, were placed before each guest. A steamy aroma lifted from a large punch bowl of macaroni and extra cheese. Endless bacon and eggs sizzled on hot aluminum trays. A ten layered lasagna with cheese and sauce dripping out of it was stacked like a skyscraper. Each bottle of beer was served in its own little bucket of ice. They spared no expense for their leader's appetite, XD3.

Grizz's first response was, "Whoa, this almost makes a four square meal."

Grizz immediately reached out and took some of the fried chicken. "Uh, uh, uh!" XD3 said with his index finger raised. He wanted Grizz to wait for something, but Grizz paid him no mind as he stuffed his face further with steamy macaroni and extra cheese. "No table manners, buddy?"

Grizz snorted like a beast who no one would disturb when eating. The punks were quite surprised by Grizz's appetite and the aggressive way in which he ate. He made a terrible noise and when he drank, it was even messier.

XD3 looked Grizz over, up and down and said, "So, yo eat my food. Least yo could do is show a little consideration and be somewhat O a hospitable guest and tell us yer story." Seeing Grizz was not a talkative person, XD3 asked, "Who are yo?" The leader, XD3 did not seem to be intimidated by Grizz's obvious physical advantage.

Grizz had no intentions of answering, rather he continued to slop the food around in his mouth before looking up at XD3. There was something different in the confidence of this punk's eyes. Grizz came up with one of his typical responses. "I'm from nowhere." A sense of the two men exchanging thoughts became pertinent from their locked gaze. Then, Grizz elaborated a little further. "I'm a government secret experiment that went terribly wrong, a weapon, but I escaped. Now I am here. The end." Grizz answered quickly and went back to stuffing his face with lasagna.

The punks broke into heavy laughter. One of the punks who appeared to be out of her mind and bound to a wheelchair, didn't stop laughing and actually became louder. This punk's name was Lips. She had a bleached white skin tone and bald with a long tuff of hair growing from the top of her head. Her eyebrows looked like they were stretched up into the wrinkles of her fore-head. The corners of her smile were cut into her cheeks to give her the most hideous smile with the strangest puffy lips and sharpened yellow teeth.

Grizz stopped eating and looked up at Lips with grub hanging out the corner of his mouth.

"Someone gag Lips, now!" Commanded XD3.

A punk immediately put a ball and strap around the laughing head of Lips. With the ball in her mouth as it was tied at the back of her head, she seemed to continue with her insane muffled laughter. Her sharp teeth biting into the ball.

With Lips still giggling, XD3 continued. "Okay, so let's say yo're a top secret government experiment that went terribly wrong. Are there any other terribly wrong experiments walking around like yo?"

Grizz stopped eating and glared at XD3. XD3 was not comfortable with this in the least. Everyone else at the table became very quiet as well in anticipation of Grizz's response. "There were four others. They were my Brothers."

"Where are yer brothers now?" A punk asked.

Grizz stood up and slammed his hands down on the table top tray, "They're dead!" he told them flatly as every punk in the lair pointed a fire arm of some sort at Grizz. When the sound of guns cocking ended, Grizz looked around and swallowed hard.

Just as Grizz eased off, XD3 smiled and was about to break into laughter. The punks slowly lifted their weapons and went back to carry on with the party like nothing even happened. As Grizz sat back down, he watched as a suspicious fellow entered the lair and approached their main table from the upper walkway behind the booth. Wearing a long black trench coat, the mysterious new comer drew a sawed off shot gun and pointed it down at XD3. All the while, Grizz watched what was about to happen as XD3 hadn't even a clue he was in trouble. The man in the trench coat shouted, "Taste Justice!"

XD3's head snapped back to look up at the shouting voice.

As everything began to move in slow motion, Grizz lashed out faster than the blink of an eye. He exploded through the table as he drove his whole body forward and

278

slammed his fist into the chest of the black trench coat. The rifle did not have a chance to get a shot off as it was crushed under Grizz's powerful fist. The man was hit with the force of a speeding truck which sent him through the air to slam into the wall at the far end of the room.

The music stopped instantly and the punks dancing seemed to have rifles pop out of their arm pits. Noticing Grizz had attacked a stranger, the punks did not open fire right away. XD3 quickly gave the hand signal of cease fire.

The punk leader sat up and stared at Grizz with his eyes more intense than ever. It wasn't until Rat and Roach explained the situation to XD3 when he finally understood what was going on. Until then, XD3 thought Grizz was trying to attack and kill him. When XD3 realized Grizz had in fact saved his life, he said, "I owe yo one, man. What're we supposed to call you?" Grizz had no intentions of telling them his name. XD3 looked at Rat and remembered him referring to Grizz as the Blackguard. It really didn't matter what his real name was anyway because all of the punks had custom punk names to cover for their real names. "I'm gonn'a call yo, the Blackguard." XD3 told him when he realized Grizz was not about to say anything.

With a snap of his fingers and a quick finger point at Grizz, XD3 had signaled for some other ladies to get cozy with Grizz and show him some affectionate attention. Grizz was not used to young women regarding him so. Never before had Grizz been in the presence of a man like XD3 who had such influence and power over others.

"I owe yo fo save'n me life." XD3 told Grizz. "All men have desires, Blackguard. Tell me what yo want and I'll do what I can ta make it happen."

Feeling content with a lifted sense of freedom since

279

he was out from under the authority of the Government, Grizz hadn't thought about wanting anything more, but could it be, if he searched, he did wanted more?

Examining his feelings, Grizz closed his eyes, he went deep inside himself and touched a place he didn't previously know existed. Seeing the big picture of his entire life, Grizz could see clearly. "I want to understand what it is to be still, quiet and at peace. I want the pain and the hatred to stop, but it is so integrated into my very being, I don't see how it could be possible. Like I said, I'm a weapon. No man on earth can help me…"

XD3 just glared at Grizz for a moment. Poison discretely slid a bullet into the chamber of her pistol, before she whispered discretely, "This'll make'm still, quiet and at peace." XD3 shook his head and waved Poison away.

A smile cracked across XD3's chiseled features. "Blackguard, yo've come ta the right place!" The others surrounding the leader broke out in laughter.

XD3 sat back and brushed his vest open to reveal a series of leather pockets attached to his wide belt. He opened a pocket and plucked out a small red pill. "This, my friend, is the answer to yer desire. It'll make yo feel the peace you so rightfully deserve." With his other hand, the punk leader began to take out more pills one by one and place them in his open hand. "This one'll make yo bigger and stronger, this one'll make yo smarter. Problems with anger? This one'll fix that. We've got a pill fo everything." Grizz saw how XD3 was not only the punk leader but also a punk drug pusher.

"Pills don't work on me very well. They never have." Grizz told him.

"These're super pills." XD3 spoke with amusement and a chuckle, "Yo'll be powerless ta their affects." he added.

Grizz thought about it. A pill to feel, normal? Grizz looked around the dark musty tavern of party goers and saw how everyone seemed to be really enjoying themselves, but none of them were *normal*. Those in the close vicinity were looking at Grizz with eyes of expectancy. To turn down the offer might have unexpected consequences or side effects. Though Grizz was certain the pills would not have any affect on him, he would very much like to try them for the off chance he could experience what it would be like to live detached from anger, even if for a short time. Curious about what people have said about living a peaceful life, Grizz considered the offer.

"Why not?" Grizz said, he felt he had nothing to lose. If the drug worked it would make him feel great or he would be correct and the pill would have no effect on him. The punks were very happy to see Grizz take the red pill. They laughed and watched him carefully. An attractive young lady, Vamporess, wearing heavy mascara and a broad smile, offered him a glass of something to drink. Her lipstick was thick, glossy and blood red.

After popping the pill into his mouth, Grizz took the glass and drank it all back. *'They had it all figured out? The punks?'* Grizz looked at his drink. *'Everything has been tainted with a drug of some sort, hasn't it?'* He wondered to himself. These people could not be trusted. Grizz stood up from the table and felt a slight dizzy spell wash over him. "Washroom..." he blurted. Some of the onlookers pointed to a direction for him to go. Grizz dizzily made his way through the crowd of dancers. Dragging his toes as he walked Grizz envisioned his legs turning into hollow paper machae. He had to use table tops and chairs to assist him with the final distance. The drug was not meant to make Grizz feel better, it was

281

meant to sedate him, he figured out that much. It must have been a very powerful drug because he hadn't felt such powerful effect ever before. Somehow Grizz *did* make it to the bathroom where he found someone throwing up, while the skinny punk rolled off the toilet and sat up on the wet floor, Grizz could see he had recently been shooting up. A fresh cup of coffee was placed on the floor next to the man who had been vomiting. A small ziplock bag of powdered drug with some crumpled tin foil and a rubber surgical tube also laid about spread around the pathetic punk. The bathroom was disgusting. "Does anyone ever clean this dump?" Grizz asked, though his eyes were swimming in his head. "Is that dried blood on the walls?" The mirror had been smashed and broken glass was scattered on the tiled floor.

Grizz realized there was a big problem with the punks. They took drugs as the answer to their problems. Grizz began to sweat from his fore-head profusely. He hunkered down and crawled along the grimy floor as he made his way to the punk who had recently been shooting up. Grizz spoke to the punk drug addict, "Give me your name."

"I-I'm Switch." replied the punk with great effort and slurred speech. It was then; Grizz focused on Switch's face and noticed a long pink scar which ran diagonally across his face. He was sick and old looking.

"Do you know how bad your situation is?" Grizz asked Switch with the tone a father might use on his son.

Switch replied to Grizz's question with slurred speech, "Yeah, I'm dying, I know. Believe it er not, I'm only 26 years old. I came here because I had no choice, but it was like making a deal with the devil."

"What do you mean when you say you had *no choice?*" Grizz asked Switch though he had difficulty training his eye on one thing.

Switch gave Grizz a slight sneer. He didn't like to be cut off in the middle of a thought. "It was either, get high or die." Switch responded. Others listening and watching from the door of the bathroom giggled. "I wanted to live the good life like these punks preach. They know just what to say to lure you in, but there is no perfect pill. Your first pill will be so good, you will want another, but it always leads to another, because it'll wear off and leave you feeling so low. To get that high back, you will need the pill again, but it won't be the same as it was the first time around, so you begin to experiment to find that first high again. As you try other drugs your body takes a phenomenal amount of punishment, but you think you can handle it or even fix it. It's hard to accept the pill has a hold on you. Each pill brings its own set of side effects. The side effects, weather it is head aches, stomach aches, depression, sleep disorder or whatever, just causes you to have to take more pills."

Grizz, felt the sensation of his immune system fighting off the affects of the red pill. He imagined the potency of the pill being secreted from his pours as he sweat. Burning with heat, Grizz's body caused even more sweat. Though he felt like his body was one big fever, Grizz could feel his head clearing, he was feeling better.

The onlooking punks at the door were confused as to how Grizz was not in a deep sleep yet from the pill he took. From a deep sense of obligation, Grizz instinctively found himself helping Switch. As Grizz rolled over to get up off the dirty bathroom floor, he cut his hand on one of the shards of broken glass. Grizz used the sink for support as he arose. From the edge of the sink a drop of Grizz's blood fell into the cup of coffee which was set next to the poor doped up fellow. Switch did not notice the drop of blood fall into his cup as he lifted it to his lips for a sip. No one observed the drop of blood fall into the cup except for one, XD3. Sleepily, Switch drank the coffee and felt an immediate change in himself.

Switch set the cup back down on the floor with his energetic eyes wide open. "Wow, I am feeling warm from my head to my toes." As Switch said this, Grizz could see a healthy colour and glow begin to grow in the punk's face. Grizz wondered if the powerful volk agents in his own blood were somehow cleaning Switch.

Grizz saw a second drip of his blood fall from the sink and hit the rim of the coffee cup. At seeing this, Grizz realized what had happened. "You have been given a second chance and you are now free from your addiction. Get out of here and never touch a drug again." Grizz told the punk.

"Wha? How did you do that?" Switch asked with amazement as he felt the amazing affects transform his body from the inside.

Many other punks, with XD3, stood at the open door of the bathroom and tried to make sense of what Grizz had done. They were openly upset because Grizz hadn't experienced the affects of the red pill they gave him. They marched in cautiously. Though the punks wanted to over power Grizz, it was obvious, Grizz's strength was practically fully restored. With chains and switch blades exposed in a threatening manner, a few goth punks took the lead with slow careful steps; Stint, Zom-Buckle, Enemi, Poison and Lips.

Stint, wore a green mohawk in spikes which were nine inches in length. He was very skinny and known as a wise cracker. Stint had a talent for laughing like a hyena.

Zom-Buckle, was a strange man with a long filthy, bushy beard from his chin to his stomach. His eyes are sunken into his eye sockets with dark circles and deep creases. The complexion of Zom-Buckle was like the dead. He looked like a hideous Zombie.

Enemi, was a young lady who looked like she was the victim of abuse her entire life. She was however, a product of her own making, though she may not have been able to understand it, because she continuously found herself attracted to men who were abusive, mean and hurtful.

Poison, had proven herself to be a formidable but deadly silent killer. She was wanted by the police but her punk friends protected her. Her eyes had the ability to send chills up and down your spine. Poison was rarely without her dark sun glasses even in dark places.

Lips, was a tall, thin, gangly woman with sickly and eccentric facial features, but the most noticeable thing was her big inflated lips and hideous smile of crooked, sharp, yellow teeth.

Grizz barred his teeth and growled a threat of his own at the strange ensemble of characters who approached him. Somehow, as Grizz growled, he seemed to be able to read into the thoughts of the morbid looking punks. He recalled the sensation back to when his brother Narl had last, telepathically invaded his thoughts, only this time, Grizz was in control of sending and receiving somehow through his growl. Though his ability was to the lowest power, it confirmed what he saw in their eyes and the eyes of the punks did not lie. They were ready to kill him.

XD3 pushed his way forward, shouting as he lumbered forward powerfully and forcefully. "Wait! Look at Switch!" XD3 pointed out. "He's changing before our eyes..."

The punks backed off slightly, as they too began to notice a change in their companion.

Though Switch was still quite thin, his face quickly began to flesh out his complexion. His skin colour was restored to a healthy tone and the reddened scar across his face became less noticeable. Switch, solemnly placed his hand to his chest where he could feel his heart pumping faster and stronger. He jumped to his feet and said, "Whoa, do I ever feel better. Its like a huge weight has been lifted." pausing for a moment in thought, Switch added. "You know? I don't think I'm an addict any longer. Yes! The craving has left me... It is a clean life for me here on out!"

Many listening shook their heads in disbelief and chuckled, but XD3 was not so sure. Could Switch's statement be accurate? XD3 actually knew the implications would be catastrophic. The more XD3 thought about it, the more it ate at him. How could Switch be restored of his drug addiction? Whatever had happened had certainly caused a profound restoration to his body.

XD3's attention turned from Switch to Grizz. The others also focused on Grizz.

"It appears there's a much deeper mystery under yo skin, eh, Blackguard?" Came a sinister tone from XD3. Clearly the drugs which were administered to Grizz were not taking the desired affect after all. "Come with me." XD3 spoke as Vamporess and Darkade came along side Grizz and helped him to walk and follow their leader. Grizz could have gone crazy any moment and tore a path right through the punks, but he decided to see what they had planned for him. XD3 escorted Grizz to a locked back room which they referred to as the private chamber. Using a key, XD3 opened the heavy metal door and nodded for Grizz to follow him. With XD3, Grizz and Darkade inside the private chamber, Vamporess closed the heavy door and left them alone together.

The interior of the private chamber was the remains of an old meat locker which would never function properly ever again. There was a table in the middle of the room with a couple of vacant folding chairs around it. Grizz saw police files on the table along with some maps. An old beat up filing cabinet was tucked into the far corner and a light bulb hung a couple of feet from the ceiling. No evidence of an electrical outlet or a venting system had ever been installed.

Practically everywhere XD3 went, Darkade followed. The two of them where almost inseparable. Darkade was XD3's second in command and his profession in the world, believe it or not, was as a lawyer.

Darkade was the first to have something to say to Grizz, "I have had to represent XD numerous times in the past in the Metro court of law. We're able to blend into society very well. No one wants to quit their day job."

From a small refrigerator, XD3 took two glass bottles and twisted off the bottle caps in his grasp. Offering Grizz a beer, XD3 said, "I want yo to understand. It's because O the world O free enterprise, one I have worked very hard at ta build ta what it is today. Now, I don't know what yo did to make Switch well, but I do know it can't be good fo business... My business, Sucker!!!" Within a moment, XD3's dark mean streak was revealed to Grizz. XD3 had been covering a darkness of anger, resentment and hate deep inside.

"Look, XD3, I'm new here. I don't care about your business." Grizz said clearly.

XD3's mind was filled with calculated thought as to how best to deal with Grizz. He had dealt with other strong headed punks in the past and XD3 had been very good with his intuition for knowing the best way to deal with them. Grizz was a threat to his business, *'But is it the right thing ta have the Blackguard killed?'* XD wondered. *'If the blackguard is a government secret then he must be someone of some substantial dollar value. How deep are the blackguard's secrets? I'll give him one chance but if he's too much trouble, if the threat's too much, I'll kill'im myself.'*

"Yo *should* care about my business because I've decided ta cut yo in on it." XD3's comment sparked Grizz's curiosity. XD3 could see the confusion in Grizz's eyes, "Tha's right, *Blackguard*. I'm make'n yo my business partner... Yo up to it?"

Grizz took a step toward XD3 with his hand held out to shake on the deal, "I'm up to it." Grizz spoke confidently.

XD3 just looked at Grizz's out stretched hand then back to Grizz's eyes. "I don't do that!" Grizz took his hand back. "There're a few stipulations yo need ta know; Yo'll make ten percent O what I make. Yo'll carry out orders without question. Yo'll speak only when spoken to, and before yo begin your new position, yo must first pass, *the initiation*."

"Initiation?" Grizz questioned, "Buddy, there are a few, *stipulations* of my own you need to know. I make no less than 90% of the gross revenue. No one tells me what to do. I say what I want whenever I want to speak, and you can shove your initiation right up your..."

"Hold on!" Discouragement painted the face of XD3. "If yo don't want ta co-operate, fine! Be an idiot an pass up on an opportunity yo'll never get again, or anywhere else fo that matter."

Grizz took a deep breath and let it out through a low grumble. He peered a sharp gaze of stone cold authority at XD3. Finally, Grizz said, "First step, what's this *initiation*?"

Chapter 9

XD3 explained how the initiation was set to take place in the old Historical Benson Building Museum, where Grizz will have to fight three challengers. Each one will try to subdue Grizz but Grizz must subdue each one of them without getting killed. People have died during initiations in the past, but it is not *supposed* to happen.

Grizz insisted on starting the initiation right away. XD3 knew it wouldn't be difficult to organize. When they rejoined the others, XD3 was surprised to find the band was no longer playing and everyone was very quiet save the voice of one man speaking.

The voice was of no other than Switch again, "...The big guy, what was his name again?... Oh, ya, the Blackguard. He's so massive and he crawled on the bathroom floor to me." Switch chuckled, "I know, right? But he did, he looked into my eyes and did some sort of magical thing. I can't explain it but all I remember is I didn't care about anything at that moment. Nothing mattered, not even my life, but just look at me now!!! Fully restored. I am rejuvenated. I feel younger and stronger than I ever had in my life. Thank you, Blackguard." Switch announced as he raised his attention to XD3 and Grizz as they approached.

When the others noticed Grizz was there, they flocked to him. Each one asked Grizz to help them with a problem of some sort like he was some sort of mystical healer. XD3 understood a new threat which Grizz posed, the threat of popularity, authority and ultimately leadership. Already, Grizz had proven he had the ability to take addiction away from customers. This would put

XD3, and all the Bleeding Heart Punks, out of business. It was with this decision XD3 decided he would make the challenges of the initiation unforgiving. *'If the Blackguard dies, all the better.'* thought XD3.

Grizz, wearing old soiled and torn spandex which reeked with the smell of decay was led into the old Benson Museum, blindfolded and bound. With his hair greasy and scruffy, he scowled as though he could see right through the blindfold at the punks who escorted him. The smooth marble floor was very cold under his bare feet. Grizz could feel hands loosening his blindfold and bindings. Before the blindfold fell from his eyes he could hear the feet of two punks skittering out the large double doors. The doors closed heavily and the sound of the iron lock echoed from the great walls as it was secured.

The wide haze of a blue moonbeam was cast to the floor from a beautiful domed skylight above. Grizz saw a figure bound from out of the shadows and move quickly through the distant light. This was followed by the sound of glass shattering. Cautiously, Grizz, also using the cover of the shadows, drew near to his opponent.

Across the hall Grizz could see something stir. He looked harder and found it was two night-time security guards who were bound and gagged together. Despite Grizz's large size, he could run very fast with the silent feet of a cat.

As Grizz came closer, he could hear his punk opponent clattering items of some sort. It sounded like the punk was searching for something. Grizz was close enough to hear the punk grunting and breathing. When Grizz was right beside the display, he could see the punk had broken the protective glass of the museum display and was inside going through the contents.

'*I'll rush him…*' Grizz thought just before he swung around the corner of the broken display window and lept at the punk.

To Grizz's amazement, the punk was going through a Chinese Samurai presentation. The punk held a samurai sword, wore a warrior's helmet and blew a ball of fire from his mouth at Grizz. Grizz was so disoriented from having a fire ball blown at his face. He crashed into a Chinese paper wall. The thin dry wood and paper immediately started on fire around Grizz. Trying to rise to his feet, Grizz had to move fast to avoid the sword the punk was trying to attack him with.

The samurai sword moved viciously as it sliced through the air at Grizz again and again. The danger triggered Grizz's training to explode into action. He dodged and used a shoulder plating from a manequin to deflect the sharp blade. As Grizz rose up and gained a stable footing, he quickly assessed the skill of the punk's sword's play. It was not long before Grizz detected the slowness and overall sloppiness of the punk's attack.

Almost effortlessly, Grizz spun around and swung his hand out at the punk plucking the sword right out of his hand. As Grizz rose up, he filled his lungs with air. Distinguished and confident, Grizz lifted the samurai sword high over his head. Before Grizz delivered the fatal strike, the punk caught Grizz unaware with another fire ball blown at him. Spinning and rolling away from the tumbling flame, Grizz sought cover from the great heat. He rolled right over another samurai manequin because his chest was on fire. Clumsily, Grizz's legs knocked over an ancient weapons rack display. Patting out the flames quickly, Grizz sprang up and took hold of a fist full of spears from the Asian weapon's rack. Taking aim Grizz hurtled a spear at the fleeing punk.

"That's right, run!" Grizz shouted after him, "I'll find

you soon enough..." A life size rendition of a ninja stood next to him who was made entirely out of wax, but the straps criss-crossed at his chest were quite authentic. Taking the straps from the wax dummy, he admired how they held true renditions of throwing stars within the decorative stitching. Around Grizz's neck and upper chest, his tight fitting outfit had been burned. At his feet Grizz found a manequin wearing black Chinese shoulder protection. To cover the burns which Grizz saw as a form of weakness or failure, he took the shoulder protective gear and pulled it over his head.

Bounding out of the samurai display, holding the sword and a second spear, Grizz looked for the punk. Still in his bare feet, Grizz thought it wise to head out in search of some footwear. Slinking down the great hall, Grizz was alert to detect the whereabouts of the fire breathing punk. The punk was very quiet and the museum displays were quite distracting as the punk could be hiding anywhere or even disguised as a manequin.

Stepping in front of a Viking display, Grizz saw a giant size rendition of a Viking King sitting in a great throne with a battle ax at his side. The physical nature of this warrior king was astounding and unnatural. With regards to the Viking's height and build, Grizz was reminded of volks, but where volks were hairless; this Viking had a great bushy beard and a helmet with the horns of a bull coming out from the left and right. Grizz examined the Viking's biceps, before looking down to admire his own. The audience of on looking punks laughed at Grizz, but he ignored them. Looking down at the Viking's feet, Grizz noticed the sandals were laced and not at all something he would consider wearing himself.

The next display over had a knight in dark armor standing in it. This was no ordinary Knight for he too was a slightly exaggerated in size. It was a mid-evil Knight in black armor riding a stuffed black horse which also wore dark armor. Grizz looked down at the metal boots of the mid-evil warrior and knew he had to have them. Lifting the spear, Grizz hurtled the projectile at the display window, shattering it in a loud echoing noise.

Looking from side to side and listening intently, Grizz tried to get a fix on the fire breathing punk's location, but there was no sight or sound of him. Grizz climbed into the display and began to tear the Knight apart. Grizz put on the heavy metal boots, the gauntlets and gloves along with the helmet. The gauntlets had a hidden spring loaded knife controlled from the glove. The ten inch double blade had of the fore-arm could pop out and retract easily from a simple switch. As for the helmet, it covered Grizz's entire head with a grill like visor of slits to protect the eyes and an angled piece of shielding to cover over the lower half of his mouth.

A sound of metal striking the marble floor couldn't have come at a better time. Grizz seemed to fly from the display window as he ran in search of the one he was required to destroy. The crowd from above was very impressed with Grizz as he ran after the fire breathing punk like a tyrant. It was not long before Grizz had tracked the sound to its source but he had the sense this was a trap and Grizz was running right into it.

Standing beneath the skeleton of a Tyrannosaurus Rex, Grizz knew the punk was close. Instinctively, Grizz stepped to the side as a dinosaur rib bone came crashing down on his position. "That was a big mistake, hot-head!" Grizz announced as he activated his gauntlets to make the twelve inch blades spring out over his fists. Grizz quickly turned and chopped at the legs of the T-Rex and the bones shattered. The punk rode on the back of the T-Rex skeleton as it crashed to the ground. The entire assembly of carefully set bones came crashing to the floor with the fire breathing punk at the top of it. Midst the fossilized bones breaking part and spilling out over the floor, the punk rolled out flailing his limbs.

The punk sat up quickly, he was obviously dazed from the fall. When he turned and noticed Grizz walking toward him, he let out a scream of terror like the sound of a tea kettle whistle. He cradled his left elbow as he was injured.

Grizz continued to approach, lifting the helmet off his head and kicking the scattered bones out of his path. The punk stopped screaming and became fidgety. He lifted a small device to his mouth and blew another fire ball at Grizz, but Grizz quickly filled his lungs and blew a great breath of his own at the ball of fire, which sent the flame back at the punk's face.

The front of the punk's mohawk was singed and smoking and he did not have any eye brows any longer. Grizz had to chuckle at the fire breathing punk's stunned expression and wide comical eyes.

With his hand lifted for Grizz to stop, the punk began to scream again in stark terror.

"Shut up!" shouted Grizz with no patience for the irritating screaming punk.

This petrified the punk as he thought Grizz was about to kill him. Then Grizz spoke to the punk more calmly and asked, "If you think I'm going to kill you, why don't you run?"

The punk spun around hastily and ran with his arms and legs flapping ridiculously. Little spurts of high pitched screams were made as the punk got slipped on a bone and fell down with a struggle to find his next footing. He did this again and again making very little distance between himself and Grizz. Letting out a breath as he shook his head, "Oh, brother..." Grizz commented to himself.

Standing up straight, Grizz cleared his mind and watched as the next challenger was escorted in through the main doors. This punk was wrapped up in a strap jacket. Under the direction of two other punks, this new challenger stood under a flickering damaged light. It didn't take long before the punk in the strap jacket caught sight of Grizz. With her Grizz could make no mistake about it. This was Lips, a punk he was introduced to earlier with the deformed mouth. Even at a great distance, Grizz could make out the hideous smile and the sharp, crooked, rotten teeth. Unable to help himself, Grizz gave Lips a disconcerting eye before he fit the black knight's helmet back over his head. Lips stopped laughing and became viciously serious.

Looking up, Grizz responded to the sound of many feet stomping in over the open upper level balcony. The punks there hung over the railings yelling and laughing like monkeys. From there they taunted Grizz with warnings.

Then they began to chant from above, "Lips, Lips, Lips..."

Grizz leveled his attention back to Lips as her two escorts cut the bindings loose from her strap jacket with a bowie knife. In a blink of an eye, Lips spun around as her arms tore the final straps which flew from her like rubber bands. She turned the bowie knife on one of the punks and bit the other one on his shoulder. With the two punks screaming and writhing in pain, the audience above began to shout and cheer, like a bunch of gorillas.

Lips spun around again and charged in at Grizz. The eyes of Lips were wild and she laughed mindlessly.

Grizz stood his ground and let Lips come to him. In readiness, Grizz lifted his sword above his head preparing himself to decapitate the psycho. At the final moment before contact, while Lips was still at her full running speed, Grizz swung his sword forward with such great force as to make a whistling hum as the blade cut through the air. Lips dropped down falling backwards unexpectedly. Sliding across the polished marble floor, the thin lanky punk seemed to float between Grizz's legs where she struck him in the crotch. Grizz hunkered forward and dropped to his knees as he shouted a guttural sound which echoed throughout the great halls of the museum like thunder. Grizz's sword clattered to the floor as Lips ominously rose up behind Grizz. The taste of victory was upon the lips of Lips. She licked her big fat lips with an unusually long tongue as she seemed to relish in the presence of Grizz's pain. The satisfaction for Lips could not peak for she was still hungry. At this point only death would full fill her hunger, but she could not take it all at once, and not to be too hasty to be sure. Lips wanted to savour the moment.

The anticipation made the on looking crowd build with their senseless cheers. Lips stepped closer to Grizz like a demonic clown, predator moving in on her prey, but Grizz half turned and their eyes met even through the tight slits of his cumbersome helmet. Lips lunged forward. Grizz met the speed of Lips and caught her by the throat. All of the screaming applause ended immediately.

Fighting to take in air, Lips clawed at Grizz's grip which was too tight for her anyway. The eyes of Lips rolled up and back into her head. Grizz growled as he knew he was about to take the crazy woman's life. Again, as he growled, Grizz was able to tap into a telepathic ability. He found a scrambled mind of buzzing insanity within the crazy lady's thoughts.

Amazing, a part of his brother, Narl, assisted him in

a small way. He was granted quick little glimpses through a train of thought and his deep growl.

By some eerie twist of reality, Lip's eyes bounced back and seemed to protrude from her eye sockets. Her long thin hands closed in around Grizz's thick gauntlets which he wore around his wrists. Like a statue, Grizz was unmoving, except to tighten his grip.

Lips revealed the depths of her crazy mind as she smiled and slithered out her incredibly long tongue. Oddly, Lips began to squirm uncomfortably. She lifted one leg and set her crooked foot on Grizz's thigh. Grizz thought nothing of it, *'Won't be long now and it will all be over.'* Grizz told himself patiently, but Lips continued to climb up Grizz's body. Higher and higher she climbed, right up to where Lips finally placed her scrawny feet with long, yellow, chipped toe nails on Grizz's shoulder blades. *'This punk must be double jointed.'* Grizz thought. Through it all, Grizz did not loosen his grip from her bony throat.

Grizz felt like he was not holding the throat of Lips anymore, only her spine. Lips reached out to Grizz with nervous, shaky hands and removed the helmet from off Grizz's head. The bulgy eyes of Lips fixed on the unshielded eyes of Grizz for the first time. Lips realized Grizz was quite possibly crazier than she was. Lips quickly began to work her disgusting foot into Grizz's mouth as she repeatedly kicked at Grizz's throat with her other bare foot. A couple of quick kicks impacted Grizz's face and eyes. Grizz had enough, *'Why aren't you dead yet?'* Grizz wondered with Lips still gripped by the throat. Grizz pounded her to the hard marble floor. Spitting out her bony dirty foot, Grizz used his free hand to pound at the face of Lips. After three punches, her long thin pointy nose was completely crushed.

Grizz knew, if he added the slightest bit more

pressure to the throat of Lips, her neck would crack like a walnut in his fist. *'I always thought no one could be crazier than my brother, Oblit, but this woman, her mind is twisted beyond return. So her fate will have to come to this moment where Lips will die by my hand.'*

XD3 could not take one more second of the punishment being administered by Grizz. He popped a couple of colorful pills into his mouth as Vamporess injected a drug into the base of his neck.

Turning to Vamporess, XD3 demanded, "Give me another!"

"No, XD, it'll kill you." Vamporess was not only surprised, but also openly concerned.

"Don't argue with me, just do it!" Spat XD3. Vamporess tried not to show any emotion as she quickly and obediently, administered a second dose of the powerful drug. She jabbed the needle in and pushed the plunger down injecting the intrusive drug into the body of XD3.

His veins grew larger, harder and darker as his heart began to pump in over time. Without fear, XD3 lept from the upper level and landed on his feet with a heavy thud. "Release her, Blackguard!" Ordered XD3 forcefully, but Grizz did not respond.

The other punks came running down the stairway to make sure Grizz did not hurt their leader. XD3 came up behind Grizz and punched him in the ribs. The drugs in his system gave him unusually enhanced strength. Grizz reared up in response to the pain. He subsequently let go of Lip's throat. Grizz turned to XD3.

"What is this?" Grizz asked as he turned, humored by the surprise attack. "Are you the third challenger?"

"No, Blackguard. I'm not supposed ta be, so don't tempt me. I want yo to leave Lips alone! Yo've done enough!"

"I thought this initiation was supposed to be to the death?" Inquired Grizz.

A punk girl, Enemi ran over to Lips and knelt down beside her. Lips appeared to be dead, but Enemi placed her hand gently on her chest to be sure. Leaning forward to listen, Enemi felt Lip's heartbeat racing in panic with a weak breath of air wheezing from her hideous smiling mouth.

"She's still alive." Enemi announced just before she leaned forward and assisted Lips in breathing with mouth to mouth.

Grizz had to look away in disgust because the sight of Enemi touching her lips to the ballooned lips of Lips was repulsive. Another couple of punks came with medical supplies. They carefully loaded Lips onto a spine board and put a neck brace on her before she was carried away.

In the thick of the confusion a punk got into Grizz's face, "Yo, you not legit, dope! You mo psycho dan Lips! Yo, draw blood from Thrash and Lips! We call fo retribution!"

"Retribution!!!" the others shouted. The punk flicked out a switch blade and stabbed Grizz's arm without warning.

Grizz roared in painful surprise as the punk continued, "Blood fo blood!"

This did not settle well with Grizz. From a mighty back hand, Grizz responded and the force of his strike sent the punk flying over the gathering. Others began to react with hostility. Grizz reached out and grabbed a punk from the crowd and used him to beat the others.

XD3, smiled a crazy smile which seemed somewhat related to Lips. His eyes became all bugged out and squirrelly. He threw himself between Grizz and the punks knowing all the while he could be the next one to be used as a baseball bat.

Striking Grizz on the side of the head with surprising speed and agility, Grizz's dark knight helmet was knocked off. Though Grizz was momentarily dazed, he turned ominously to XD3 and sneered with a chest growling full of thunder. Grizz could see his thoughts and XD3 was aware of it. This fueled XD3's anger.

The display of Grizz's thunderous growl, emanating his warning and power seemed to go unnoticed by XD3. A telepathic hint of XD3's rage was transmitted to Grizz through his growl. An insane shout broke forth from XD3 which was not a roar but caused the hairs to stand up on the back of Grizz's neck. XD3 mastered the look of the beast in his eyes and for a moment, Grizz, not knowing the limitation of XD3's strength and anger, wondered if he was out matched.

Though XD3 was a former body builder and had doped himself up with, who knows what, Grizz knew he had little to fear because he had volk blood coursing through his own veins.

The surrounding crowd backed away to make a clearing for the fight. XD3 flew at Grizz, punching, scratching and kicking. Grizz seemed to be taken by surprise and over powered by the punk leader.

As XD3 moved in to deliver a second volley of punishment, Grizz grabbed the incoming fist of XD3 and raised his other mighty iron clad fist to teach XD3 about true power, but Grizz stayed his readied fist as a deep ominous voice bellowed throughout the great halls of the museum.

"XD3! You are not the next challenger! I am!... The Blackguard is mine!!!"

Grizz looked up at the shadows to find the person belonging to the deep voice, but he could not find him.

Everyone began to retreat back up the wide stairway

301

as they prepared to let the third and final challenger enter. Grizz realized, XD3 was breathing erratically, like he was hyperventilating.

"Let go of him!" Vamporess shouted at Grizz anxiously. "He's overdosing!" At this announcement everyone in the museum stopped and turned to look back at their leader, XD3. He was convulsing and foaming at the mouth. Suddenly obvious, XD3 was in more trouble than the others thought. He began to gag as he was choking.

With a quick swipe of his hand, XD3 managed to slap some blood from Grizz's knife wound and touch it to his mouth. After this, XD3 blacked out.

Other punk men returned and helped to drag XD3 away. He was still alive. One of the punk men accidentally bumped Grizz's shoulder with his own, though it was obviously on purpose. "I'd hate to be yo right now!" he chuckled.

The room grew darker and a low laugh broke the silence echoing throughout the museum halls before the punks cleared out. *'These punks are crazy, the initiation is expected to continue?'* Grizz took a step back as he listened for the approach of the final challenger.

A projectile of some sort came whistling through the air from a great distance. Grizz turned his head in response to the whistling sound as the object came out of the darkness and pegged Grizz in the fore-head. Thrown backwards from the impact to the cold hard floor, Grizz quickly began to search the darkness to find his helmet. On the floor Grizz found the small metal marble which had struck him.

Grizz's frustration quickly escalated to a deep burning anger as he could feel blood trickle down between his eyes and beside his nose. "Now I know what direction to find you." Grizz said quietly to himself. Something stirred in the shadows. Grizz arose with a loud booming roar. He charged into the darkness. There, he found a little punk girl sitting on a box. She sang while she played with her yo-yo. Grizz hardly looked at her at all as his senses were in a buzz. With sudden movements, Grizz cautiously looked this way and that. Without making eye contact with the girl, Grizz spoke to her, "Wha?! What are you doing here?! This is no place for children! You're in great danger! You have to get out of here, now!!!"

"I am, Kiki Vixen... You remember me don't you, Grizz?" The little girl spoke so sweetly, but her words broke Grizz out of his *on edge* search of the darkness. He looked at her and realized he did, remember her. It was the same young little Kiki he knew from the Knolix Island. Heavy black mascara was painted around her eyes and her hair was spiked green on one half of her head. She was dressed in a new punk outfit not so dissimilar from the one he first saw her in. Countless bracelets decorated her wrists with studded leather around her neck and waist. Her clothes were torn but stylishly. She wore a dark blue mini skirt over cargo pants and a small leather jacket over a red zebra striped shirt. She fit in just fine with *this* crowd of punks. "I'm board. Do you want to play?" The little girl asked.

Grizz turned his head from side to side as he, again, looked for his next challenger. Knowing the challenger might strike any moment, Grizz's awareness grew. "You're wha? Who? No! Look, just stay close to me. Don't you realize the danger you're in here?"

"I just wanted to tell you, I am really thankful for you saving me from the plane crash, but don't you realize the danger you are in here?" Kiki asked.

"Kid, I can't always be there to save..." At Kiki's

words, Grizz figured out the catch of the little girl and how she was in ca-hoots with his mysterious challenger. Kiki had been purposely placed to distract him. Grizz took Kiki by the hand and began leading her out to the exit door of the museum. She ran to keep up behind him.

"Grizz?" Kiki called out. Grizz turned in time to get a yo-yo smashed in his face. *'It can't be...'* Grizz thought with dazed stars in his eyes. Then he realized the impossible truth, *'Kiki is the challenger.'*

Kiki backed away from Grizz as she giggled at him. She sounded like a child playing *'Catch me if you can.'* Kiki took one step which made her seem to completely vanish before his eyes.

Kiki's giggling stopped and an eerie silence filled the museum. "Hey, Kiki, come out here. You're a good kid. A little mixed up at the moment, but I know you'll make the right decision. I don't want to hurt you, you're just a little girl." Grizz explained carefully.

"Oh, you won't hurt me." Kiki's voice seemed so distant and the echo bounced around Grizz from every direction. "You said it yourself, I'm just a little girl."

"Alright, now I've had enough of this. If you think for one moment you can toy with me, you're surely..." A dart came zipping in at Grizz from the darkness and planted itself ever so accurately in Grizz's thigh. "Ow! What the..." Grizz pulled the dart out from his leg and looked around. "Kiki, I'm not going to tell you again, now stop it!" Another dart fell from a height and stuck itself into Grizz's shoulder. "I don't want to fight you!" Grizz shouted as he stumbled forward. He could feel his leg begin to tingle and give out under him. Then his shoulder began to have the same effect. "You drugged me? What is this? I'm going numb." Grizz fell to the ground when his leg could no longer support his weight. "This won't work, Kiki. Right now my body is fighting off the affects of your drug and when I can stand again, I will hunt you."

Darts fell on Grizz like rain from a sudden cloud burst. Many of the darts missed their mark or bounced off Grizz's armor, however, the darts that did find Grizz's flesh were too many to count. Grizz's unprotected back looked like a porky pine with all of the feather end darts sticking up out of him.

"Oh, that's it! You're going to suffer for this. Do you realize what kind of enemy you have created in me by this betraying…" Grizz was unable to finish his sentence because the drugs in his blood stream had moved throughout his entire body.

The crowd of punks cheered and hooted as XD3 found the strength to sit up at the balcony railing and join the others as he watched the initiation. Kiki came skipping out from the darkness and stopped near to Grizz's head. Grizz could move his eyes in a drowsy and uncoordinated way as he tried to look at Kiki. Drool dripped from his limp mouth and pooled on the floor.

With a giggle, Kiki began to play with her yo-yo. She spun it out and it went down and wound out all of the string where it stopped, but it didn't actually stop because it was still spinning. She gave the string a little flick and the yo-yo coiled right back up to her hand. She revealed she held a second yo-yo in her other hand. With quick rolling motions, Kiki rolled her hands around in tight circles letting the yo-yos swing in and out impressively. Her skills seemed to improve as Kiki executed further tricks at increased difficulty. Each time she tried something, she pulled it off with perfection. It was like she had a telekinetic power over the yo-yos as they would shoot out in any direction and return to her flawlessly. She let the yo-yos fall down her back and then they would seemingly climb back up her back to her hands.

Kiki was a young little rouge who thought she was bigger than everyone else. *'Mind over matter,'* she would tell herself and prove it to others with every chance she had.

Kiki let the yo-yo drop down and crack Grizz over his head. Grizz moaned, but otherwise didn't move a muscle. "Now, you know why I was sent to the Island?" Kiki bent down with the yo-yos moving in and out above her like an aura of power, then she whispered into Grizz's ear. "I am more dangerous than you can imagine." Kiki began to walk around Grizz's unmoving body as she struck him with her yo-yos time and time again. Each time she did so, she would thrust the yo-yos down on him harder and harder. By the time she made her way around the body and back to Grizz's head. She would let the yo-yo go behind her where she swung it around and drove it down upon him with incredible force. The sound of the solid porcelain yo-yo impacting flesh was disturbing.

She began to concentrate her efforts on Grizz's unprotected head. He made fists with his hands and curled his arms in. Kiki could see the affects of the drugs wearing off and she didn't have any more darts.

Grizz pushed at the floor and managed to flip himself over. Many of the darts fell out of his flesh. Kiki seemed to become a little worried. She was no longer in the mood to giggle. All of her efforts went into striking Grizz's face as fast and as hard as she could. She broke his nose and pummeled his head so severely his face looked like ground beef with a couple of swollen eyelets to see through.

Grizz shot his hand out and caught one of the bloodied yo-yos. He yanked at it and Kiki jerked forward. She felt as though her finger was about to be torn off with the yo-yo string.

"Ouch! Grizz, you're hurting me!" Kiki pleaded

with a sound in her voice like a cat's meow.

Grizz wanted to say something but regardless of the drugs, his lips were mashed and swollen. It made no difference as Grizz's moan said enough.

Kiki stepped close to Grizz as she dropped her other yo-yo. She dropped her free hand to her boot and pulled a knife from its sheath. She made two quick strokes with it. With the first she cut the string between her and Grizz as her second stroke slashed out at Grizz and nearly cut his throat.

Grizz decided his disadvantage lacked purpose. He rose up and began to chase Kiki. As Grizz hobbled after Kiki like a monster, she screamed and ran from him. Climbing the stairway to join the crowd of on looking punks for protection, Kiki was reminded of the one rule where no one is allowed to intervene the challengers until the leader deems the fight finished or someone dies.

Grizz took quick wide steps to keep up to the little terror. Kiki reached to her back taking hold of something she had tucked in the back of her pants, but before she could reach it Grizz grabbed her by the back of her leather jacket. Grizz's huge hands moving over Kiki were twice the size of her head.

Kiki looked at Grizz and saw something there no one else did. She decided not to scream or fight him in any way, rather the cunning little girl simply went limp in his arms and relaxed.

When Grizz noticed what Kiki was doing, he drew his face in real close to hers and roared loud enough to rattle windows. Still Kiki remained unmoving. Grizz was confused. He went after Kiki because of the pain she inflicted on him, but once he had her, he wasn't sure what to do with her. Grizz couldn't hurt Kiki this way, whether she was playing possum or not.

In the blink of an eye, Kiki had slipped out of her

leather jacket and out of Grizz's hold on her. With extreme skill and speed, Kiki spun around holding a sling shot in her hand. Pulling back on the elastic, she released a small metal ball bearing. It bounced off Grizz's skull again with a sound like, "TACK!"

Grizz seemed to stiffen his entire body before he fell backwards and tumbled down the stairs. At the sight of this, the entire crowd went gonzo with deafening cheers. Grizz the unbeatable, was struck down and defeated by the third challenger, a little girl.

Grizz attempted to roar some more as he fell down the stairs. Kiki had proven to be the most challenging adversary he had ever fought in his life. A realization came to Grizz as he figured out how Kiki was about to defeat him and there was nothing he could do about it.

Rolling out at the bottom of the stairwell, Grizz just laid there, motionless. Kiki stepped down to Grizz with the crowd in an uproar of disbelief. At this point, Kiki knew she was expected to kill Grizz once and for all. Moving in for the final death blow where Kiki would easily take his life, she saw how Grizz was in agony and pain. Looking up at Kiki through one partially open eye, with the other eye totally swollen shut, Grizz surrendered for once and accepted the inevitable. To be powerless and defeated was a new experience for Grizz.

Examining the crowd of punks above, Kiki saw XD3 looking down at her. Motioning his finger across his throat, XD3 wanted to see Grizz die. Grizz saw Kiki pull out her knife again, and Grizz knew it would all be over soon, then he would be dead.

As Kiki looked down at the great warrior, she took pity on him. Kiki was not used to the sense of pity though she found herself putting her knife away before she announced, "I release the Blackguard!"

Grizz began to lift his head. Rolling over Grizz rose

to a crawling position. XD3 did not approve of Kiki's decided announcement. If Grizz was to be released, XD3 was the only one in authority to do so. XD3 rose up from the rails of the upper level and shouted his discontent. "Destroy him now, Kiki! I'm commanding yo to do it!!!"

"No one commands me…" Kiki replied in repugnant defiance. To XD3's surprise, Kiki went to Grizz and began to help him rise to his feet.

XD3 turned and vanished amongst the crowd, indignant of the blatant defiance.

As Kiki assisted Grizz and they were about to make for the door, a thunderous sound rumbled through the museum. Grizz and Kiki turned to look up the stairs and there at the top was XD3. He had mounted a motor bike and three punks stood at his side. Each of them sticking one needle each into the thick neck of XD3. They pumped him up with even more steroid drugs. XD3 throttled up before he kicked it into gear and came driving down the steps on his Harley Davidson. He bounced his feet up onto the seat when the bike came to a short landing mid-way down the stairs. He lept from the motor bike and flew through the air like a wrestler before colliding into Grizz. The dangerous tackle knocked Grizz off his feet and they both tumbled to the floor.

Grizz knew not from where his new found strength came, but he took up a shield from the floor and found his samurai sword. XD3 lifted a spiked club over his head and brought it down on Grizz, but Grizz lifted his shield to protect himself. The only problem was both items were completely made out of wax so they both broke apart immediately.

XD3 was quickly upon Grizz where he gripped Grizz's hand which held the hilt of the sword. As they battled for the sword, XD3 realized Grizz's strength was quickly returning. XD3 drove his knee into Grizz's groin with the expectation the sword would be released.

Grizz was not prepared for XD3 to fight so dirty as he did let go of the sword and it clattered to the floor. XD3 reached down to take hold of the sword, but Grizz could not allow that. Grabbing XD3, Grizz twisted around causing the punk to spin, before he pivoted with enough leverage to send XD3 over a barrier of the in floor mid-evil torture display.

Grizz turned to walk away as XD3 surprised everyone and popped back over the edge of the barrier. Grabbing Grizz by the armor plating of his shoulders XD3 pulled him back with him. They both fell twelve feet into the deep display.

Many torture devices were organized in a musty setting of log and iron. Everything seemed to be fastened together with huge knobby black bolts. Wax dummies were positioned to depict the way in which the devices of pain were intended to be used.

XD3 shuffled to get up muttering threats as to how he was going to kill Grizz. Grizz, however, had already risen up on one knee. Next to a long heavy chain, Grizz began wrapping it around his wrist. XD3 stomped his feet as he ran up from behind Grizz. Using the weapon of heavy black chain around his fist and fore-arm, Grizz spun around and struck XD3 square in the stomach with incredible force. XD3 fell backwards and looked up at Grizz with wide eyes of surprise. Grizz arose to his full height as he loosened some of the chain and let it fall limp to the ground. XD3 was rising and about to charge at Grizz, but Grizz used the chain like a whip and cut right through a wax torture device of spikes which was designed to tighten into its captive slowly. XD3 thought he could move fast enough to evade the chain whipping and attack Grizz, but Grizz was faster than he looked. Swinging the chain at XD3 it wrapped itself around his neck. Grizz gave the chain a little tug and XD3 stumbled to him. When XD3 was close enough, Grizz punched him in the face. The chain loosened from around XD3's neck and he collapsed to his knees gasping for air. The tension to XD3's neck was obviously too strenuous for him.

Scampering away, XD3 searched for a weapon of his own, but there was nothing real, only what was made of wax. Then XD3 found a chain of his own and began to quickly wrap it around his own wrist. Eyeing Grizz as he was about to use his chain against him, XD3 seemed to get some of his strength back.

Grizz, seeing what was coming, began to rewrap his chain around his wrist again.

XD3 stood up, charging and yelling as he swung his heavy arm at Grizz. Grizz also swung his chained arm at XD3. When their chained fists met, they clanged with a heavy thump and sparking sound of a crack.

The crack was the breaking of XD3's hand under the immense pressure of the over tightened chain and coupled with the powerful impact. "Ugh!!!" shouted XD3.

Sweat poured over XD3's face as his body fought the effects of the drug. It was not long before XD3 realized the effects of the drugs he had just taken were not nearly as powerful as he wanted them to be. XD3 could literally feel the drugs nullify in his system. This angered him as he pointed his good finger at Grizz and blamed him. "Yo, it's yo! Yo're the reason I can't get high. I bet none O my drugs will work on me ever again because I tasted yer blood."

"Hey, man, if it weren't for my blood you'd be dead right now, due to an overdose!" Grizz told him flatly.

XD3 tried to attack Grizz again as he swung his chained crippled hand at him. Grizz easily blocked the punch as he could see XD3's strength had left him.

XD3 fell to his knees as he had caused himself much more pain. Blood began to seep from the black coil of chain which encased his fist and fore-arm.

The initiation was over. With the satisfaction of overpowering XD3, Grizz stood straight and tall and let his chain unwind from his gauntlet and fall completely to the wood flooring.

The challenges had ended and Grizz could no longer be bothered to toy with XD3. XD3 understood this and he realized how the punks, who have always looked up to him, were now looking at him as unfit to lead. He felt it was not fair how, due to one failure, XD3's time as leader had ended, for no punk would follow weakness.

For a moment, Grizz expected XD3 would signal the others to kill him but instead XD3 stood up to address the crowd. Though he was in great pain, he announced clearly, "I promote the Blackguard ta take my place as yer leader."

The punks were not very interested in long boring speeches. This statement was a big surprise to everyone, especially Grizz. Before Grizz could say something of his own, XD3 quickly added, "The Blackguard'll lead the raid tomorrow night. Obviously, he's worthy O this task. He'll need yer co-operation. Accept Grizz now as one O us!" he told them.

The crowd of punks began to clap and cheer but they only put in half as much enthusiasm as XD3 had expected.

"Oh, come on!!! Give it up fo the Blackguard!" shouted XD3 as he turned to leave. The crowd responded much more enthusiastically at XD3's request.

Grizz looked up at the punks who surrounded him cheering. Though he had seen better days, he did enjoy the attention.

With the sound of approaching emergency sirens, everyone quickly disappeared from the initiation museum into their respective holes to lick their wounds. XD3 and Lips were driven to separate hospitals. Thrash was injured but he did not need hospitalization.

Many punks wanted to speak to Grizz, especially Darkade, but the museum was no longer the time or place for any of them. Grizz was not sure where he should disappear to, but Kiki Vixen felt responsible for Grizz's condition. Because Kiki shared a history with Grizz, and she really liked him, she took him back to her place.

Kiki had to take Grizz on the subway in order to get him to her apartment. Neither of them were able to conceal themselves very well in public as they attracted the attention of many night owl commuters who had somewhere to get to in the early morning hour. Metro City never slept.

Kiki noticed how Grizz seemed to get stronger as they made their way from the subway station to a building complex. Grizz was beginning to assist Kiki up the staircase. She led him to a door marked 32. Fiddling with her keys, Kiki unlocked the door and led Grizz inside.

"You need to keep it down, alright?" Kiki told Grizz quietly, "Don't wake my roommates." Kiki took Grizz directly to the bathroom where she assisted in removing his shirt. Kiki cleaned Grizz's wounds and bandaged his face. Examining Grizz, Kiki followed the scars of his body with her finger, up and around the curves of his large muscles. Finding a few patches of grey volk skin worked into the puzzle of skin grafts, Kiki began to question him. Grizz was silent as he decided to keep his secrets about such things as volk muscle implants, to himself. Not entirely himself, Grizz kept his feelings deep inside as he was suspicious about revealing too much to the girl. No one could be trusted.

"Boy, I really kicked your butt." Kiki tried a new approach. As she spoke to Grizz, she snickered and reflected on the recent fight while tending to cleaning and dressing his wounds.

Grizz snorted his discontent, but made no further comment. He required rest.

Kiki was a strong young girl. Using her small Barbie sewing kit, she was able to stitch up the knife wound on his arm with three stitches. Grizz growled at the pain. Shortly, a knock came to the bathroom door. "Kiki, you Ok?" Came the voice of a young lady.

"Yeah, I'm fine." Kiki answered. Giving Grizz a frank look, she blamed his growling for waking her roommates.

"Oh, I'm hearing some strange sounds, what's going on?" asked a roommate.

"I have brought a friend home with me and he's been hurt a little. I won't be long." Kiki hoped this was the end of the conversation, "Go to bed, I'm fine."

"Did you say, "he?" Listen Kiki, I really need to use the bathroom, can you finish up in there... now?" insisted the roommate.

"She's just being protective." Kiki whispered into Grizz's ear. "We'll be right out, sheesh." She spoke louder to address her roommate outside the bathroom door.

Grizz could hear other voices outside the door. Kiki had more than one roommate, "I told you she would be trouble, she's into all that *punk stuff*. Next thing you know, this place'll be full of punks. Then we'll get robbed or worse..."

Grizz was not sure if Kiki could hear what was said as well as he could, but he acted like he didn't hear anything and stood up, "Let's go." Grizz told Kiki.

Kiki opened the door and walked out with Grizz. Kiki's roommates were a couple of young women in their late teens or early twenties. They each looked at Kiki first, but when Grizz emerged from the bathroom, their eyes went up to him in horror. They had never seen a person as inhumanly large as Grizz before. His bandaged face frightened them to start screaming, but Kiki put out her hands and quieted them down right away.

"No, no! You don't understand. Its' okay, he's with me. He's my friend and he won't hurt you..." When Kiki could see the young ladies had settled down after their initial shock, she told them, "His name is, Grizz." Kiki looked up at Grizz. "Grizz? These are my roommates, Kathy and Farrah."

Grizz grunted. His face was very sore and swollen still and it hurt him to talk. When Kiki saw Grizz was not going to say anything, she felt prompted to explain for him, "Grizz had gotten into a scrap earlier tonight and had his butt whipped." she giggled like the little brat she was.

Grizz growled at her little insinuation how it was Kiki who gave him the mentioned butt whipping.

Though Kathy and Farrah did not like the idea, they let Kiki give their couch to Grizz for the night.

Later, when Grizz was fast asleep and the sun would soon begin to rise, Kathy and Farrah woke Kiki to have a little private talk with her. They hadn't had Kiki staying with them for more than a couple of nights, and they didn't know her very well. To keep from another episode like this from re-occurring, Kathy and Farrah tried to be as polite as they could when they told Kiki she was not welcome to stay with them any longer. Both Farrah and Kathy said they didn't approve of the punk way of life, or her punk friends, like Grizz. Punks were just too dangerous and unpredictable for Farrah and Kathy.

With all of her belongings packed into a box, Kiki walked out of the apartment building in the morning sounds of people starting their day. Grizz came out of the building behind Kiki and much of the sounds from the street came to a grinding halt. People could not keep themselves from locking their gazes on Grizz as he still wore the same armor and wounds from the previous night.

Together, Kiki and Grizz returned to the punk hide out under the warehouse. Grizz had removed much of the gauze which was wrapped around his face for his swellings and wounds had healed quite well in the short time since the initiation. They show up like a couple of derelicts with no place to live, but once they stepped foot into the basement, they received a hero's welcome.

Both Grizz and Kiki were praised and honored with a loud crazy party. Grizz put his helmet on and the response was of a crazy cheer, much like a shrill. They chanted "Blackguard, Blackguard, Blackguard..." Most of the attention was on Grizz, Kiki didn't mind at all. In fact she loved it, because Kiki knew Grizz favored her and she wanted to be his number one more than anything. Never in her life had Kiki known anyone to be like Grizz. There was no other like him. Not even Eddy Evon was like Grizz, because along with his heart stopping presence and charisma, Grizz was larger than life. In Kiki's young eyes, Grizz was as a picture perfect icon of cool. Grizz knew he held favor in Kiki's eyes, but he didn't know he was her number one fan.

After a few hours, when the punk rock party had died down some, Grizz was prompted to explain the plan for the assignment he was given from XD3 to lead the punks on an important raid.

Remembering XD3 mention something about a raid,

Grizz really hadn't given the assignment much thought, nor was he aware the due timing of this particular event was so soon.

Darkade appeared next to Grizz and address the crowd, "The Blackguard will certainly fill you in on the details shortly but there are some details about the layout of the location I need to bring to his attention. We'll talk and return shortly."

The crowd was in an impatient up roar as they wanted answers from Darkade immediately.

Despite the negativity from the frustrated punks, Grizz followed Darkade across the crowded floor. Kiki took hold of Grizz's finger as she followed along. Darkade noticed at a glance how Kiki figured she would be involved in the arrangements of their plans. Turning and bending down to Kiki, Darkade said. "Kiki, I'm sorry. This will be a private meeting." he addressed the crowd who also wanted inside, "That goes fo all O yo as well." Darkade pointed out toward the angry punks.

Kiki let go of Grizz and her hand dropped to her side, as she let Grizz move away into the crowd. Grizz looked out after Kiki as she clearly said. "Things are not the same Darkade!" Wanting desperately to be with Grizz Kiki made her will evident through the tone of her voice. "The Blackguard is not like XD3!" Kiki cried.

Darkade acted like he couldn't hear Kiki shouting after him as he and Grizz made their way to the private chamber. With the door open, Kiki could see Grizz speak to a large punk body builder guard. The chamber guard pulled out a cell phone with a camera as Grizz pulled up one of his protective iron shoulder guards. The punk guard took the picture of the tattoo on Grizz's shoulder before Grizz glanced back at Kiki. Grizz followed Darkade into the chamber where they locked the door.

Darkade reported, "XD3'll be out O action fo some time due to his injuries. When I spoke to him last, in the hospital, he told me he wouldn't be returning. I can't believe that. I am telling you, between you and I, we have the makings of greatness. XD3 and I have accomplished so much together and he trusted me completely. You and I need to establish the same relations if we are to have even a fraction of the success I am used to. When I am not a punk doing what I can to disable an already disabled system of society, I am a lawyer, a very successful lawyer."

"I am not used to having any support. I have to depend on myself, trust never came easy to me." Grizz explained as his words trailed off.

"I understand *that*, Blackguard. Listen, XD3 has basically quit and it hurts me to do this but he's given me the keys to his home and his ride and I am giving these things to you. You will overtake what was once his. If you screw everything up and XD3 returns, I will personally return these things to him."

Grizz plucked the keys from Darkade. "I *won't* mess this up... *You* can trust me..." Grizz shook the keys and they tinkled before he slid them into his pocket.

Darkade smiled through his thin goatee. Letting out a deep breath from his nose, Darkade added, "Ok, listen, I suspect, because XD3 had a bone to pick with you, he likely, in Secret, wanted to see you get taken down at the hands of the police. I have looked into his plans for the raid and found a few key operational tactics which were over looked. Such sloppiness was not like XD3, you see, for one thing, if we don't want the police to interfere, we can take care of that. The way the original plan was set up, potential dangers existed for all punks involved. I can't see how XD3 intended to lead this raid at all. It's as though he had *you* in mind for this from the beginning.

318

There wasn't even a back-up plan or an escape route for any of us, much less for the one to lead this raid."

Grizz was not happy with this news.

Outside, many punks, along with Kiki, wanted to enter the Blackguard's chambers to speak to him. The guard standing outside the chamber doors, Cratorface, addressed the punks, speaking with his scratchy voice, "I twas told strictly, not to allow no other ta enter unless dey bore a certain tattoo like da one da Blackguard has on his shoulder."

One by one, the punks began to show Cratorface their tattoos and he rejected them all. "Nope, nope, seen it before. Awe, come on Jett, I've seen dis tattoo a billion times, I don't wan'a see it again... It's disturbing."

Kiki stepped up to Cratorface and lifted her sleeve. She showed him the tattoo she received from the government. Kiki's tattoo design was of a planet and eagle with the words, "Property of the U.S.A." Burned below the tattoo were four small numbers; 2211.

"Oh, hold up just a beat here, Kiki. What is dis?" Cratorface dug his cell phone out of his back pocket and flipped it open. Touching a button, the picture of Grizz's tattoo popped up on the guard's display. The light from the phone cast dark shadows over Cratorface's pitted skin making his features seem somewhat spooky. Kiki liked it. Cratorface was surprised when he compared the photo to Kiki's tattoo. The tattoos were the exact same tattoos both Kiki and Grizz had received from the Knolix Island.

"You're so weird, Kiki." Cratorface whispered as he shook his head and chuckled before he moved to the side just enough to let Kiki in. "Always full O surprises." Cratorface added.

"Wha? The girl?" Darkade questioned.

319

"She's with us! I insist she stays." Grizz spoke flatly. Kiki ran to him and slapped her arms around his rock hard waist.

"She hasn't been with us very long. We need to be cautious of spies. This is the reason I wanted to speak with you privately, in here." Darkade explained nervously.

"The girl and I share a history together..." Grizz turned to Kiki and began to lift his shoulder guard. "Show him." he told Kiki bending forward and flexing his biceps.

Kiki knew exactly what to do. Lifting her sleeve, Kiki presented her tattoo next to Grizz's. Kiki was also flexing her tiny biceps.

Darkade was surprised at first but he soon narrowed his eyes in sceptic thought, "I knew the two O you were different from the rest O us, but I didn't know yo were cut from the same cloth."

"As I said, Kiki and I share a history, but *we* are not the same. I trust her and so should you." Grizz huffed.

Darkade raised his eyebrows and shrugged his shoulders, "Fine, now let's get down to business then."

"Perfect, first of all, what are we raiding? And why?" Taking charge, Grizz asked persistently.

"We need to storm the mansion O Dwergmal & Tannis. Both Dwergmal & Tannis were punks until they mysteriously found themselves swimming in an endless supply O cash. They disappeared from our punk group and began to live the good life on snob hill with all the other rich snobs where they snubbed all O us. We would have liked to see some of their money but they obvious were not interested in sharing any O it with us. We don't have a problem with this at all. They can keep their money fer all we care, but the purpose O the raid's to acquire the talisman O the bleeding heart ruby. They volunteered to keep it fer us fer safe keeping, in a difficult time, but they refuse to return it. *We* want it back." Darkade rolled out a map on the table top. "These are the schematics O Dwergmal & Tannis's home." Grizz and Kiki sat down with Darkade and they worked through the plans thoroughly until they deviced a plan and presented it to the punks. The plan was both simple and effective, the kind of plan everyone had confidence in.

From the pale light of the evening moon, through the darkness of the alley ways of Metro City, Grizz, with Kiki accompanying him, tried out XD3's old key. The apartment, previously belonging to XD3 was found at the corner of Hastings and Bradner. Though Grizz had removed his armor, he was dressed in leather with studs and chains. With the dark tattoos around his eyes and his messy long hair, Grizz looked more goth than punk, but next to Kiki they were a matching pair.

Kiki and Grizz went directly to the location of Hastings and Bradner where they found themselves not only in the middle of the busy city, but standing in front of a posh hotel, the esteemed five star Rosetta hotel. The doorman stopped them and asked for some ID.

"We will be staying in XD3's place." Kiki told the doorman as Grizz dangled the key before him.

The doorman took the key and inspected it. "Very well. Be sure it is checked out at the front desk, enjoy your stay." Grizz took the key back and dropped it in his pocket. Kiki and Grizz looked at each other and shrugged their shoulders before stepping into the large glass double doors of the Rosetta hotel.

Almost as immediately as they entered the hotel's main doors, the manager of the hotel trotted up to them. Trying to keep his voice low the manager said, "You, you two, this is a private hotel. We don't allow just any old rif-raf off the street to come in here. To stay here you need to have money. A lot of money. I'm going to have to ask you to leave." The manager wore a penguin like tuxedo, custom fit for his small frame. Bald on top of his head, the manager, protecting the reputation of the hotel, sneered under his thin French moustache.

"I am registered here." Grizz insisted as he dug into his pocket with his hand to find the key. Grizz tore his pocket removing the key because his leather cloths fit so tightly. He held it out to the hotel manager. "I was at a costume party."

The skinny manager was shocked as he took the key from Grizz, "Indeed." Inspecting the key, the hotel manager realized the error of his assumption, "Oh, oh my, this is..."

"XD3's room." Kiki finished the manager's sentence for him.

"I am terribly sorry sir. Please forgive me." With his tail tucked between his legs, the manager tottled off behind the front desk to a computer where he was able to verify the information. Shortly, the manager returned.

"Everything checks out, sir. I was expecting XD3, but a verified message confirms the room is now yours." The manager's cheeks were red as he was rather nervous and embarrassed. Apologizing until it became annoying, the manager escorted Grizz and Kiki to the suite personally. The key fit perfectly, unlocking the door. Stepping into a separate elevator the manager inserted the key into a keyhole on the buttonless panel and gave it a half twist. A green light lit up. The doors slid shut and Kiki gave Grizz a nervous grin as she began to wonder if they had stepped into some kind of trap. Grizz put his hand on Kiki's shoulder as the elevator softly lifted off. The elevator took them to the suite at the very top of the tall hotel, the penthouse suite.

The elevator stopped and the doors slid open. Before Grizz and Kiki was the interior of a beautiful and spacious suite which was nothing less than royalty. So much was white with gold trim and extravagant designs. Grizz and Kiki had to pinch themselves as they felt like they were looking through a doorway to heaven. "The best of the best, of course, sir." The manager remarked with a snobbish roll of his tongue as he removed the key from the elevator panel.

The manager waved his hand for Grizz and Kiki to step out of the elevator. Grizz and Kiki were speechless though they tried to step out like they had done it a million times before. Kiki began to grin senselessly as she was beginning to lose the battle to keep her cool. The manager handed the key to Grizz, and Grizz held out his hand. The manager placed the key in Grizz's hand and in turn held out his own hand. Grizz looked at the managers open hand and could not figure out, he was waiting for a tip.

Raising one eyebrow, Grizz placed the key back into the managers hand. The manager shook his head and gave the key back to Grizz then he opened his hand again for a tip. Grizz thought this was very strange behavior. He put the key back in the manager's hand again and again the manager gave the key back to Grizz.

Grizz was fed up with the silly game as he snorted and pushed the manager into the elevator. Twisting the key in the panel and removing it, Grizz let the elevator doors slide shut.

"That's enough of that." Grizz told the young manager before the doors were completely closed and the manager was on his way down, empty handed.

Grizz turned to see Kiki running around the Suite with her arms stretched out wide. She was laughing and excitedly checking out the entire pad. Laughing, Kiki jumped up onto the couch and picked up an arm full of pillows. Hugging the pillows before tossing them up into the air, Kiki fell down on her back to the couch with the pillows, laughing all the more. "I can't believe it, Grizz. This is like a dream come true! I am living the high life, here, with you. I must be dreaming. Pinch me!"

"It is all ours." Grizz said in a low covetous voice.

Kiki found a remote control on the glass coffee table. Pressing a button Kiki was surprised to find HD flat screen begin to rise out from the floor. She found the latest gaming console with a countless assortment of games and movies. Pressing another button, some classical music started up and filled the room. Kiki didn't like the music so she frantically hit more buttons. A panel slid open on a wall and a wine collection swivelled out from a hidden compartment. Another button from the remote started a fire in the fireplace. Finding the controls for the apartment's music Kiki quickly changed the radio station to one she was familiar with. Guitars buzzed like the sound of chain saws and a deathly scream was sounded. Grizz covered his ears with his hands. Kiki saw she was disturbing Grizz so she quickly shut everything down and tossed the remote control onto the coffee table. When Kiki smiled sweetly up at Grizz, he wondered, *'Could I ever be angry at her?'* Certainly, he could not stay angry.

Kiki screamed in excitement and ran around some more, in amazement. Grizz walked through the suite and looked around a little. He was not sure if it was all a mistake or perhaps a joke, but he was skeptical if his knew life of luxury was going to last.

Kiki had to be the first to open every door and see what was behind each one.

"There are many bedrooms. I'll take this one…"

Kiki paused and looked at Grizz. He seemed less than thrilled about the new place. "...Unless you want it, Grizz. Are you ok?" Kiki asked with care.

"None of this seems real to me yet, Kiki." Grizz answered her honestly.

Kiki peeked her head into another room, "Oh, no way! Grizz, you've got to see this!"

Grizz marched right up to the door. He thought XD3 was a strange guy and the room did not look like a room for a punk leader. *'Now,'* he thought, *'We'll see something disturbing that'll make more sense.'*

Grizz threw open the door and there before him was a room chalk full of various exercise equipment.

"Isn't it great? You'll probably get a lot of use out of this room." Kiki pointed out gleefully.

"I won't be stepping foot in there." Grizz said as he slowly closed the door.

"Why not? I figured a muscular guy like you..." Kiki started.

"No." Grizz cut her off, "It reminds me of when I was a kid. I was forced to use equipment like that, but it was a nightmare for me. I felt like my life was worthless, empty and full of pain. I might use that equipment on my own terms, but not if it makes me feel... I just want to be free from my past."

Kiki hugged Grizz and he received her kindness.

They wandered into the huge living room near a gas fireplace in the middle of the room. It was designed from ancient Greek mythology and the designs were worked into the marble all around it. Kiki bent down and petted the polar bear skin rug, "Ooo, soft..." The soft fur through Kiki's fingers engaged a reaction which expressed her sensation.

Grizz looked at the bear skin rug and huffed. Grizz respected bears for more than just the strength they

325

symbolized and he cared as much to see one skinned as he did to see himself skinned.

One wall of the apartment was dedicated to a sound stage with an assortment of musical instruments. There was a keyboard, electric guitar, base guitar, electric drums along with an assortment of brass wind instruments, a violin, a mandolin and a cello.

"Are you sure we have the right room, Grizz?" Kiki asked. It was a good question for there were many items that did not fit as the property of XD3 at all, at least not the XD3 they knew.

"The key led us in here didn't it?" Grizz was a little cocky because he liked the place and wanted to enjoy it a little.

Kiki walked to the stage and let her fingers play over the different instruments, while Grizz was inspecting the sword collection. The intense sound of the electric guitar erupted and squealed. Kiki stood at the micro-phone on stage with the guitar's shoulder strap taking the weight of the guitar on her little shoulder. She had one hand on the reeds of the neck and her other hand stretched to the ceiling with a shiny silver guitar pick pinched in her hand.

"Let's make some noise!" Kiki shouted into the mic and strummed the electric cords. Grizz closed his eyes, hard. It was indeed some noise.

Later, Kiki asked Grizz what he thought of her performance.

Grizz lied and told her he loved every moment of it. He didn't have the heart to tell her a couple of guitar lessons wouldn't hurt.

Kiki noticed a silver mug on the kitchen counter shaped like a skull with rubies for eyes. Engraved on the back of it was typed in large lettering, 'XD3.'

"We definitely have the right place." Kiki told Grizz

as she passed him the mug to inspect. Walking through the spacious kitchen to some sliding glass doors, Grizz and Kiki were hand in hand. Opening the doors, Grizz went outside where he looked over the sights and sounds of Metro city.

Kiki soon joined him out on the beautifully kept grounds of the terrace. They walked to the rails where a bench was nearby. Kiki said, "Grizz, don't you see? We are on top of the world! The whole time we were on that God forsaken Island, they were just trying to keep us from getting here. Well, who has the last laugh now?" Smiling, Kiki looked at Grizz and she wondered why others would look at Grizz like he was an evil monster. She knew he was so much more. "One day you could be president of this," Kiki turned to the city lights and lifted her arms wide and high, "Our great nation! First, we just need to change the views of society."

"This *great Nation?*" Grizz seemed to be somewhat upset, "You think I am blind? You think I can't see what's happening to *this great Nation?* Look out there at all those lights. Let's say each light represents one life."

"That's a lot of dudes." Kiki said playfully.

"Everyone is living comfortable lives. No one wants to lift a finger to get involved in other people's problems or to, heavens forbid, get a little dirt on their hands. People are lazy, and they don't know it, but life is passing them by. They're passing up on opportunities to really make a difference. A difference that is deeper than what they believe to be most important, *greater profits for self.* It disgusts me."

"I agree." said Kiki, "Whoever made up that saying for children, *'Don't talk to strangers,'* was full of fear. This is where people have such thoughts embedded in their subconscious from the beginning, how it is better to keep to yourself than to get out into the world and meet new people. I have never obeyed this rule and look at me, I am a better person for it... A stronger person."

"You've got it, girl. Another thing I don't understand, is the homeless. What? In *this great nation*, people are struggling? Isn't this still the land of opportunity? If people can't make a life for themselves here, where in the world do they think they can do better? People need to stop giving hand-outs or they might begin to depend on them... Oops, too late for that. Let's get them motivated. One day I plan to rule this planet and I'll fix all kinds of things."

"I maybe a little rough around the edges but I am not the bad guy. I understand, however, to effect change, some kind of action must proceed the change... I *am* some kind of action."

"Does it always work?" Kiki asked doubtfully.

"No, actually, but it is what I am built for so I have to try." Grizz told her.

"Well, I don't know, but if you want to rule the planet, perhaps you should further your education." Kiki responded.

Grizz just looked at Kiki for a moment. He didn't expect her to say that. Grizz finally agreed with Kiki but he began to show signs of being very tired. They went back inside where Grizz decided to take a shower and go to bed.

As he felt himself drifting off to sleep, he could hear Kiki in the next room singing. Kiki was not tired at all and so she softly sang her song;

Moon-light,
Aura so bright.
Dark forebodings
In the shadow of the night.
Can't hide from the Spector

328

Can you hear the guardian's whisper?
At the end of it all,
Will you still love me,
For who I am?
At the end of it all,
Will you still love me,
For who I am?
Don't you remember me, Don't you remember me…
I'll wait for you on the other side
Don't remember me…
I'll see you on the other side,
Don't wait for me…
I'll love you on the other side.
Don't remember me, Don't remember me, Don't
remember me…

Chapter 10

A cool stillness slowed the night air as tension built from the darkness. Dwergmal and Tannis believed they were safe. Taken completely unaware as the raid was about to awaken them.

Four tri-axle black commercial transport trucks came to a stop at a four way intersection. Each truck idled at a separate stop sign. Air brakes hissed into the night like serpents preparing for the hunt. A few seconds were spent to check for suspicious traffic, but there was no sign of other vehicles on the roads at all. One of the identical trucks fired up its' engines and kicked into gear. The others waited as it crossed over to the adjacent road where it stopped and lowered the back door of the trailer. A large bulky vehicle blundered out and down the ramp to the street. Once outside, it was clear how the vehicle had filled every square inch of the trailer.

The new vehicle was custom built for this specific operation and tied in with XD3's original plan. A make shift battering ram which started out as a school bus. Heavy structural eye beams were welded and bolted to the frame work with layers of dura-steel plating covering the entire body including the underbelly. Multiple spikes seemed to protrude from the flat front nose of the battering ram. No guns or such projectile weapons were built into it, rather it was rigged with countless charges that would burn hot and slow. This was the preferred reaction over a messy explosion.

Grizz drove the battering ram with Kiki next to him riding shotgun. Besides her mascara loaded on around her eyes heavier than usual, Kiki wore a quiver of feather ended arrows and a bow over her shoulder. Kiki's seat was raised quite high so the little girl could see through the narrow slots in the armor plated windows.

Behind them sat Darkade and Zom-Buckle who were assigned the task of setting the charges and laying down a suppressing line of fire to protect Grizz and Kiki.

One rule, everyone understood, was not to kill. Wounding people was permitted but only if necessary. The goal was to go in, retrieve the talisman of the bleeding heart and escape without being identified.

Grizz slowly drove the bulky battering ram down the street toward the mansion of the punk traitors, Dwergmal and Tannis. The other three transport trucks took turns driving through the intersection just as the first one did. Each trailer unloaded various punk vehicles from motor cycles to trucks, jeeps, and supped up cars that had funky lights and nitro.

As the caravan of vehicles rode through the quiet suburban neighborhood, they tried not to draw a lot of attention to themselves, however as they drew closer to the mansion they increased their speed.

Grizz pushed the school bus engine to its maximum before he hit the nitro switch. Flames shot out from the sides of the battering ram as the other vehicles equipped with nitro also joined the sudden acceleration.

With Grizz leading the pack, he broke through the tall iron front gates. No one was alerted with all perimeter alarms disabled. This was possible because an undercover punk security technician paid a little visit the day before.

Tall trees lined the long windy driveway as the punks sped faster and faster. A large rounded alcove encircled a monumental water fountain out front. The battering ram chewed through the fountain and careened up the front steps before exploding through the large double doors. The school bus battering ram settled in the center of the open lobby hissing and spewing flames.

The occupants of the mansion were awoken with a mighty rumble and the forceful shaking of walls. All were asleep in the mansion at the time of the disturbance, both owners and hired help flew into action but they were no less dazed and confused.

The school bus side doors of the battering ram opened. Kiki hopped out and disappeared into the shadows of the mansion quickly. Darkade and Zom-Buckle had finished setting the charges in the school bus as Grizz headed for the door. In mid stride, Grizz paused to speak to his associate punks. "Don't you have somewhere to be?"

Zom-Buckle and Darkade immediately took up their rifles and followed Grizz outside. They only took one step before they were forced back as bullets ricochet and sparked all around them. Dwergmal had opened fire on them from the overhead balcony. Tannis was at his side and the both of them wore only loosely fitting sleepwear. The displeasure for their rude awakening was written all over Dwergmal and Tannis's faces.

Dwergmal was a rough cut individual who was often teased for having a face that resembled a pig.

Tannis on the other hand was young and beautiful with flowing long angel blond hair. She didn't seem too concerned how her lightly covered see through night gown was revealing much of her bare cleavage.

The punks entered on foot through the broken front doors. The mansion's security personnel entered the lobby as well from a back door of the main level. Everyone took positions before everything froze to a stand off.

"How dare you, XD3!!!" shouted Tannis, burning with anger.

Dwergmal leaned in to Tannis to calm her quietly, "Easy, darling, I'll take care of this." Dwergmal returned his gaze to look down upon the smoldering battling ram, "Don't be a coward, XD3. I know you're out there. Show yourself so I can repay you for this untimely intrusion."

Grizz answered with his loud deep voice which broke forth like thunder. XD3 no longer leads the Bleeding Heart Punks! I do!" Grizz began to stand up to look at Dwergmal, "I am…"

-Rat-at-at-at-at-at!!!- Dwergmal's machine pistol prattled off a shower of bullets. Grizz was interrupted from his introduction and forced to duck back for cover. Tannis stepped out from behind Dwergmal brandishing both, her true colors and a pump action grenade launcher. The heavy gun spat a round at the giant crystal chandelier which hung over the center of the lobby providing the main light to the spacious room. It came crashing down upon the battering ram. Crystals sprayed all over everyone as Tannis shouted her command to all, "Fire!!!" Turning her rifle toward the punks Tannis began to blast like there was no tomorrow.

Everyone began to fire. Shots rang out in every direction.

Kiki did not disappear, she had merely snuck around behind the mansion and climbed her way in through the open bedroom balcony door. She came out of the bedroom skipping rope and chewing bubble gum.

Dwergmal and Tannis were taken off guard when they turned around and found the little girl innocently approaching them. Of course, when they saw she was a punk, they pointed their weapons at her. This was a mistake.

Springing into the air, Kiki spun and twirled with her jump rope sailing around her like a halo, until she snapped it down like a whip twice and disarmed them both. With a controlled snap of her wrist, Kiki bound the ankles of Dwergmal and Tannis causing them to fall to the floor. With wide movements, Kiki tied a second jump rope into a slip knot around Dwergmal and Tannis's necks. Throwing the long end of the jump rope around the banister, little Kiki created leverage for her choke-hold. As Kiki tightened the jump rope around their necks, she drew her face in close to theirs and blew a bubble until it popped in their faces with attitude.

Grizz, Darkade and Zom-Buckle could feel the heat quickly rising from within the battering ram. Bullets from the main floor continued to be fired with no sign of slowing soon. The punks could no longer use the school bus for cover any longer. Tearing the heavy steel plating door from its hinges, Grizz used it to shield them-selves as they ran for it.

Darkade shouted to Grizz, "There're too many O them! They've got us pinned down. We didn't know there'd be so many guards."

Though Dwergmal could only manage a little air through the constricting of his throat, he said, "You have made a big mistake, little girl!"

"Ground me, daddy!" Kiki spoke back playfully. It was clear who was in charge.

Tannis shouted out to her security, "Help us! She's going to kill us!"

This grabbed the attention of the security who were otherwise preoccupied on the main floor. One fired a bullet at Kiki as she was doing some tricks with her yo-yo. The bullet tore through one of the liberty spikes of her green hair.

With a quick fluent motion, Kiki slid the bow off her shoulder with one hand while simultaneously loading an arrow onto it. Crouching low, she pulled back on the bow string and aimed carefully before releasing the arrow at the guard who shot at her. The arrow embedded itself into the guard's shoulder just as he got off a second shot at Kiki.

Grizz looked up and saw Kiki go reeling backwards to the floor of the balcony.

"No!!!" Grizz shouted with his mind on fire... Unable to remove the image of Kiki falling back from the impact of the bullet. Over and over, Grizz saw the same image through his mind's eye. He had to get to her. Throwing the metal shield, a guard was struck down. With such force, Grizz brought his fists down on a fancy coffee table which smashed it to pieces. Grizz roared with such pain and frustration it left a sense in the air that something was terribly wrong. Spinning around with the table pieces in his hands, Grizz began to throw them. Like a horizontal explosion of debris causing both guards and punks to run for their lives or be pummeled by the projectiles, nothing could stop Grizz from moving closer to Kiki.

Grizz went berserk attacking the guards, his anger dangerously welling up inside him to overtake him as it had his brothers. Pounding his legs like pistons, Grizz motored his way up the arced stairway to Kiki.

Kiki was laying on her back next to Dwergmal and Tannis. Grizz took his helmet off and put his ear down low to Kiki's mouth to see if she was still breathing. As he listened he could feel a gentle warmth from her mouth before Grizz heard a whisper, like giggling. Opening his eyes, Grizz looked Kiki up and down, before running his hands over her shoulders to find the bullet hole, but there was none. Her eyes were full of laughter as he realized the joke was on him. "You silly old bear." Kiki told him, "I wasn't hit, Grizz. Did you do all that for me?"

Grizz was silent and frustrated as he sat up against the wall with his arms crossed. Kiki thought he was pouting so she leaned forward and kissed him on his head and said, "Thank you." she spoke so sweetly, before popping a bubble gum bubble in his face.

Grizz snorted and Kiki laughed. She tickled him and asked, "Where's that smile?" she taunted him, "Oh, come on, I know it's there." Though Grizz fought it, a smile finally did crack across his face. Grizz stood up and threw Dwergmal and Tannis's gun's into the fire of the brightly burning battering ram.

"Untie them." Grizz spoke heavily to Kiki. She took her jump rope by the handle and gave it a snap and a pull before it snaked its' way free from Dwergmal and Tannis's throat.

As Kiki wound up her jump rope, Grizz, towering over Dwergmal and Tannis said, "Get out of here, now, or you will burn to the ground with this house." Grizz hoisted Kiki up and she sat on his shoulder proudly. Carrying Kiki, They went downstairs, to where the talisman was kept. It was easy to locate, but it remained behind a glass encasement. The room was a games room with an adjacent bar, but the talisman of the Bleeding Heart ruby was displayed over the fire place of white river rock. The entire room was made with the theme of a Viking castle with heavy wooden beams, metal plate supports with big bolt heads tightened in.

Darkade followed Grizz down the stairs. "Now, getting this out of the protective case will be tricky. There are three stages of alarm trips." Grizz huffed with amusement before he stepped forward and put his hands through the glass case. Wrapping his hands around the golden rod of the talisman Grizz pulled it free.

The alarm screamed immediately as the punks scattered to get out as fast as they could. Grizz, Kiki and Darkade bolted up the stairs and outside the burning mansion. There they met up with Zom-Buckle and hopped down the damaged front steps to the waiting punk vehicles. The fire was spreading quickly as they climbed aboard the various vehicles. Grizz, holding the talisman, climbed into the back of a pick-up. Kiki hopped onto the back of a Harley with the light blue skinned Phan-Tom driving.

Successfully, they took off down the long driveway before the police had arrived. The battering ram was left to burn the mansion to the ground. The punks left through the broken main gates of the property and sped through the neighborhood. As the sun began to paint golden highlights into a new break of day, Grizz began to believe he finally found a place in this world where he belonged.

The four-way stop still had the four commercial trucks and trailers waiting for them. Each of the trailers had their ramps down toward the center of the intersection. The punks hastily drove their vehicles right up the ramps and into the cargo trailers. From the intersection, the four black truck split up to take alternate routes back to the punks lair. The emergency vehicles passed right by one of the black trucks without a clue to its involvement in the destruction of Dwergmal and Tannis's home.

From the vacant, abandoned warehouse lot, the sound of music was barely heard, but stepping inside and going down to the basement, you'd find the lair of the punks and the scratchy noise they call music, would drowned out your thoughts. If there was one special ability all punks shared, it would be their ability to party. Grizz, or as they referred to him as, the Blackguard, had earned a whole new level of respect. There were many who said, "No leader can compare ta the Blackguard." And they also said, "He's far more sick than XD3 ever was."

A shrine was built along the wall opposite the stage.

The shrine was a collection of countless punks who died over the years. Most of them lost their lives to drugs. Many candles were lit and many more tears were shed. Some of the ladies like, Enemi, Snapdragon and Dirty Sherry looked at Grizz as he passed by. Their tears caused their heavy mascara to run. "Stab was my boyfriend. If yo're so powerful, bring'im back ta life, Blackguard." Snapdragon pounded on Grizz's chest, "I loved him, damn it! Now he's dead!"

Grizz just looked at her as she cried. He could feel her pain, but he could not do anything for her. He made a vow, deep in his heart to do something about the problem of drugs in the lair of the punks. "I can't bring your boyfriend back, but I may be able to keep your friends from following his way."

"What do yo mean?" asked Snapdragon through her distraught emotional state.

"I can't explain. You'll just have to trust me." Grizz told her with as much emotion as he could muster.

Walking away, Grizz made his way to the kitchen where he began to inspect the food and tools. Lifting a butcher knife from the table top, Grizz pointed it at the master chef and said, "Be sure everything is always washed thoroughly and carefully, understand?"

The chef swallowed nervously as though he wondered if he would become the special of the evening, "Of course, Blackguard. Of course, we're already very diligent but we'll tighten our efforts." The chef answered.

"Very good." Grizz said sternly. Moving on, still toying the butcher knife in his hands, Grizz eyed everything carefully. Spying the kegs of beer stacked at the far wall, Grizz began to take a special interest. With an inconspicuous slip of his hand, Grizz made a small cut to his fore finger. With quick twists to the keg caps, he made like he was inspecting them, but in actual fact, he was wiping a small amount of his blood on the inside of the caps and putting them back on. Knowing there were many eyes watching his every move, Grizz shot a suspicious look at the punk cooks. Conviction in the hearts of the punk cooks caused them all to look away. Grizz was very methodical and careful proceeding with one move at a time.

When Grizz's inspection was complete, he pointed the butcher knife at the chef once again and said, "Put those kegs out as soon as you can. People out there are thirsty." Twirling the butcher knife in his hand Grizz handed it over to the master chef, handle first.

"Yes, Blackguard. R-right away, Blackguard." Sweat began to trickle down the chef's fore-head.

Grizz watched carefully as the beer was brought out to the punks. He watched Kiki dance around like she was throwing punches and kicks, to the lyrics of yet another intense punk song.

"I want to start a fight, tonight!"

"I want to start a fight, tonight!"

At Grizz's table, punks were lined up to take a close look at the talisman of the Bleeding Heart ruby. When Grizz felt everyone had some of his blood tainted beer, he whispered to Darkade to stop the music so the talisman could be replaced in its rightful place before he spoke to his punks.

Shortly, the screeching music ceased for a ceremonial moment. Spider and Scorpin-X lifted the talisman of the Bleeding Heart ruby and placed it on the wall on the stage behind the band. A few seconds of silence followed when the talisman was hung. Spider and Scorpin-X stepped back, but only for a few seconds before the cheers erupted from the crowd of punks. Grizz made his way onto the stage dawning his mid evil shadow knight helmet. Abruptly, Grizz took hold of a pitcher of beer and carried it with him on stage. The cheering became even louder at the sight of the famous Blackguard. Grizz raised his arms and the punks almost went out of control. He was trying to quiet them but raising his arms it didn't help, it only caused the opposite affect, so Grizz addressed the crowd, "Shut up!!!"

The crowd became silent as they waited to hear what their new leader had to say. "Punks! Everyone of you! Bleeding heart punks! We were a success today!" The cheering broke forth louder than ever. "The talisman is back and I couldn't have done it alone! When I walked in here today, I saw the mourning of those of you who lost friends to drugs. I have decided, all connections to the drug trade ends here and now! This is my gift to all of you, as leader. We are strong together, but we are not strong if we are dead! Taste the future of clean living!" Taking hold of his shadow knight helmet, Grizz threw it to the stage floor like he had just made a touchdown. With his other hand, Grizz lifted the pitcher to his mouth and began to chug his beer. Though it was quite obvious Grizz was referring to the beer, no one caught on that it was tainted.

The punks were not sure what to think of Grizz's speech. Certainly, they understood the drug trade was the source of their money and power.

Darkade shot to the stage and spoke into the microphone. "Don't be alarmed..." A nervous glance was barely present in Darkade's shifty eyes. "The Blackguard has many plans. All will be discussed with all of you before any decisions are made. For now, let's party!"

The punks shook their heads and jumped up and down with excitement. As Grizz stepped off the stage, the band began to rip with the drums and bass making a rolling thunder.

Grizz noticed two punks smoking a joint and

laughing together with lazy, sleepy eyes. They both stood up from their table and went to get a mug of beer each. After they filled their mugs and went back to their seats, they began to goof off again. As they laughed and drank, they began to find the smoke had lost its magic and just tasted terrible.

As the two punks sobered up they became increasingly alert. "Hey man, why do we dress up like this? Punks're so nineteen eighties, this is two thousand thirty and why does my beer taste like crap?!"

"Yo, let me get this straight, you're angry at the date? You want a fight?" challenged the buddy.

As Grizz was making his way back to his table he could see one of the bar tenders, Jakebrake, shouting and waving his arms in distress as he tried to get Grizz's attention. Grizz changed his course and stepped up to the bar. "We gotta get them dudes to choke up! Switch is on the box... On the news, man!!!"

Glancing up at the flat screen above the bar, Grizz could indeed see Switch bound in cuffs and struggling as two police officers escorted him into a court of federal law. Grizz turned to the band and party basking punks, "HEY!!!" Grizz shouted. The music stopped and everyone turned to look at Grizz. "Switch is on the box!" Grizz announced.

All eyes went to the monitor and the room fell to a deathly silence. Jakebrake turned up the volume for all to hear the news report.

The news reporter was an attractive woman who wore librarian glasses and had her blond hair tied up at the back with curly locks dangling from the sides of her head. "A punk rock kid decided to go on a rampage early this morning, keeping authorities very busy. The young man, who's name hasn't been released, was fortunate not to get himself killed as those who reported him had told nine, one, one, to beware of a weapon, possibly a gun. The area of the fifty fourth block has been quartered off as the scene of the crime, as an ongoing investigation is well on the way. Drug use is suspected. Once again, a punk rocker goes berserk in the middle of the day and in the center of Metro city. Witnesses described the man as hate filled and dangerous. He fought a couple gang related rockers, which has started speculations of a possible gang, blood war uprising. Hold on... I have one of the eye witnesses here with me right now. Sir, could you please tell us what you saw?" the news reporter held her microphone out for a young man dressed in a suit and tie.

"Well, this punk kid with the blue Mohawk and everything, came running out here angrier than a rabid pit-bull. He was growling and shouting, with blood red eyes and foaming at the mouth. He went after the rockers and fought them for no reason. Least no reason I could see... What are these kids smoking now a days?" asked the computer tech who wore bifocals and a tie.

"Well, you've heard it hear on WPCX news, first. An act of hatred. A random act of violence at that, but Constable Peter Fisher, had this to say,"

"We have contained the incident and if this kind of thing happens again we will be ready for it. No one was seriously hurt and the individual who lost control was arrested and registered to the Westbank Mental Asylum. The public should not worry about this isolated incident and return to your regular lives without fear." The police officer smiled awkwardly as he crinkled his nose and bent his moustache.

The news reporter, June Anderson, continued. "Meanwhile a lavish home in the suburbs has burned completely to the ground. Questions are being raised as to why the authorities took as long as they did to arrive to the scene. I'm June Anderson, with WPCX news. Up next, the weather."

Jakebrake turned down the volume and everyone seemed to break up into groups as they spoke about the tragic fall of one of their brothers. Grizz watched the reactions of the punks for a moment. He knew it wouldn't be long before they began to blame him for what happened. Grizz waited at his table patiently, but no one seemed to accuse him of anything at all. Grizz found it very strange how he was not targeted by the punks. Everyone knew Grizz had given a drop of his blood to Switch, which freed him from his drug addiction. Obviously, there was an unknown side effect though in hind sight it would seem rather obvious. It was such a simple test, the ingestion of a small dose of Grizz's blood, the scientists of the Knolix Island must have figured out the positive and negative effects of Grizz's volk-human blood years ago. It would have been handy if such information of such dangers were shared with Grizz. As it was, Grizz was not made aware of the affects of his blood or he would have made sure his blood never came into contact with others. Unfortunately, Grizz had already spiked the kegs of beer and all of the punks have had some of it to drink.

It was not long before the punks began to piece everything together. As they talked amongst themselves, Grizz began to see a very big change come over everyone. They were happy Grizz hadn't cured them like he had Switch, but soon after this statement was made; they began to notice they no longer had a buzz, nor the need to get high. Skepticism spread like wild fire. "The Blackguard must'a done somethin to us. Like he did, Switch."

"Sure, it only makes clear, man. He basically told us

so on stage, remember? The Blackguard said, "This is my gift to all O you, as leader. We are strong together, but we're not strong if we're dead! Taste the future O clean living!""

"Yeah," the chef spoke holding the butcher knife, "We checked him out in the kitchen earlier fo a strange inspection. He must'a contaminated something. Maybe he's like magic and contaminated everything and we ate it." Grizz began to receive looks from the punks and it could mean only one thing, the punks had figured out the beer was tainted with the Blackguard's blood.

Many of the punks were still confused. They felt they had been duped because they weren't given a choice. Though many punks felt great with a sudden charge of energy, clear thinking and cleanliness, they were now aware of a certain side effect they were sure to expect... Like Switch, they would soon face insanity. Though the punks were angry, they were also thankful, because they were free from the hold the drugs had on their lives. With their confusion came a sense of embarrassment not knowing whether the change was for the better or the worst. No one spoke a word to Grizz as they left the lair, except Darkade who said, "If yo're guilty O something here, we'll be coming fer yo... *Justice'll* be served."

The punks who were heading for the exit of the lair, stopped in their tracks when they heard what Darkade had said. They turned back to Grizz in search of answers. "Hey, man! What did you do to us?" A punk began to shout with hatred at Grizz. The masses began to approach Grizz at once. They held spiked clubs, chains and knives. They knew to challenge Grizz could be deathly fatal and they wanted to avoid such a dangerous conflict, but they did not know any other way of dealing with their situation.

Grizz brought his heavy fist down on the table

which split it in two. Standing up, he pulled out his swords in defence. The crowd of punks took a defensive step back. Kiki ran up beside Grizz with her jump rope twirling at the ready. A stand off to a fight was initiated.

"Easy man, he was trying to help us, weren't yo, Blackguard?" Darkade attempted to be a mediator but the only problem was, he had a stake in the situation as well, because he too had drank three mugs of beer. "Yo have some answers for us, isn't that right, man?"

"That's correct, now, don't be afraid." Grizz tried to explain, "All you need to do is listen to me very carefully and you won't lose it. Look at me, I am not insane, I am strong. I can walk you all through this. I didn't know about the side affect until the news broadcast. We need to bring Switch back here so I can help him. You see, I have to live with the madness every second of everyday, but I can tell you it will get better. You just need to know a couple of effective techniques to manage it."

"Techniques? We're go'n ta all go insane and it's all yo're fault!" Zom-Buckle shouted. He looked so much healthier, even through his big bushy beard which covered much of his face.

"Chill it to the bone, man. We don't need the Blackguard gett'n angry on top of it all." reasoned Darkade.

"I just wanted ta have the ability ta make the choice fo myself, man!" Zom-Buckle explained. Many punks began to walk out, while others tried to vomit out everything from their stomach.

Grizz noticed a few other punks standing next to the kegs pouring more mugs full of beer. Perhaps they did not clue in that the blood was in the beer, or perhaps they knew full well what they were doing so they could contain samples of it and sell it to the highest bidder.

"Listen, man!" Darkade seemed to be turning on

Grizz as well, "Can yo fix this?"

Grizz looked Darkade in the eyes and answered, "Yes I can."

"We need yo to do better than a little advice. We need yo to create a formula, a serum or antidote that'll completely counter act the affects of yer blood."

"You got it! I just need a little time." Grizz told Darkade.

"Fine, We'll give yo six hours. Now, yo best get go'n. Yo know where ta find us or we'll find yo. In the meantime, we keep Kiki. She, we know, you care about most. It's the only true collateral we have." Darkade laid it out clearly.

Grizz just stared at them. He was fuming. "This is a dangerous game you're playing, Darkade." Grizz warned as he didn't have a clear idea how he was going to fix the problem, but he knew one way or another he would not abandon, Kiki. Looking up at Grizz with a surprised helplessness in her eyes, Kiki asked Grizz, "You won't leave me like this. Will you?"

"Do you want me to kill everyone so you and I can blow this joint or do you want me to try to help them, Kiki?" The answer to Grizz's question was obvious as the punks were important to them both.

Kiki's strength and confidence returned to her, "I can take care of myself. You know I can, so for now, it has to be this way."

Grizz hated the situation, but he was still the leader of the punks. His anger would solve nothing. "I won't fail you, Kiki. I won't fail anyone. Now, just co-operate for me."

Darkade placed his hands on Kiki's shoulders and motioned for her to sit down on a chair as others approached her with ropes. Kiki did not take her eyes off Grizz as a tear rolled down her cheek with the tightening of the ropes.

Grizz took a step to attack Darkade, before he stopped to ask, "What do you think *you* are doing?"

"Just an added incentive, Blackguard. Now go, and don't let us down." Darkade stretched out his hand for Grizz not to approach any further. Grizz burned with frustration reddening his eyes, before he turned on his heels and motored toward the staircase.

Shortly after Grizz had left the lair, Darkade went to the bar and sat next to Vamporess. There he asked her, "Yo okay? Yo seem ta be in deep thought. Need ta talk?"

Vamporess continued to stare at the stairs leading out of the lair long after Grizz was gone. Without looking away from the stairs, Vamporess told Darkade, "I don't know. I usually have a very enlightened morbid sense O humour. I'm not easily disturbed, but our new leader, he continues ta disturb me as time goes on. I'm so skeptical O him and maybe I'm crazy but I just can't help it. Something about the Blackguard." Vamporess dropped and shook her head before adding, "He's wrong fer us. I mean, look at him... Is he a villain? You know what makes him a great villain? He's always pissed. He's rough, he's tough, and he's successful, but what is he doing now? He is taking the drugs away? XD3's legacy, gone, just like that and is XD3 going ta be remembered as the villain after all is said and done? What about the money, Darkade? No drugs means no money! Is no one else worried about this? Who does the Blackguard think he is now? He came in here like the devil, now he acts like our saviour preaching clean living. "Drink my blood and yo will be cleansed." What exactly have we gotten ourselves into here?" shaking her head, Vamporess continued, "This place sucks! I mean, yo want clean living? Go fer it, but Switch looks like a pretty good indication O the long term affects of ingesting his, so called, *'magical blood.'* It just ain't natural. When will the insane hate wear off? Does it wear off?" Vamporess began to weep. "Oh, Darkade, I'm so scarred." Vamporess sucked a long drag from her cigarette and began to cough as her lungs rejected it. She butted out the rest of her cigarette in an ash tray.

"Yo heard the Blackguard, he didn't know his blood would lead to madness. He'll return. Whether he can help us or not, we will soon find out fo sure, but fo as much as he wants us ta believe he can fix this situation, I think we're about to see the Blackguard at his weakest." Darkade could not offer much hope to Vamporess, only the support of his company.

"Not this time, Darkade. I will die, or be cured. Either way, I'm going to quit the Bleeding hearts. I'm sorry. I've seen too much. I can't do this anymore. I'm not the only one, also. There was a time when being a punk meant something. A time when all O this was cool and fun. I don't know what it is anymore, but it's not cool, and it's not fun, either." Leaning into Darkade's shoulder, Vamporess sobbed. Darkade placed his hand on her back and stared out into nothing as he filled his mind with deep thoughts.

"You're so pathetic!" Kiki called out to them from the tight ropes that bound her to the wooden chair. "You don't know the Blackguard at all. He will not let anything happen to me. Not ever! The both of you are still learning."

It was almost as though the life was draining out of Grizz with each breath he took. The heaviness of the guilt that weighed upon him was far greater than he had ever known before. How would he help the punks who adored him just moments ago? He told them he would help them but truthfully, he was not in any position to help them at all.

Midnight, as Grizz made his way through Metro city, he became increasingly skeptical of anyone who looked his way. Were they spies? Were they going to try to attack him or call the authorities. Everyone seemed so edgy. Grizz just needed a quiet place to think. After heading back to his penthouse suite, Grizz marched out onto the terrace as it began to rain. He couldn't believe how quickly his world as leader of the punks fell apart on him. Just coming into possession of the immaculate penthouse suite, Grizz would now likely have to give it back. Worst of all, his best friend in the world, Kiki Vixen, was in trouble and likely feeling a sense of betrayal because he abandoned her to the punks.

Grizz literally had nothing. He needed his blood tested. How would he get an antidote prepared when he had no time to do any of it. He was still so new and unfamiliar with the city and the world, and Grizz had no idea how to get plugged into the social network.

'Would Kiki die because of this mistake?' Grizz wondered. 'How can this be? I was finally trying to do good. Now all is lost...' Grizz threw his head back and roared to the world. As he did so Grizz could feel a sense of his telepathic ability reach out and touch many minds who occupied the hotel from the lower floors. Through this, Grizz found he was no closer to finding the solution to his problem. Letting all of his breath out with the powerful roar Grizz was left feeling exhausted. Sitting down on the bench Grizz took in deep breaths of air as the rain trickled down his face. He went back inside his mind to moments of his youth. Thinking about his brothers and all he went through with them, Grizz admired not only their abilities, but the way they functioned with an air of invincibility as a team. Desiring

349

the company of his brothers at this low point of his life, Grizz's thoughts wondered to his parents and how he wished things could have worked out differently in his relation to them. Thinking about his father in particular, Grizz remembered a special connection he held with Dr. McNeil. Perhaps he was still connected to him. The last time Grizz saw Dr. McNeil, his father had written his phone number on Grizz's tattoo.

Though the number no longer existed on Grizz's tattoo, Grizz had memorized it. *'Of course, Dr. McNeil... He holds the answer to my problem.'* Grizz's mind brightened up as everything suddenly came together so simply. *'Dr. McNeil and his group of scientists must have tested my blood in everyway imaginable. If there was anyone I needed to talk to about my blood, it would be Dr. McNeil.'*

Grizz stood up in the rain and looked out over the city lights as a flash of lightning lit up the night sky. This was followed by a mighty rumble of thunder. Grizz marched into the suite and picked up the phone. He punched in his father's phone number. Placing the receiver to his ear, he listened as it rang three times. Finally, the call was answered as a voice from the other end picked up. "Hello?"

Amazing, Grizz never thought to hear the voice of his father ever again. "Dr. McNeil?" Grizz asked with his unmistakable deep voice.

"Domin? Or should I say Grizz?" Dr. McNeil asked to be sure.

"It's me, Dad." Grizz spoke with the tone of a wayward son.

"Very good, son. I wasn't sure if you would ever call. Is everything alright? I thought I'd lost you just like I lost your brothers. Where are you son. Let me know and I'll come and get you right away."

"No! I don't want none of that. I'm in trouble, dad. You hear me? I have tried to help people by administering a fraction of my blood to them. I found it makes people strong and healthy and it can break any addiction."

"Yes, Grizz. This is true. Your blood is very potent and amazing, but our research has found this to be for the short term. You can imagine how we felt when we thought we had stumbled onto a medical breakthrough in you. However, the long term affects are always the same. Madness. It takes a very special kind of person to be able to deal with the affects of volk blood. You will find you are a very special person. You seem to be born with an abnormal inner capacity, no doubt from my extensive biochemical research. It's what keeps you from falling under the strength or influence of that alien volk blood."

"Alien?" Grizz asked as if the thought never occurred to him. Sure, Grizz had thought of volks as aliens, but it sounded no less extraordinary when spoken out loud.

"Yes, son. The blood, the tissues, muscles and organs spliced into your body are not from this world. That's why it's so important for you to return to us." Dr. McNeil explained.

"Get this straight! I'm not coming back. Not alive anyway! What I need to know is what I can do to help the people whom I've infected with my blood."

"Sure, I have that information, but I can't give it to you unless we meet." Dr. McNeil insisted.

Grizz snorted into the telephone receiver and it reminded him of his new found telepathic ability. Growling into the phone, Dr. McNeil began to get nervous.

"W-what are you doing, son. Domin! Stop that!... Grizz, I want you to calm down this instant, you sound like a mad dog, for crying out loud!" The doctor was frantic and nervous as he was about to hang up the call.

Grizz stopped growling, just before he said, "Vitamin B? That's the answer? But that's so simple."

"How did you do that? We did not find your mind to ever function at the level of a telepath."

"A little gift from my brother, Narl." Grizz told him.

"Okay, that's it! I'm coming to get you right now. I'll see you soon, son." with Dr. McNeil's level of genius, he was tracing the call.

Grizz ended the call immediately. He headed for the elevator with a whole new sense of purpose.

After ransacking the nearest pharmacy, Grizz made his way back to the Bleeding Heart Lair with all of the Vitamin B the store had. Grizz quickly swallowed a handful of the pills to see if he could find any effect. He took Vitamin B100s and remembered the effects from his childhood. When Grizz was given an unlabled shot to calm him, he was actually being given vitamin B supplements. Like always the calming effects were short lived, but Grizz liked it while it lasted. For him, it was a chance to feel a little closer to being more like everybody else.

From the darkened, dank streets of the abandoned industrial lot, Grizz returned to the warehouse of the basement punk lair where he found a large group of punks outside fighting.

Somehow, Grizz should have predicted this would happen. The punks were throwing punched and knee jabs while cursing all sorts of verbal abuse. When Grizz saw chains knives and other weapons come into play, he charged in amongst the rioters. Spinning around at the core of the mini brawl like a massive beast, Grizz caused the punks to disperse and back away.

Grizz was welcomed with only high expectations, "Yo better have an antidote, pal." Fang was not cheerful to his leader. Many of the punks readied their weapons.

Fan-Tom dropped his spiked baseball bat in his hand, as Roach tightened a chain around his fore-arm. What Grizz said next was likely to unleash the anger building within the punks.

"I have what you need." Grizz told them. Immediately, Grizz began to hand out bottles of the vitamins to waiting punks. He also gave them explicit instructions, "Don't just gobble them up, okay? Only take them when you feel a darkness come over you. It is better to make these last so just take enough to lift your anger when it comes over you."

Grizz went inside to Darkade, Vamporess and many others. He gave them the same instructions.

"Vitamins?" Darkade questioned, "Yo can't cure us with vitamins, buddy!"

"No." Grizz answered. "I don't think there is a permanent cure, but you can offset the affects with Vitamin B." Grizz twisted off the cap of one of the bottles and carefully shook out a couple of tablets to the palm of his hand. He went to Kiki and put them in her mouth. As Kiki worked to swallow the vitamin tablets dry, Grizz began untying her.

"What do yo think you're doing?" Darkade asked with growing frustration, "Yo didn't uphold yer end O the deal. All yo did was give us a temporary fix. We need a cure!"

"Let me clarify this for you. All of you!" Grizz spoke loud and clear. "You are all better now than you ever were. You can fight off any drug in your system along with any virus or sickness. You are also able to heal faster than you could before. As for the anger that over powered Switch, he had no idea what was coming over him at the time, *you* all do. You now know you can take a vitamin to suppress these effects or you can draw strength from your anger as you have seen me do. It can be a source of such power and strength, you won't believe it. You will want to throw your vitamins out. How many of you have tried very hard to connect with your darker side, huh? Every one of you do this and you embrace it for all it's worth. Stop thinking of my blood as a poison or a setback, because what I gave you is a gift. Now, Quich yer crying and deal with it! By rights, each one of you will live unnaturally long lives."

Grizz slid out one of his samurai swords and cut the ropes that held Kiki. She jostled about to let the ropes fall off before standing up from the chair. Grizz lifted Kiki to one of his shoulders prior to walking out.

The punks quietly remained behind within the lair to discuss, not only what Grizz told them, but the changes they would undoubtedly have to make for their future. Nothing would ever be the same again for the members of the Bleeding Heart Punks. The blood of the Blackguard changed everything, but Grizz knew, with a little time, they would all come around and eventually regard him as the greatest leader of the Bleeding Heart Punks.

Chapter 11

Lost in the world of 'Smack & Grab Street Wars.' Two warrior clad punk fighters duke it out on main street. The two fighters had the appearance which was almost identical. They sported tri Mohawks, leather studded vests and tight leather pants with bands around their arms and high boots. One man dressed in Red and the other in Blue.

Repeated jabs were exchanged left and right, before Blue fell backwards landing hard on the black top. Red lept into the air, jumping right over Blue. Red got back up on his feet almost instantly as Red spun a round house kick striking Blue down again to the road. As Red ran toward Blue, Blue rolled along the pavement to a rocket launcher. Grabbing it and lifting it to his shoulder, Blue launched a rocket at Red. With a direct hit followed by a large explosion, Red was thrown backwards against a bus. Blue dropped the rocket launcher and walked over to a dumpster where he lifted it up with ease and threw it at Red who was just rising to his feet next to the bus. Red fell again and Blue began running toward him. Red quickly stood up turned and lifted the bus over his head. Turning with the bus lifted high, Red quickly threw the bus at Blue with incredible force. Blue was knocked off his feet where he remained sprawled out on the road, defeated.

As Red jumped up and down celebrating his victory with his fists in the air, large block letters began to flash;
"GAME OVER"

Kiki laughed, "Ha, ha, ha! I win again, Grizz! Again, again! I just love whip'n your butt!" her bright smile told how happy she was and her eyes spoke of the excitement she felt. Kiki had Grizz all to herself as they played the video game. Grizz was her best friend in the world. Sure, Kiki liked it when Grizz would invite other punks over and she played video games with them, but to her, Grizz was the best. He was Kiki's most special companion. Though Kiki was very young, she could not imagine meeting anyone who could hold a candle to her friendship with Grizz.

"Yeh, you remain undefeated to be sure." Grizz told her. "This is enough video games for me, Kiki. We've been at this since three in the morning! I can't sit here any longer." Grizz stood up from the couch and walked toward the kitchen.

"One day, some genius will make a video game about us, Grizz." Kiki spoke to Grizz, though he was behind her, or so she thought.

The immaculate suite had taken on a rather lived in look with Chinese food cartons and cola cans littering both tables and floors.

While Kiki put the video game console away, Grizz had seemed to disappear. "Grizz?" Kiki called, "Did you go outside?" Kiki went to the sliding glass door and found Grizz hadn't gone that way. She turned and headed down the hall and knocked on the door to Grizz's room. "Grizz? Are you in there?" twisting the door knob, Kiki found it was unlocked. Opening the door, Kiki peeked inside, but there was no sign of Grizz. The bathroom door was open and Grizz wasn't in there either. Concerned, Kiki ran out of the room calling out, "Grizz!!!"

A sound like a distant clang came from a door they had rarely ever opened. Kiki opened the door and found Grizz laying on his back on a weight lifting bench. He was bench pressing, 1000 lbs easily. As always, Kiki was amazed at the power Grizz possessed, as he was like a machine.

Kiki silently watched Grizz workout until he could hardly lift the flexing bar anymore.

"You know, if you're going to lift that much weight, I don't think I'm going to make a very good spotter." getting Grizz's attention, Kiki observed.

Grizz grunted, sitting up nursing his sore muscles. Chuckling, he replied, "You're probably right. That sure felt good though. I'm not expecting you to ever spot me." Grizz looked at Kiki like he was very proud of her. "Kiki, what was it that attracted you to want to be a punk?" Grizz asked kindly, preparing for his next workout. Sliding down the bench a little where he looped each of his legs through the padded bars, Grizz continued his exercise lifting more weights. With his legs powerfully working the extra-ordinary weight, Kiki decided to climb onto the bars as Grizz pushed them up and down.

Enjoying the free ride, Kiki explained to Grizz why the life of a punk was for her, "The everyday normalcy of life is boring, Grizz. We are punks. We don't want to be like everybody else, or society's narrow minded version of how we're all supposed to be. One mold, only we don't fit that mold. Look at us. We are punks! Each individualized and unique. Honest to who we are on the inside by expressing ourselves on the outside. Not one of us is pretending to me someone we are not, like a saint. People who seem extremely good scare me, because they must be covering for something. They must have something to hide. Punks are real people, even more real than average people who are just controlled by the rest of society. We are walking works of art and each one is beautiful to me, but not everyone shares my opinion. Punks scare average people because they think we clash against their life style, but they don't understand. They probably don't even realize the masks they are all hiding behind." Kiki shuttered, "You see why *that*, to me, is scary? If everyone was true to who they are on both the inside along with the outside, could you imagine how much more hideous the average man, woman and child would look? Perhaps then punks wouldn't seem so out of place." Kiki almost lost her footing on the pumping apparatus. Grizz pause in mid repetition before she continued, "Now let me show you what punks are all about. First, you must know the punk society is segmented in various outfits and within each outfit we have multiple levels.

"Like gangs?" Grizz questioned her under pressure.

Kiki was not comfortable with this comparison, but after she thought about it, she answered, "A few similarities could be argued as parallels, but we are far more complex than some random street gang. We have a wide range of people who come from the very rich and successful, to the average young dreamer and we are all mixed together into one place. How deep you want to go depends on what level your capable of managing. It requires a punk to be very strong, and you Grizz? No one is stronger than you, but all who join must prove their loyalty first, as you did, with an initiation."

Grizz rose up from his workout, "That's it then? You simply have some sort of insight as to what a true punk is so you wanted to be one? Somehow I thought your story was deeper than that." Grizz was a smooth operator. He knew how to work his words to press Kiki's buttons and get her to talk to him.

"You want deeper? Fine," Kiki took a breath before she dived into the meat of her past. "My real father and mother were punk rockers. My father was killed in a knifing. My mother lost it and through a series of misfortunes that led to her jail sentence she could no longer support my brother and I. She, herself was an outcast so there was no other family to fall back on. She gave me and my brother up to a foster home. My brother was a professional yo-yo expert. I learned a lot from him and whenever I use my yo-yo, I am reminded of my brother. It was from him and our fun play fighting techniques where I learned to use my yo-yo for the real thing. My brother and I were going to always stick together, but when he was adopted into a separate family, we knew we would never see one another ever again. I was finally adopted by a strange Vietnamese family. My new step mom worked very hard at a law firm. My new step father on the other hand, worked as a professional clown. His name was Bolo Chiba and his professional name was Bolo the Clown. He was a lot of fun and he sure knew how to make me laugh… but he knew how to make me cry too. Bolo was trained in the martial arts because he could do things that defied gravity. He made me do one of three things for twelve hours straight each day, either jump rope, throw darts, or shoot archery. Bolo taught me a few of his clown tricks as well, but if I made a mistake or couldn't get it right, he would make me do painful exercises. As a clown, he was a top notch professional and there was no other who could compare. Bolo had it all, but it took a lot of discipline. Funny and fluent, Bolo didn't have to speak English to do what he did. I was with that family for four years. I hated them. I needed to find out more about my real parents. I cried to see my mother in prison, but no one would take me. I was just a girl, right? So I became louder and louder until they had no choice. They took me to the prison with the idea that if I saw my mother I would become a good girl. When I finally sat down across from my real birth mother, I found she was a burnt out soul of a person. She couldn't recognize me. When I looked in her familiar but distant eyes, I found she had given up on everything.

Even though I couldn't speak to my mother, I did have all of my questions answered from my mother's personal psychiatric nurse. I needed to know the history of my parents and the history of my family. I saw her face haunting my own reflection whenever I looked into the mirror. I decided I would never again be the helpless little girl, the good girl, forced to accept a life not my own or let myself go so unprotected that I end up like my mother. I stood up to my foster parents and fought Bolo Chiba. Bolo hurt me real bad but he couldn't finish me off. I was a little girl and he took pity on me, the same way you did, Grizz."

Grizz waved his finger, "Uh, uh, uh... Let's not go there, ever again, understand?"

Kiki half smiled as she looked away to ignore him. "I left their home and I have been rotting inside ever since. Well, until I met you, that is. You make me feel alive. I selected this specific punk look from what I remember from pictures I was shown of my real mother and father when they were young, in their prime and in love with each other. I became a homeless street kid and I learned not to ever set boundaries for myself. Learning to depend on myself became a welcomed freedom. One I highly value."

"I lived day to day and once I was picked up by police as they conducted a spontaneous raid at a shelter. They questioned me, but I had no records or history to tell them about. The police finally matched me up to a missing girl report. I was told they would soon send me back to where I came from, so I took care of matters, *Kiki style*. The police won, but I didn't make it easy for them. Rather than sending me back to where I came from, they sent me to a strange interrogative professional who tested me to find my limitations. It was many days and very intensive. I had to keep my wits about me. I had to fight with everything I had. After that, I was sent to the Knolix Island where I first met you."

"I reason for myself now, for example, to be alone is merely a deepening thought of self pity. Being around people will not make you accepted. You can live in a home full of people and still feel very alone. It is a perception from someone who is their own worst enemy. Happiness does not come from anywhere else but from within. I hope that advice will help you, Grizz."

"Thank you, Kiki, for sharing your story with me. I wish we had a moment like this back when we lived on the Island. You're a smart girl, smarter than any other ten year old girl I have ever met. I feel I know you so much better now." Grizz told her sincerely, "So where do you see yourself going from here?"

"I go where life takes me, but if I could choose the course, I have always wanted a man to one day treat me well. My father was not that man. I just want to be number one in someone's life. Someone special. He and I would go out to an extravagant dinner like the one, I heard my father made for my mother many years ago. Mainly, I don't want to live a poor life ever again."

Kiki's comment intrigued Grizz, so he questioned her, "But I thought you said you value your freedom. *I* was the most free when I was poor. If you take the beauty out of this place, it could quickly become the dungeon at the top of a tower." Grizz told her.

Kiki realized Grizz did not know the importance of money. "Grizz, having money means you do not have to be hungry. Money means a place to live, clothes to wear, you know what I mean? A life! Without it you are poor and it can be very hard to get. Just ask Jim Vanderwal, he owns the Mulberry Bryor Casino and is the most wealthy man in Metro city. Here, you can read about it." Kiki tossed Grizz a magazine of the Metro Daily Times which featured an article about the extravagant life of Jim Vanderwal. Grizz flipped through a few pages of the magazine. Not seeing anything too spectacular, Grizz did notice the article mention something about how Jim Vanderwal was the only man to posses the Kamisauri Dragon Heart medallion. Though Grizz couldn't see anything suspicious, he was somehow interested. Perhaps a potential opportunity was here somewhere.

"Money is for the weak!" Grizz told her bluntly, "If you want something in life you just have to go out there and take it."

Kiki laughed at him, "Oh, Grizz you can be such a joker."

Grizz was very serious, "It's no joke, Kiki. Tomorrow, I will show you. The world can be yours if you just go out there and take it."

Kiki shook her head trying to contain her smile, "Heh, okay, Grizz, tomorrow you can show me what you're talking about." Kiki got up and her eyes seemed to widen in a daze of realization. "That reminds me, I have something for you. I was waiting for the right moment and, well, now is as good a time as any." Kiki ran to her room as Grizz wandered into the kitchen again. Kiki returned with a white box and slid it onto the counter in front of Grizz. The young girl was bouncing as she was so excited. "I'm sorry, I didn't wrap it."

"Am I supposed to care?" Grizz asked. He opened the box easily and to Grizz's astonishment he found a large round white object inside. "Hhph, ah, ya, thank you Kiki. It is very nice." Grizz told her and he turned like he was going to walk away.

Kiki quickly stopped Grizz by holding him back with her hands. "No, wait, do you even know what it is?"

"Sure, it's a gift and I am very grateful." Grizz replied as graciously as he could, but he was truly feeling very tired and was wanting to go to bed.

"Not just a gift. It's a yo-yo, only it's not like any yo-yo you have ever seen before. This was custom built by my specifications from a very good wood worker who's also a Bleeding Heart member. Please, please try it out." Kiki tried to lift the yo-yo out of the box, but it was large and awkward. Grizz easily pulled it out of the box and lifted it up. It was ten inches across and larger than any other yo-yo he had ever seen. Kiki found the string and a large wide band at the end of it. Taking the band, assisting Grizz to slip it in place, Kiki said, "This has to go over your right hand. You see, mine is tied to my middle finger, but yours is so big it would tear your finger from your hand." Kiki told Grizz as she tightened the band snug.

Grizz had never used a yo-yo before in his life. He tilted his hand and let the yo-yo roll out. It unwound as it descended until the string was at length before it began to recoil up the other way. Grizz did not add any momentum to the yo-yo so it finally just wound out.

"I will never get this one, Kiki." lifting the yo-yo up Grizz used his free hand to coil the string around the center axil.

"This will define you, Grizz, and you will become so famous." Kiki told him. "How can you live in this penthouse without fitting into the role?"

"Famous?" Grizz asked Kiki what she meant.

"You will be famous. I believe it. I'm also going to be famous. It's what I've always wanted and I'm going to do it by just being myself. People have never taken me seriously. For one thing, I'm a girl. I'm also a very young girl. But mainly it's because I am a punked up young girl!" With a giggle, Kiki nuzzled in close to Grizz. She too was feeling drowsy. Grizz lifted Kiki up into his arms as colors of fire brightened the distant sky.

As the sun continued to light up the clouds with golden linings and the first beams of the sun stretched out from the horizon, Grizz and Kiki became very tired and decided to go to bed, for they were night people. They each made their ways to their own bedrooms where they locked their doors. With the magazine sporting a featured article of Jim Vanderwal, rolled up in Grizz's back pocket, Grizz hurried to bed for he had some interesting night reading to brush up on.

Grizz liked nothing more than to spoil Kiki as much as he could. When the two of them awoke, to the buzz of their alarm clocks at the start of another night. After ordering pizza and potato chips, Grizz and Kiki ate within the theater room where they enjoyed an action suspense movie in 3D.

Grizz began putting together a list in his mind of all the things he wanted to do, but he knew there was not a lot of hours in the day to accomplish everything.

"Let's get on with our day, Kiki. I found this key in the drawer of my night table. I called Darkade to ask him what it was for and apparently, a car is waiting for us to take it for a spin." Grizz shook the new keys and they twinkled in his hand.

Kiki's smile stretched across her face. The two of them took the elevator all the way down to the parking garage. Grizz knew to use one of the keys to unlock a separate garage door. When the large door lifted, they gazed wondrously upon XD3's old hummer. It was dark blue and in immaculate condition.

Jumping into the hummer and checking it out, Kiki said, "If we knew this was here we wouldn't have had to do so much walking."

Grizz fired up the engine and turned on the high beams as they rolled out of the private stall. Kiki took over the satellite radio as soon as they drove out of the underground parking.

They drove around the city streets until they became bored and decided to stop at the largest mall in the world, the Metro-City mall. Though Grizz and Kiki didn't fit in with the other people at the mall, they ignored the odd glances and pretended the other people did not exist at all. They ate at the food court, Kiki tried on some clothes for Grizz and he bought her what she wanted. Kiki played around with some of the make-up but she wore it like it was heavy paint which made the sales lady upset.

After browsing the different stores, Grizz drove Kiki to the Metro amusement park at the ocean's edge of the city. They went on every crazy ride there, but the one they rode the most was the Colossal roller coaster. This one had the seats suspended from the over head tracks and it twisted every which way, even all the way around in loops.

As Grizz and Kiki walked together along the board walk, each eating cotton candy, Kiki stopped and froze up when she spotted a clown walking in her direction. "Is that Bolo the clown?" Grizz suspiciously asked though the odds were not very likely it could be the Bolo the clown.

"No, he isn't. I just hate clowns is all. Let's go." Kiki cuddled into Grizz and added, "I want to go home right now."

As they walked past the clown, Grizz tripped him causing his arms and legs to flail about before he fell head first into a garbage barrel. Everyone who saw this laughed.

When Grizz saw how Kiki was exhausted he checked his to do list and found there was just a couple of things left he wanted to do.

"Come with me, Kiki. I have somewhere special I

want to take you now." They drove to the main casino in town. It was the Mulberry Bryor Casino. As they drove near they saw it was covered entirely with decorative blinking lights. It looked like the casino was plucked right out of Las Vagas.

The valet parked the hummer and Grizz strolled into the casino with Kiki on his arm.

Upon entering the casino, Grizz and Kiki's eyes were opened to the wealth and magic of the casino. Looking around, the two of them were amazed at the excitement, energy and resourceful advanced technology of the gambling scene. The busy people and ringing sounds created a mood that seemed almost hypnotic. A lucky feeling was shared by all who attended. Recent big winners were advertised on huge digital billboards both inside and out. The gamblers visiting the Mulberry Bryor Casino had dreams of have there own names showing up on the magnificent bill boards.

There were multiple levels which Grizz and Kiki could look upon. The different levels divided the casino into slots, black jack, craps, roulette along with every other contemporary type of gambling means. "No wonder Jim Vanderwal is the richest man in the city." Grizz pointed out in awe.

"Grizz, did you bring me here because of the magazine I showed you?" Kiki asked with a knowing smirk.

Grizz looked down at Kiki who was looking up at him expecting an answer, "I am here to prove a point to you." Grizz explained.

"If you want something, just take it?" Kiki recalled some of Grizz's wisdom.

"That's right." Grizz looked back out across the wide expanse of activity. "Only, this will not be taken by any primitive means. I will have to give this one a little more thought."

"You don't have to do this, Grizz. Let's just enjoy ourselves and who knows, perhaps we will win big tonight."

"Win big? Don't shoot so low, girl. I want this Mulberry Bryor Casino and by the end of the night it will be mine. It will *all* be mine." Grizz told her with a sense of arrogant power in his voice. "For now, let's have a little fun."

Grizz went to the counter to get some coins for the slot machines. The attendant charged Grizz for two buckets of coins and handed them to both Grizz and Kiki. "Nice outfits. Is the circus in town?" The attendant asked hoping they would laugh at his little joke, but both Grizz and Kiki just gave the attendant a serious glare.

Quickly forgetting about the rude comment, Grizz and Kiki joined the crowd to play some games.

As Kiki walked with Grizz, she passed near to another young girl who was about her age, walking in the opposite direction. The little rich girl was dress to the nines with a thin white dress. She had beautiful blue eyes with her blond hair done up high. Around her neck was a pearl necklace and draped over her shoulders was the softest white fur scarf. She looked at Kiki as her eyes became tense with the expression of repulsiveness.

Kiki half smiled as she had dealt with her kind many times in the past. When the two girls were next to one another, Kiki said, "Hey, snob, you tired of your boring life yet? Call me when you're ready to loosen up and party." Making a punk rocker hand gesture, Kiki opened her mouth in a big smile and hung her tongue out.

The little rich girl was not impressed by Kiki in the least and replied with, "Get out of my face, punk." The little rich girl quickly shuffled away from Kiki to catch up to her parents.

Kiki played the slots quickly. In no time, all of her coins were gone and she was none the richer. Kiki did not care that she didn't win anything, she was determined to have fun. Still blowing his coins, Grizz was playing to win while Kiki began skipping around. Kiki soon stopped and leaned against Grizz to watch him play his last few coins.

She watched as Grizz put a coin into a machine and nothing happened. Grizz shook the machine and one of the casino's staff walked up to Grizz and said, "Sir, you must not shake the machines."

"It took my last coin." Grizz told the man. "My lucky coin!"

"Very well sir, we will get you a new coin." The casino staff member suggested politely.

"I don't want a new coin!" Grizz told him strictly, "I am about to win with this machine, that's why it jammed. Don't you see? My last coin was my lucky coin. I bet it's designed to do this so I don't win!"

"Sir, I assure you that is an absurd suggestion."

"Forget it! I'll fix it myself." Grizz told him and turned to the slot machine.

"Oh, brother…" Kiki said as she stepped back.

Grizz gave the slot machine a couple of light kidney punches in hopes of loosening up his coin. "Sir, I demand you stop what you are doing at once!" Grizz was told. When he found he was not getting his desired results, he pulled the clear plastic display window off and moved the little rollers inside. He turned the little fruit pictures until there were cherries, cherries, cherries. The lights began to blink and the bells began to ring and the money came pouring out.

"Awe, I knew it!" Grizz said as he placed his bucket low to the inner tray which was quickly filling with coins. As Grizz scooped coins into his bucket, he looked to his left then to his right but Kiki was nowhere to be seen.

Meanwhile, the staff security bouncers were called to the scene. Grizz was told the coins were not his and they asked him to leave. One bouncer tried to take the bucket of coins from Grizz but Grizz would not relinquish it. Another bouncer hit the bucket and it flew from Grizz's hand and spilled across the floor.

"Sir, you must leave now! Don't make us call the authorities." Shouted the casino staff worker.

At that moment, the lights went out. Grizz seized the opportunity and escaped the bouncers. Once outside, Grizz soon found Kiki. "Hey, did you?..." noticing a new necklace around Kiki's neck with a medallion of a golden dragon curled around a red ruby, Grizz seemed to speak to Kiki by simply locking his gaze with her eyes, whereby he just knew what she was thinking. It looked like the medallion was very expensive, but Grizz was still getting to know her. He thought, perhaps it had been there the whole time.

Smiling and shrugging her shoulders, Kiki answered, "Maybe I did." Kiki's smile suggested she was getting away with something. Later she told Grizz how she used one of her darts to cut the power at the main breaker box and disable all of the power to everything, even the security system.

A ring tone was heard and Kiki responded to it, only she didn't carry a cell phone on her. She looked at Grizz and said, "You are ringing."

Grizz looked at her as though awakening from a daze. Twisting this way and that, Grizz inspected his hips. Grizz was not used to carrying a cell phone, but he did recall tucking one away in his back pocket before they left the penthouse. Finding the cell phone on his night table, Grizz finally decided to carry it with him but he never expected it to ever ring.

Kiki plucked the phone from Grizz's back pocket which proved she had some experience at pick pocketing. Opening the clam shell phone Kiki said, "Hello?" Kiki looked at Grizz and smiled. "This is Kiki. I know this is supposed to be the Blackguard's phone, he is very busy you know. He's right here, I'll get him for you." Grizz was very curious as to who the voice at the other end of his call could possibly be. Kiki held the phone out to Grizz and said, "Oh, it's for you."

"Who is it?" Grizz asked.

"Darkade." Kiki answered. "He wants to know if you can meet with him."

'Darkade?' Grizz thought, *'I might be able to use his help.'* Grizz began to formulate a plan. "Hello." Grizz said, "I'm not able to meet with you today, I'll have to see you tomorrow, I'm about to enter some heated business negotiations with Jim Vanderwal."

Darkade asked Grizz about the details of his business pitch to Jim. He warned Grizz of the dangers of doing business with some of the city's top dogs, but Grizz was going to have contact with Jim one way or another. Darkade referred Grizz to another Punk, Digger. Digger by trade was a highly successful banker and investor. He had connections to many other esteemed investors and philanthropists. His professional name was Doug.

Grizz took Darkade's advice and called Digger. Digger was happy to speak to Grizz, he had some questions as to what exactly Grizz was after but though it was somewhat far fetched, Grizz expressed the importance of the punks to have a dependable source of income which would be more profitable than the drug trade ever was. Digger asked Grizz, "What are you planning to do, execute some hostile take over?"

Grizz answered, "I think of it more like a hostile

business agreement."

"Well, let's try not to hurt anyone with this one, alright?" Digger advised while walking the edge of being offensive. Digger picked up on the awkwardness of the silence and quickly continued, "So, in short, you want to have the Mulberry Bryor Casino as the new source of income to subsidize our losses in the drug trade for the Bleeding Heart Punks?"

"Correct!" Grizz answered.

"I'm in, let the negotiations begin." Digger hung up on Grizz and immediately called Jim Vanderwal's personal banker. The personal banker listened to the proposal before he called Jim Vanderwal to see if the fish would bite at the bait.

Digger proved to be very dependable as he had a keen understanding as to what Grizz was after. He had faith and guts along with information, but before he hung up, Digger had a few comments to make to Grizz about how his blood was working out in his life.

Jim asked his banker, "Is this offer for real?"

Jim's banker answered, "I have checked him out thoroughly. His name is the Blackguard. He's legit. He's been rising up as the new leader of the Metro City punks who call themselves the Bleeding Hearts. He has taken over for XD3. The punks think the world of this new leader, the Blackguard. Apparently he can be very dangerous. He has targeted the Mulberry Bryor Casino and wants to buy it."

Jim's first reaction was laughter, "It's not for sale." Jim said as though the whole idea was ludicrous.

Jim's banker was quick to respond, "Very well, sir. I'll let him know, before I let him go."

Jim, However, had a change of heart as he was about to let the whole thing go. He hated to let a good opportunity pass him up. "Hold on, how much was he offering?" It only made sense to look into it further, for the deal would never have to go through unless he agreed to it.

Jim's banker answered, "He offered $100,000,000.00"

The said amount surprised Jim, "What? Is he good for that much dough? Hmmm, I'll make him a counter offer, $300,000,000.00. Let's see what kind of response we get from that."

This led to Jim's banker and Digger engaging in some heated words. After Digger called Grizz and told him how the deal was going, Grizz insisted they all join in a four way call. Kiki hit a button on the key pad and the tiny cell phone switched to external speakers to she could listen as well.

After this link was agreed to and established, Grizz spoke directly to Jim Vanderwal, "I won't pay as much as you suggest, but I would be willing to make a trade, my hotel for your casino, straight up. Business for business. The esteemed five star Rosetta hotel for the stand alone, top casino of Metro City, the Mulberry Bryor Casino."

Jim didn't even seem to think about the new offer, "No, I change my mind. Forget it!"

"You're making a mistake." Grizz told him with his flat low tone.

Jim did not respond well, "Don't try to muscle me, you punk." With a jab below the belt, Jim tried to establish dominance and control over Grizz before he added, "Understand this pal, you've heard my decision. I never go back on my word. You and I are finished!"

"Want a bet?" Grizz asked with a sly sense of confidence.

"Huh?" Jim was momentarily caught off guard.

Grizz continued, "Let's make this next wager really

worth your time. I'm new here. This kind of business is a strange field to me. Let's just make a simple bet then. I win, I get the casino. You win, you get the Hotel. I have never been any good at gambling. I have never placed a bet in my life until now, with you, here, now. This is very simple. All you have to do is answer my riddle and you get the Metro Hotel."

"So what's the riddle?" Jim asked, knowing he hadn't agreed to anything.

"First, I have a question for you. Do you know of a golden dragon that is clawed tightly around a red ruby. Perhaps a necklace of sorts?" Grizz asked.

Kiki was shocked Grizz would say this. Reaching up, Kiki held tightly to the medallion that hung around her neck. Grizz put his finger to his lips for Kiki to be quiet, next he whispered to her, "It will be fine. You'll see." Grizz tried to calm Kiki with a reassuring wink.

Kiki was no less worried. When Kiki knocked out the power to the casino earlier, she was able to gain access to a safe in a back office. With incredible speed Kiki, with her amazing talent, felt she was owed the right to snoop through the contents of the safe. Her fingers played over the contents and stopped at the touch of the medallion. Before Kiki decided to take the medallion, it was in her possession as she bolted back into the crowd of gamblers.

Now, since Grizz figured out Kiki's little secret, she suspected he was in the process of turning her in.

"Awe, yes, it seems you've read the article about the Kamisauri dragon heart necklace in the Metro Daily Times. It is very rare and valuable. Now, enough of this, what is your riddle, Blackguard?" Jim was becoming impatient. It sounded like he was about to hang up any second.

"Very well, you have been very patient, here is the

riddle. There is only one necklace called the Kamisauri Dragon Heart. Is it safely in your possession, in the possession of Emperor Kamisauri or in my possession right now?"

"Blackguard, is this your riddle?" Jim asked. Grizz could hear Jim cover the phone and speak to someone else who was with him at the time, "This guy's like, retarded or something."

"Yes, I told you I am not very good at this, but if you accept the bet and try to answer my riddle, I will ask you to provide details to the item's location."

Jim was silent for a moment as he thought about the strange riddle. He couldn't believe anyone would know the location where the medallion was, much less the combination to the safe where it was kept. Looking at his phone, Jim knew if the medallion had been moved, his phone would have rung with an extension of the security alarm. Either the computer would have contacted his phone or his staff would have called to report it missing. *'No, it is a trick. They want me to doubt myself using a pathetic intimidation tactic of uncertainty. They won't mess with me. No one will.'* Finally Jim answered, "I accept your riddle, but you must know, when I give you the correct answer, ownership of the Rosetta Hotel will be signed over to me immediately. Our bankers are standing by."

"I'm such a sucker. Very well, Mr. Vanderwal." Grizz answered with a tone of his own self doubt.

"Is the link established?" Jim asked the two bankers who were still listening on the line.

"The link is established, sir." each of the bankers answered.

"Very good, the location of the Kamisauri Dragon Heart is locked safely within a state of the art safe in the back room of the main floor of the Mulberry Bryor

Casino. It is virtually impossible to get into the safe and if ever someone was able to break into it, an alert signal would be sent to me via computer to this phone. This is how I know with complete certainty that the necklace is still there."

"Very good, Jim." Grizz said to everyone.

"Ha, I am a Hotel richer. Let me know when the deed has been transferred to my name." Jim said to the bankers, before he added, "Thank you, Blackguard. There are no heart feeling in this matter I presume because it was your idea after all. It was a pleasure to have this encounter with you, I would like to thank you in person if you would be willing to do so."

"Not exactly." Grizz told him. "Doug, do not complete a transfer of any kind."

"Hey! You made a deal. Now, you are obligated to honor it!" Jim was getting very frustrated. "I'm going to have to ask my lawyer to join us on the line."

"That might not be necessary." Grizz explained, "All we need is for someone to verify the location of the Kamisauri Dragon Heart and we will be able to finalize this deal."

From the four way call, Jim called the casino and asked the manager there to check the safe. Jim was informed of a power problem throughout the entire establishment before a possible sabotage was reported. Finally, the manager reported the Kamisauri Dragon Heart was stolen. "You are a dirty under handed thief, Blackguard and I will not make a deal with the likes of you. Because of your trickery, I expect you to return your stolen property to me or I will call the authorities and throw the book at you."

"You have already, legally agreed to the deal. I will have the medallion returned to you in the hour, and don't call me a thief. I am an exceptional businessman. One you won't be forgetting anytime soon."

Grizz closed his cell phone and held his palm out to Kiki. She knew she had to give the medallion up to Grizz, but Kiki didn't like it.

In honor of the agreement, the bankers signed the deed to the casino over to the Blackguard, but Grizz insisted for half of the ownership to be signed over to Kiki as well. There was a problem with the signing because of Kiki's age, but Grizz continued to press for her to be included because if it weren't for her steeling the Kamisauri Dragon Heart medallion, the deal wouldn't have gone through at all. Digger informed Grizz they would meet the following day with Darkade where the papers would be signed and finalized.

Jim ranted and raged on the other end of Digger's line as he shouted obscenities about how he was tricked and robbed.

Bending forward, Grizz closed Digger's cell phone hanging up on Jim. Grizz turned to Kiki and said, "This whole place is now ours, fifty fifty. Come on, let's go get something to eat. It'll be my treat."

Grizz drove Kiki to a very luxurious and expensive dinner with a spectacular ocean view. The first thing he ordered was an apple juice and to have it poured into two wine glasses, for Kiki was far too young to drink wine. It wouldn't have mattered, of course, if they did drink wine, because the volk blood in their system would counter act any drug, poison or alcohol but the apple juice was a choice that wouldn't be questioned.

Looking out across the ocean, Grizz wondered what was happening on the Knolix Island. He remembered Eddy Evon, his half brother volk which led his thoughts to his father. Grizz shook his head, for he was at dinner with his best friend and he didn't want to bring

377

unpleasant thoughts to mind while he celebrated with her. Lifting his glass of apple juice in the fancy wine glass, Grizz made a toast. "As I said, 'If you want something, just take it!' Cheers!" Grizz noticed a red sparkle come from the ruby of Kiki's medallion.

Kiki touched the rim of her champagne glass to the edge of Grizz's and giggled before saying, "Lesson learned." Kiki took a sip, "You do realize, of course, if this deal doesn't work out and you fall flat on your face, I'm going to tell you, I told you so." Kiki giggled some more. "Grizz, don't you feel different now?" asked Kiki.

"Should I?" Grizz counter asked.

"Well sure, don't you see? You're much more than the leader of the punks. You've become the Kingpin of Metro cities gambling monopoly. You have power over the rich."

Grizz snorted with a half chuckle like Kiki was over exaggerating. Kiki giggled even more. "You said money was for the weak. Now, however, you will see just how powerful money can make a man."

Chapter 12

A delivery was made to the penthouse of Grizz and Kiki. Grizz was not sure if he should accept the strange package, but when Kiki heard there was a package that needed a signature, she jumped up and ran to the elevator.

"Let me see who the sender is!" Kiki said ecstatically as she seemed to recognize the company who sent the package. It read Zentarus Aerotechnical division. "Oh, it's here! It's really here!" Kiki signed for the package and asked Grizz to pay the delivery person.

Grizz did so and he figured out he was always expected to give a generous tip. As soon as the delivery guy was on his way down the elevator, Kiki ran to the dining table and put the package on it. Tearing the package open right away, Grizz's curiosity grew.

Walking up behind Kiki, Grizz craned his neck to see what was in the package, but Kiki was already busy trying to explain what it was through her excitement. "I had a dream of you and I against the world, and the only weapons we had were our sling shots. I know my sling shot and it was the same one I used in my dream but you had something with the most interesting design." Kiki's sling shot was not a special design in any way, but when she pulled out a sling shot from the box, it was like nothing Grizz had ever seen before. The handle was loaded full of metal ball bearings and the base of the handle had a fore arm brace for added wrist support. The top of the "Y" was extended out by two feet with the elastic tubing attached out there. The elastic tubing was not much longer than Kiki's sling shot but to pull it back would mean by an extra two feet.

"Alright, listen, I contacted this company Zentarus

Aerotechnical division because they specialize in the latest sling shots. I did this shortly after I returned to the mainland but I didn't know I would ever see you again. I showed them my designs and they liked them. They also added a specialized rubber to it. It's something new with twice the stretch of typical sling shot rubber tubing. When you shoot this puppy off, it will be like the compound bows of sling shots. It has the power of a gun and the ball bearings they sent with it are shaped like cute little footballs." Kiki lifted one out of a pouch. "See? Streamline for speed and solid for destruction. We could design some that could detonate on impact. That'd be cool."

Grizz lifted the sling shot in his hand and examined it. "Is this a gift?" He asked with a shrug.

"Yes it is. Only someone with your strength could use it. I also designed it to fold up in a compact way so it won't be cumbersome to carry around." Kiki answered.

Grizz turned to Kiki and set the sling shot back in the box, "Thank you, Kiki. It is the most thoughtful gift I have ever received in my life. Well, next to the yo-yo you had also designed for me." Grizz told her as he bent down and gently gave her a hug.

With a few quaint weapons packed away in a duffle bag, Grizz and Kiki drove to the punk lair to meet with Darkade and Digger. There, many of the punks were present. Darkade had previously prepared the punks to hear news from the Blackguard. As Kiki and Grizz walked in, side by side, they heard the surrounding punks snickering at them.

Kiki caught sight of the stage and her eyes twinkled with excitement. She looked up at Grizz before telling him, "I think I'll skip the meeting this time, Grizz. A girl's gott'a practice once in a while you know." Kiki smiled and krinkled her nose before she ran to join Vamporess on the sound stage with the band.

Cratorface opened the door for Grizz to enter the private chamber. Within the private chamber, Grizz met with Digger and Darkade. Quickly greeting one another before getting down to business, Digger briefly went through all of the necessary paper work which finalized the deal of ownership of the Mulbury Bryor Casino.

"I had ta git pretty involved with Digger ta bring everything ta a head without having it get messy and go ta court. Jim Vanderwal was beside himself, he totally came unglued, but he understands the world O business and when yo make a poor choice yo ultimately have ta live with the circumstances. We will have ta lay low fo a while in hopes that time will help us ta disappear from his radar or Jim'll retaliate and it won't be pretty." Darkade explained.

"So, we don't need to worry about Jim? He's not a threat?" Grizz asked.

"Jim'll always be a threat ta us fo now on, potentially." Darkade answered. "Now, what I called yo here fo was our pressing new business. The Snake Skull Rocker's leader, who goes by the name, Warhead, who has declared a turf war on us. They know XD3 no longer leads the punks so they're under the impression we're weak and leaderless."

"I wasn't aware we ever had a problem with the Rockers in the past." Grizz said, "I thought they were our allies. I mean, they're just like us, practically, aren't they?"

Darkade provided a prompt answer, "Yo're right Blackguard, but something has changed and I'm not sure what it is. They're not our allies anymore. They want ta push us out and take over our turf. They would never try this when XD3 was our leader, but like I said, they think we're weak and they have more guns than we do."

"I'll show them who's weak…" Grizz added his comment with reputed indignation.

"They're planning on coming here, right ta us, tomorrow night. They intend ta wipe us out an take our lair as there own. Don't get me wrong, this's a very real threat." warned Darkade with fear quivering in his eyes.

"We need to inform the others." Grizz told them.

"We're not strong enough ta stop'em, Blackguard. We'll surely lose this one." Darkade told him.

"You're incorrect. We're just getting started and nothing is going to stop us now!" Grizz laid it out for him, and reminded him of the preparations they had made. With that said, Grizz stood up and marched out of the private chamber.

Kiki was on the stage during the meeting. Kiki had a unique friendship with Vamporess and she loved to practice songs with the band. In the midst of their practice, Vamporess stopped Kiki and walk with her to a private table. There, Vamporess lifted Kiki onto her lap and asked her quietly, "Kiki, I don't know how ta say stuff like this so I'll just cut right ta it. I'm yer friend and I'm here fo yo. I want ta help yo, if you need it. Yo're only ten years old, but yo're not alone." Vamporess took a deep breath. "Has Grizz ever tried anything inappropriate when yo were alone with'im?"

Kiki was surprised by the suggestion, however she smiled calmly and told Vamporess, "If Grizz was a bad person, I'd beat him up again and I think he knows it." Giggling Kiki added, "Don't worry. You have nothing to worry about. There's no man more honourable than Grizz."

Grizz went straight to the stage where the band was sitting around lazily. No music was being made. Stepping up onto the stage, Grizz began to address everyone, "I have been informed we are under threat of the Snake Skull Rockers who will be invading our turf tomorrow night to drive us out or extinguish us entirely, but I say this is a great opportunity for you to put your anger to the test. We will not fall, rather we will turn this situation against them and take their turf!"

The punks were eating it up, "Yeah!" they cheered.

"If they come at us with a fist they better be prepared to get punched. If they come at us with a knife, they better be prepared to get cut. If they come at us with a gun they better be prepared to take a bullet. What ever strength they use against us, by the same strength it will be used against them, plus a little extra. Lay off your vitamins and feel it! Let the anger course through your veins and give you power and strength. Do you feel it? You are invincible and no one can stop you!" Grizz ended his encouraging speech with a low rumbling growl.

Cutting his growl short, Grizz was surprised to find he'd come into a little knowledge through his limited telepathic ability. The punks could not fully give their attention to Grizz because to them there was an elephant, of sorts, in the room. Though, Grizz was aware of how the punks believed there was some inappropriate activity between himself and Kiki. This news inadvertently astonished Grizz as he wanted to ignore the rumours how he was being looked upon as a cradle robber. The punks were not comfortable with Grizz, their leader spending all of his time with a girl as young as Kiki.

However, because Grizz was standing on the stage when the information came to him, he said, "Hey!!!" Glaring at each punk in the room, Grizz made sure he established eye contact with each one. "I get the sense, many of you do not feel comfortable when you see me and Kiki Vixen together." *'Sick minded fools.'*

Grizz looked at Kiki and she made eye contact with him and there was something he saw in her eyes he had never seen before. Grizz found something apparent within his grizzly heart at that moment though he did not say anything about it, but they loved one another despite the fact their friendship was without romance. The unmeasurable respect Grizz felt for Kiki prevented him from ever contemplating hurting her or ruining their special friendship in anyway.

"I am going outside now to warm up and practice before the brawl. You are all welcome to join me. Perhaps I can teach you something new. If any of you still wonder about what is going on between Kiki and myself, I ask you to stay behind, as Kiki will take the stage to answer any and all of your questions." Grizz told them.

Grabbing the duffle bag, Grizz headed up the stairs. Many punks followed Grizz outside. Many of the punks had a new found sense of respect for Grizz as he calmed much of the waves of suspicion the punks felt for his close friendship with Kiki.

After Grizz climbed the stairs out of the lair, Kiki did step onto the stage all by herself. The punks told her to be strong and not to lie. They would be able to provide protection and professional help if in fact there was some sort of abuse between her and Grizz. Kiki only became all the more defensive and she wasn't sure if it had something to do with the anger affects of Grizz's blood.

"You all have Grizz labelled wrong. Grizz and I connect on multiple levels, sure but the reason he and I share the same tattoo is because we share a deep history together. I trust him with my life and you should too. To make a friend like Grizz is very rare for anyone in their lifetime. The friendship, Grizz and I share is not romantic at all, but somehow we share a closeness in our friendship which has somehow grown deeper than I could have ever imagined." Scanning the room, Kiki found many punks had heard enough. Convinced Kiki was not in any danger, many of the punks left the lair and joined Grizz upstairs, but not all of the punks were so easily swayed by Kiki's words for they knew how clever a victim of abuse can be to avoid detection of their problem.

Noticing not everyone was satisfied with her answer, Kiki continued. "Grizz is more than just my friend. At times he is like the father I never had. Our friendship by definition is nothing more than that. If you still don't understand, then too bad, time will just have to tell the truth for you." Dropping the matter there, Kiki left the stage to join the others up stairs.

They gathered in the abandoned industrial area where Grizz began practicing a series of Asian warm up and defence moves. The other punks stood around Grizz and mimicked his ever move.

When everyone was tired and had worked up a good sweat, Grizz called Kiki over to him as he unzipped the duffle bag. Grizz pulled out the bow and quiver of arrows and let Kiki show the punks what she knew. Kiki chose targets of the surrounding old structures, all of which were dangerous for anyone to venture through for the level of disintegration accompanied with their age of abandonment. Kiki let other punks try her compound bow, and even Grizz gave it a couple of shots. They moved onto practicing with darts, swords and finally Grizz brought out his sling shot. Firing off some shots to the base of a couple of the structures Grizz was proud, he brought them toppling to the ground. The punks were very impressed, but no one was as impressed as Grizz. He was so proud that Kiki had the imagination and will to make such a powerful weapon a reality. *'Ingenious.'* Grizz thought.

Brandishing his yo-yo, Grizz spun it out to the ground. When the yo-yo line came out, it immediately began to coil up again. The punks were impressed by the size and power behind Grizz's yo-yo. Kiki began passing out yo-yos to the other punks as she said, "Don't be intimidated by Grizz. It's not the size of the yo-yo that will save your life, it's how you use it that makes the difference. The punks tried their best to keep up with Kiki but her yo-yo skills were far too advanced. Grizz, on the other hand, was able to do quite well. Kiki was impressed with how naturally he was picking it up.

"You're good at this." She told him as she giggled and continued to impress everyone with her tricks.

"I like this yo-yo a lot." Grizz responded. Kiki and Grizz could have continued on all night in use with their yo-yos, but they could see they were losing the attention of the on looking punks.

Grizz and Kiki decided to put their yo-yos away and continue training with many of the techniques Grizz was taught when he was at training with his Brothers. Kiki revealed how some of Grizz's move complimented many of the moves she learned from Bolo the clown. Into the late hour, Grizz and Kiki went on and on with their practices even long after the punks had given up and left.

After showering up and putting on fresh new clothes, Grizz decided the time had come for his wardrobe selection to expand. Clothes were not easy for Grizz to come by in his size. He and Kiki went down to a custom fitting store that stocked upscale business suits. Grizz had a few suits tailor made for his unique size. He slicked his hair back into a pony tail and wore a nice hat from the nineteen forties with his new get up.

Kiki was impressed and had trouble taking her eyes off him. "What is it?" Grizz asked. "Is it too much?"

"N-no, it will just take me some time to get used to it." Kiki told Grizz truthfully. "You don't look like a punk at all, but you don't exactly look normal either. You still look cool, and I'm not sure if I like it, but I'm sure after a while I won't. It will take me a while to get used to it because you look like an entirely different person." She eyed him carefully up and down, "I would like it more if you grew a three foot Mohawk of blue spikes."

Grizz raised his eyebrows and said, "Maybe next time, Kiki…"

Grizz felt so good dressed in his new threads, he thought it would be a good idea to go to his new casino and get used to sitting in the president's chair of his new office.

Walking into the main doors of the Mulbury Bryor Casino, the bouncers recognized Grizz and Kiki right away. "Sir, you have been kicked out of here and you are never welcome to return. Now if you will kindly turn around and leave we won't have to make this harder than it already is…" spoke the bouncer rudely.

"For starters, do you always welcome your guests in this manner? Or how about your boss, because you are fired!" Grizz told the bouncer, "That's right, as you have likely heard, this casino is under new management and I am the Blackguard."

"S-sir, I-I was only trying to protect your investment. Now, had I known…" The bouncer pleaded to keep his job, but Grizz knew he would have more pull within the ranks of the establishment if he let someone go right off the hop.

"You heard me, and like your prior owner, I never go back on my word." Grizz added as he walked on looking fine in his new suit.

Kiki was dressed as punk as ever and she giggled as she told Grizz, "You walk different in a suit, like your butt is tighter or something." shooting look at Kiki, everyone wondered if Grizz was about to fire her next, "What? Did they leave the pins in?"

Grizz answered Kiki with a low voice which was almost a whisper, "Shut up, Kiki."

Grizz and Kiki took an elevator to the top floor of the casino where they walked into the secretary's office. Connected to the main secretary's office were other glassed in offices with personnel busy calculating like there was no tomorrow.

When the secretary noticed Grizz and Kiki enter the office, she quickly stood up and tried to compose herself, with last second fixes to her hair and dress. When she spoke her red lips glistened from the added lip gloss. "Oh, oh my, hello, I-I mean, welcome, sir, um, Mr. Blackguard, right?" A nervous giggle was not well received. The secretary had long red hair and she wore it up high at the back. Her glasses were black rimmed and her dress was tight like evening wear.

She held her hand out to shake hands with Grizz, but he ignored her and walked past as he replied, "Yes, yes I am." At the sound of Grizz's low rumbling voice, all work from the other offices stopped and all eyes went to Grizz.

"I am Kissandra, your secretary and personal advisor. You've just missed Mr. Vanderwal. He was here earlier clearing out his belongings. Jim gave us a description about you though he said he never really, actually, ever met you. He waited around for awhile hoping you would show up."

Kiki approached Kissandra's desk and blew a pink

bubble from her bubble gum until it popped in her face. "Hey, chicky, your babbling and making a fool out of yourself. Zip the lip, kay?"

The secretary was openly surprised by Kiki's forcefulness, "Well, I've never in all my years…" the secretary quickly caught herself before she said something she might regret. Like a snap change of expression, Kissandra smiled a big fake smile full of teeth and asked, "And who are you? Mr. Blackguard's little sister?"

"I'm Vixen, Kiki Vixen. Don't forget it." Kiki said playfully. Grizz began walking toward the main double doors to his office.

"Oh, I won't." Kissandra said as she did a bad job covering how much she disliked Kiki.

Sticking out her tongue at the secretary, Kiki skipped along behind Grizz as he opened the great oak doors to his new office. "Oh, wow, Grizz, this place is spank."

"Right, totally spank." Grizz replied.

Grizz closed the doors behind him and looked around the office with Kiki. The two of them spent some time looking out the large window together. They could look over the intricacies of the casino's design for the roof below them revealed much from the many levels of the structure's complex design. They could see the cars in the parking lot as well with a view not only over the city but up and down the main street in front.

Grizz sat in the chair at the desk. Putting one of the Cuban cigars in his mouth and crossed his legs with his feet upon the desk top, Grizz put his hands behind his head and smiled. "Yeah, this is a boring life, Kiki. If this is all I am expected to do here, I won't be coming to work much."

"You look pretty comfortable to me." Kiki observed.

"Ill just get soft in this self made prison. No, it's not me."

"Then why did you want it so much?" asked Kiki with a curious tilt of her head.

"I just wanted to make a point, that's all." Grizz told Kiki truthfully. Setting his feet back down on the floor Grizz inspected the office junk which cluttered his desk. When Grizz noticed the intercom, he immediately spat his Cuban cigar into the waist paper basket. Reaching out, Grizz pressed the call button on the intercom and the secretary answered.

"Yes, mister, um, Blackguard. What can I do for you?" Kissandra's smooth voice answered back.

Grizz replied, "I would like to see some schematics or charts or whatever you have of the past few year's profits. Could you have those on my desk, stat?"

"Oh, y-yes sir. Right away sir." Kissandra replied nervously.

Grizz released his finger from the intercom and said, "That felt good." to Kiki.

In less than a minute, Kissandra was walking into the room carrying a stack of folders and rolled up charts. She tripped a little on her heels but managed to bring the entire stack to Grizz and slide them onto his desk.

Kiki saw a potential threat in Kissandra right away. She was an attractive woman and Kiki didn't like it. To Kiki, Kissandra looked like a sophisticated tramp.

Kissandra looked at Grizz with her hair slightly coming undone and her glasses sliding down her nose a little. "Anything else sir?" Kissandra asked, Kiki saw Grizz also take notice how his secretary was attractive in her unorganized sort of way.

"Looks like a lot of material." Grizz observed, "Wasn't anyone else able to help you?"

Kissandra looked back at the door with

discouragement as movement of shadows scurrying was detected. "Everyone is very busy right now." she told Grizz.

"You mean those wimps just outside the door?" Grizz spoke loud enough for the ears on the other side of the door to hear. At these words, the scurrying quickened as the employees outside scampered back to their offices to look busy.

Kissandra turned back to face Grizz. "Let me help you to get started, sir." Kissandra walked up behind Grizz swinging her hips seductively. She leaned over Grizz's shoulder to examine his first file report from the top of the pile. Pushing her breasts up against Grizz's shoulder and sliding her other hand down to the end of her dress, Kissandra hooked the thin fabric onto an adjusting lever on Grizz's chair.

Kiki wasn't comfortable with Kissandra so close to Grizz so she walked around to the front of the desk where both Kiki and Grizz exchanged glances. Kiki wanted so badly to warn Grizz of the seductive woman, but to her horror, Kiki could see Grizz was lost to Kissandra's intoxicating advances almost immediately.

Grizz closed the file as he did begin to feel a little uncomfortable being so close to Kissandra. Grizz backed his chair away from the desk as Kissandra wobbled backwards. A tearing sound of her dress was heard. She made a seductively surprised sound like "Oops!" She tried to be as innocent about it as she could but Kiki couldn't believe how bad Kissandra's acting was. In an instant, Kissandra's dress had practically been torn right off. Her milky white long legs seemed to shine like beams of light. Surely Grizz would be able to see through Kissandra's act as well, but to Kiki's surprise, Grizz was clueless of her seduction. Kiki's idea of Grizz, being such a strong and powerful man, was shattered and her respect for him began to sink.

"Kiki, go get something to help Kissandra fix her dress." Grizz called. Kiki left the room quickly as she was burning mad. Feeling like she had been tossed aside like yesterday's news, Kiki marched right to the elevator. Tapping her foot impatiently, Kiki pushed the elevator call button numerous times. "He dumped me just like that? How dare he..." she said to herself quietly.

Grizz stooped to help lift some of the torn dress. It was quite torn and he looked up accidentally catching sight of Kissandra's kinky underwear. Grizz shifted his eyes to look away quickly, "Do you have a change of clothes?" Grizz asked, but it wasn't clear if Grizz was speaking to Kissandra or to her underwear.

Kissandra did not seem to be shy with Grizz at all. She began to talk to him comfortably, "Hey, Mr. Blackguard, why don't you stop playing babysitter for one evening and start making plans for when you will take me out to dinner?"

Grizz seemed like he wasn't paying attention to Kissandra until he shook his head and said, "You don't know what you're talking about. I-it's complicated. My life, I mean, me." Grizz told her.

"What? Are you kidding? You mean between you and Kiki?" Kissandra shook her head, "You don't know what you're missing." Speaking seductively Kissandra lifted what was left of her skirt to reveal her bare, silky smooth leg. "Oh, come on, Grizz, she's just a kid. What does she have that I don't have? There is no way she can give you what I am capable and willing to give you."

Leaning down and kissing Grizz on his mouth, Grizz settled back into his chair melting just as Kiki walked back into the room. Kiki stopped, frozen in her tracks. *'What's this strange feeling that's come over me...*

jealously?' Eyes pooling up with tears, Kiki thought, 'I can't let them see me.' But it was too late. Both Grizz and Kissandra turned their heads to see Kiki bolting out the door with her face in the palms of her hands.

"Kiki?" Grizz called out after her. "Kiki!!!" Standing up, Grizz was about to go after her, but Kissandra slid her hand over Grizz's wide shoulder and down his chest before she kissed Grizz again, "Can't she take care of herself?" Again Grizz gave into her affections. Grizz figured this would be a great way to end the rumours amongst the punks that he was a cradle robber, especially if he had a girlfriend, no matter if it was just for a short time.

Kissandra was able to repair her dress and the two of them had a good time together trying to fix it. Taking Kissandra on his arm, Grizz treated her to a dinner downstairs amongst the busy activity of the casino. Kissandra was a whole new experience for Grizz, but while they enjoyed their meal, Grizz found Kiki did not leave the casino. After catching Kiki's scent, Grizz found her lurking nearby.

While, Grizz and Kissandra enjoyed their red lobster and steak dinner, Kissandra asked, "So will you be inviting me over later to see your crib?"

"Crib?" Grizz questioned the expression with a smirk, "If you mean my penthouse home at the top of Metro City's Rosetta Hotel, perhaps…" He teased her.

"Oooohhh… The penthouse of the Rosetta Hotel? Sounds like the nicest crib in Metro city." Kissandra complimented Grizz with twinkling eyes of excitement.

"It would be the perfect place for someone who was suicidal." Grizz commented strangely, "It's a long way down."

Though Grizz had lost sight of Kiki, he soon found she was again not far away. Kiki, feeling a rats nest of emotions, kept a close tab on Grizz and his date from Hell. At a glance, Grizz noticed Kiki was crying. Rising from the table, Grizz tried to approach Kiki and help her with whatever it was that troubled her, but when Grizz came near to her, Kiki would get up and move away. Grizz suspected jealousy was Kiki's problem, but as hard as it was, Grizz knew the experience of her seeing him on a date was for the best.

With his loud and intimidating voice, Grizz shouted amongst the happy gamblers, "Come upstairs and we will talk when you are ready, but moping around down here is not going to make things better." Grizz told Kiki which caught a lot of attention though Grizz and Kiki hardly noticed.

Grizz and his secretary made their way back up to the office. As Grizz headed for his private office, Kissandra followed, but Grizz told her, "Please, Kissandra. Dinner was fun but this will have to be enough for now. I want you, to take the rest of the day off."

"Oh, but Mr. Blackguard…" Kissandra began.

"Don't argue with me, just trust me." Grizz kissed Kissandra again before he backed into his office closing the doors behind him.

Soon after Kissandra left, Kiki slunk sheepishly into Grizz's office.

Kiki and Grizz talked and Grizz clearly laid it out for her. "I'm not emotionally attracted to you. I am your friend and you are my best friend. Nothing will take this away from us. One day you will find a boyfriend who is your age and you wouldn't want me standing in your way, right?"

Kiki went to the window where she sat on the window sill looking at Grizz. Agreeing with a sniffle, a shrug of her shoulders and a slight nod of her head, Kiki tucked her knees up to her chest and hugged them with her arms. An odd smile crept across Kiki's face as she could see Kissandra, in her red dress, walk out to her car in the parking lot below. Many of the valet were standing around her car scratching their heads because the body was scratched and dented with all four tires popped and the windows blown out.

Kiki could almost hear Kissandra say, "What happened to my car?" but Kiki fixed it. She fixed it real good. Kiki took a small detonator out from a pouch of her belt. Flipping a residual switch Kiki armed the device before pressing the small red button. In that instant, Kissandra's beat up vehicle exploded in an impressive show of light, sound and fire.

Secretly, Kiki had sworn to take revenge on the tramp because Grizz had taken Kissandra out to dinner at a very expensive restaurant. This was something Kiki wanted to be special, exclusively for her and Grizz.

Together, Grizz and Kiki talked well into the morning.

While Grizz was going over some of the charts from over the past years profits, some well dressed business men came walking in through the large double doors of the office without appointments. They demanded to speak to the Blackguard.

At first sight, Grizz thought they were Jim Vanderwal's men. Ready to tear out of his new suit and fight, Grizz stood up and patiently waited to hear what they had to say. The men introduced themselves as the ones who started the punk gang and who gave XD3 his power and authority.

Grizz told them, "I'm sure you have done well in the past, but I am the future. The punks don't need you... I don't need you. You are no longer useful to us."

"It doesn't work that way." the men told Grizz with a sneer.

"It does now! Get used to it and get out!!!" Grizz shouted at them before he raised his mighty arms and brought them down, full force upon the desk. The desk top collapsed through and the men fell to the floor in astonishment.

Kiki's heart skipped a beat as she was not ready for Grizz's sudden out burst. Stepping over the broken desk, Grizz continued to approach the men. One of the men screamed in high pitched fear. Grizz was almost right on top of them. They looked up in stark terror with Grizz towering over them.

"You're still here? You want to Die?! GET OUT!!!" Grizz roared at them and they scampered and crawled for their lives to get out alive.

Grizz turned to Kiki, who looked at Grizz like she too was scared of his presence. "Too much?" Grizz asked her.

Kiki nodded, "Ya, j-just a little too much." Kiki smiled as a tear trickled down from the corner of one eye.

Grizz went to Kiki and put his arms around her for comfort, "Hey, I'm sorry. I was just mess'n with them." Though Grizz explained his actions to Kiki, he learned how Kiki was not always as tough as he perceived her to be. She was still a ten year old girl. "You know me well enough by now, don't you?" Grizz questioned, but Kiki would not answer him, she just glared at him until he became so uncomfortable, he had to leave.

Later that evening, the men returned to Grizz's casino office. Grizz was sitting at a new desk and the office looked so clean and organized, as if Grizz's earlier temper tantrum had never happened. The well dressed men had recomposed themselves and as before, they did not make an appointment. They also seemed to carry a new air of confidence with them. Grizz saw clearly how the men were smug and full of confidence in themselves.

Grizz questioned the men, "Back for more? Did you come with back up or don't you have any sense? I was expecting a lot more of you guys to show up." Grizz attempted to intimidate them by standing up at his desk quickly but the men were not easily scared. Kiki quickly trotted out of the room when she figured it would be safer to wait outside the office this time.

Kiki turned to look at the main door as it began to open. A police squad entered the room. Kiki hustled back into the office with Grizz as the police were right on her heals.

Grizz was relieved to see the police had shown up because he would not have to call himself. Grizz was also felt a low sense of conviction because he didn't do anything to harm the men when they first came to see him. Grizz felt it was his turn to be smug as he said, "Well, the law is here..." Folding his arms across his chest as best as he could, Grizz knew he might tear his suit, "They will settle this."

The men respond calmly, "They certainly will."

Grizz realized quickly, the police were there under the command of the two men. The officers drew their tazers and pointed them at Grizz. Knowing there was no time to run, Grizz spun around quickly scooping Kiki into his arms and smashing through the great window.

The tazers bit at Grizz's back for a fraction of a second as many of the electrical tips touched him but did not stick. Landing with a tuck and roll upon the roof below his office window, Grizz ran carrying Kiki like she was a football. Leaping from one lower existential multi level to another Grizz came to a rather large glass dome. Sliding down the beveled lower level of the roof, Grizz came to the flat area of the parking lot.

The men shouted after Grizz, "You don't get it do you! You'll never win! We are the law!!!"

Grizz acted like he could not hear the men as he made his escape.

Hours were spent amongst the punks as Grizz and Kiki continued to work hard to fortify their lair and more importantly the entire area within the abandoned industrial complex. With the guidance of Grizz, the punks made weaponized stations which were disguised so the invading Rockers would not be able to recognize where they were. Nor would they be able to recognize the misleading traps which were also put in place by Grizz's design.

Within the lair, the punks reunited with Grizz to hear their leader repeat the plan for their defence and also their offense, for the time for war had come.

"We will need the five to move like shadows and keep from being seen as the majority of us, led by myself, meet our challengers head on and keeping to protocol…"

Roach came bounding down the stairs, "Heads up punks! Our retarded Rocker brothers have arrived!"

"Let's go!" Grizz shouted to everyone. With a subtle glance at Kiki, Grizz added, "Kiki, you stay here! We'll be back soon."

"No, Grizz, not again!" Kiki protested, as she sat in a dark corner on a stool where she tucked her knees up to her chest and hugged her legs, pouting. Kiki watched as everyone turned and charged up the stairs. She felt a sense of being trapped, 'Grizz is over protective.' she thought. Grizz had been arguing with her on and off for the past four hours how he wanted to keep her out of harms way. Grizz was so adamant about it, but he didn't understand. She was trained for this sort of thing. Kiki ended up feeling like she just wasn't having any fun anymore. Kiki wasn't even sure if she liked Grizz anymore. Kiki warned Grizz to stop with the lectures, because she took responsibility for her own decisions no different than anyone else. Grizz began threatening Kiki, how he would lock her up because he cared for her so much.

Kiki just laughed at Grizz's threat and didn't seem to realize just how serious he was about assuring her safety.

After the punks had all left the hideout, Grizz spoke to Kiki alone, "You know I have a bad feeling about tonight. So much could go wrong. I don't want you out there!"

"I might as well be dead then, if can't go. You're treating me like a kid! This is exactly the kind of thing I don't want to live with anymore and it's why I left my foster home in the first place! You have a bad feeling about tonight? Well, so do I! I have a feeling you will need me to protect you and I won't be able to do that. Besides, I'm not sure how to tell you this, but I think the punks will soon turn on you and betray you."

"You'll say anything for me to reconsider, but it won't happen. You stay!" Grizz spoke with words of concrete definition.

"Why don't you think I can take care of myself? I defeated you at our initiation, didn't I?" Kiki knew she had Grizz, but she also knew it wouldn't be enough to change his mind.

"What?" Grizz reared up. "You're a little girl. You had me at a disadvantage!"

"Disadvantage? Can you hear yourself? This little girl could have taken your life!" Kiki's eyes quivered as she wondered how much she had angered Grizz this time.

"I couldn't fight you, much less hurt you, but there

are others out there who wouldn't give killing you a second thought... I am responsible for you..."

"No, Grizz you aren't! No one is. I can take care of myself!" Kiki warned, with her eyes a flare.

Grizz liked her tenacity and half smiled. "Kiki, please..." Grizz spoke softly. "How do you think I would feel if anything ever happened to you?"

This comment surprised Kiki. She didn't understand how it was possible for her to mean so much to anyone. It was what she had wanted from the moment she met Grizz, but the whole idea was so fantastic she actually only believed it in her heart, or so she thought. And what about Kissandra? Grizz was very clear he could never love Kiki that way. She was a little confused about her feelings. Now she felt confronted with them and they distracted her. "Well, get over it. We're not married, you know."

Opening the door to the private chamber, Grizz said, "Get in!"

"I'm not going in there! You can't make me!" Kiki lept off the stool and tried to bolt it for the stairs, but Grizz took a couple quick wide strides and swept her up in his arms. Kiki kicked and punched at Grizz, but she couldn't free herself from his grasp. With a kick twist, Kiki elbowed Grizz in the eye with her bony little elbow.

Grizz roared and tossed her into the private chamber, before slamming the door shut and locking it from the outside. "You make it sound like you're in love with me!" Kiki shouted after Grizz, through the thick metal door.

Grizz knew he certainly had no romantic attraction for Kiki, but she did start something in his grizzly heart he thought was impossible. Grizz knew he loved her when he was struck with the realization that he would give his life if it would save hers. Grizz was usually very confused about feelings of love and compassion because he was not very familiar with such powerful emotions, but one thing he did know, Kiki was not going to be put in harms way while he was around.

Grizz quickly caught up with his punks under the light of the moon and organized them before he led them to the Rockers. The punks moved quickly and Grizz thought they looked like creepy angry zombies possessing a great deal of energy. As the punks came through the tall gangly structures and across a narrow dirt road, they approached a wide empty lot.

A great number of punks followed closely to Grizz's lead to hear what he had to say, "We're gonna win the fight! We'll go at it at midnight! First, destroy every light! We're take'n what they have! We're take'n everything in sight! I don't care if the world stops turn'n, or if we burn the city to the ground! We're wound up too tight! We're crazy with no fear and hungry for the fight! Let the anger burn inside you, cause soon you'll be scream'n like rabid demons. We got no class, no taste, rough'em up, line'em up and take it to the end! How's yer blood punks? Tick'n like a time bomb, take'n Rockers till they're all gone! We're beasts, unchained, unlocked, turned loose and can't stop! We'll bring mighty turbulence and brute force to the riot. We'll be blasting eruptions of thunderstorm'n earthquakes. Each one of us is a fire breathe'n dragon! Storm the Rockers with a wild running rampage. Indulge your selves with ferocious excitement, pump'n scorch'n hot blood of vengeance." the punks hung on every word, the Blackguard spoke, as he stirred them into readiness for whatever challenge the Rockers might have in store for them.

There, at the opposite side of the lot, the Rockers were very busy assembling equipment and hooking up countess spools of wires. Lighting rods were erected to supply light to the stage and surrounding work areas. A stage was fashioned from existing materials and upon the stage were large towering speakers. Musical instruments, like drums, guitars and keyboards had been carefully positioned.

The leader of the Rockers stood on the stage commanding orders of preparation. "Get that scaffolding up, come on, people! You think you have any time? Get it Done!"

One rocker shone a bright flashlight around at their surroundings and caught sight of Grizz coming through a jumble of metal pipe work and wooden frames.

The Blackguard, dressed in his black armored gladiator outfit, wore a gun metal gladiator helmet and large metal shoulder pads. He also wore black gloves with spiked brass knuckles and metal forearm gauntlets with six double layered razors along its' edge, also a long pointed metal blade protruded out from the bottom ends of his gauntlets and passed his elbows. To protect his elbow from the metal spikes he wore elbow pads, with many little sharp studs covering the surfaces. Across his chest were two straps that criss-crossed at the center. One strap was full of explosives, the other had small throwing stars.

On his back, Grizz wore a bow and a case full of arrows. Between that was a sharp metal throwing disk and tucked under the back of his belt were nun-chucks.

On the outer side of his left metal boot was a small gun. The opposite boot contained a knife. The boots looked very heavy, and it was amazing how easily he moved in them. At the front of the rim, near his knee, the metal of the boot pointed into a long spike. Metal plates protected his thighs. Also, his utility belt was made up of many small weapons; a pouch of ball bearings for his sling shot, darts, the large unique yo-yo, two samurai swords, rope and grappler hook.

The distance between the rockers and the punks was roughly like that of a football field. The light quickly played upon other punks who followed their leader as they too filtered through the old structural remains. With them, other nearby punks climbed high over towering metal structures and catwalks.

"The punks have arrived, lord Warhead!" shouted the rocker with the flashlight.

Darkade stepped close to Grizz and whispered, "There, the one at the center of the stage, *he* is Warhead, the leader of the rockers."

"Am I supposed to be impressed?" Grizz asked with a strong sense of attitude.

"Apparently, you have done nothing to scare *him*." Darkade added with a smirk.

"After tonight, you will never be able to say *that* again..." Looking at Darkade without turning his head, Grizz spoke with his threat dripping with blood.

"Let's go, rockers, formation!" commanded Warhead. At the sound of the loud command, the rockers began filtering out from behind the stage. They took positions in front of the stage in single file. Row by row the rockers seemed to keep coming with no end to their number.

Eventually, there was an end. The rockers numbered nearly three hundred in all. This was a far cry from the punks who numbered one hundred and twenty. A thunderous beat started up from the rocker band on stage like a huge diesel engine. Ripper, the rocker guitarist began tearing a sound which was kind'a like a wining buzz saw.

Meanwhile, the rockers who were standing in formation began to lift their knees high and stomp their boots in unison as Warhead directed.

In an act of intimidation, the music stopped as did the marching on the spot. The moment of silence was quickly broken when the rockers shouted.

"Raugh!!!"

The wicked music and mechanical stomping resumed.

The punks seemed unprepared to say the least. "Oh, forget this, man." Thrash waved his hand in the air and began to walk away, but a mighty hand pressed against his chest.

"Don't be a wimp." Grizz told Thrash, with one arm around the waist of Kissandra. Nuzzling into Grizz with her dainty hand on his wide solid chest. Grizz straightened and addressed the multitude of punks, "Don't let these low grade punk rockers intimidate you. Remember your training. We will cut their number down to size quickly, but first, you know the drill and how we have agreed this would all begin. Before we can even get started, we will need to take positions... Send in the truck!"

Behind the mass of punk rockers a great mechanical behemoth came rumbling through the abandoned industry with the sound of a growing thunder. It was one of the huge black commercial trucks that came charging down the dirt road. The wheels bounced over the potholes and the long trailer box shook as the whole thing slowed to a stop, hissing air breaks. The rockers looked on as the trailer opened up at the side. The entire side of the trailer folded down to become a music stage as well.

The punk stage was in full readiness. Huge speakers towered on either side of the band members who were all in their places. Multiple colored lights were fastened and assembled along wide scaffolding rods above the stage. Just under the series of lights was the body of Lips who was tied to two poles in the form of a crucifix. Lips wore a neck brace and a very punked outfit of tattered black leathers. Smiling with her hideous open smile of sharp pointed teeth, Lips laughed in her crazy high pitched way. Scorpin-X was directly below Lips on the drums, while Roach was at the synthesizer, and Zom-Buckle held a base guitar which was fashioned to look like a mid-evil battle ax. Jakebrake took up a position near the lead singer with his bone structured electric guitar. Vamporess stood at the mic with her straggling jet black Mohawk drooping down over one eye like skeletal fingers. Attitude was conveyed from her smoky shadowed eyes.

"Kick it!" Vamporess spoke into the microphone. Though she didn't try to speak very loud, the powerful speaker towers carried her soft voice to all ears. Zom-Buckle began to finger a base line which was quickly supported by the drums.

The punks also stomped their feet and made additional gestures of slapping their shoulders. One of the punks who wore a helmet with a big bushy bright red Mohawk pasted to it, broke formation and decided he would take off his helmet. As he did so, he revealed his own hair was fashioned with the same bright red Mohawk which sprung up from underneath.

Regarding Kissandra and giving her a little kiss on the mouth, Grizz turned away and marched to the front of the punks where he faced the rockers.

Surprisingly, Warhead remained on the stage as another person took the responsibility of moving to the front of the pack. Accompanied with the loud sound of a motor, the newcomer slowly rode a Harley Davidson between two leashed tigers that had been obviously pumped up on steroids. The tigers wore iron helmets and shoulder armor with clusters of six inch spikes protruding. Grizz thought he was looking at cows at first because from a distance they didn't even look like tigers. The person who led the tigers was someone who had a bone to pick with Grizz.

The punks were amazed when they recognized their former leader XD3 taking up a position at the head of their rival rockers. The music from the punk stage ceased as every jaw dropped open. Darkade felt he was standing beside himself. XD3 seemed stronger than ever, with the support of the two tigers and the legion of rockers behind him and that wasn't all. Built upon his body was the mechanical robotic technology of an exoskeleton.

Unknown to anyone else, the government agents had supplied it for him. XD3 felt he needed it if he were to defeat Grizz, because the drugs he used to rely on to enhance his strength no longer had any effect in his blood stream. Along with the strength enhancing exoskeleton, XD3 had a blind pride which was fueled by his hatred of Grizz.

XD3's plan was to defeat Grizz, restore his honor amongst the punks and become the sole leader of both, the rockers and the punks. It was a dream he was determined to make reality that night.

Grizz took the first fearless step out toward XD3. When he did this Kissandra shouted out to him, "Blackguard! What are you doing?! Are you crazy?! You're going to get yourself killed! I have to go! I can't watch!!!" Kissandra turned and disappeared behind the stage.

XD3 began to walk out toward Grizz with his

monster sized tigers, one at each side. XD3 was used to being the number one leader of the punks. There was a time when he was feared as the biggest and meanest boy on the block, back when it was he who was leader. Grizz wondered if XD3's jealousy over Grizz's success was as obvious to the punks as it was to himself.

Without warning, XD3 shouted a command to his tigers, "Kill him!" With the release of the leashes the tigers immediately charged at Grizz to attack him. At that moment, the rocker band struck their cords and interjected powerful music of charged energy into the approaching fight;

> Someone's going to nuke the entire nation,
> They're gonna do it for the pure sensation,
> We're gonna bring you hurt like a military hive,
> You're gonna wish you were never alive.
> This Rock's come'n at your head
> You're gonna wish, you were dead
> We're gonna start this fight!
> We're gonna start this fight!!!
> WE'RE GONNA START THIS FIGHT!!!
> Come on! Let's Fight!
> Bring it!

The tigers bounded toward Grizz with thunderous heavy paws. They leaped into the air brandishing pointed white teeth and long sharp claws. Grizz fell backwards in a roll. When the tigers came down on top of him he kicked his legs out which threw the tigers sprawling right over top of him. Quickly, Grizz flipped from his back to his feet and went on the defensive as the tigers came right back at him. With one arm Grizz grabbed one tiger in a headlock. The tiger struggled to be free but Grizz was too strong, for the moment. His other hand balled into a fist which Grizz used to thump the head of the other tiger down to the dirt. As the tiger arose, Grizz ended up getting it into a headlock as well. In this position Grizz attempted to apply a lot of pressure. He had a mind to squeeze them to death, but because the tigers thrashed about so much, they proved to be quite a challenge for Grizz. The tiger began to run and Grizz was pushed in reverse and unable to achieve the footing to stop the big cats. The tigers pushed Grizz across the field and right into the mass of punks. The crowd of punks disperse and ran for their lives. Grizz was pushed right through the distracted punks to where he slammed into the stage with his back. The impact caused Grizz to release his hold on the tigers. They stumbled back a little before they gained their moorings once more and attacked again. The tigers were not interested in anyone else, they only had eyes to kill Grizz.

The tigers roared as they swiped their ferocious claws at Grizz. Taking in a deep breath of air, Grizz bellowed out a roar of his own. As he warned the big cats with his primal expression of hostility, Grizz touched a couple buttons of his gauntlets which quickly extended an eight inch double edged blade from his gauntlets. The tigers were distracted by the power of Grizz's roar and stumbled back for a moment before they lept at him. With lightning reflexes, Grizz ducked and slid to the side narrowly dodging a leaping tiger. Within the midst of a spin, Grizz managed to grab the armor of the tiger as it was in mid leap. Using his momentum, Grizz swung the big cat around and knocked the second cat back before he threw the one in his hands up into the air. When the tiger was tossed, it flew over the punk stage and further over the heads of Vamporess and Scorpin-X. The tiger hit the wall below the feet of Lips who was laughing at the air born tiger uncontrollably.

The tiger Landed heavily behind the drum set and Scorpin-X's eyes grew to the size of baseballs. He scrambled to get away from the drums as the massive tiger came bounding back over the entire drum set.

The musicians fled from the stage screaming in outrageous panic and fear. While Grizz could fight the one tiger, one on one, he naturally let his extensive training surface. Grizz could defeat a wild beast when he could get inside its' head and predict its' next move. Like an animal himself, Grizz paced a half circle around the tiger as it was sizing him up. Grizz too was figuring out his opponent. When the tiger moved to attack, Grizz lept into the air above it and executed a back flip.

XD3 watched, and almost missed the fluent and quick motion as Grizz reached out from above the tiger to smash its' head between his fists, before landing on his feet. The tiger collapsed to the ground and there it remained unmoving.

XD3 rose up from the seat of his motor bike, "No!!! It can't be!" kicking the bike into gear he began moving forward.

The second tiger waved its' tail from side to side before it lept at Grizz from the stage. Grizz did not back down in the least, rather, he drove both his fists up at the tiger's chin. The tiger fell upon him, but Grizz kicked it off. Unclipping his large yo-yo from his belt, Grizz prepared himself as the tiger did what it only knew to do and press the offensive. As the beast moved in on Grizz, Grizz surprised the huge cat as his yo-yo sprang out and cracked the animal on its' skull. The cat reeled backwards and in its weakened state, Grizz drove his elbow blades down upon it.

Rain began to fall from the sky and Grizz welcomed it. He felt the rain was somehow fitting with how he felt inside.

As XD3 looked upon the death of his beloved tigers, he kicked his bike into high gear and punched it into full throttle causing the front end to rise high in the air.

Turning and noticing the other tiger rise up, Grizz leaped into the air in a spin before he came down hard driving his sharp metal elbow blades into the second cat as well.

The punks cheered for Grizz and by this time, XD3 was going out of his mind with frustration, "Yo'll die for this, Blackguard... I promise yo this... I'm going ta kill yo right now." XD3 spoke his oath out loud to everyone.

A mechanical grappler hook dropped down slightly at XD3's side from his hand. He began to swing the grappler hook around from its' tethered nylon rope. As XD3 rode his bike past Grizz, he threw his grappler. With a touch to the ring on his finger, XD3 activated the grappler and it gripped a hold onto Grizz's gauntlet.

Before Grizz could react to the incident, the line became taut and Grizz was lurched away from where he stood. Suddenly dragged behind XD3's motor bike in a wide turn, Grizz rolled uncontrollably from behind. XD3 was heading back to the rockers with his trophy, Grizz where they would have there way and execute him right in front of the on looking punks.

When the bike was dragging Grizz in a straight line toward the rockers, Grizz found he was able to stabilize himself. Rising up on his knees behind the bike, Grizz found he still had his yo-yo strapped to his hand. He loosened the yo-yo from his hand and quickly used it by throwing the entire thing at the back of XD3's head.

XD3 was knocked forward and he spun his handle bars which caused the whole bike to pop up into the air and topple end over end as it crashed.

The front wheel was bent pretty good, but XD3 did

411

not seem hurt at all. Rising up quickly before Grizz, the two warriors found they were completely surrounded by the crowd of rockers.

XD3 laughed at Grizz and mocked him, "You do make your mistakes, don't you?!"

Grizz was like a rock and was unaffected by anything XD3 had to say. Emanating a power of pure anger Grizz kept the rockers at length, except for one.

Burnit, a rocker who desired to make a name for himself in the ranks, came running out from the crowd and blew a breath of fire in Grizz's face. Grizz did not feel the danger as he had been throw this sort of thing on his initiation with the punks.

Burnit believed he would not only be proving himself as a great rocker, but he would be rewarded for being the only one to protect XD3.

Grizz put his hands to his face and shielded his eyes from the immense heat and growled as he stomped his feet in annoyance.

"How you like that, eh, Blackguard? Not so tough now, are ya! Betch'a never met the like of me before, eh? How you like gett'in fried? Or would you rather be, extra crispy!" The surrounding rockers laughed at Burnit. Burnit fed off the attention. With renewed pride and confidence, Burnit began spraying more flames at Grizz but Grizz leaned in at the rocker and roared a deafening, rolling, thunderous threat. With lungs full of air and a mighty stomp of his foot, Grizz blew the flame back at Burnit before it was extinguished completely. "Heh-heh-heh-heh-heh…" Burnit chuckled like a chipmunk.

Grizz had it with Burnit, and everything else about the rockers. They fought dirty and Grizz felt it was time he too fought dirty. He bent down and took hold of Burnit by the ankles in one hand. Using Burnit as a floppy stick Grizz wildly struck the crowd of rockers with him.

XD3 walked up to Grizz and took Burnit right out of his hands and threw him to the crowd. This was followed by a left hook to Grizz's jar jaw. Grizz spun and went down on one knee as he stroked his sore chin with his hand. Grizz felt the strength from XD3 was incredible.

Quickly, Grizz rose up and pushed XD3 away. As the rain evaporated as steam from Grizz's hot body like he had just stepped out of the pit of hell, Grizz realized XD3 possessed an added strength which was not his own. XD3 laughed while he took a couple of steps back. A large warrior clad rocker stepped near to Grizz from behind XD3.

With a new surge of confidence, XD3 said, "Blackguard? I'd like to introduce you to, Iron Hammer." The large rocker was one foot taller than Grizz and full of empty pride. With long black hair falling over his face wearing a studded leather jacket, Iron Hammer held a large sledge hammer with both hands. Swing his sledge hammer from side to side in a figure eight motion, Iron Hammer began to move in on Grizz. Leaning back, Grizz tightened his fist before he tightened his entire body, springing forward and stretching his fist out at the huge rocker's abdomen. The impact made a low muffled thud which caused onlookers to shrug their shoulders and tighten their faces.

Iron Hammer flew backwards from the after shock of Grizz's powerful blow. The rockers who stood behind Iron Hammer were all knocked off their feet also. This cleared an instant path.

Grizz turned back to address XD3, "I've let this go on too long… I've had it with you…" Grizz rose up and struck XD3 repeatedly in the head breaking his nose in a multiple different ways. XD3 reached out with one hand and caught one of Grizz's fists. Grizz looked into XD3's crazy eyes. With his face covered with mud and blood,

XD3 smiled back at Grizz, but It was not a drug induced crazy person Grizz was looking at. XD3 was a pure and simple, blind rage crazy, who was even more dangerous and powerful than he was when Grizz fought him last. This new image of XD3 would remain with Grizz long after the rumble, providing he survived it. Grizz lashed out with another fist and XD3 caught that one as well. Grizz could hear a strange sound come from the servos of XD3's exoskeleton. The robotics which covered over XD3's hands began to buzz as they worked under load. A great pressure built up around Grizz's fist squishing out mud from between XD3's fingers. XD3 attempted to crush all the bones in Grizz's hands. Grizz quickly became aware of the danger as XD's hands continued to close in on Grizz's fists. Wasting no time, Grizz shot his foot out with a mighty kick to XD3's crotch.

XD3 was actually knocked two feet into the air as a result of the impact. Released his hold on Grizz, XD3 fell right down to the ground as he cupped his hands to his painful area. While XD3 rolled around on the ground writhing in pain, Grizz approached him with the intent to finish him off. Just as he took the lives of the tigers, Grizz lifted his arms with his elbow blades reflecting the dim lights of the stage. The blades, coated with tiger blood, poised at the ready to come down like giant vampire fangs, when suddenly, the rockers crowded in on Grizz and attacked him. They knew they were powerful in numbers. Grizz turned his attention to the rockers who tried to cut him with knives. Someone broke a glass bottle over Grizz's helmet.

Meanwhile, the punks were able to pull themselves together. They watched how gallantly and hard Grizz fought the rockers. They began running across the field to aid their leader, the Blackguard.

Someone had the bright idea to cut the bonds of Lips and assist her to climb down from her cross and go free. The punks knew how dangerous Lips could be and they needed all the help they could get. Lips disappeared into the crowd as the Punk band reassembled on stage to back their people with music charged with dangerous punk energy;

Give me more, give me more, power!
I'm gonna give you power
You're gonna give me power
I'm gonna show you all my power
Because I am Power!
Power! Power! Power!
I need more, I need more, I need more, POWER!
Feed me!
Tonight, you're gonna get it.
Bleed into me!
You get the point don't make me shout!
Give your power up to me!
We're gonna give it to ya.
We're gonna cram our vengeance down your throat!!!
We've brought our killer punk moves,
And tonight, You're going to know our power,
More than you can handle,
Too much power,
More than you can handle,
Power! Power! Power!

In the midst of the rocker's rage, Grizz proved he was a one man army. Sweeping his fists across the crowd, many rockers fell at the might of Grizz. When the rockers wised up and stood back a distance from Grizz, Grizz found a stack of wooden pallets nearby. Taking the pallets off the stack one by one Grizz threw them at the rockers like Frisbees. From the rocker's stage, a Chinese rocker lept from the stage holding a long thin sword. He intended to come down on Grizz from behind and drive the sword into his back and out through his chest, but Grizz seemed to have eyes in the back of his head. He unsheathed one of his own swords to block the attack. The Chinese rocker was thrown backwards where he skillfully landed on his feet.

Grizz studied his new attacker for a moment as the surrounding rockers backed away. From the way the Chinese challenger moved, Grizz knew he was trained in the arts of the ninja. The ninja rocker exploded in an array of twisting flips and sword handling. Grizz stood his ground until the ninja show-off came a little closer. Grizz impressed the ninja as he deflected his attacks, blow for blow.

The surrounding rockers advanced on the face-off with the charging punks when the ninja was in the midst of engaging Grizz. With close cutting strikes, lights reflected and flashed from the fast paced movements of the swords. Slashing through the air ferociously, Grizz noticed a rocker throw a punk at him as he had his swords thrashing about, but with quick thinking and quicker reflexes, Grizz caught the punk out of the air and spared him. In the midst of Grizz quickly spinning his body, he threw the punk back into the crowd of rockers.

An observing punk made the remark, "Oh, not cool, man."

Grizz proved how he had the advantage with quicker speed and exceptional strength. When the ninja found he was bested by Grizz, he had the smarts to disappear from the challenge quickly.

When Grizz saw the ninja had bugged out, he turned to retreat, but before he could he found XD3 standing before him with the confidence of his second wind.

Covered in mud from head to toe, Xd3 sucker punched Grizz in the abdomen. As Grizz bent forward, XD3 lifted Grizz up over his head and slammed his body down into the muddy ground. Grizz quickly rose to his hands and feet as XD3 approached him. Shooting out his foot, Grizz kicked XD3 in the stomach knocking him off his feet and onto his back with a splat. Grizz crawled onto XD3 and quickly worked his arm into a twisted kind of wrestling hold. Lifting his boot to XD3's face, Grizz pushed on XD3's chin. XD3 powered up his exoskeleton and jolted his body enough to throw Grizz off. Stepping up to Grizz, XD3 again lifted him up over his head. The mud entirely coated their bodies making them both the same color. From the increased strength of the exoskeleton, XD3 was able to jump ten feet into the air while carrying Grizz over his head. In mid air, XD3 threw Grizz down onto the stage of the rock band as they continued to play their music.

XD3 lept onto the stage where Grizz found himself at the mercy of both XD3 and now also Warhead. Pulling his grappler hook from his belt, XD3 locked the powerful jaws of the grappler onto Grizz's shoulder. Grizz shouted out in pain. Warhead grabbed Grizz by the throat and lifted him up.

Many of the Punks who were still running to join the fight with the Rockers slowed to a complete stop as they saw the Blackguard on the stage being tormented by XD3 and Warhead. They were not sure if they should stay and fight or go to the aid of the Blackguard.

"You sure are entertaining, Blackguard. I'll give you that, but you will not survive this night unless you do exactly what I tell you." Warhead spoke to Grizz like he was his master. "The first thing I need you to do is surrender and allow us to bind your wrists and ankles. I have some friends who would like to ask you a few questions. So, what will it be? Will you co-operate?"

The grappler tightened and released on Grizz's shoulder, before it tightened again, when Grizz noticed how XD3 was controlling the mechanical grappler in the remote control of his sophisticated fore finger's ring.

Grizz looked at Warhead as he bit back the pain of his shoulder. Slowly, Grizz held out his wrists for Warhead to attach the bonds. Warhead quickly pulled out some plastic zap-straps and used them to bind Grizz's wrists.

"Look at him, XD3." Warhead observed, "He's exhausted. I've secured him, you can release your hold."

"Oh, I don't think so..." XD3 told him.

"Hey, I've got it from here, now let him go." Warhead told XD3.

Shaking his head, XD3 said, "Fine, but I won't be responsible for..."

As XD3 released the grappler hook from Grizz's shoulder, Grizz quickly spun around and snapped the pathetic plastic zap strap bonds like they were made of licorice. In an instant Grizz reached up to XD3 and pulled his exoskeleton from the side of his head and crumpled it like it was made of paper. "I've lost power..." XD3 realized. Doing the same thing, Grizz tore apart the exoskeleton from XD3's shoulders, hips and legs. Grizz literally unpeeled XD3 like he was a human banana.

Warhead snuck in from behind and forcefully swung a prybar down against Grizz's back. Grizz was not bothered by this. Examining the mechanical parts of the exoskeleton in his hands, Grizz found a familiar logo. Spinning around Grizz snatched the prybar from Warhead's hands.

Warhead began to laugh as he was somewhat

418

embarrassed as to the ease in which Grizz was able to take the prybar away. Warhead feared Grizz would kill him for beating his back so hard.

"Does this look familiar to you?" Grizz asked as he held the section of metal exoskeleton close to Warhead's face to observe it. There, upon a very small servo motor, was a plate with a symbol of an eagle over a planet. Warhead looked at the symbol closely before he looked at Grizz and shrugged his shoulders. He didn't understand what Grizz was trying to tell him. Grizz threw the prybar down like a spear and it embedded itself into the floor of the stage. Throwing down the piece of broken exoskeleton aggressively, Grizz expressed his frustration. Pointing to his shoulder, Grizz lifted his armored plating and revealed a tattoo which was identical to the logo of the exoskeleton.

Warhead saw the strange and undeniable similarity of the two depictions. Not sure what it meant, Warhead looked at XD3 with skepticism. *'Could XD3 be a government spy?'* Warhead wondered. *'How deep were the ties between XD3 and the Blackguard, and how far back did their history go?'*

At that moment, XD3 was completely powerless. He felt naked before Grizz and wanted to flee.

One of the rockers brandished an AK47 attack rifle and began shooting it into the air. As the rocker lowered the barrel of his weapon at the group of brave punks, Warhead shot him and he collapsed to the ground. "No guns!!!" Warhead shouted, as he lifted his smoking gun. Speaking much quieter, almost to a whisper, Warhead added, "Not yet, anyway."

The punks saw the whole thing through the heavy down pour of rain and were amazed. Their bodies were steaming from after their run.

419

Chapter 13

Grizz pulled out his sword and held it to XD3's neck. "Give me your ring." Grizz commanded, XD3 stalled, but Grizz pressed the sharp blade of the sword to XD3's throat and drew blood. XD3 pulled the ring off his finger and held it out to Grizz.

Grizz, in turn, took the ring. Warhead pulled a flesh colored ball with a blue stripe on it from his belt. "Hey, Blackguard. How would you like to have one of my custom made punk grenades?"

Grizz and XD3 turned their heads to Warhead and saw he was holding a grenade that was painted to look like a punk's head with a blue Mohawk and thin sunglasses. The pin looked like a nose piercing.

Warhead pulled the nose ring from the grenade which armed the thing before he tossed it at Grizz's feet.

Grizz tossed XD3 away and dived off the stage. Commencing a forward flip and landing on his feet with ease, the stage floor exploded in a brilliant cloud of fire behind Grizz. The sound of the explosion combined with the flash of great heat knocked everyone to the ground and caused a buzz of feed back from the speakers.

With the ring pinched between his finger and thumb, Grizz examined the ring. The top of the ring was gold plating with a spider sculpture attached to it. Under the ring were two small buttons; one button to open the grappler and the other to cause the grappler to close. Amongst the two buttons were micro sized electronics with a tiny red light which came on when the grappler closed and a green light to indicate the grappler was open.

Grizz slipped the ring onto his finger and turned

back to find XD3 laying on his back in the mud. Grizz approached XD3 as he scrambled to get away. Grizz reached out to grab XD3 by his tattered and bent exoskeleton, but the pieces just peeled away easily. Grabbing the grappler hook which was coiled at his side, Grizz found the clasp snapped open easily and the coil of nylon rope remained in good condition. Grizz watched as XD3 disappeared in the chaos of the rumble.

The rocker's band was quick to rise to their places on stage once more. They worked hard to intimidate the punks as they ripped on their guitars. XD3 rose up amongst the rockers on the stage once more and spoke into the microphone, saying, "Don't be intimidated by the Blackguard. We can defeat him and we will!" Swellings altered the features of XD3's face and Blood poured from his crushed nose.

A voice from the shadows called to XD3 and whispered, "Over here, XD. Come quickly."

XD3 limped near to the shadow near the edge of the stage, "Make it fast, pal, my body burns in pain all over and I think my nose has been pulverized."

"It's me, XD, *Darkade*. We've always been a great team together. I'm here ta help yo. What do yo say we get out'O here an I make the whole thing disappear. I'll take care O yo and yer wounds." Confusion filled Darkade's mind as he was not sure who's side to take.

XD3 lifted his head as he could not see Darkade very well through the black and blue swelling surrounding his eyes. XD3 surprised Darkade as he struck him and said, "Yo've already chosen yer side, bud. If yo were really interested in protecting me, yo would've fought off the Blackguard to protect me. I know what a coward yo are. Yo gave everything I had to the Blackguard, fool. Now, get out O here!"

Darkade did as XD3 said, with reluctant shame and

a heaviness of guilt and humility, Darkade's confusion continued as he was still not sure who's side to take.

Grizz ran out to join his punks where he told them, "None of you will be going back to your former leader anytime soon. Can you believe it? XD3 has turned tail and joined forces with the enemy, the traitor."

Grizz noticed Kissandra was amongst the crowd of punks. He was surprised she returned to the field and ran right into Grizz's arms, "I just couldn't leave." Kissandra told Grizz before he addressed his punks and gave the command to, "Attack!"

Zom-Buckle continued to support the battle with his low Base, as Scorpin-X supplied the thunderous beat.

"Power! Power! The Blackguard is POWER!" The punks chanted and shouted. Grizz continued to fuel the punks new found anger.

"They're already defeated, now let's get in there and finish them off!" Shouted Grizz victoriously.

When the punks could wait for battle no longer, Grizz finally shouted the command for them to attack. The punks raced into the awaiting crowd of rockers as the conflict went into full effect.

Grizz heard the voice of a young female punk singer scream into the micro-phone along with Vamporess. Grizz stopped in his tracks for a moment as he was curious who was behind the familiar voice. Sure enough, it was as he feared, Kiki. Grizz was disappointed in Kiki. He didn't want her to come and when Grizz found how prepared the rockers were, he really didn't want Kiki to be there.

Kiki, however, was equally disappointed in Grizz because he had Kissandra in his arms. Grizz sent Kissandra back to the stage with a strict command. The punk's fought within the rain swept expanse between the two rock bands.

As Grizz fought viciously, he kept an eye on Kiki. Not wanting to carry such a distraction, Grizz knew it made the conflict more dangerous for him. Kiki took the microphone from Vamporess and began singing. She was a girl of many talents and Grizz knew, as long as he could hear Kiki singing, she was safe from harm.

As Grizz powerfully chewed into the crowd of rockers relying on his personal weapons mostly, he kept his focus on the words Kiki sung;

You can't run, You can't hide,
He can smell your fear inside.
The Blackguard's gonna find you.
When he find's you, he's gonna eat you!
Remember how you feared the dark,
As you did once as a child.
The Blackguard is the monster you once feared in your dreams,
The Black guard is the monster of your nightmares.
The Blackguard's gonna find you.
When he find's you, he's gonna eat you!
He'll creep up on you, and devour you.
Like a ghost of the night, he'll consume you.
When I grow up, I'll be coming for you.
You'll be begging me to stop.
I won't stop till you drop.
When he find's you, he's gonna eat you!
He'll creep up on you, and devour you.
Like a ghost of the night, he'll consume you.
When I grow up, I'll be coming for you!

Amongst the brawl, in the down pour of heavy rain, through the flying and pounding fists the permission was given to both sides allowing the use of knives. The knives were upgraded to swords and spiked baseball bats. Grizz noticed chains and prybars were also added to the brawl. The brawl had obviously progressed to the next level and Grizz could put his practiced yo-yo skills to the test. Quickly pulling arrows from the quiver at his back, Grizz took care of some distant targets with his new love for archery. A dart came in handy for a rocker who decided to go on the offensive at a closer vicinity. Looking for the appropriate opportunities, Grizz used all of his weaponry and skills throughout the brawl.

With Grizz's help, the punks manipulated the hostile confrontation to lead the rockers to the traps which were set throughout the abandoned industrial complex. An M16 attached to a standing tripod was the perfect bait, where any rocker who saw it and tried to use it, would meet with a rigged floor. When a rocker stepped on the bogus floor, it did not support the weight of the rocker and tripped. The rocker fell into a deep pit filled with shallow water. Meanwhile, above the trapped, live captured rocker, the floor flipped all the way around to reset the trap with a new M16 of equal measurements and proportions to deceive the next rock to make his way by in search of a weapon.

XD3 seemed to have disappeared, but when Grizz found a group of rockers standing alone, he surprised them by throwing an ecology block at them like he was a bowler knocking down bowling pins.

One rocker attempted to swing on a rope to the punk's stage to attack the band members with a machete. Vamporess pulled Kiki to her, then she stood in front of her, to protect the young girl from the attacker.

Grizz responded when he noticed the sudden silence as the punk music stopped. Lifting his head, Grizz looked to the stage and saw the punk musicians were in trouble. Doing what he could to fight his way out of the brawl, Grizz began to work harder to make his way in the direction of the punk's stage.

Zom-Buckle charged at the attacker shouting in anger and power. A vicious sight to behold was Zom-Buckle as Grizz had obviously rubbed off on him. Evidence of the additional power coursing through the veins of the punks was clearly evident as the punks, though out numbered by the rockers were superior fighters. The punks knew the only reason they could win was due to a taste of Grizz's mysterious angry blood.

Holding his base guitar by the neck, Zom-Buckle attacked the rocker. His uniquely shaped guitar was altered to look like a viking battle ax and when Zom-Buckle swung the instrument, it looked as impressive as the real thing. Zom-Buckle chopped at the rocker and knocked him down to the stage floor. The machete clattered to the stage floor and slid under the drum set. The rocker moved to get up on his hands and knees but Zom-Buckle kicked him in the face. With stunning aggression, Zom-Buckle forced the dazed rocker's head in front of the massive base speaker of the huge on stage speaker tower. Zom-Buckle maximized the volume knob of his guitar before he strummed the cords. The sound was so powerful, the rocker was literally blown right off the stage to the ground, five feet below. Zom-Buckle looked down from the stage and saw the rocker writhing on the ground. A hideous goblin like smile and laugh came from Zom-Buckle as he was not finished with the rocker, yet. Pushing the fourteen foot tall speaker to the edge of the stage Zom-Buckle heaved it hard enough to tip forward, right over onto the rocker. "Eat the beat, pal." Zom-Buckle said with dark emotion.

Zom-Buckle turned to the rest of the band and

smiled to receive their approval. High fiving Vamporess, Zom-Buckle struck up a rhythm once again with his base guitar, and the rest of the band joined in on que.

Upon the rocker's stage, a lady rocker was getting right into the intense moment as she sang with a male rocker. From out of the brawl, a brick came flying and hit the female singer in the head. She dropped to the floor immediately with her wet hair flapping through the air like a flag as she fell. The male stopped singing and the entire band also ceased. The lead singer bent down to see how bad her injuries were. "I need assistance up here!" The lead vocalist shouted into the microphone. He was incredibly angry. "Kill those punks!" the rocker singer shouted. "We need to get Val to a hospital right away!" In the thick of the chaos, the lead vocalist quickly realized, Val was not the only person in need of medical attention. The rumble was not settling down in the least. Rather, it was just getting more dangerous. The level of vicious acts only multiplied. Many rockers and punks made the mistake of attacking their own kind because there were just too many bodies and the rockers and punks were dressed so similar in the darkness and the rain.

The weapons used in the brawl were upgraded again to Guns and explosives. Both punks and rockers disappeared into the shadows as it became too dangerous to remain in the open.

One of the punks released another trap on three rockers as a high dump truck bucket, suspended by cables, spilled sand and chunks of rock over the three dangerous rockers.

Grizz certainly had a lot of energy as he continued to fight through the crowd of rockers until he finally broke

426

free from the rumble and began charging toward the punk stage. Grizz could still see Kiki. Because of Grizz's one track mind, he could not see how his actions were causing punks to follow suit and turn from the battle to followed after their leader on foot. The rockers were not defeated and when they saw the punks running out on them, they too gave chase.

With Grizz running at the lead, and the large group of punks behind him, with the equally large group of rockers taking up the rear, all headed for the punk's stage. Grizz ran quickly to get to Kiki, like a predator bearing down upon its' prey. The rockers began to reveal weapons like spears, bows and arrows and rifles.

Kiki, again, was under attack on stage where she defended herself masterfully executing some acrobatic clown tricks and fighting off the intrusive rockers.

Grizz pumped his legs harder as he sped to protect Kiki as fast as he could. He imagined his legs were two great pistons of a powerful diesel engine. Grizz was not in danger of the rockers but he reacted to the sound of motor cycle motors growing louder as they approached.

The rockers moved in on the punks with motorcycles bolting out from behind their stage. They rode into the battle field with a wide course which headed around to the outside of the running crowd of punks. Warhead joined the bikers with his own custom built three wheeler as he pulled up from behind the rest. It was evident, Warhead was gunning for, Grizz. His trike had one front wheel extended forward with high handle bars and a wide back seat between two rear tires.

Preparing his specialized sling shot, Grizz loaded it with an aero dynamically shaped trajectory bearing. Leaping into the air and conducting a single spin, Grizz pulled back on the elastic, targeting a rocker motorcyclist who was moving to attack the punks with a ball and chain. Releasing the harness of the sling shot, the motor cycle exploded into the air as it flipped end over end multiple times. Before the motor cycle crashed back down to the muddy earth, Grizz had landed and continued to make his way to the punk stage.

When the punk musicians on stage noticed the entire rumble heading toward them, they immediately figured the rockers were winning the brawl. Gunshots rang out at the punk stage. Kiki and the others felt like helpless targets on the open platform. The punks stopped playing music and scrambled to figure out how they could best prepare for the danger charging toward them substantially.

Kiki struggled until she was free from Vamporess's strong protective hold. "We can't run!" Kiki told the others, "We have to make our stand here and now!"

The other punks, with Kiki, looked upon the approaching danger and shared the same sensation of anger and power. They were reminded, the source of their confidence and strength was the blood of Grizz percolating within them.

"So, help me Kiki. I actually want them to come!" Vamporess tightened her eyebrows and told the others.

"Oh, ya, so do I!" Added Scorpin-X as he flipped his lighter open and shut letting a flicker of flame exist for a fraction of a second.

"Ditto!" Jakebrake tossed in his agreement.

Zom-Buckle didn't say anything at all, he just roared and expressed what the others felt. Upon the stage, the musicians stood together in a row as they awaited their opportunity to fight.

The three wheels of Warhead's ride kicked mud

high into the air, but when he hit the turbo, the rear of his trike blew four feet of flames as he shot forward at such a speed, the mud sprayed every which way. The entire trike shook like it was about to lift off the ground like a rocket at any moment. As the trike was buffeted by the turbulence, Warhead fought to maintain control over it. Warhead passed ahead of all the running rockers and punks and even all the other bikers. This put Warhead right in line with Grizz, side by side. Grizz just ignored Warhead as he pumped his fists forward and back to keep rhythm with his legs which worked and thundered like ground shaking machines.

Warhead didn't try to communicate or toy with Grizz in the least, rather, from his reclined position, he lifted his pistol from its' holster and with a smooth even motion he pointed the weapon at Grizz and shot him right in the side of the head.

Grizz dropped to the mud immediately and slid a good distance in the mud before his body stopped and remained limp. The motor bikes behind Warhead tore past Grizz's body.

"NO!!!" Kiki screamed in disbelief as she witnessed the execution of the best friend she ever knew in her life. The others who were with Kiki held her back as she wanted to leap off the stage and go to Grizz. Stretching out her hands to Grizz, the others wrapped their arms around Kiki to hold her back before she collapsed and cried.

Kiki had never felt a pain like this for a long time, but she couldn't imagine crying like this ever again.

The punks slowed and gathered around Grizz in a sad moment of disbelief and disappointment. Meanwhile, Warhead slowed as he neared the punk's stage. The rockers, on foot, surrounded the punks pointing their weapons at them. The brawl was finished.

The punks had lost to the rockers and those who survived were considered prisoners.

The very first thing Warhead saw was the carcasses of the two armor clad tigers. He was disgusted when he saw Lips sitting in the midst of the two tigers. Laughing as she ate the raw bloodied innards, Lips was covered in the tiger's death, but when Warhead dove past her, examining her, she stopped feeding and her smile disappeared. The way she gazed at Warhead sent chills up and down his spine. Unable to turn her head because of the cumbersome neck support brace she wore, the insane eyes of Lips followed Warhead. Sick in mind, the psychotic bony body of Lips crouched in the blood and death of the tigers as she was proud to be free and to live her life in crooked glory. Warhead was certain Lips was going to attack him at any moment. Unable to take his eyes off the carnage of Lips, Warhead was disgusted to watch the gruesome smile return to Lip's face and her long tongue slither out to lick blood from her abnormal puffy lips. The uninvited image of Lips was the scariest thing he had ever seen, and repetitive nightmares of the moment would stick to him like an unshakable curse.

"You punks are sick…" Warhead was unable to keep his comment to himself.

Warhead continued on, riding his trike in a slow lazy arc, eying the stage members who were huddled together at the center of the stage floor. With an unexpected motion, Warhead bit the ring out of a small hand held object and tossed it onto the punk's stage. The small device clattered across the deck of the stage to the feet of Kiki. The other punks took one look at the object and recognized it to be one of Warhead's trademark, 'punk head grenades.' Everyone jumped away from the grenade and sought protection behind some solid object to shield themselves from the expected explosion, only Kiki did not see any danger at all. Looking down at the grenade, Kiki saw no danger. She only saw the head of a punk rock doll. Picking it up and examined the doll head, Kiki decided it was a harmless child's toy. Before anyone could shout a warning to Kiki, the grenade activated.

A putrid thick white gas spewed from the smoke bomb. The cloud of knock-out gas engulfed Kiki completely and she collapsed to the floor of the stage in an instant.

The other punks, shielding themselves on stage, screamed helplessly. They knew not to run near to the dangerous gas. It was all they could do or else they too would fall to the affects of the poisonous gas.

Warhead brought his motor trike around to one of the towering speakers which had been pushed off the stage. He stopped, letting his trike idle as he watched to see what was happening amongst the crowd in the field. Letting some time go by, Warhead gave the gas a moment to blow away from the punk's stage.

Many punks stood around the body of Grizz. No one from the outside of the circle could see Grizz's body laying in the mud. A scream of anguish sounded as Lips stood up from her paradise of carnage. With her mouth hanging open impossibly wide, Lips screamed again like nails on a chalkboard as her eyes bugged out all crazy like.

Sprinting to a run toward the group of exhausted and unsuspecting rockers and punks, Lips tensed her hands like claws reaching out to the rockers. The rockers were horrified as the demon punk, Lips, came bounding closer. As the rockers saw how Lips was covered in tiger blood, the rockers panicked. Forming a line like a battalion, the rockers opened fire on Lips. Taking multiple hits, Lips kept on coming. The punks rose up with the power and indignation of Grizz's angry blood coursing through their veins before they attacked the rockers from behind and all at once.

Unfortunately, Lips had to pay the price for the freedom and liberty of the punks as she was cut to pieces upon the surface of the muddy battle field.

The rockers found their weapons had been quickly taken over and in the hands of the punks. As Grizz told them, the weapons of their enemies would be turned against them. No further shots were fired as something stirred behind the punks with the rumbling of a low growl. To the amazement of everyone, Grizz arose.

A single bullet indent was identified at the side of Grizz's helmet as he stood up shaking his head. Elation sounded amongst the punks as they praised their leader for defying death yet again.

Grizz took a moment to gain his bearings as he drew in a few deep breaths. Looking to the punk stage, Grizz's head was still ringing from the gun shot, he began to move toward the fallen body of Kiki. Some white smoke remained as a fog disappearing quickly in the breeze.

Warhead dismounted from his trike and climbed onto the stage. When he stood up and took a step toward Kiki's unconscious body, Jakebrake, Scorpin-X, Zom-Buckle, Roach and Vamporess stood up from the equipment at the far edges of the stage. The punks were ready to defend Kiki's body.

Warhead quickly drew his pistol and aimed at the threatening punks. Targeting each one in turn, Warhead stepped closer to Kiki. Bending down, Warhead found Kiki's body was as limp as a wet towel before he lifted her onto his shoulder. Quickly, Warhead made his way to the edge of the stage and climbed down. The punks followed Warhead cautiously, not taking their eyes off him for a moment.

Zom-Buckle stepped forward holding his battle ax base guitar like it was a weapon, "I can't let yo take the girl, Warhead… She's like family ta us." dropping the guitar to the stage floor, Zom-Buckle opened his empty hands as a sign of his surrender, "Take me instead." Offered Zom-Buckle with defeated self sacrifice.

"No, take me!" Vamporess shook her head and spoke up quickly.

Warhead slid Kiki off the stage and held her awkwardly in his arm as he held his pistol to her head. "No thanks, sorry, but she's the bait I need for a bigger fish." Dropping Kiki into the back seat of his trike, Warhead fastened the center seat belt around her waist. With haste, Warhead mounted his motortrike and spun the tires in the mud leaving two deep trenches in his place before racing away.

Still distracted from being shot in the head, Grizz perceived everything happening around him too fast and all at once. With a terrible sense Kiki was being taken from him, like deja vue, Grizz couldn't tell what was real. He could see Kiki actually being captured. Her limp body was pulled right off the stage by Warhead, but it was all so surreal.

Grizz thought, *'Okay, this isn't fun anymore!'*

Somehow, Grizz found he had covered the distance to the punk's stage. Leaping to the motortrike, Grizz was just shy of getting his hands on Warhead.

There was no doubt about it, Warhead did take Kiki and for *that* Warhead would pay with his life.

Stumbling forward when he failed to grab hold of the motortrike, Grizz did not stop running. Regaining his balance, Grizz practically flew to the cab of the black truck. Tearing the door from its hinges, Grizz forced the cab of the truck open.

Dropping himself into the driver's seat, Grizz Twisted the ignition key on and released the parking breaks with a hiss. A loud sound broke forth from the radio and shook the cab. Grizz sneered at the sudden explosion of punk rock music. Gritting his teeth and tightening his face, Grizz's fingers franticly played over the buttons and dials of the radio to turn it off but his efforts had no effect.

With the rig running, Grizz shoved the stick into gear. The whole transport truck lurched forward. The punks who were still on the stage fell to the decking as the entire thing moved with the truck. The truck pulled the open stage, quickly ramping up to a violent high speed.

Grizz had no mind for the safety of those who might be on the stage, rather he preferred to clip the stage on some large structure to tear it loose from the tractor because it was cumbersome and only served to slow him down.

Roach, Jakebrake, Zom-Buckle, Scorpin-X and Vamporess struggled to keep from letting the momentum slide them right off the stage to their deaths. While Vamporess was laying flat near the edge of the stage, she could see an old silo dangerously close to their path at the edge of the road. Trying to get up and run, the bouncing from the deep dirt road potholes kept Vamporess from rising to her feet.

The radio, still blaring its' annoying noise, angered Grizz. Wincing, Grizz punched the radio and it shattered as it was forced into the dash. Through all of Grizz's influenced handling to fix the radio, it still functioned. Even louder than the radio came Grizz's frustrated roar.

Swerving close to an old rusty silo, the main platform of the stage caught its' edge on one of the vertical support legs. The result tore the second extension of the stage free from the rest of the trailer.

Scorpin-X and Jakebrake were able to lean out and pull Vamporess to them for safety just before the dangerous clipping occurred. Clearly, no one on the trailer realized right away, how Grizz was trying to knock the trailer off. The punks only figured Grizz was a terrible driver.

As Grizz journeyed out from the abandoned industrial complex, he caught sight of Warhead's motortrike parked in the middle of the road at the main gate. Warhead was standing beside the back seat where he was bent over, binding Kiki's wrists to her ankles with duct tape. Kiki had also been gagged in case she awoke from the knock-out gas. To be sure no one would try following him, Warhead wrapped a heavy chain around the inner poles of the main gate behind him. The moment Warhead noticed the black rig barreling toward him and how the rig caused the silo to teeter over and crash to the road, he quickly fastened a pad lock to the gate chain and bounced back onto his trike and sped away like the devil himself was after him.

Despite the wind and propulsion of the momentum the punks encountered, Scorpin-X and Jakebrake cautiously climbed through the musical equipment and past the drums as they attempted to get to the cab of the tractor. The two punks rounded the wall at the head of the trailer. Holding onto the red and blue coiled air supply hoses for added support, Scorpin-X led the way across to the back of the truck's cab. The engine wined and roared as it was abused by Grizz's inexperienced driving.

435

Sounds of mechanical snorts, grunts and grindings were a frequent occurrence as the mad driver forced gears and pushed the engine to maximum.

Jakebrake was the next to try to get around the wall at the trailer's front end. As he swung around and reached for the air supply lines, the speeding rig plowed through the chained and secured main gate. The impact caused the whole rig to lurch aggressively. Jakebrake lost his footing but his hold of the air lines saved him. Dangling for a moment, Jakebrake finally regained his stability.

The towering speaker at the very back of the trailer tipped forward at the impact of the main gates. Vamporess and Roach thought the speaker tower was going to crush them but as the rig sped past the gates, the speaker tilted back into position with a loud thud.

As Grizz turned the rig to a hard right onto the main road of 400th avenue, Roach, Vamporess and Zom-Buckle were forced against the wall of the trailer along with all of the musical equipment. All eighteen wheels squealed, kicking up an impressive cloud of dust. Jakebrake and Scorpin-X almost lost their grips from the force of the high speed tight turn, which tipped the entire truck and trailer slightly to its' side. Grizz hit the breaks and the truck settled back down to all eighteen wheels once again.

The engine thundered as black smoke blew out from the tall exhaust stacks. Blinded to all things, Grizz only wanted to get Kiki back. Forcing other vehicles off the road, Grizz became the road hog master of road rage.

Once off the gravel road and onto the pavement of the main road, Jakebrake and Scorpin-X were able to climb around to the cab's passenger door. Opening the door, the two punks climbed halfway in before they paused to take a good look at Grizz.

Grizz had his right foot up in the air as he had

pivoted himself to kick them out, however, Grizz did not take this course of action as he recognized the two punks in time.

"I thought you were rockers for a moment there." Grizz told them as he shifted his weight and put his metal boot back under the steering wheel to the gas pedal again.

Struggling to take in each breath, Jakebrake seemed like he had just run a marathon. Looking across the dash Jakebrake couldn't help but notice the damaged radio, "What did yo do ta the radio, man?"

"I just wanted to turn this noise off. It's not normal, can you turn it off?" Grizz asked without taking his eyes from the road.

Jakebrake smiled and answered, "We fixed it so it wouldn't turn off. It's better this way..." Grizz glared at Jakebrake and his point was quickly received, "It's really cool..." he added meekly.

"It's broken!" Grizz barked.

Scorpin-X and Jakebrake looked at one another, then they looked at the radio and Scorpin-X remarked, "Yes it is..."

"Yo sure put us through hell back there!" Jakebrake told Grizz as he was still breathing heavily.

"There're no rockers on the rig, but Vamporess, Roach and Zom-Buckle're still in the back O the trailer." Scorpin-X added.

"Or what's left O it... Yo ever drive a rig before?" Jakebrake asked childishly.

"The trailer is slowing me down! I was *trying* to get rid of it." Grizz explained like they should have known already.

"We're heading away from Metro city. Where's Warhead taking Kiki anyway?" Jakebrake asked as he fastened his seatbelt.

"It doesn't matter. We will dog him until he finds a

destination or runs out of fuel, then we get Kiki back. I only hope she doesn't get hurt…"

Grizz frowned with hell burning in his eyes.

The police finally caught up to them. Three police cruisers raced down the road of the on coming lane with their red and blue lights punching and screaming to let all the world know they were on approach. A highway patrol helicopter flew low along with the police caravan. Warhead sped past the police. Unknown to anyone, Warhead pulled the piercing like pin from another punk head grenade. Tossing the round grenade high over his head, Warhead smiled at the idea of him alone up against the world.

The outer molding of the grenade was a molded rubber which caused the grenade to bounce down the road behind him until it landed on the hood of a police truck and detonate. It exploded into a fiery mess of engine parts and black smoke. This incident caused the line of police vehicles to slow down immediately. The authorities remained in their lane as Grizz barreled past them in the black truck and trailer.

Grizz's truck was obviously out of control by its' insane speed, but when he rammed through the smoking ruins of the police truck, he started a new war. The highway patrol helicopter changed direction and took up its' new targeted course on the tail of the dangerous punk and rocker vehicles. All of the police vehicles turned around and sped toward Warhead and the punks in full speed pursuit.

Enroute, passing through Liberty town, which was situated at the outskirts of Metro city, Grizz had managed to get very close to Warhead's motorcycle. When Warhead saw how close Grizz was, he retaliated by throwing many of his bouncy punk head grenades. Both Grizz, and the police, drove through the onslaught of

438

random explosions.

The people of the little town came out to the road side to see what all the noise was as the explosions approached. Warhead did a lot less grenade throwing as they entered Liberty town. Fearlessly, Grizz drove right up behind Warhead's motorbike to intimidate him and make it perfectly clear how serious he was.

The police vehicles, with lights and sirens pulsating, made their way up beside the rig and trailer stage. Vamporess, Roach and Zom-Buckle made eye contact with the officers. The police officers began firing at the punks who were on the open trailer stage.

"They're shooting at us!" Shouted Roach as he ducked low to avoid taking a bullet.

"Well, I'm not going to let them take me!" Vamporess shouted, she took one of the brass symbols from the drum set and threw it at the police cruiser. The symbol embedded itself into the windshield and the police car as the glass shattered like a spider web. Both scared and surprised, the police slowed to the shoulder of the road.

The punks drew strength from the successful result of fighting back as Zom-Buckle congratulated Vamporess, "Good idea!" Zom-Buckle shouted as he threw his battle ax guitar at another police vehicle.

In toe, Roach pushed the entire drum set off the stage and let it crash all over the road to slow the police down.

In the cab, Grizz told Scorpin-X and Jakebrake, "Go get Kiki!" The punks obviously didn't want to get out of the rig at such high speeds. Decisively, Warhead tossed another of his punk head grenades which exploded over the nose of the rig. The black metal hood and side body of the front end and grill had completely blown away. The windows shattered and crumbled and the engine was on fire.

The road began to wind to and fro. Zom-Buckle fell to the floor of the stage and almost slipped right off. He struggled to climb away from the edge.

Warhead hit the turbo and sped away. As he left, Grizz noticed Warhead's turbo flash and sputter like it was practically out of fuel.

Nearing the town's only intersection, Warhead flashed up his turbo accelerator for the very last time. Using up the last of the fuel, the turbo just kind of popped. This was enough for the motorbike to conduct a single wheelie under the momentary boost of speed. Warhead ran the red light and sped through the intersection, a mass of fast moving congested vehicles passing through and cutting off the path. Warhead magically made it through the traffic without a scratch. Grizz followed, full throttle as Scorpin-X and Jakebrake screamed with their knees brought up high and their arms crossed before their faces to protect them from the crash.

Grizz plowed into the side of a delivery van as multiple other vehicles were also damaged within a few seconds of total chaos.

The tall speaker tower fell forward to the stage upon impact with the delivery truck. When the speaker tower fell, it crushed Zom-Buckle like a fly swatter.

Coming through the intersection, Vehicles ran into the trailer as the speeding rig slammed into several other vehicles. Cars slammed into the side of the truck and trailer on both sides as though one look at the fiery punk rig was a curse of certain destruction. A garbage truck locked up its breaks but speed and momentum caused it to collide with the back end of the trailer stage which split it in half. The great speaker, along with the rear axiles were torn away and thrown through the air. Scattered crumpled vehicle parts were strewn over the compromised traffic. The magnitude of destruction was overwhelming for Vamporess and Roach.

With the rear axiles missing, the trailer was dragged over the road with a shower of sparks spraying out twenty feet behind. As long as Warhead was riding, Grizz would not give up the pursuit. The stage was angled to a downward slope and grated across the road. Vamporess and Roach saw saw the remainder of the sound equipment slide away. They held on for dear life as the rig felt like it was not going to slow down anytime soon.

From the moment of mass destruction at the intersection, the pursuing police slowed down. Many police vehicles remained to assist other emergency response teams to tend to the casualties, however several other police vehicles maneuvered past the scene. With their anger peeked, the police gave chase with feet heavier on the accelerators and a burning aggression in their souls.

Chapter 14

In the wee morning hours, the busy commute of regular morning traffic had already filled the streets of Metro City. Before the road ways and city streets were at their busiest, the highway exits saw the most congestion. Roads looped and crossed over to allow drivers to head in their desired directions, only this particular morning was like no other. This morning, Grizz was on his way to work.

As Warhead motored down a connector to merge with High way traffic, he tossed one of his trademark punk grenades so it was bouncing down the road behind his motor trike. The explosion of tarmac and concrete immediately tore up the off ramp to the high way. Grizz steered away from following Warhead. He had no other choice but to avoid the damaged section of road pitted with one very deep hole. Taking such unnecessary risks would not help him get to Kiki.

Driving across the over-pass and choosing to drive against the on coming traffic, Grizz steered for the on ramp. All on coming vehicles were forced off the road as the burning truck and broken trailer dragging behind approached.

The truck began to slow more and more as Grizz found they were losing power. Grizz wrenched on the steering wheel, turning the truck to cut off all three lanes of on coming vehicles. The fire from the engine came up from under the dash board and Grizz, Scorpin-X and Jakebrake quickly hustled out the side doors before their legs were burned. Their ride was dead. Grizz watched with a knot in his stomach as Warhead sped off into the distance with Kiki.

Jakebrake and Scorpin-X ran to the trailer as soon as they jumped out. Their faces were blackened and stunned by the engine fire when they found Vamporess and Roach climbing down from the trailer. Under regular circumstances they would split up and disappear but they were not at the end of their high speed life threatening ordeal.

Sounds of police sirens approached from the distance. Motorists began to come out of their vehicles as they tried to determine a sensible way to help, but at the sight of Grizz and the punks, logic kept them from getting involved.

Grizz immediately led the others to a Greyhound transit bus. The driver refused to open the door for them, but Grizz began to work his fingers into the door jam before he began reefing on it. The whole bus shook and the passengers expressed their fears and concerns. As the door was beginning to bend and come loose, the bus driver opened the door. Grizz took the first step in. His arms braced the opening so the door would no longer be able to close.

Jakebrake stopped in his tracks and expressed a concern, "Hey, we can't leave without Zom-Buckle!"

"Ya, does old Zombie need a hand?" Scorpin-X offered his friendly assistance as he began to make his way back.

Vamporess stopped Scorpin-X with her hand on his chest, "He didn't make it." she told him in a flat tone of doom.

"He didn't like Grizz's driving." Roach added with his hands on his hips. With his head down and turned, he tried to fight back his sorrow for the loss of his friend.

"Stay and die for all I care!" Came the last words from Grizz before he disappeared into the bus. Forcing the bus driver into the back with the other dazed and nervous passengers, Grizz found the bus to be loaded with a group of elderly men and women.

The punks thundered their steps as they too boarded the bus. Grizz dropped into the driver's seat as he threw it into drive and stepped the throttle to the floor. The bus jumped forward and nearly clipped the burning engine of the truck. Grizz had the steering wheel cranked all the way to the right as he barreled through the cement meridian to continue his pursuit of Warhead.

In their wake the truck exploded providing the perfect cover and diversion for their escape. As the bus increased speed the further it traveled down the now baron high way, a couple of high way patrol motor cycles sped up behind the bus. Grizz looked in the mirrors and thought, *'Oh, we don't need any more of this.'* But to his surprise, the two patrol officers passed them by. They were obviously in hot pursuit of Warhead.

Because Grizz and the punks possessed a different vehicle, they were no longer targeted fugitives, they had a new disguise. Grizz liked the fact a bus was not a suspect, but he knew it was likely just for the short term. Grizz resumed the chase though he lost sight of warhead.

An elderly fellow amongst the complaining passengers spoke up, "You're going the wrong way, you young punks."

Grizz shook his head as Scorpin-X grabbed hold of a CB receiver and spoke into it, "What'd yo know, old man? Yo think yo can drive? I don't think so!" The voice of Scorpin-X came through the speakers loud and clear. Grizz found the bus was at its' full speed.

Grizz swiped the receiver from Scorpin-X and said, "Listen, I have only one rule on my bus, 'sit down and shut up!!!' Break that rule and I toss you off the bus."

Grizz's statement was followed with silence until an

elderly woman corrected Grizz, "That's two rules!"

Grizz stood up from the driver's seat and turned to face the passengers. Scorpin-X was surprised by this and scrambled to get hold of the steering wheel. The bus shifted from side to side, but Grizz had the elderly woman locked in his gaze and he wouldn't let go.

"Come on, lady. You can be first." Grizz glared at her.

The old woman just sneered back at Grizz in a death stare.

"Ah, Warhead. There yo are…" Scorpin-X said leaning over the steering wheel and keeping the bus going.

Grizz spun around and confirmed it was indeed Warhead but he was still a good distance ahead of them. The pair of high way patrol officers were quite close behind Warhead.

Grizz waved Scorpin-X out of the driver's seat, before he took over again. He held the steering wheel tightly as he willed the bus to go faster. Grizz figured Warhead was up to something because he seemed to be slowing down slightly.

Near to them all was a low flying highway patrol helicopter who was either reporting the events.

Warhead smiled at the patrol officers as one pulled up next to him on the right and the other pulled up on his left. With pins in his mouth which Warhead had bit out from the two punk head grenades he was holding.

The highway patrol motorcycles recognized their dangerous situation. They reduced their speed and held back a distance. Everyone was watching as Warhead drove under an overpass and threw the two grenades, one at either side of himself as he sped through. The grenades exploded at the support beams of the overpass but the structure did not fall.

445

The commuters, who were using the over pass above, quickly cleared off the ramp and no one used it further after the clouds of smoke and dust from the explosion rose up over it. The two police bikes pursued Warhead passing under the shaken and unstable over pass and through the wall of smoke.

"Jakebrake, take the wheel!" Grizz shouted as he stood up from the driver's seat again. Pulling on the lever, Grizz opened the tall folding exit doors.

For a couple of seconds, Jakebrake was in a daze as he looked at the empty driver's seat. Quickly snapping out of it when Jakebrake realized the bus would not be able to drive itself for long. Jakebrake jumped to the driver's seat as though his butt had been shocked by an electric currant. Quickly settling in, he took control.

Grizz took his sling shot from his belt, unfolded it and prepared an aero dynamic bearing. As they passed through the cloud of smoke under the over pass, Grizz shot out one of the main support columns of the overpass. The structure cracked and buckled under the second shock as the bus quickly passed through the dust from underneath. The entire length of the overpass collapsed one section at a time and fell like a wave of broken concrete and dust.

The massive pile of broken concrete served as a wall, holding the pursuing authorities at bay. All except for the police helicopter. The copter's mandate was to do nothing more than to be the eye in the sky and give continuous, to the minute, reports of the positions of the motor cycle, but with the strange involvement of the greyhound bus it was quickly discovered how Grizz and the punks had hi-jacked it.

The police quickly considered the stolen bus to be a hostage situation so they did not target it, rather they followed it.

Warhead, preferred a fight, over being followed. As before Warhead released a grenade behind him and it bounced down the road between the two police motor bikes. When the police were close enough to Warhead they were blown off the road, one to the left and one to the right.

Jakebrake shouted with raised eyebrows, "Warhead's taking the next exit!" He pointed his finger at Warhead as they sped past the smoking ruins of the patrol officers.

An elderly woman, smaller than the first boisterous passenger, began shouting, "Hey, you hooligans!"

'Oh, brother.' Grizz thought as he crossed his eyes at having to deal with the elderly passengers again.

"You're taking the wrong exit, you big goof!" after speaking, the woman showed a little fear through her courage as she pushed her large glasses up the bridge of her nose.

Grizz turned to the old lady, "Sit down and SHUT UP!!!" he nearly stopped her heart.

Thinking about his earlier threat to throw one of the passengers off the bus for being noisy, Grizz had to convince himself this would be inappropriate. Shaking the thought from his head, Grizz focused on Warhead. They found themselves in the midst of thick traffic once again.

Grizz knew they would eventually drive right into a trap set by the police if the helicopter remained in the air to constantly give away their position. Grizz pulled back on his sling shot and blew the tail router off it.

The copter began to spin as the pilot did all he could to slow their descent and crash with as little force as possible.

Warhead was still a great deal ahead of the bus but

Jakebrake purposely kept his distance. Warhead believed he had given the police the slip, but Jakebrake hoped Warhead didn't suspect the bus was also after him.

Slowing to blend in with the traffic around them, Jakebrake ended up right behind Warhead. Not turning to look at the bus, Warhead seemed to still believe his troubles were miles away.

Following Warhead, Jakebrake commented, "Warhead's heading through a smaller town of West Key on the pacific coast a few miles out, next to Metro city."

The morning sun had risen over the horizon and lit up the soft strips of clouds with golden light. Grizz tried to remain inconspicuous as he was almost able to look right down into the back seat of the motorbike and see Kiki. Blending into the surrounding traffic, Warhead and Grizz shard the same idea. Unfortunately, the morning traffic of commuters was only getting thicker the closer they came to the popular public beach. Warhead's motor bike proved to be able to maneuver through the congestion far easier than the bus. Everyone just wanted to get ahead of the bus which made it move even slower. Grizz and the punks lost sight of Warhead's bike and the bus was only going to have to slow down.

Frustrated beyond measure, Grizz whaled on the horn and shouted at the other drivers.

Jakebrake stroked the stubble on his chin as he said, "Easy, man. Statistics show a rise in road rage these days."

"Pull over and open the door. I'm going to get Kiki by foot right now." Grizz commanded with the veins in his fore-head throbbing under his helmet.

"No, Blackguard. Yo'll never make it. Stay in the van, I think I know where he's going." Jakebrake said before he pursed his lips. "As I look around, it's all coming back ta me. I was a rocker once, but it was a lifetime ago."

Jakebrake drove the bus professionally, which was too slow for Grizz. With a short fuse, Grizz quickly lost patience with Jakebrake. "How can you drive like this? Just go through them! What are you waiting for? Do it, now!" Grizz protested.

Motoring cautiously through a full parking lot, Roach spotted Warhead's motorbike. It was parked but Warhead and Kiki were no longer anywhere near it.

Driving to a designated bus stop, Jakebrake parked like driving a bus may have once been his profession. The passengers along with everyone else inside the bus were frazzled, and no one was more so than Grizz. Grizz addressed everyone in the bus nicely, first asking them to sit down and shut-up again. "Take some deep breaths people and settle down. The ride is over." The passengers and the punks were too tired to disagree or to do anything but co-operate. No one wanted to see Grizz get angry and perhaps be persuaded, in some forceful fashion, to co-operate.

Under Grizz's instructions, the elderly were told not to call for help or to bring attention to them. From the windows of the bus, the elderly watched as Grizz and the punks departed the bus smiling and waving at the people who were looking at them from the sidewalk. Grizz made eye contact with a young family who had a little daughter with them.

"Look, mommy, is the circus in town?" asked the little girl. Her parents placing a protective hand on their daughter's shoulder as they eyed the punks questionably.

Grizz smiled as best as he could, "Hey, hey, don't miss the show later, okay?" the punks went along with Grizz's enthusiasm like they were part of a circus or something.

When Grizz and the punks headed down a flight of stairs toward the beach and were beyond line of sight from the bus passengers, the elder bus passengers stepped off the bus screaming and shouting about their terrible ordeal. Concerned pedestrians tried to understand the elderly, but they misunderstood them and thought they might be some kind of European tourists group. The bus driver finally explained their problem soundly and the authorities were called.

At the sound of bus passengers in a panic, Grizz and the Punks knew they only had minutes left to figure out how to take Kiki back before disappearing into their dark world again. Running as fast as their feet would carry them, the punks raced to the West Key boat docks. Grizz easily took the lead as he could run substantially faster than the rest.

The sights and sounds of the popular West Key Muscle Beach in the morning had a wonderful vacationing spirit about it accompanied with the aroma of bagles and coffee in the air. As they headed down to the beach and the little strip mall of shops, Grizz carefully glanced at the faces in the off chance he might notice Warhead.

Descending the many levels and flights of stairs to the beach front area, they could see from their height, the left side of the bay was cluttered with a maze of floating wharfs to allow access to countless private boats. To the right of the bay was the ever famous stretch of wide West Key beach.

From just above a rise from the boat dock, Grizz bounded across a small road which was for boaters to gain vehicular access to the docks. Bracing himself and slowing at a railing, Grizz stopped and studied the people on the dock intently. While he searched for any sign of Warhead, the punks were able to catch up to him.

When they arrived, they were quite winded. The punks took a moment to catch their breaths.

"I need a drink..." Roach commented as he folded himself over the railing.

"Good idea. When all this is over, I'm going ta have me some O the hard stuff." Jakebrake added as he leaned back against a light pole and let his feet slide out so he was sitting on the boardwalk looking up at the sky. "I was built fo driving not this running thing."

"I meant water, motor mouth..." Roach was half joking with his friend, "I could use a big tall glass O ice cold water." The others visualized the same mirage before them.

"There he is..." Grizz announced to the others. Their fantasy of nourishment popped and disappeared like a bubble. "I have you this time..." Grizz spoke like Warhead was right in front of him listening. "He is the one five docks over carrying the bright red sports bag." Grizz pointed out.

"Kiki is in the duffle bag no doubt." Vamporess added with sharp eyes.

Oddly, Warhead craned his neck and looked around suspiciously, then he stopped in his tracks as he spotted Grizz and the punks watching him from the upper boardwalk.

He began to run down the length of the dock once he was aware of his immanent danger. Grizz leaped over the railing to the docks below to save time while the others charge down to the boat docks together. Knowing they were so close to saving Kiki, they ignored the pain in their unexercised legs and raced along the wooden wharfs to Warhead. Warhead had already joined a group of five strange men, all of whom were wearing sunglasses. The man at the center wore an expensive suit and tie, while the other four men who were with him wore a strange design of army fatigues. Their identical uniforms were grey but their boots, belts and other accessories like watches and elbow pads were all black.

As Grizz thundered his way along the wooden dock, the man in the business suit gave an order with a gesture of his hand and the soldiers pulled out pistols and aimed them at Grizz. Grizz was the first of his group to confront Warhead. It was Grizz's intention to hit Warhead so fast and so hard he would simply be out of the picture before he knew it, but he didn't want to risk injury to Kiki.

Finally, Grizz's plans were put on hold when Warhead turned around with the tight shoulder strap of the red bag pulling on him. Kiki was certainly in the bag when Warhead lifted his pistol from its' holster and pointed it to Kiki's head. The threat was more than Grizz expected to deal with. Kiki meant nothing to Warhead and in a desperate situation of life and death, he wouldn't think twice about shooting the girl.

The four punks came charging up the dock behind Grizz until they saw men with guns. They stopped in their tracks. Behind them four more soldiers stepped up onto the dock from a boat and ordered the punks to put their hands on their heads. After arresting the punks and shackling their wrists behind their backs they were escorted closer to Grizz and the others.

Warhead gave Grizz an evil eye when he spoke to the soldiers behind him, "Arrest that thing!"

Grizz complied and let the soldiers arrest him without resistance. The soldiers had some complications getting the shackles to fit on Grizz's wrists.

"I must admit, I am impressed you pulled this off, Warhead." The man in the suit commented as he fixed his tie. "We might have to consider adding you to our payroll." he chuckled at his own joke. Grizz couldn't help but to wonder who these guys were anyway. Of course, if he was told he really couldn't care less. They were just an added annoyance.

"It went better than I had planned. For a time I thought I'd actually lost him." Warhead replied as he smiled contently to himself.

"We have been trying to track him for months and here you actually deliver him to us. We are impressed by this set up." Added the man in the business suit rather robotically.

Grizz raised an eyebrow and snorted, "Setup? What's the big idea? You took my friend. Didn't it occur to you, I would come for you? If you didn't fear me before, you *will* fear me now."

Warhead shrugged his shoulders as he holstered his pistol. He didn't fear Grizz once the shackles were fastened tightly to his wrists, "Yo, you know I don't have a problem with you punks. I would like to see other punk organizations start up just like yours. Punk the world for all I care, but I am not your enemy."

Grizz took a step toward Warhead and the soldiers got a good sense of the strength Grizz was in command of, "Don't try to sweet talk your way out of this, *Warhead*. Now that you've attacked and kidnapped one of mine, there is no going back. You *will* suffer."

The sirens of angry police vehicles screaming toward them caused the group to get moving. They all hustled into the back of their fourteen foot outboard speedboat and headed out to sea.

At the back of the long boat, Warhead reclined in a padded seat and relaxed where he could get a good look at Grizz and the punks. He kept the red bag with Kiki inside, at his feet. "You might want to think twice about your threat, pal. Look, I get it. You're upset."

"Oh, I'm way past upset." Grizz groaned.

Agent Cawston ordered his troopers to search the

prisoners and collect all of their weapons. They collected knives, a small and large yo-yo, a couple of sling shots. They also removed body armor from Grizz and the punks, along with a coil of rope and remote grappler.

"Leave their weapons here. The further away they are from them the better their stay with us will be." Agent Cawston pointed out wisely.

Warhead leaned forward to make his point to Grizz, "None of this was our idea, you know, Blackguard. Our hands were tied and we were blackmailed, forced, duped into betraying you. Of course they knew you would come for the girl. Everyone knew *that*. Everywhere you go, there she is. She is your akilies heal. It didn't take a genius to figure that out. You've played right into their hands, perfectly."

Grizz broke the chain of his shackles with ease. The soldiers raised their pistols to Grizz's head, "Freeze!" One of them shouted.

Grizz raised his hands to surrender and back down. He stared deep into Warhead's eyes before asking, "Talk fast, who are *they*?"

The man wearing the suit and sunglasses spoke up as he stroked his chin, "He is referring to us. I am special agent Cawston of our government's secret service and these are specially trained Knolix troopers."

It dawned on Grizz just how much trouble he was in. If he let Agent Cawston have his way, he would find himself back on the Knolix Island and chances were he would not have anywhere near the freedom he used to have there, "Knolix? As in the Knolix Island, no doubt. Warhead, you're in ka-hoots with these guys? Oh, I get it, so this was all a set-up? The brawl and everything? I bet you don't even have Kiki. I just saw some look-alike. The real Kiki is still locked away where I left her, isn't she?"

Warhead bent forward and unzipped the red duffle

bag. To Grizz's horror Kiki was revealed bound inside in a fetal position. When he saw her sleeping face, he could see she was the real Kiki.

They seemed to venture along the shore line for hours. Not a word was spoken as it was very difficult to hear anyone over the loud noise of the boat motor. Grizz noticed the red sports bag begin to move. Kiki was waking up. Her eyes blinked open and Grizz was happy to see her through the opening of the bag. She seemed quite dazed as she tried to figure out where she was for she was still bound and gagged. Her exposure to Grizz's blood was the key to enabling her body to fight off the affects of Warhead's knock-out gas.

Warhead couldn't understand how she was able to wake up so soon but not one of the punks felt obliged to explain it to the rocker.

Finally, they turned the boat into a deep and private alcove. Trees and tall stones surrounded a wide area of water and at the center of the area were four houseboats. The motor boat approached the houseboats which were tied together with specialized shock absorbing rods with ball joint hinges. The specialized rods served the purpose of keeping the boats together, even in turbulent weather diminishing the possibility of friction or collision.

"Nice little trap you've put us all in..." Grizz observed as he looked at their surroundings.

"You see a trap. I see privacy." Warhead replied with an obnoxious smirk.

"You can't hide anywhere. The police will find you and bust you." Grizz predicted a warning.

"I have already called them off. I assure you the police will not be bothering us." Agent Cawston informed.

"Oh, let me guess, you own the police?" Grizz inquired.

"Should this surprise you? We are the government." Agent Cawston looked at Grizz like he was dumb.

"Seems everyone owns a piece of the police these days." Grizz mentioned in hearing the statement as it was made in the past.

The motor boat approached the houseboats slowly until they just drifted in for the last few feet. There were no other rockers seen anywhere on the houseboats. Every one of them had attended the rumble, however, Knolix troopers were in no short order.

Without warning, agent Cawston held his finger in the air, before he brought it down to point at the prisoners. At the signal the troopers opened fire and began firing one shot at each of the prisoners. Each one was shot in their shoulder.

Grizz saw his punk companions fall around him with what looked like a little yellow flower on one of their shoulders. He looked at his shoulder and found he was shot with the very same tranquilizer dart as the others.

Grizz flopped forward like a weakling and it made him very angry.

"What good will they be to us now?" Warhead tried to figure out the advantage of tranquilizing the prisoners. "I thought you wanted to question them."

Agent Cawston smoothened out his jacket and adjusted his sunglasses as he explained, "You do not need to concern yourself with our methods. For one thing, the tranquilizer will keep them under control. Grizz has proven to be very unpredictable. Also, it is a test. Drugs have no effect on Grizz. I am curious with how quickly the young one has fought off the effects of your knock out gas. I would like to know if the others have the same ability. Besides I have another cocktail in mind for anyone of them who prove to fight off the affects of a simple tranquilizer."

From the deck of the houseboat the troopers assisted in tying the motor boat and unloading the prisoners. The troopers were amazed to find each one of the prisoners were not entirely unconscious. The punks fought hard to keep awake. The troopers helped each of the punks up and they moved forward with heavy feet dragging with each step. Assisted from Knolix guards, the prisoners walked in single file, not certain what fate awaited them. Within the houseboat, it was clear how the agents had converted the space into their mobile base of operations. They had sonar, radar and satellite linked computer systems. A buzz of networking and operations was in full works as personnel were so busy they barely looked up long enough to notice Grizz and the punks as they were being brought through. Clearly it had not been long since the agents had set up base upon the floors of the houseboats. Tools, like hammers and drills, amongst a few soda pop cans cluttered the kitchen counters.

Guitars still hung for display on walls as were some rock band posters. One of the walls of the base area within the main room was made of glass and countless snakes could be seen slithering together under a dark light within. Grizz was disgusted by the sight of the snakes moving together with pegs built in to assist them while sandwiched between the two panes of glass. A sign was engraved in wood above the glass which read, 'The nest.'

Within the nest were countless snake bodies of various sizes and colours. All of them were in a tangle but they could still move, or slither. There was one snake in particular which stood out to Grizz. It was a fully grown boa constrictor and it could have easily taken up the space behind the glass all on its' own.

When Warhead saw Grizz examining the wall of snakes, he flipped a switch on the wall and announced,

"Feeding time!" The switch opened a small hatch which allowed about four white rats to fall in and land on top of the slithering bodies. The slithering immediately began to speed up as the snakes reacted to the installation of a live scurrying meal.

Warhead could only laugh when he saw the expressions on Grizz's face.

Quickly, the rats were pushed against the glass or otherwise strangled in tight coils where others underwent far quicker deaths as the snake heads rose up with wide mouths to devour their pray, whole.

The prisoners snapped out of their wild life lesson when agent Cawston went to the main computer system and lifted a micro-phone to his mouth. "Agent Cawston here, make ready the Aquatica to accept six prisoners for interrogation proceedings."

A female operator was engaged in communication at the console. The voice of an Asian man replied over the com. "As you command sir, the interrogation room is in readiness. Would you have Eddy Evon with you?"

"No, but I have his brother, Domin. I repeat, we require immediate approval to board Aquatica."

"Of course sir, Captain J. Chan, out."

Once again, Grizz and the punks were escorted through the houseboat to the deck, only this time they were on the inside of the circle of houseboats. Each one of the prisoners could feel their strength returning and as it did, their anger rose.

Looking around everyone could see how the houseboats were attached at each corner. This created a rather large area of surface water at the center of the square, circle of houseboats. Nevertheless, the prisoners were confused, "What're we doing out here?" Scorpin-X asked with slurred words as he looked around nervously.

Before long, a strange bulbous object emerged out

from the water's surface. It was attached to a long neck, but it was no creature for in the broad daylight it was quite obvious the object was metal and man made.

Jakebrake thought it was all part of the funky hallucinogenic drug they were given. "Whoa, far out! It's like, the Ogopogo, man, only it's a robot."

Agent Cawston began to explain, "One of the advantages of this particular location is the depth. If you look around and notice the tall stones, you will also find they are even more impressive underwater. They are vertical cliffs of approximately five hundred feet below the surface."

The object at the end of the pole which protruded from the water's surface, resembled a camera of strange design. As it rose up from the waves, it was attached to a much larger metal body housing. The great object was painted gun metal grey.

"This makes such a location ideal to hide a submarine." The object emerging from the water was, a submarine periscope.

The submarine was huge and facing the prisoners as they watched from the deck. The bow of the sub came up high enough to slightly lift the houseboats which were in front and behind the periscope. Water poured off the emerging sub and when it had stabilized, they opened a gate of the houseboat and guided the prisoners across the wet skin of the submarine to a hatch which opened at the side of the conning tower.

Within the sub, an elevator lowered the disoriented punks, two groups at a time because the size of the elevator was not designed to take them all at once. Accompanied by two troopers, the first group, with Grizz, Roach and Vamporess, were taken deep inside the belly of the Knolix Island sub. Behind them, Kiki, Scorpin-X and Jakebrake were led by two other troopers.

459

They found themselves in a dismal room with pipes running along the walls, a bright red fire extinguisher attached to a bracket, no tables, no shelves, but many chairs. Everything was painted the same dark gunmetal grey.

The elevator let them out in the submarine's brig. Grizz was immediately taken to a separate room or cell with chains and shackles on the floor which were specially designed for Eddy Evon. A red button within a glass box was mounted next to the cell door. Grizz was directed to sit in a metal chair which was bolted to the floor. When the heavy shackles were locked to Grizz's wrists, he began to growl angrily and shake off the affects of the drug. He was curious to find thick electrical cables coming up from the floors and connected to the shackles along the chains. As Grizz tugged at his bonds, he realized it was a situation he would not be able to win with strength alone.

The other punks were brought into the next room which was a tight spaced stockade. There, the Knolix troopers tied each punk securely to metal folding chairs. The sound of the submarine's engine drives could be heard vibrating through the walls. Along the wall, which was a sloping inner hull of the sub, many conduits of different sizes ran. A wide flat screen monitor was positioned over the assorted pipes.

Grizz was able to see everything going on in the next room. Kiki was the last one to be brought into the room. They had run out of the folding chairs so a few wooden chairs from the mess hall were brought in as well.

Within Grizz's cell, agent Cawston strolled in, "Like the view?" The agent asked Grizz with a smug smirk on his face. Warhead came walking in behind him as he observed all they did. Grizz noticed Warhead only had his last two punk head grenades attached to his jacket. Agent Cawston wrapped his knuckles upon the window. "This shatter proof glass is six inches thick." Next, agent Cawston tugged at the titanium steel chains, "Even if you were to free yourself from the chains, you wouldn't be able to get out of this room." He stepped out of Grizz's cell and closed the heavy steel door behind him.

When all of the prisoners were secured, Doctors entered the room wearing the familiar white lab coats which Grizz and Kiki recognized from the Knolix Island. There were six doctors in all and each of them stood behind each of the prisoners. They all held a syringe. Preparing the syringes, the doctors removed the protective caps from the small needles and pointing the needles upward, they tapped for the bubbles to rise and squeezed out the air.

Again, agent Cawston gave an order with a silent hand gesture, and the doctors inserted the needles and pressed the plungers to administer the new drug. When the process was finished, the doctors left with their empty syringes as quickly as they came.

Agent Cawston stepped in sight of the prisoners with his hands clasped at his back. "You have all been given two kinds of drugs. One is to temporarily paralyse you and the other is a truth serum. Such a dosage would mess up any regular mortal for a week at least, but you six, however, are not so regular... Are you?!"

"What do you want?..." Grizz asked with droopy eyes and tired speech.

Agent Cawston responded to Grizz right away, "Primarily, we want you, Domin, but more importantly, we want your brother." Walking to the window and speaking to the glass, agent Cawston asked, "What do you know about the present location of Eddy Evon?"

"You lost him?... I have no idea where he could

be…" Grizz answered before dropping his head.

Agent Cawston used a small key attached to a long necklace chain to open a small clear box next to the door. "Not good enough!" Agent Cawston shouted forcefully as he slapped his hand against the red button and Grizz was electrocuted.

Grizz stood up from the chair and roared to the ceiling as voltage cooked through his body.

More awake now, Grizz realized the agent was in a panic to find Eddy Evon. He would try to act cool but it was just a front to establish dominance. "No more games, Grizz. Tell me where Eddy is now or I will remove the information from you in the most unpleasant fashion. Our sources have confirmation you were with Eddy recently. Now, where is he?!!!"

"Your sources are mistaken, I have no information for you." Grizz told the interrogator.

Agent Cawston was fired up with anger as he punched at the red button sending electrical jolts through Grizz's body.

Finally, when the electrical current ceased, Grizz sat back and sagged into the uncomfortable chair. His shoulders and head were smoking. "Now tell me where you last seen Eddy and I promise the pain will stop. Why should you protect him? He can take care of himself." Agent Cawston stared at Grizz for a moment, but when he could see Grizz was not going to give him any information, he walked to the punks who were tied to their seats. "Perhaps if you will not speak under your own pain, then maybe you'll have more to say when one of your friends are in pain. Now I can be a reasonable man. I have a way to benefit us both Domin. You see for my benefit, I will provide a buddy system where we have one trooper to each one of these low life punks. Rather than terrorizing one at a time, they will all feel the same pain at once. The benefit for you is I will let them all go at once if you simply tell me Eddy's location... Why, heck, if any of you punks want to share some information, I will be happy to listen." He snapped his hand in the air and the troopers put away their rifles and took up positions behind the prisoners.

Though the punks were drowsy, they were no less frightened.

Agent Cawston puffed up his chest and spoke loudly, "First question, and it goes for you smelly punks, as well. When did you last see, Eddy Evon?"

"Who *is*, Eddy Evon?" Jakebrake asked.

Agent Cawston drew a remote control from a video monitor and used it to turn the screen on. He clicked through a series of slides and showed a few pictures of the eight foot tall, grey muscular volk.

Grizz knew there would be little chance of any of them getting out alive when the punks were being shown photos of their precious top secret jewel.

"I have answered your question, now, won't one of you answer mine?" But no one responded. Agent Cawston nodded his head and the troopers beat the punks with metal rods. They seemed to beat them for an eternity before agent Cawston nodded his head again and the terrible beatings stopped. The troopers were careful not to strike anyone in the mouth because agent Cawston wanted to be sure the prisoners would be able to speak.

Clicking through a few more pictures, agent Cawston paused on another interesting photo. "This one is of Eddy Evon walking on a sidewalk in the middle of Metro city. It was taken yesterday. What have you all got to say about that?" asked agent Cawston with his skeptical eye examining each one.

Warhead could see, none of the prisoners were going to answer the question and agent Cawston was about to give the signal for another beating. Quickly, Warhead said, "It's not necessary to beat them all. There is just one whom the rest have a soft spot for. Choose her and your efforts will be far more effective."

Walking along the line of punks, Warhead stopped at Kiki and dragged her out tied to the wooden chair.

Agent Cawston looked at Warhead with a half grin smirk, "Very good, Warhead." Nodding to the Troopers he signaled for them to leave the room and they did so. He addressed the prisoners again, "Once more, does anyone have any information about where Eddy Evon is? Or do we have to watch this young girl get beaten to death?" Agent Cawston's tone was heartless. He waited for an answer. When none was given, he personally struck Kiki across the face.

Grizz struggled to be free, but the shackles only cut into his wrist. A line of blood trickled from the corned of her mouth.

"Oh, big man!" Came the voice of Grizz through an intercom speaker. "You don't get what you want, like a spoiled child, so you hit a defenseless little girl?"

"Ya, why don't you pick on someone your own size?" Added Vamporess.

"Well, I did get something I wanted." Agent Cawston told the others as he turned away from Kiki to glare at Grizz. He slapped his hand on the back of Kiki's head and patted her like a pet. Violently, agent Cawston gripped her spiky green hair and tugged it back. Kiki's face cringed in pain. "I've got a strong reaction from you." He threw her head forward and tore her shirt before swinging around and striking Kiki again on her other cheek. "Do you think I care if any of you die?" He turned away from Kiki again and spoke to the ceiling. "At least I can tell my superiors I did all I could… They just wouldn't talk." Agent Cawston began to shout at Grizz

464

through the window, "He is your brother. Knowing how close you were to your other brothers, you must not be reunited with him. Luckily, we now have you. Soon, we will have Eddy as well, and we will take you back to the Knolix Island where we will implement mind control devices."

Grizz roared and thrashed against his bonds again. Though he caused himself a lot of pain, he felt the affects of the drugs had nearly worn off completely. Studying the behaviour of the punks, Grizz realized they too were fighting off the drugs.

Agent Cawston noticed Grizz fighting against his bonds and commented, "You might as well stop struggling. We created you pal. Do you think we don't know the limitations of your strength? Those are high density titanium steel rods anchored four feet into the frame work." Agent Cawston looked at everyone, "You all disappoint me. Still, no one has an answer for me? Looks like I am going to have to take things to the next level." Pulling a small pistol out from his holster, which was hidden in his jacket, Agent Cawston pressed the barrel of the gun against Kiki's fore-head.

Grizz's whole body became tight, as his veins bulged and coursed with dark red blood. Stiffening his muscles, like Grizz was a statue of solid die cast metal. With his eyes fixed on Kiki in madness, Grizz could only think about one thing. He could not bare to let harm come to her. "Come on, *Domin*, you know what I want…" The gun barrel was pressed up against Kiki's temple as the agent began to count backwards. "Three, two…" The gun fired and Kiki's head went down immediately. The metal under Grizz's feet bent under his stress and the metal rods began to stretch out. With Grizz's eyes fixed on the other room, he noticed Warhead standing behind Kiki's chair as he brought his smoking gun down. He had fired into

465

the air. Kiki lifted her head back, unharmed. She was breathing heavily with tears streaming down her face…

'She was not shot.' Grizz couldn't believe it. It was all just a scare tactic. They approached Kiki to rough her up some more, when Warhead noticed a strange tattoo on Kiki's arm under her torn sleeve. "Hey, agent Cawston, what is this? I know tattoos and this one is not normal. It looks…"

"Government…" Agent Cawston finished Warhead's sentence. "We will have to verify the tag to find out if it is authentic."

When agent Cawston turned away for a moment to call someone else into the room to have the tattoo verified, Kiki, with a bruised eye and cut lip, looked up at Grizz and smiled before she winked. Grizz perked up curiously. Relaxing her body, Kiki pushed her shoulders down low. She then wiggled a little from side to side lifting her elbows up at her sides and the ropes simply slipped up over her head as easily as taking off a T-shirt. Kiki was free and the agent turned around to look at her as she spun around lifting her chair and cracking it over the agent's head breaking his four front teeth out. The agent fell down and Kiki struck him several times with the chair. When Warhead approached her, she growled like Grizz as she came in touch with his blood influenced anger. From this burst of new strength, Kiki hit Warhead with the wooden chair so hard the chair broke to pieces and Warhead sprawled out on the floor like a rag doll. The door to the compartment opened and Kiki rushed the oncoming troopers. Throwing some of the broken chair pieces, she struck the troopers in weak unprotected areas like eyes, throats, noses and stomachs. Kiki used the broken pieces of the chair like police batons. She was untouchable and uncatchable as she jumped around putting her clown training to good use. Kiki's fluent movements were so professional, she seemed to defy gravity with impressive clown tricks. Stepping up onto Jakebrake's chair to his shoulder, Kiki leaped into the air and kicked out the lights. The room went dark as she landed. Kiki moved through the shadows like she was floating and gliding weightlessly as she subdued the remaining troopers. "I need more lumber!" Kiki shouted as she broke the other punks free from their chairs. As the other punks were freed, they too began to roar like Grizz as their anger empowered them also.

Agent Cawston came to laying next to Warhead. Warhead was also groggy as he shook his head to rise up. Agent Cawston caught sight of one of the last two punk head grenades dangling from Warhead's jacket. Grabbing the grenade, agent Cawston asked what is this, a doll's head?" as he plucked the grenade from the jacket. Warhead tried to slap the agent's hand away and protect the grenade, but his finger snagged on something. The two men backed away from one another and found the agent was holding the grenade and Warhead was holding the pin. When they realize the grenade had been activated, Warhead jumped up and began to run shouting, "Do you know what you've done?!" Pushing punks out of his way, Warhead bolted for the door.

Grizz pounded and struggled against the bonds ensnaring him tightly. He began to hammer his fist to be free as the shackles cut into his skin. "No, no, no... Run!" Grizz shouted through the thick glass.

Agent Cawston wasn't sure what had gotten into Warhead when he asked, "Is this supposed to be a bomb?"

-Ka-Boom!!!-

The grenade was so powerful, it blew agent Cawston into tiny meaty fragments. Warhead was blown out the heavy submarine door as he struggled to open it. All of

467

the punks were forced to the floor and they all momentarily lost their hearing. Water was spraying into the sub.

Grizz saw Kiki get tossed against the six inch window in the blast. The window was as high as the ceiling and as low as the floor and it was on the floor where Grizz saw Kiki's eyes go wide with shock as she took a quick deep gasp of air. The life seemed to drain from her face as pain was in her eyes. Kiki fell to the floor and writhed as she tried to reach around to her back and remove a hot embedded shrapnel fragment. When Grizz saw the blood coming from her wound, he could feel a shiver run through his own spine and he could imagine feeling the hot piece of metal protruding from his own back.

With sea water slowly filling the room, somehow Kiki found the strength to ignore the pain and look up at Grizz with unexplainable eyes of pain and strength. With unfounded determination, Kiki began to crawl. Grizz had never seen such strength as he had seen in this remarkable ten year old girl. She closed the door to his little cell with a locking click, then turned away in an attempt to save Vamporess.

The pipes which lined the wall were blown apart along with the monitor which seemed to no longer exist. The outer skin of the sub had buckled and continued to moan under its weakened position from the blast. The broken pipes hissed with steam and hydraulic fluids sprayed out.

Grizz fought harder against the chains holding him.

The other punks were crawling on the floor as well. Their faces were red on one side like they were sun burned, with some blistering.

Though Kiki couldn't hear or talk, Grizz could see from the movements of her lips, she wanted him to stop trying to break out of the cell. She pointed out how he would just drown with them. As she pointed to the moaning wall with fluids and steam spaying from it, the whole thing was compromised. The wall tore open from the water pressure on the other side. Cold sea water flooded the small interrogation room in a violent instant. All Grizz could do was watch as Kiki drowned before his eyes.

Kiki was loyal to Grizz to the very end. She gladly died for him, so he could live.

"RRRRRAAAAAAGGGGGGHHHHHH!!!!!!"

Going out of his mind with frustration, Grizz's veins thickened and pumped with dark red blood. With each agonizing moment, the bolted plates slowly tore their way right out of the floor. Once he had torn one arm free, he turned to the other chain and found where it was connected at the floor he could twist it and unhook it.

Next, Grizz went to work on the six inch thick window. He punched and kicked at it as he could see Kiki floating like the dead on the other side. Besides Kiki, the other punks had a breath each and were trying to swim though they were not sure where to go. The window wasn't about to let go easily, but the punks tried to kick it to help Grizz get out. They desperately needed Grizz to save them and he vowed to do just that.

Working his powerful fingers into the torn up flooring, Grizz began to tear chunks of the floor away. He was planning on going under the window. With a good pull he jarred something important out because cold salt water began spraying into his cell. He had to move faster, but as the supports around the seal of the window were torn away, the great pressure of the water against the window on the other side aided in pushing the window in. Water flooded Grizz's cell immediately. The glass wall was loosened from its edges, but its size still took up a lot

469

of room. Grizz took a great breath of air and worked his way around the six inch glass. Pushing his way out of the cell, Grizz believed he would be free. Through a little mind over matter, Grizz made his way to his punk friends. The punks were still alive but on the verge of losing the air they held.

Pulling a red fire extinguisher from the wall, Grizz gave the punks the chains which still hung from his wrists. He took Kiki from where she floated unconscious and held her under his right arm with the fire extinguisher under his left. As he made his way out through the large hole in the side of the submarine's hull, he broke the end off the compressed fire extinguisher canister. They were all rocket propelled upwards.

As Grizz rose quickly from the sub, he could see the punks begin to lose it one by one. They let go of their air prematurely, then they let go of their grip. Grizz struggled to keep a hold on each one.

Finally, they broke out at the water's surface and Grizz helped them to cough out the water in their lungs. Each of them had swallowed a lot of water, but not long enough to lose consciousness as Kiki had. They coughed out the water from their lungs and they were not able to do it in a quiet fashion. Grizz thought they would be found out for sure but none of the troops were outside on the deck. Grizz grabbed hold of the railing and lifted himself up high enough to get a peek inside the main houseboat. He could see Warhead was already inside speaking to the others. Injured but not nearly enough, Warhead was dripping wet as he reported what happened in the sub. All eyes were fixed on him as Warhead spoke quickly in a loud panic. One of the troopers were bandaging up Warhead's burns.

Pointing at a couple of troopers, Warhead instructed them, "Get outside and guard the houseboats in case the

Blackguard survived." The troopers left the room right away, but as they left, Warhead remembered how Grizz was locked away inside his cell and it was highly unlikely he would have been able to get out of it.

"Security breach! Security breach!" Shouted a trooper as he discharged his magazine with a volley of bullets.

Warhead jumped to the door and opened it a crack, "Report trooper, what did you see?"

"I think I saw Domin, sir. He was running through the eastern houseboat. I fired on his position but I think he got away, diving into the sea on the other side." The trooper explained professionally.

"Well round up your boys and go over there to take a look." The trooper looked at Warhead as to question not only his authority, but his plan. "I'll back you up." Warhead added quickly as he cocked his pistol.

The trooper cocked his automatic rifle also, which made Warhead's pistol look like a pee shooter. "Yes, sir."

Warhead watched intently as the troopers scoured the waters from the deck of the eastern houseboat.

Grizz, a strong swimmer, glided through the water like a shark. The troopers detected Grizz from time to time and unloaded their ammunition into the ocean. As Grizz toyed with the troopers, he distracted them enough to go after the stabilizing bars which held the houseboats together. It did not take long for Grizz to force the bars free, disconnecting each one from the two corners of the eastern houseboat.

Warhead was peeking out from the corner of the window through a narrow opening from the curtain, when he noticed Grizz tear one of the stabilizing bars away. Jumping out from the door, Warhead fired his pistol at Grizz.

"Over here! I got him! I got him!" shouted Warhead

to warn the troopers.

As the troopers hustled through to the opposite side of the houseboat, Grizz quickly dove under the houseboat where he drove his fists into the flotation pods. The troopers felt the impact of Grizz's power as his strength slightly lifted the houseboat. Warhead fell and his pistol slid off the deck and sank into the sea. As the pods quickly filled with sea water, the houseboat sank and with it, the heavily armored troopers.

Grizz climbed aboard the next houseboat and smashed into the room where he confronted the stunned Warhead. Pieces from the thin wooden walls flew throughout the room and damaged some of the computer equipment which was set up as various stations. Grizz stood menacingly over Warhead which was when Warhead realized he no longer had his pistol with him.

As Grizz took a wide step forward and pushed a table out of his way, Warhead slid his hand quickly and discretely into the jacket pocket of his vest and pulled out a small glass vial. He wrapped his fingers around the vial and squeezed until the vial broke.

Just as Grizz moved in on Warhead to strike, Warhead threw his fist out at Grizz and released the peppery powder into his face. Grizz reeled backwards for a moment and sneezed out a small cloud of the powder. The affects of the powder became realized as Grizz's eyes began to burn infectiously.

With his hands pressed to his eyes and rubbing, Grizz was momentarily disoriented and Warhead knew it. Rising to his feet with a hop, Warhead spun through the air to deliver a perfect round house kick to the side of Grizz's head. Slumping over to one side, Warhead lifted a pry bar from the counter of strewn tools and used it to pound at Grizz. He kicked Grizz in the stomach and Grizz toppled to the floor. There Grizz remained with one

472

hand over his eyes as his other hand stretched out to locate Warhead.

Roach and Jakebrake were outside where they could hear the sound of a fight going on inside. The two punks carried the body of Kiki across the deck of the houseboat to the same motor boat they arrived in. Scorpin-X went ahead to be sure the way was safe as Vamporess followed up from behind. They all made their way to the motor boat, where they gently laid the body of Kiki on the floor. Jakebrake went to the driver's seat and fired up the motor.

While Grizz was laying on the floor, Warhead balanced himself upon a stool as he smashes the glass wall out with the pry bar. The glass shattered and all of the snakes fell out and spread across the floor slithering toward Grizz.

One snake slithered right into Grizz's shirt. Grizz struggled as he was bit many times. The largest of the snakes was surprisingly quick to coil itself around Grizz as well. The boa constrictor began to apply pressure and though Grizz was impressed by the snake's strength he wondered if it was all the snake had.

"Ha, ha! Ya! Get'im boys!" Warhead laughed. "You don't know how happy it makes me to see you wallow at my feet."

At the sound of Warhead's words, Grizz stopped struggling. He stood up like the snakes didn't even exist anymore. Grizz snapped the neck of the giant boa constrictor and it released its' hold and dropped to the floor where it wiggled around as a reflex to its' deathly wound. Struggling to see through bloodshot eyes, Grizz proceeded to grab the tail end of the black snake which was deep within his Shirt. He pulled out the slithery tail of the snake's glistening, slick, scaly hide. Hand over hand, Grizz began to pull the snake out. Before the black snake was pulled out of Grizz's shirt, Grizz found resistance. The snakes fangs were locked onto the flesh of Grizz's chest. Warhead chuckled with satisfaction, but Grizz just frowned and pulled the snake harder until the fangs released.

Grizz and Warhead were at a face off alone in a houseboat, the floor alive with the movement of snakes and the flickering lights of damaged computer equipment. Grizz glared at Warhead, holding the vicious black snake, as he said, "You know, you put yourself on a tall pedestal, Warhead, but it only means, you have a longer way to fall…" Grizz tossed the black snake at Warhead as he also kicked the stool out from under him. Warhead fell to the floor where he twisted and turned amongst the poisonous snakes as he fought to protect himself from them.

"The poisons have no effect on me, Warhead. How are you doing?"

Warhead jumped up in a frenzied panic as he squealed an insane scream. Snakes had bit Warhead multiple times when he fell on them, but when he was back up on his feet, he pulled the last punk head grenade from his jacket and pulled the nose piercing activation pin free from it. Grizz knew what to expect from one of Warhead's potent grenades. He turned to run when he felt a subtle click on his back. It was no mystery, Grizz knew just what it was. Warhead had attached the grenade to his back. Grizz swung his arms as far as he could behind his head and back but he could not reach the grenade with his thick muscled arms. Quickly, Grizz bolted for the large opening he made in the wall when he entered. Jumping through the jagged edges of the opening, Grizz made a conscious effort to graze his back across the opening's edge. Using the jagged edge of the broken framework, Grizz managed to knock the bomb off.

When the bomb fell, Grizz plummeted over the side into the sea water. The last thing Warhead saw was the smiling face of his last punk head bomb mocking him with the look in its painted eyes. The bomb blew up and the houseboat hideout flew apart in a great explosion of wicked fiery light.

The punks watched from the motor boat as Warhead was consumed with his snakes in the magnificent blaze of destruction.

Jakebrake drove the boat near to Grizz and Grizz was able to climb aboard from the back of the boat. The salt water seemed to wash out much of the pepper sting from Grizz's eyes. He found the Punks in the motor boat were quiet and delirious. Jakebrake drove the boat like he was trying to outrun the devil. Following the coastline, Jakebrake took them back the way they came. Through reddened and less irritated eyes, Grizz looked to the floor and saw Kiki laying there, "Stay with me Kiki!" Grizz shout while on his knees next to Kiki. He lightly slapped her on her cheeks to wake her. "You're the strongest person I know. Be strong now, stronger than ever!"

Grizz supervised as Vamporess blew into Kiki's mouth gently to breathe for her. Scorpin-X performed chest compressions as he counted, "One, one hundred, two, one hundred, three, one hundred…"

Grizz wouldn't dare take over for he was worried he might hurt Kiki if he tried to revive her with CPR. Scorpin-X carefully push on her chest, but there was no heart beat or breathing. Blood was mixed with the water on the floor of the boat. Kiki's lips were visibly turning blue and her eyes were open like she was already dead, but Grizz wouldn't accept that… he couldn't.

Like an impossible miracle, Kiki coughed up water

but she was obviously in a lot of pain. The punks looked on along with Grizz in disbelief as to how Kiki was still with them. At the same time, none of them could accept losing her again. Grizz assisted Kiki by lifting her up a little, letting her cough out the water to her side. As Grizz had his hands around Kiki he could feel the piece of metal lodged in the right side of her back. He found, as he rested her back down to the floor and slid his hands out from behind her, blood coated his hands. Kiki was bleeding too much.

As Jakebrake manned the heading of the motor boat, a green military helicopter flew to their location where it followed them carefully. They saw many police lights on shore as emergency vehicles raced to follow the boat from land. Grizz quickly dressed back into his armor and attached his weapons to his belt again for everything was still in the boat where it was first removed. Grizz took over the driving from Jakebrake. He wrenched the steering wheel to the right and headed the motor boat right up onto the beach of the eastern peninsula of Key West. It was an abrupt but soft stop amongst the sunning bodies of the beach.

Grizz slid out of the driver's seat and wept when he saw the pain in Kiki's eyes. Her skin was pale. Kiki had lost so much blood. Whaling with tears of pain, Grizz carefully lifted Kiki's limp frail body out of the boat.

Quietly, Kiki muttered something about her brother. Though Grizz couldn't fully understand her, he knew some of Kiki's final thoughts were of her brother who was her last remaining living relative. Grizz could relate to Kiki. He was certain his final thoughts would also be of his brothers, but he couldn't shake the thoughts he had for his last remaining living brother, Eddy Evon, as the late agent Cawston had reminded him. *'Eddy, too had escaped the Knolix Island? Could he have found his way to the same city on the coast? Metro city?'* Grizz wondered as he looked out at the tall buildings of Metro city in the distance.

An innocent young voice came from Kiki. In Grizz's arms Kiki made an uncomfortable sound of tightness under the stress of the great pain she felt. Opening her eyes, Kiki looked up at Grizz, she seemed so lost, like she was not going to win this one.

Unable to believe Kiki could perish, Grizz asked her, "What can I do for you?" A thought struck him, "Hospital! I'll take you to a hospital."

Groaning as she spoke, Kiki said, "No Grizz... It's too late, you know that... I'm just a freak to them anyway... Uhgh, Neither of us will be taken seriously and we will both die... just hold me until I have gone... Ouch! Here in your arms is where I want to be. Nowhere else..." Kiki spoke to Grizz as if she were trying to calm him.

Grizz dropped to his knees in the sand as Vamporess, Roach, Scorpin-X and Jakebrake approached from behind and set their hands on Grizz's shoulders. Opening eyes, tight with pain, Kiki looked at Grizz with helpless innocent eyes. "I want you to forget about me Grizz... Never speak of me and never bring me back to your mind..."

"No! I will never forget you, Kiki. I will save you!" Shaking his head as he fought back his tears to be strong for her, and to encourage her.

"I don't think so, Grizz. Not this time... I love you, but you must forget me!!!"

Holding Kiki a little closer to himself, Grizz rocked her back and forth. Within the moment of grief and sadness, Kiki, began to sing a familiar song. It was the same song she sung when they first met and once again as friends.

Moon-light,
Aura so bright.
Dark forbodings
In the shadow of the night.
Can't hide from the spector
Can you hear the guardian's whisper?
At the end of it all,
Will you still love me,
For who I am?
At the end of it all,
Will you still love me,
For who I am?
Don't you remember me, Don't you remember me…
I'll wait for you on the other side
Don't remember me…
I'll see you on the other side,
Don't wait for me…
I'll love you on the other side.
Don't remember me, Don't remember me, Don't
remember me…

When Kiki's song had finished, her breaths began to grow noticeably shorter. She looked at Grizz with slow tired eyes. "You've saved me, Grizz…" Kiki told Grizz, "You always save me…"

Realizing, finally, Grizz was sitting in an ever widening circle of Kiki's blood. He told Kiki to rest. Each breath drew more faint than the one before. She closed her eyes and fell asleep in his arms then Kiki passed on quietly and peacefully.

As sad as the punks were for Kiki's passing, they could no longer ignore the sound of police vehicles as they drove through the wooded park enroute to the beach area to arrest them. Jakebrake was the first to run, with Vamporess and Scorpin-X close behind. Roach pulled at Grizz's armor and shouted, "Come on, man! Yo're going ta have ta forget her, she's gone!" Grizz would not respond. Roach looked this way and that as his opportunity for choices quickly diminished. Finally, he fled along with the others.

Police vehicles came swarming in at Grizz from every direction. Hitting their breaks, the patrol cruisers and vans kicked up a lot of dust. The police lept out of their vehicles and drew their weapons, "Hands up! Move and we will shoot you dead." The police were not sure what they were looking at. Grizz continued to whale, moan and cry in pain over the death of his best friend as though the police and the danger of the police didn't exist around him at all.

The police tell Grizz to put the girl down. Gently he did just as they instructed. The surrounding authorities were able to see the young girl was lifeless. Because of the amount of blood and the metal piece of shrapnel protruding from her back, the police immediately assessed Grizz had murdered Kiki.

The police opinion from their quick scene assessment was; *'This insane character, who is a danger to society, had killed the girl.'* Following code was their mandate, but in this situation the police were not comfortable with the rules. The police could not recognize a difference between Eddy the volk or Grizz the half volk. To them, Metro City was in danger because of a threat and the government was not clear as to what exactly the threat was. The police believed destroying the creature would solve the problem and keep the innocent lives safe from harm. Again the police threatened Grizz's life. "One false move and we will cut you down right here and now!"

Grizz shouted back, "Go ahead! Kill me!!! Kill me, now! You'll be doing everyone a favor, including me…"

Just as the police were about to pull back on their triggers, a command was given for them all to stand down, "Hold your fire!"

The government's secret agents arrived on scene. They came to protect and to help Grizz. Twisting and shifting his body, Grizz slumped down next to Kiki. Looking down at the girl's face, Grizz couldn't take his eyes off her and he appeared to have a distant look in his eyes. Grizz allowed the agents to shackle him. Again, he had his weapons confiscated. Grizz seemed to have surrendered, but actually he had just given up on fighting. Standing up, Grizz walked with the Knolix agents willfully to their van. Looking back, Grizz saw Kiki get zipped into a black body bag and get loaded onto a stretcher. She was carried into the back of an ambulance and Grizz knew it would be the last time he would see her.

The agents sat Grizz in the back of an armored transport van. While Grizz, shackled, rode in the van with five other agents, he just stared at the floor. *'It's not fair. How could Kiki expect me to forget her. I can't get her out of my head.'* Grizz's grizzly heart felt swollen with such great pain. It was as though the weight of a planet was upon his shoulders. Grizz looked at the agents who sat around him one face at a time. He did not recognize any of them. Grizz wondered what he could do to get the agents to shoot him in the head. All Grizz wanted was to die. He was certain it would bring him closer to Kiki, and if it didn't, at least his pain would end.

One of the Agents turned to Grizz and spoke to him, "You didn't kill her, did you? She wasn't just your friend, she was your best friend. Am I right?... I know what you're going through."

Grizz looked up at the agent with the eyes of a wild caged beast. His dark dirty wet bangs hung low over his eyes. *'The audacity of this fool to believe he knows anything about me at all.'* Grizz thought.

Grizz felt like there was no fight left inside him anymore. He just leaned his head back and closed his eyes. Kiki's death was still very fresh in his mind. As he recalled, he remembered when Kiki's life lifted from her mortal body, how something profound began to occur deep within Grizz's soul. He realized how Kiki was the one to show Grizz every good emotion he otherwise wasn't able to connect with; feelings of friendship, of sharing, of acceptance, laughter, joy and love.

Now Kiki was gone and Grizz was not only in shock, saddened and grieving, but he was becoming immersed into a very dark place within his soul. In such deep despite, Grizz did not know such a dark place could exist inside. Such a profound and deep journey, Grizz had never travelled here before and the experience scared him. It was a dark place of the mind that killed most of his brothers. Because Grizz recognized the deep journey his nature led him was a dangerous place, the place where his brothers never returned from, he resisted the temptation to let the dark dimension of pure anger overtake him and possess him with blind rage.

On the surface, Grizz was co-operative and complied with everything the agents asked of him, yet little did they know, Grizz's fuse was short. Burning from the inside out, the true result of what was manifesting at the core of Grizz's soul was about to surface.

Holding on as long as he could, Grizz became charged up from the power of anger. It was time for him to initiate the beginning of his own demise. It was

481

obvious, if he just sat there and went along with the instructions of the powers that be, the agents would never attempt to kill him, and death was the reward he had earned long ago. Grizz reasoned it was his time now to accept his reward.

When the incredible emotion came to a head, Grizz moved like lightning and smashed his fist through the wall of the van which separated the prisoner hold from the driver's cab. As the agents reached for their weapons, Grizz reached his arm deep into the driver's cab and gave the steering wheel an aggressive spin. The van made a turn which was too sharp for its speed, causing it to tipped right over onto its' side. Crashing upon the pavement in the middle of daytime traffic, the van slid approximately thirty feet, grinding sparks. Agents were strewn about the hold. Through their injuries, they were either unconscious or too over taken by their own pain to react as they needed to.

Out in the street, Grizz could hear the wheels of police cruisers squeal to a stop and take defensive positions.

Tearing the large case open, Grizz retrieved his armor and weapons again. Making his way to the head of the hold, Grizz tore open the hole which he had started until he could fit through it. The armor used between the hold and the cab was the weakest. From the cab Grizz opened the driver's door and climbed out.

The first thing Grizz realized, he was no longer in West Key. They had driven through to the next town over, which was Burbanks. Burbanks was more developed than West Key and still situated at the edge of Metro city, only the smaller city of Burbanks was further away from the coastline.

In the midst of Burbanks center, at the intersection of St. Elmo Street and Hunter Avenue, Grizz emerged from the armored truck where he was exposed in broad daylight for all of the countless and clueless commuters to see.

Grizz realized his suicide attempt was what earned him his freedom. The surrounding police cars mysteriously did not fire upon him. This frustrated Grizz and his muscles hardened as his veins thickened to dark red branches over the surface of his body. Grizz decided he would give the police good reason to kill him so he began throwing nearby commuter vehicles at the agents and police vehicles. Grabbing a car by the front end with both hands Grizz swung around, 180 degrees, to build momentum before he let go of it. The cars sailed through the air, one at a time before they landed on the police cars. The police officers lept from their rides to keep from being injured in the collisions. They must have been somewhat stunned by Grizz because not one of them fired a single shot at him.

Finding a small smart car, Grizz was able to toss it far enough to hit the police cruiser which was the furthest emergency vehicle away. After the mayhem, Grizz stood with his anger kindling in his irritated eyes. All who could see him were astounded by his intimidating presence. Grizz couldn't just wait around to be shot at so he instinctively escaped into the city of Burbanks and where no one could easily find him.

Chapter 15

Wondering into a quite little church, Grizz's presence was not well received. The other few people who were there to pray quickly gathered their things and left as though the devil himself had entered the holy sanctuary. The pastor of the church had his eyes fixed on Grizz the moment he entered the house of prayer. He could see Grizz was in turmoil over something. A struggle was taking place within Grizz's soul. Recognizing the unease and conflict in Grizz, the pastor felt compelled to approach the mysterious visitor and offer what he could to relieve the suffering tug of war between his emotions.

The pastor sat down near Grizz, but not too close for a sense of danger was about him both outwardly, because of his armor and weapons, but also inwardly because what was detected in his eyes. Grizz wanted to get angry but he fought to suppress it and remain calm. He collapsed into the pew and relaxed. He held his hand up before his face and saw it was nervously shaking. The involuntary shaking was a sign of weakness and how he was losing control. He made a fist and tried to keep the control to himself, but he could still feel the reverberation in his tight fist.

"Greetings, friend," The pastor spoke, "This is a house of prayer and all are welcome here. God loves you. If you are troubled, give your worries to he who is far more capable to deal with them than ourselves." The pastor waited to hear a response from Grizz but Grizz gave him none. When the pastor realized Grizz was not going to say anything, he began to pray for him.

With a deep breath, Grizz tuned out everything the

pastor said as he prayed. Closing his eyes Grizz let the things which were out of his control, just go and leave him. Though this was a new idea for Grizz, he felt nothing but found it was better than to feel something. Kiki was gone and Grizz knew he would never be the same again.

Grizz drew in unto himself and shut out the world around him. He cared for Kiki a great deal. He would have given his own life if it would serve to save hers. He felt he was at the epidemy of deep depression as he mourned her loss.

Though Grizz was not sure how much time he spent at the church, he finally left and wandered the back streets and alleys to keep from calling attention to himself. Before he knew it he found himself near the Mulberry Bryor Casino. Crossing the street and trying to enter the main doors, Grizz was hassled by his own staff. No one who worked for him recognized him right away because he was very dirty and still wearing his armor and weapons. One of the employees pointed out no one else was as big as the Blackguard so it could only be him.

Nevertheless, Kissandra was called to the front door to verify if it really was the man they referred to as the Blackguard.

At the main entrance, Kissandra finally arrived. With one look at Grizz, she knew it was the owner of the casino, the Blackguard. Though Grizz looked the way he did, Kissandra the secretary greeted Grizz cheerfully, "Good morning, Mr. Blackguard." As an after thought she added, "Can I just call you Mr. Black?" Grizz did not answer.

Kissandra immediately led Grizz up to his office. She noticed a tension about him as everyone else did also, "Where is the cute punky girl who's usually with you?" Kissandra tried a little small talk.

"She died…" Grizz spoke grimly.

"She what?... Oh, no! I'm so…" her words were cut short.

Grizz marched into his office and slammed the door behind him.

"…Sorry." Kissandra finished.

Shortly, after a time of allowing Grizz a moment alone, Kissandra opened one of the double doors to Grizz's office. There she could see he was busy writing something in his day planner at his desk at the far end of the spacious office. When Grizz noticed Kissandra had walked in, he stood up slow and menacingly. He was ready to yell and tear a strip off her and to tell her to get out, but as he watched her approach and with the way she moved her hips, slinking her way in like a cat, Grizz slowly calmed himself and sat back down.

"That's far enough!" Grizz told her with the palm of his hand held out to her. He didn't want her to be able to see what he was writing.

Kissandra couldn't shake the sense of danger she felt from Grizz, "I-I know you don't know me very well, Mr. Black, sir, but I can see you're hurting..."

Grizz dropped his pen and closed his day planner.

With his head still down at his desk, Grizz raised his eyes to her. The sight of his angry eyes sent chills through Kissandra's spine.

Grizz's voice was low and dry as he asked, "Do you have something important to tell me? If not, go!"

"Oh, um, well, there is something." Kissandra was not prepared for Grizz's reaction. She pushed her glasses all the way up her nose and quickly composed herself. "Mr. Vanderwal paid a visit here while you were out. He wants desperately, to speak to you and he is willing to make an appointment for your earliest convenience."

"What does he want?" Grizz cut to the point.

"Primarily, he wants his casino back." Kissandra revealed.

"Give it to him… I didn't really want it in the first place." Grizz was not just serious, he was dead serious.

Kissandra's mouth dropped open. "You're just going to give it back to him? Wha? No fight?" Kissandra didn't want to provoke Grizz and she cleared her throat and considered how Mr. Vanderwal would take it back. She shook her hair out and continued as she wiped a tear from the corner of her eye, "But we will no longer be working together… I-I thought you liked me, Mr. Black?"

Grizz opened his day planner and looked at Kissandra as he chewed on the end of his pen a moment, "I do like you, Kissandra, that's why you shouldn't be around me. Sooner or later, you're going to get hurt…"

"Like the little punk girl?" asked Kissandra with the feeling it would be the words to cause him to blow his top.

Grizz was disappointed how Kissandra could not have the dignity Kiki so deserved to have her name remembered. No, people who knew her would only know her as the punk girl… a low life… but Grizz knew she was so much more than that.

"Yeah," Grizz replied with sadness, "like the punk girl." he repeated. Like a snap, Grizz was suddenly all business, "Be sure to set up a meeting with Jim Vanderwal, right here, this evening at nine O'clock. On you're way. Thank you."

Kissandra turned on her heels and left the office closing the tall heavy doors of Oak behind her.

Nine O'clock came and went with Jim Vanderwal

losing his cool. Though he respected punctuality, he knew this was the moment to be most patient as Mr. Black was not only late but willing to hand the entire casino back over to him. The secretary, Kissandra, tried to call Grizz but he was not answering his phone. The group of business men was a compliment of about twenty men and some of them were bankers, lawyers and muscle. They hounded Kissandra to find the Blackguard. They really pressured her and she was very frightened of them even though she used to work for them. Kissandra tried to make excuses for Grizz, but the men wouldn't have it. Truly, Kissandra didn't like being caught in the middle and she didn't have a clue what more she could do to find Grizz. The meeting, to the men, was too urgent. Finally, Kissandra opened the doors to Grizz's office. As she expected, Grizz was not there. She noticed his day planner was left on the desk top. She opened it to get an idea of what else he may have had planned to do before the scheduled meeting. When she turned to the page of the current date, she read; *'Midnight, the penthouse – the end for me is near.'*

What she found disturbed her because she was the one person who was able to instantly connect the dots and realize the severity of Grizz's suicide note. The penthouse was one of the highest towers of the city. Grizz commented to Kissandra in the past how if he were to end his life he would like to go out by leaping from the height of the penthouse. Looking at her wrist watch, she saw it was 11:35 pm. Kissandra realized with a nervous start, the note was real and in the works, but she still had a small window of time to make a difference. She vowed to do all she could to prevent Grizz's untimely death. There was not much time left, but Kissandra just might make it to Grizz before he followed through with his plan. Rallying the group of men together Kissandra showed them the note in Mr. Black's day planner.

"You see? Mr. Black wants to kill himself!!!" Together, they all raced out of the casino to the Rosetta Hotel.

In the lobby of the Rosetta Hotel, Kissandra and her group coincidentally ran into a group of fifteen concerned punks which included Vamporess, Roach, Scorpin-X and Jakebrake. Kissandra quickly explained the situation to them as she pointed to what Grizz had written in his planner. It was decided the situation was truly grim for the clock read; 11:48 pm. All together, they raced to climb the tower to the top. Some waited for the elevator but most took to the stairs. Kissandra stayed behind in the lobby where she insisted, the hotel manager do one of two things; give her the key to the private elevator to the penthouse, or accompany her to the penthouse. It was a life or death situation and the manager would be held accountable if he did nothing. Kissandra was dedicated to do all she could to save Grizz.

When Kissandra finally had the cooperation of the hotel manager, in marched a second group of pushy punks through the front doors. This new group of punks were noticeably more aggressive than the others. Kissandra was not interested in wasting any more time. She envisioned the others at the penthouse before her, trying to talk Grizz out of taking his own life. It was there where she needed to be, so she dropped her gaze to the floor and tried to shuffle her way through the crowd to the private elevator quickly with the manager at her side.

Using the key, the manager opened the door to the elevator and they stepped inside. With the use of the key again, the door began to close behind them. A large arm from a studded leather jacket plunged into the elevator just before the doors had fully closed. The sudden presence of the big arm surprised Kissandra and the manager and for a split second they thought the arm was going to be severed.

The elevator doors reopened automatically. The punk who belonged to the arm was Cratorface. He did not know Kissandra or the hotel manager, but he did recognize the private elevator and he knew exactly where it would take him. "We have business with the Blackguard." he told them as the elevator was quickly crowded with punk rockers.

The elevator delivered them to the penthouse where, when the doors opened they came out expecting to find Grizz. Kissandra looked around, but the entire room was barren. "Mr. Black!" Kissandra shouted but she did not receive a reply. Knocking and pounding came from the front door to the hallway. Unlocking the door, Kissandra allowed the others to enter. Many who entered were out of breath from their long hard climb up the stairs. Kissandra ran out onto the terrace with the hoard of others. They all called out to Grizz at random. Before long everyone realized Grizz was not there. Kissandra looked at her watch and found the time was 12:04 am.

Gasping, Kissandra ran to the edge of the terrace and looked over the edge to the tiny lights of traffic far below. The hotel manager went to the telephone and made a call to the front desk.

"I think... we might be too late, boys." Kissandra told them without believing the words she produced from her own lips.

Many people headed to the railings where they inspect the ledges. They wanted to make absolutely sure, one way or the other, if Grizz really did jump, but there was no evidence to support it.

"If that's true it'll make our job far too easy. We are here to kill that sucker. He infected us with his blood and caused the death of XD3 and many others." Spoke Enemie with Cratorface at her back as though she had decided to step up as leader of the Bleeding Heart punks.

Vamporess approached her, "We need to talk. You obviously have everything all wrong about the Blackguard."

"My sources tell me the Blackguard has just walked into the main doors of the hotel. He is not a pancake on the sidewalk, he is on his way up here!" reported the hotel manager after he hung up the phone.

"He is playing us, Vamporess. Don't you see? He only uses us for his own selfish needs. He doesn't care about us. He's not even a punk! Yet you guys hail him as our leader! It's pathetic!" Enemie spat at Vamporess.

At the glass door of the penthouse, Poison stood out of trouble where she could see everyone arguing. She was the first to hear the ding from the private elevator, just before the doors opened, she shouted to the others, "Take cover! The Blackguard is here!"

Instinctively, everyone ducked into the nearest shadows where they remained motionless. Sure enough, stepping out from the elevator, Grizz marched through the penthouse suite. Stopping at the open sliding glass door, Grizz was curious as to who had left it wide open. Standing at the door for a long minute Grizz listened and sniffed the air. His sharp eyes scanned the darkness but detected nothing unusual.

Breaking into a stride, Grizz made his way across the terrace to the railing. With his hands curled around the cold metal of the rails, he took a deep breath. Gazing out at the lights of Metro city, Grizz brought his sights in closer before he bent over the rails and observed the people on the walkways below. They were so far away they could barely be seen as specks. He pondered his self worth and then his death as though the two thoughts went

491

around and around in his mind like a broken record.

A shuffling sound alerted him from behind. Grizz quickly twisted around to see a mass of people standing before him. Grizz was startled like it was some sort of surprise party.

"Nice night, eh Blackguard?" Jakebrake asked carefully.

Grizz did not reply, he just kept looking from one face to the next as he recognized many of them while other faces were not remotely familiar at all. "Yo don't want ta do this, alright? Now just take a step toward me nice and easy, okay?" Jakebrake held his hand out to Grizz.

"Yo have got to be kidding me?!" Enemie stepped in with anger, confidence and power. "Our true leader, XD3, was the one who put our world together from the beginning and now he is on the other side and it's all the Blackguard's fault!" she shouted as she pointed a finger of accusation at Grizz. "Payment is required and the Blackguard must pay in blood! Let's just kill him now and get it over with."

"Yo've got it all wrong!" Scorpin-X butted in, "The Blackguard saved our lives. If it weren't fo him we would have died a thousand other deaths." Looking right into Grizz's eyes, Scorpin-X added, "I will repay yo, man. One day very soon, I will save yer life, I promise."

Enemie blew her jet black bangs out of her eyes and stroked her red tattered Mohawk, "The Blackguard must be very clever, ta split up the Bleeding heart punks like this, but I'm not so easily convinced, and I'm certainly not ready ta die fo him." Enemie spat contemptuously.

The punks were split up as some agreed to kill Grizz while others preferred to follow him. Feet shuffled as those who supported Grizz stood before him with weapons and fists drawn as they faced the others. The

492

protective punks, like Vamporess, Roach, Jakebrake and Scorpin-X were well out numbered by the others who began to move in offensively.

Jim Vanderwal stepped forward from his own little circle and said, "You owe me a great deal as well, Blackguard. I will take it all back, plus extra to cover damages. Yes, I did not come here to save you but to find out for myself that you're dead. Never before has a man humiliated me the way you have."

At the words of her former employer, Kissandra ran to Grizz through the crowd of haters. She threw herself at Grizz's feet where she begged and pleaded for him not to kill himself.

"Oh, please Grizz, you must reconsider. Taking your own life is a bad choice. You have so much to live for." Kissandra told him with passionate emotion and tears.

"No, Kissandra! Don't you get it? Kiki is dead, and I don't belong in this world anymore! Look around you, there are far more people here who would rather skin me than to join me. I told Kiki I would save her and now she is dead. It's all my fault. I've failed her. I've failed myself. I've failed everybody. I don't know what to do… I don't know what to do…" Grizz wrapped his arms around Kissandra and wept.

Kissandra looked up at Grizz and he could see she was crying as well. "I love you!" she told Grizz. "And do you know why?... You are strong, smart and you have been created to do great things."

"I have been created to be a weapon of destruction…" Grizz added.

"And I believe I was created for you." she told him, though Grizz knew Kissandra's words were hollow. "If you live, I just know you will rule. You'll change the world. It is in your nature and I saw this from the moment I first met you." These were important words for Grizz to

493

hear. "I have a vision of you and I raising a large household of powerful children. Each one will look just like you." she kissed Grizz again and again on the mouth as tears streamed down her face.

"Children?" Grizz did not realize how possible it was for a woman to feel so strongly for him.

"Oh, yes and you can love them the way you loved the little punk girl." Though he did not feel anything for this particular woman, Grizz was hopeful he would find the right woman for himself one day. Perhaps he could find the strength to love again, in a variety of other ways.

"Her name was, Kiki! Learn it, know it and never ever forget it." Grizz told Kissandra sternly. The confrontation had a profound affect on Grizz and he could feel how he was changed on the inside. By this unexpected encounter, Grizz felt a needed sense of usefulness. It was no longer clear if Grizz should end his life... Grizz wondered, *'I might have unfinished business. I may still be needed.'*

"So you will stay with me and forget this ridiculous attempt to take your own life?" Kissandra caught her breath as it was aggravated by her emotional stress.

"I will stay, but not with you, woman." Grizz lept up onto the railing and balanced himself upon it. "This world is mine!" Grizz announced loud and clear.

Such a statement upset a lot of people. Weapons were drawn and a command was given, "Kill him now!!!" shouted Jim Vanderwal.

As the guns began to fire at Grizz, he jumped over the ledge of the tall hotel and he vanished. As everyone crowded toward the railing, they believed Grizz was dead this time for sure, as he *had* completed his suicide mission.

What they found was a strange robotic, claw like device attached to the rail where Grizz was standing a moment before. As Jakebrake inspected the robotic claw, he felt a taut line connected to it. Jakebrake was forced away from the robotic grappler as the various people gathered at the railings to find Grizz. Through the darkness some people believed they could see Grizz swinging out to a neighboring tall rooftop. Jim Vanderwal's men attempted to cut the rope so Grizz would fall to his death. Before anyone could touch a blade to the rope, Grizz used his ring remote to release the mechanical grappler hook when he had swung himself to safety.

Jim Vanderwal pounded his fist on the railing, "No! He got away? He was supposed to die! Don't you people know how dangerous he is?" Jim fixed his eyes on Kissandra, "And you... What was that all about? You love him and you want his baby?... We should throw you over the ledge with him!"

One of Jim's thugs took Kissandra by the arm forcefully. It scared the wits out of her and caused a stir amongst the others who were present. Roach and Scorpin-X stepped in front of the thug to prevent him from approaching the rails with Kissandra.

Jim Vanderwal was content with his threat alone. He nodded his head at the thug and said, "Let her go. She's not important. We need to go after the idiot who just jumped over the ledge. Any of you punks who joins our cause will be added to my payroll. Let's go!"

Everyone took off for the elevators and stairs as they raced to descend the building in the same anxious way they came up. Within the masses, the punks were unable to determine which of them were for Grizz and who was against, but it would all soon become clear when they found who branched off with Jim Vanderwal and who chose not to.

With the use of satellite radio, the Internet and the national broadcast system, the people of Metro city and surrounding towns were notified of a deadly terrorist who was loose and very dangerous. Pictures of Grizz circulated through multiple forms of media as a wanted man with a reward of fifty thousand dollars for anyone with information leading to an arrest. All civilians were instructed to remain indoors and await further information.

The Metro city police force had set up road blockades in strategic locations based on the information they had in conjunction with the information they were currently receiving.

Traffic commuters were quickly allowed through the blockades to allow the innocent to leave the areas which were considered hot zones. The potential was too great for people to find themselves in the middle of danger. More importantly, the less civilians in the area meant less casualties and it would make it easier for the authorities to do their jobs.

From the descriptions the officers of the blockades had, they knew they would be looking for a person of abnormally large proportions. Understanding this, they were able to let small vehicles through with little inconvenience. Very few instances arose where the police hassled large people like body builders or the obese.

A dark blue hummer approached the blockade and an officer knocked on the door of the vehicle for the driver to roll his window down, but the driver was not responsive. The officer called others to assist because all of the widows of the hummer were tinted and the driver was not cooperating. The vehicle ahead of the hummer was allowed to pass. With each passing second, suspicions rose and a dark blue hummer was at the top of their suspicious vehicle list.

496

Many of the officers found it highly unlikely they would see the actual dark blue hummer with the suspect in the driver's seat at a vehicle check, but it had to be verified.

The officers were momentarily distracted as a large group of people came running down the road past the line up of cars. They were on their way to the police shouting words of importance. The police were trying to figure out what the people were trying to tell them, when the horn of the hummer sounded. It was long and drawn out, then the motor revved up.

The officers scrambled as they heard the voice of one of the people running to them shout, "He's in the hummer!"

A patrol car moved in front of the hummer to block its' exit. The hummer jerked forward, the horn still sounding. The police officers were in a buzz, they seemed to be looking for orders from their superiors. The hummer lurched forward again and the police flinched and stepped back.

The hummer began to drive forward slowly in four wheel drive. It scratched into the police cruiser, but it didn't stop there. The front tire, with thick wide tread, gripped the bumper of the cruiser and lifted as the entire hummer drove up and over the police car. The hood caved in and the officer in the driver's seat just barely escaped in time. Driving over the roof, it too caved in blowing out all of the glass and munching up the red and blue emergency lights. It was like being at a monster truck rally.

The hummer left behind a totaled patrol car. It drove a short distance down the road and turned to the left where it stopped in the middle of the road. The driver's window rolled down and Grizz glared at the blockade.

Rolling up the window, Grizz turned the hummer

back toward the police blockade so the officers opened fire on it. The punks, with Jim Vanderwal's hired help, joined in with the police as they too lifted what guns they had and targeted the hummer.

Grizz was not interested in escaping the police, he wanted to dominate them. He dropped his foot to the floor and raced toward the blockade. The bullets bouncing off the hull of the hummer stopped as the people at the blockade scrambled.

"Take cover!!!"

Ramming through the blockade, police vehicles were punched off to either side. As the hummer barreled down the road, the police vehicles, which were not damaged, squealed their tires and tore off after the hummer. At the first intersection, the hummer took a hard left turn.

Just when Grizz thought he would be leading the authorities on some huge complicated chase throughout the Metro city streets, he came nose to nose with a low flying patrol helicopter.

Grizz turned his steering wheel to the left as he hit the breaks and locked up his wheels. The hummer almost flipped over as it tipped onto two wheels. Gravity finally pulled the hummer back down to its' four tires again. Pointing in the direction of the blockade once more, Grizz headed down a back alley between tall buildings.

Jim Vanderwal stood with the police chief. They were so comfortable with one another, it was obvious they shared a history together.

As the chief received word of the hummer moving in their direction, Jim lifted a megaphone and addressed his men and loyal punks. "The Blackguard is coming down a back alley toward us. You can head him off. Take Willard's street right here! Go! Go! Go!" he pointed with his outstretched arm, and the feet of his people were in motion.

Prior to engaging the authorities, Grizz had tied the loose end of his rope to one of his arrows. The mechanical three fingered grappler claw at the other end of the three hundred feet of rope was locked onto the center roll bar within the hummer's cab.

Opening the driver's door, Grizz targeted the helicopter. Pulling back as far as his compound bow would allow, Grizz shot his arrow with enough force to sail through the helicopter's down draft and through the hull. The shot was a direct hit where the arrow disappeared into the underbelly of the helicopter. The helicopter reeled back and up as the pilot figured out something was very wrong. The rope tightened up quickly. Grizz strummed the tight rope and it reverberated a base tone like a string instrument. Bracing himself at the ready to leap form the open driver's door, Grizz felt the helicopter's momentum begin to lift the hummer off the pavement. Rising past each story of the surrounding buildings, Grizz held his breath. The helicopter began to roll into a spin as did the hummer.

The masses, consisting of five police officers, ten punks and three of Jim Vanderwal's thugs, ran one block down Willard's street, between the buildings. The group began to slow as they neared the corner because they could hear the sounds of the helicopter's rotor blades, the engine of the hummer at full throttle and the sirens of the pursuing patrol cars.

The group, armed with various guns, lept around the corner in a surprise attack and began blasting at the hummer. The driver's door was open and Grizz hung half out with one hand clutching the rope which was attached to the bottom of the copter along with the hummer. With his other hand, Grizz pulled out a long knife and held it at the ready.

From the sunroof of the hummer, the rope was pulled, and like magic, the hummer rose up off the road before the eyes of the group. The hummer wheels spun at top RPM as though it would make a difference to the escape.

Gun barrels continued to flash with the discharge of ammunition as the target lifted over their heads. The hummer swung out toward them before it was quickly hauled up and away, with Grizz along for the ride.

Near the roof of the building, Grizz tapped the release button on his remote ring controller which caused the grappler to release the hummer. The people shooting from below found themselves scrambling for their lives as the hummer came crashing down upon them.

Grizz continued to rise into the air as he still had a firm hold of the open grappler. Using his knife, Grizz sliced the rope just above the grappler and he fell a short distance to the rooftop below.

The grappler, of some importance to Grizz, would not be discarded unless it was necessary.

Despite the release of the hummer and Grizz's weight, the helicopter pilot was still challenged with finding a way to gain control. What added more trouble to existing problems, was what happened next. The rope sprang back at the helicopter and became caught up in the tail rotor. The propeller wound in the rope until it became seized.

Grizz watched as the patrol helicopter spun out of control and soon crashed into the glass building side of a Metropolitan bank tower.

Grizz threw his fists into the air and shouted from the building top, "The world is mine!"

Making his way across the rooftop to an access door, Grizz easily forced it open and ran inside. As Grizz made his way down through each level of the apartment complex, he would examine the hallways to be sure they were clear. With each floor he saw the residents standing outside their rooms wondering what all the comotion was all about.

Grizz shouted at them, "Get back to your rooms! This doesn't concern you!" At the sound of Grizz's powerful deep voice, the people ducked back into their rooms instantly and the clattering sounds of door locks being secured was heard.

On the street, out in front of the apartment complex, police gathered as they had confirmation that Grizz was inside. The chief of police, along with the bomb squad, who just showed up with a trailer of explosives in tow, were planning to set the charges in the lobby and wait for the Blackguard to stumble across them. The chief spoke to the bomb squad as he explained, "It is better for us to lose one building than to lose an entire city."

Leaping down from one platform to the next, flying over the stairs as he descended the winding staircase. Grizz made it to ground level in record time. Opening the main doors, Grizz came face to face with multiple gunmen, police and other brave citizens who wasted no time for small talk and immediately opened fire.

Moving quick like lightning, Grizz ducked behind a concrete flower box which had pebbles adhered to its' exterior. Shredded wood, metal fragments and countless tiny shards of glass accompanied the hail of bullets which littered the floor around Grizz. *I may not live much longer, but before I go I will take you all with me.'* Grizz thought to himself in the middle of the chaos. From Grizz's state of mind, he recessed into a deeper darkness. He was trapped and he knew it. This made him even more dangerous for no one should cage an untamed beast. The noise around him just kept coming and coming. The brain of the Blackguard was stimulated with a cocktail of adrenaline, testosterone and neurons of energy as he waited for his moment to strike back.

"Cease fire!" Ordered the chief of police as he bunched his bushy dark eyebrows together with stern focused eyes. Everyone searched the dust for movement.

A deathly silence followed as tense trigger fingers twitched with each and every reloaded weapon. In the still uneasy silence, the men stood frozen with their guns hot and smoking.

Beside the chief was a rookie cop who was only supposed to attend as an observer. Holding up a mega phone, the chief's augmented voice cracked, "Come out with your hands behind your head." Turning to a small bomb squad who arrived just a minute before, "We have no time to set up the charges. Just arm the thing and we'll send it in, trailer and all. Pass me the detonator. I'll take it from here." came the words of the anxious chief of police.

More silence followed at the scene before the chief gave the order for the trailer to be sent in. Grizz wasn't about to come out just yet. It sounded like the chief was inviting Grizz out for a complimentary bullet between the eyes.

The chief of police turned to the rookie next to him, sitting in the passenger seat of the patrol car, "Hold this for me, will ya?" the chief passed the rookie the detonator. "Whatever you do, don't arm it or fire the blast." he warned before he turned his attention back to the apartment building. Through the megaphone the loud boisterous voice barked again, "This is chief Tyrell of the Metro city police department. I am giving you an opportunity to trust me here, Blackguard. If you surrender to us and come out now, we will protect you. Not even these punks will harm you." Chief Tyrell turned slightly and gave a signal for the trailer to be pushed through the main window of the apartment lobby.

The bomb squad lifted the trailer hitch of the charges and carried it down the slope to the apartment where it broke through the main glass and stopped just inside the lobby. Fear resonated from the eyes of the bomb squad men who carried the trailer in as they turned and ran back to the front line. A punk peeked over the hood of a green pinto with his reloaded pistol at the ready to fire upon Grizz at his first opportunity.

The broken glass wall of the lobby erupted and blew out at the police gunmen unexpectedly. Grizz had tossed the trailer of explosive charges at the front line and it careened through the air like a missile. Slamming into the grill of the chief of police's squad car, the rookie panicked, arming the detonator, he set it off. The chief's patrol car blew up in a spectacular explosion which was meant to destroy the apartment complex.

As a reflex, Chief Tyrell raised his arm to protect his face from the chunks of concrete which went flying at him from the impact of the explosion. The chief was so taken by the situation, he didn't even notice, through his ringing ears, a quick abrasive fragment had cut his cheek.

When Chief Tyrell looked around, he noticed how disoriented everyone else was as well. The rookie had no chance of survival at such close range to the explosion.

A strange feeling came over the chief as he felt the urge to duck into a neighbouring squad car. Upon closing his door, chief Tyrell became the first to notice Grizz at his door side, looking at him through the glass.

The others were also still looking for Grizz inside the complex. It wasn't until Grizz roared and tore the door off the chief's car, when the others located him. It was too late for anyone to react as Grizz threw part after part of the chief's car at the gunmen. Grizz's sights were on the chief mainly as Grizz came closer to him with each piece he violently tore away. First the wheels, then the fenders, the seats the roof, moving closer to the chief until they were nose to nose. The chief was not prepared for Grizz's overwhelming hostility and brute strength.

Grizz was more than capable of destroying chief Tyrell, but as the seconds passed it became clear, Grizz wasn't going to do that. Instead, Grizz just huffed in the chief's face, stood up straight and thundered down the road as the sound of more sirens approached.

A black Pontiac pulled up at the scene and an agent from the Knolix Island stepped out of the car. He was well dressed in a suit and tie and sporting a pair of large sunglasses. The agent, tall and slender, approached chief Tyrell. "Obviously, Domin has been here." The agent found no reply from the chief as he stared off into space in shock. The agent seemed to speak into his cuff-link, "Domin has crippled the civilian protection forces. Within the hour the military will be involved. The ability of the Metro police force has been depleted. More force is required."

Chapter 16

The secret agents and the city's Metro police force and fire fighters joined with Jim Vanderwal's forces. It seemed every police officer and fire fighter of the tri state area had shown up to the scene. Even a cross walk guard with her hand held stop sign came to help.

The punks organized themselves. They didn't want to fit in with society so they went ahead, in secret, to go after Grizz. They felt Grizz was their responsibility, even more so when they saw the police could do no more.

On a rampage through the streets of Liberty town, Grizz would play with the punks like toys as he bolted from the shadows like a stampeding bull. He would perform quick attacks, running very fast, before disappearing again only to pop up in the most unlikely places. Through the confusion, the punks fired their weapons in all directions at random. For them, it was like fighting a ghost.

Smashing every pane of glass, jumping through walls leaving a path of destruction where ever he went, Grizz was bent on destroying Metro city in its entirety.

Swinging from a new rope, which he acquired from an Alpine Outdoor Mountain sporting goods store, Grizz swung from one building to another and smashed his body into the base of it where he kicked and punched out the main building supports which caused the entire structure to tip over and spill out across a main street. "He is a human wrecking ball." One of the fire fighters pointed out.

The punks were saved when the authorities arrived, or so they thought. The city streets became Grizz's stomping grounds. All who opposed him were victimized by his blind rage time and time again. He threw cars at the fire engines and he seemed to have an endless supply of energy because he just kept coming.

The authorities had trouble shaking the odd feeling of inferiority. They were fighting something they couldn't hit, but what had no problem hitting them.

In the midst of Grizz's destruction, a young female journalist was on the beat, upon the rooftop of a six story building. She did her best to remain low and unnoticed as she documented Grizz climbing an adjacent building across the street. She spoke into her microphone to narrate each event as it unfolded. "Nine O'clock and the Blackguard is showing no signs of slowing down. I would love to ask him some questions, but chances are when all of this is over there won't be anything remotely recognizable left of him." The reporter adjusted her straps as she picked up her gear and moved to the east ledge. "Where did he come from and what does he want? History is being made here in our beloved city today. The Blackguard is a terrorist who will be remembered for generations to come. This is June Anderson of WPCX news reporting live. Thank you, and have a pleasant evening." she focused her telescopic lens and snapped another half dozen shots.

Frame by frame she caught sight of Grizz throwing his grappler hook from the side of a tall sky scraper. The end of the rope caught its' targeted neighboring building and Grizz swung through the air like Tarzan or Spider-man or something. He moved behind the large red awning which was draped in front of the Metropolitan theater of the arts. Countless cables ran up and down the face of the building like the mast of a pirate ship. It was behind the large red awning where the reporter, June

Anderson, totally lost sight of Grizz.

Looking for Grizz with the zoom of her camera, June spent no more than five minutes studying the streets before she realized the caravan of joined forces who were in pursuit of the Blackguard, racing in her direction. With a thud, and a shudder, June heard something very heavy land behind her. She turned to see the Blackguard had landed on her rooftop. He didn't notice her as he assumed he would be alone. Grizz was very busy working his shoulders as he wound up his rope.

June figured she could just slip away unnoticed if she remained low and moved fast, but as she gathered her things, her audio recorder slipped out from her back pack and clattered to the ground. June looked up at Grizz, and found him frozen in place, glaring at her.

Grizz scared June something awful, and as a spontaneous reaction, she dropped her equipment and ran. June couldn't get very far before Grizz caught her in his large mitts. Screaming and struggling, June could not free herself from his powerful hold. She was extremely scared as she awaited the pain and punishment June so expected, but as the seconds ticked by, she realized Grizz was not going to hurt her after all. June finally stopped struggling and slowly lifted her head and looked in Grizz's eyes. She saw the wild nature of a warrior beast, yet deeper than this, and only for a brief moment, June thought she saw a noble logic, or at least she wanted to believe that was what she saw. "Want to make a statement?" June thought the words, but she surprised herself when realized she had actually asked the question out loud. June literally saw her life flash before her eyes. She reached for her audio recorder, because June figured a recorded statement from her killer might somehow vindicate the situation and justify her life.

Releasing June and taking a step back, Grizz said, "I

am not the villain here."

June chuckled accidentally as she figured this would be the last thing he would say. She stopped grinning quickly for fear of offending Grizz, "Oh, really." June replied with heavy skepticism.

"They provoked me… and I reacted…" Grizz told her as he lifted his head to take a look at the crowd gathering below.

Fire fighters and police officers, knowing Grizz was on the building, began evacuating the people who were inside.

June crossed her arms and rubbed her sore muscles up and down where Grizz had held her, "All of this is as simple as that?" June asked with a sideways glance to be sure she was not speaking out of term.

"That simple, yes…" Grizz confirmed.

A light seemed to go off in June's mind, "So, if everyone just left you alone, you'd stop this rampage?" She felt like such a goof. June had only saw Grizz in one light, a negative light. It was like looking through the lenses of narrow sighted spectacles, Grizz was a terrorist, but now, when she stood before him June saw a quality which shattered her lenses and allowed her to see a much deeper and complex person existed inside. It was the passion and frustration of conflict within Grizz which fueled his tantrums.

Grizz smiled at June calmly, "Mystery solved." he told her.

Stepping near to the edge of the rooftop and with his lungs full of wind, Grizz shouted, "Get-Lost!!!"

Instantly fired upon, Grizz and June ducked down low with their faces to the pea gravel. The bullets chewed into the top ledge of the building, while June screamed for her life.

"You are in too deep… I have to get you away from

this danger!" Grizz told June as he began to rise.

Below, approval from Metro city's mayor gave clearance for the law enforcers to demolish the small old building where the Blackguard had last been located. Only a restricted few city structures were deemed expendable and the old building Grizz was seen on last was one of them. Quoting the mayor of Metro city, "It is better to lose one building than to risk losing the rest of the city."

When the old building was quickly inspected and clear of any occupants, save the Blackguard, the fire power was quickly concentrated on the first floor. The guns started up like a thunder from below and the whole building shook under the feet of Grizz and June.

Grabbing June, Grizz held her close as he moved closer to the edge of the building's roof. June reciprocated as her fears caused her to hold tighter to Grizz. A very loud blast wave was felt more than it was heard. Pushing June away gently, Grizz spoke softly with his rugged deep voice, "Hold on, I've got to check something…" Grizz peeked over the edge of the roof and his suspicions were confirmed from the detonation of the powerful blast. The entire building dropped a distance of one foot. Nothing about the building's structural integrity was stable any longer. Movement was felt as the building began to shift and sway.

Grizz tossed his rope out across the rooftop to uncoil it. "Get on my back and hold on tight." Grizz told June with urgency.

June looked at Grizz with puzzled bewilderment in her eyes.

"NOW!" Grizz stressed as the base of the building began to pop, grind and crumble.

Holding on tight for dear life, June wrapped her small arms around Grizz's thick throbbing neck as Grizz stepped up onto the building's ledge. Below his feet Grizz and June could see the authorities scrambling about like angry ants.

An officer at a distance was using the scope of his rifle to target a shot at Grizz when he uncovered a disturbing sight, "Hey, there's someone up there with the Blackguard!" he pointed out, but there was nothing anyone could do. It was just too late. No one could stop the building from coming down.

The building began to tip and move out toward the people below. Grizz remained focused as he began to twirl his grappler hook in one hand like a cowboy at a rodeo. June had never shut her eyes so tightly before in her life, she could feel her blood, sweat and tears pumping as fast as her heart.

As the momentum increased like a rollercoaster ride from hell, June screamed in Grizz's ear. Likewise, Grizz roared to release the beast within. Scraping along the neighboring taller building, the sound was a terrible mashing of concrete and metal. The whole building was crashing down to the earth, but June couldn't figure out why Grizz was still standing on it. The two rode the building down before Grizz tossed his mechanical grappler hook.

Grizz realized his survival would be in his precision and timing. The grappler didn't have to be thrown too far from reach for it to snap a hold onto one of the cable supports of a large and illustrious awning. The large red awning was the trademark of the Metropolitan theater of the arts.

Leaping from the building, just before it completely

decimated upon the city streets. Grizz and June swung out low amongst the bewildered authorities. An unsuspecting agent stepped in Grizz's path. Lifting his feet as a buffer, Grizz collided into the agent's chest, scooping him up from where he stood. The collision was solid, but as his momentum carried him through, Grizz found he was taking a second passenger with him.

The agent was not unconscious and he clawed at Grizz to keep from falling. They swung very high before Grizz gave the agent a slight nudge with his foot which was all it took for him to slip off. The agent plummeted one hundred and fifty feet.

Grizz let out just a little more of his rope as he came about and slid his feet across the pavement as he slowed to a stop. There he let June Anderson down at his side. She stumbled a little as though she was dizzy, but she didn't let go of Grizz. The scent of gas was thick in the air and caused everyone to feel somewhat nauseous. To linger much longer in the city was dangerous to a persons health and the threat hissed from many gas line ruptures.

Gently, Grizz gave June a nudge and she stepped away as Grizz found himself surrounded with gunmen who were lifting their weapons, hungry to unload and cut him down once and for all.

When June saw the makings of a quick execution in the works, she jumped in front of Grizz and announced, "I am June Anderson with WPCX news. You have to leave the Blackguard alone, if you want him to leave you alone!"

The men looked at June like she was not being practical. With events happening in slow motion, Grizz closed his eyes. He was ready to let fate run its' course. Going into all of this, Grizz was certain things wouldn't come to a head any other way. He was ready to accept his death.

"Fire!" came the order from a superior officer who had become far too personal with the situation.

Even Grizz couldn't have predicted he had a final ace up his sleeve. Next to the group stood Scorpin-X, who made a loud statement, "The Blackguard is the greatest warrior there is, or ever will be!"

All eyes turned to Scorpin-X as he made good on his promise to help Grizz with his lighter pulled from his back pocket, Scorpin-X sparked the flame to life with a metallic click and tossed it to the broken gas main.

The gas pipes throughout Liberty town along with much of Metro city exploded in brilliant lights and tall fires. Many roads lifted and settled again with the first initial explosion. All of the gunmen fell down to the broken asphalt.

When the worst was over, the city looked like the pit of hell with plumes of fire curling straight up into the air. The people stood up and found Grizz was nowhere to be seen.

Grizz, confused, had worked himself into an unfortunate situation. What confused him the most was how he hadn't been captured or killed. The thought of turning himself in crossed his mind but it would only be an act of weakness. *'No, I will continue. This is what I have been trained for my whole life...'* Grizz thought, *'I will fortify my defences, my property will be secure. By the end of this the people of earth will not only know me and respect me, they will honour and follow me. Otherwise, I will have a very bad day, and when I have a bad day everyone else will suffer.'*

People filled the roads at the corner of Oak-ridge and Fifty-sixth. The citizens who had watched the news casts on their televisions had followed the stories. They saw the Blackguard running down their road and took it upon themselves to go after him. For the sake of protecting their beloved Metro city, the people were willing to take justice into their own hands. The city's police and fire fighters had failed, time and time again in capturing or killing the Blackguard, but they, the people, felt they had to full-fill their part and do something.

In the middle of the street the people jumped on top of one another with tools and sticks in order to strike at Grizz. Even a few remaining police officers tried to join the crowd and get a few pokes in there. The people were so angry at the Blackguard, they became the beasts, exposing a side of themselves they never wanted exposed. The Blackguard had a talent for bringing out the worst in people.

Agile, and able to move his muscle toned power housed body with ease, Grizz fended off the clumsy humans. Catching a strong scent of a volk, Grizz thought nothing of it as the scent could easily be coming from himself, after all, he was perspiring. It wasn't until he felt a telepathic sensation touch his mind when he suspected the presence of a volk.

A crowd of one hundred men or more, fought against one. The odds were not in Grizz's favor. Grizz felt good, for he was fast and in his physical prime for his age.

He swung his heavy arms about, breaking necks and shattering noses. It took less than a second for him to grip a man's throat and crush it like a soda can. The crowd did not move the raging warrior from where he stood his ground.

Every muscle in Grizz's arms would tighten up with the potential of an industrial spring, before it lashed out.

He grabbed a man's arm as it swung to hit him with a pipe. As a result the man's arm was injured in Grizz's powerful grip. He continued to use a man's body to beat the crowd with wide sweeping strikes. Whatever it took to break him was not within the ability of the rioters.

The people didn't stop beating the Blackguard, and he seemed impervious to pain. Purposely, Grizz chopped a person with his hand, extremely quick, to the nerve cluster in his deltoid, which rendered the man's arm totally useless.

Heavy artillery from a new source opened up. A multiple amount of abused vehicles came charging in. They drove right into the area of people with no regard to the police who were also present.

With armor and weapons fitted to the brutal trucks, they surrounded the group of people. The Blackguard noticed the vehicles, and he must have recognized them also, because he began to charge wildly through the people with his swords swinging to clear a path for himself to the door of a twenty story building. As he did so, the people in his path tried desperately to get out of his way. Yelling and screaming men tried jumping over each other as they urgently moved.

Three black pickup trucks pulled up and took positions under the street lights at the outskirts of the crowd. Rebellious punks rode within the trucks. They wore tattered leather clothing, coloured hair and Mohawks. Before the Blackguard entered the building, the gang of punks arose from out of the trucks with a variety of powerful fire-arms. The Blackguard turned to face the punks at the entrance of the building.

The punks lined up, locking their targeting sights on the Blackguard.

"We made you!!!" shouted Enemie, who was the

new leader of the punks.

"You will not destroy me!!!" The Blackguard shouted back defiantly.

Enemie, the leader of the punks, shouted, "Fire!!!"

--RATATATATATAT!!!-- Heavy ammunition was massed against the Blackguard and the civilians of the angry crowd scattered. The punks weren't interested in targeting anyone else but the Blackguard. A couple of bullets sparked off his thick body armor. The Blackguard fell backwards through the main doors. He pulled, from his uniquely designed sling-shot from his weapons belt and loaded it. The sling-shot, with its' supporting wrist brace and main forks extended forward ten inches from his hand grip, was held at the ready. When the Blackguard pulled the specialized elastic strap, it stretched back across his chest, five feet long. He released a tiny ball bearing from the sling-shot. The amazing elastic energy shot out the solid ball bearing in a perfect straight trajectory across the road. It whistled over the heads of the stunned punks and into an adjacent building. Knocking out the main supports, the entire building across the street exploded and crumbled to the ground in a great mass of thick dust and smoke. The Blackguards' diversion was a success and he quickly escaped, disappearing through the main doors.

Bullets came streaming in at the building. Glass at the face of the building shattered unceasingly under the relentless shower of bullets. The Blackguard had made the punks outside very upset. The Blackguard's heavy footsteps charged up the stairs of the stair well. Grizz barreled up the stairs. His muffled heavy breathing through his black knight helmet was the only sign of his exhaustion. Grizz stopped for a moment as a very odd sense came over him. Suspicious if he was alone in the building, he tried to listen.

Mysteriously, Grizz wasn't sure what was happening as he had entered the frontier of a cloaking field. His eyes met a glowing energy blue gel, before he looked upwards where he swore he saw the energy gel waves melting over facial features.

Equally as mysterious as how the strange ghostly sight appeared, it quickly disappeared.

Stretching out his hands to try and touch what he could not see, Grizz was ready to believe he was going crazy. After shaking his head from left to right, he turned back toward a support beam connected to the stairs. He reached to his side and unclipped his large yo-yo. He threw it out and it split the support beam. The yo-yo rewound up the metallic nylon string to his connected hand strap. The stair well creaked and a punk launched himself around the corner and opened fire, with a small gun. He came within millimeters of having the Blackguard square in his sights, but Grizz was lightning fast.

Using some fancy yo-yo tricks, which Kiki had taught him, the Blackguard glanced many of the bullets away. Next, Grizz knocked the punks' gun out of his hand, before swinging the brutish yo-yo out again smashing the punk in the face. After all the punishment, the yo-yo still reclined up to his palm obediently. As the Blackguard began to turn and continue up the stairs to the next floor, the stairs began to collapse and fall out from under him. The Blackguard hurtled his yo-yo out instinctively with the hopes it would snag on something.

It was certainly something which had grabbed a hold of the yo-yo. Only to Grizz's surprise, it was something invisible.

The Blackguard was pulled up to the second floor by something very powerful. When Grizz was high enough to get a firm footing, the large white yo-yo was released as it fell from mid-air.

Never before had Grizz been so confused, nevertheless, he stood up straight and gave his yo-yo a flick with his toe and it recoiled up to his hand.

He connected the yo-yo to his belt and then pulled off his rope and mechanical grappler hook. Before he used the rope, he took one last suspicious glance behind himself. The Blackguard threw his grappler hook with a powerful under-hand toss. Using his remote control ring, the grappler snapped a hold onto the remaining stairs above. After giving two strong tugs to test the grappler's hold, he swung into the stairwell and began to strenuously climb his way up the rope. He did very well considering how much weight he was carrying.

The punks had just waited for the dust to settle when they began to flood into the bottom of the stairwell. They did not even cock their guns before they showered bullets up at Grizz. Most of the bullets glanced off his cast iron boots.

Grizz dropped an explosive charge and the punks scrambled. Grizz didn't want to be toasted when the explosive went off. Another strange incident occurred as the Blackguard was pushed from underneath him. He rose up the rest of the way to where he could scale what was left of the stair case.

The explosive blew up below as Grizz bolted up the stairs. Diligently he climbed to the tenth floor when he stopped in his tracks. Grizz heard something, so he cautiously opened the tenth story door. A fire broke out below as a result of the explosion. Quietly, Grizz slunk through the door.

"That's him!!!" Someone shouted.

Grizz threw some ninja-stars at all of the punks who had just stepped off the elevator. Powerfully, Grizz walked over to the fallen punks. Kicking a door in at his right, Grizz hauled the severely injured punks into the room with him.

Dropping them onto the floor, Grizz walked over to a window. He looked outside for a moment, before he grabbed a punk and held him close to his helmet.

"You were all like brothers to me just yesterday. Now, I need to send your pals a message and you are going to be the messenger." Grizz spoke in a slow deep growly voice.

The Blackguard pushed the face of the punk up against the glass of the dirty window. "Leave here now and I will let the rest of you live!" shouted Grizz. The punk twitched and opened his eyes as both he and the Blackguard waited for an answer from outside.

The answer came in the form of a single bullet which broke the window from outside and pierced the chest of the punk. Grizz pushed the dead punk out through the window. Broken glass followed the punk as he plunged ten stories setting the example and striking fear into those who opposed him.

"No!!!" Came a distinct voice from within the room.

Grizz turned quickly questioning, "Who's there?!" Grizz was met with no answer. "Who's there?!!!" Grizz asked even louder and prominently. Searching the room and unable to hide his confusion and frustration, Grizz pressed some more. "You better answer me, or else..." Grizz paused.

The ghost did not want to give himself away, so it remained silent. Careful to keep his body concealed and protected, Grizz shouted out the window and announced as loud as he could. "I am the greatest warrior there is, or ever will be!!!"

Knowing he would not receive any further answers from the voice through asking, Grizz came up with a test. Recoiling into the room, Grizz grabbed a second and third punk to toss out the window as well. The efforts of Grizz paid off, as the ghostly presence appeared. It was the volk, Eddy Evon as he stepped forward and took hold of the victims and pulled them free from Grizz's grasp. Grizz did not understand the strange energy clothes he wore. Swinging around Grizz saw the punks fall limply to the floor, then with equal speed he turned again to take a second glance out the window.

On the vacant street where only the punks had gathered, Grizz could see them preparing a rocket launcher. Abruptly, Grizz turned and ran out of the room, noticing Eddy had disappeared again.

The room Grizz ran out from, exploded in a thunder of destructive fire.

"Ahurg! -- Rocket launchers!" Muffled Grizz under his breath.

Smoke puffed out from the seams of the elevator doors as it groaned with a giant deep hollow warning. Then the elevator belched up a roar and blasted out the doors. The doors sailed through the hallway, spinning violently and embedded into the wall at the other end of the hall. The staircase blistered and blew apart with fire, throwing splinters and hot shrapnel down the other direction of the hall in a powerful heat wave. Sirens from the Metro Fire and police Department screamed outside. Grizz stood near the window.

"Finally!" Grizz breathed, "The cops… Now, where are the choppers?"

Unexpectedly, the ghost became visible before the Blackguard once again.

The field around the bodily form wavered and diminished, then a strange blue glowing energy gel slunk off his head as far as his neck. At first Grizz thought his brother, Narl, had returned, but he quickly recognized the volk face belonged to Eddy Evon. *'What strange technology is this?'* Grizz wondered. Somehow the volk was able to make himself invisible.

Speechless, the two of them said nothing for a long couple of seconds. Before Grizz moved to attack the intrusive form, he admired the volk standing in front of him. Eddy had thick greyish blue skin which was smooth, perfect and unscathed, which was unlike his own human skin lined like a road map of scars for every square inch. Eddy, however, was like a symbol of who Grizz wanted to be. The bone structure of a volk showed through. The crown of his head was larger than a humans' with a heavy brow and bone lumps running over the center from the front to the back.

Volk hands were three times the size of a typical man's. His muscles were beautiful and perfect where again he made the comparison to his own jumble of human and volk mismatching.

The eyes of the volk were pure black and mysterious, as they also carried with them an all knowing confidence and righteousness he has rarely found in any other. He looked right into Grizz's soul and judged him with deep condemnation, or so Grizz believed.

Jealousy washed over Grizz again as it had when he was growing up with Eddy on the Knolix Island. Before he knew it, Grizz had given into his spirit of anger again as he threw a few darts at Eddy. A sound of something like chimes accompanied shots of bright gleaming little stars from nowhere which deflected the trajectory of his darts into the adjacent wall.

Grizz growled, from the depths of his chest as he sensed his mediocre telepathic ability kick in. Eddy was not his enemy, despite the disgust he felt for Grizz. Grizz found something in Eddy which was very familiar and almost comfortable. This time, Eddy's eyes reminded Grizz of his Brothers, whom he still missed very much.

521

He couldn't remember ever looking at Eddy Evon this way in the past.

A still small voice from a deep pit within Grizz's sub consciousness spoke to him. It said, *'There is still something to live for. You are meant for bigger things.'* Though Grizz did not know what that might be, as he drew in a deep breath of fresh air, Grizz could feel the strength surge through his body... through the very blood of his veins.

Indeed, he was not at the end, his story was just beginning. An inquisitive thought as to what the future of possibilities might hold for him sparked an insatiable urge to discover all which was intended for him.

Bonus Chapter

"You disgust me." The tall, monstrous volk spoke boldly.

Grizz shouted a quote he recently heard from his friend Scorpin-X and he used it to establish dominance. "Grizz is the greatest warrior there is, or ever will be!"

Grizz ran at Eddy wildly. Eddy, with his longer arms, lashed forth first and contacted Grizz in the stomach. Grizz was swept off his feet and his back was embedded into the ceiling. A light fixture shattered and an impressive indentation marked the impact. Grizz fell straight down from the ceiling, flat on the floor where he just laid for a moment.

Grizz thought he was the greatest, but he didn't consider the volk factor.

The Blackguard rose from the floor and looked at Eddy.

"Believe it or not, but I want to help you." Eddy told Grizz.

"The only way you can help me is if you join me, otherwise, get out of my way... Eddy." Grizz knew his comment confirmed his identity to Eddy, though he likely already knew who he was. The sound of a helicopter amongst the sirens in the distance shone a spotlight on their floor. The beam of blue light lit everything up like day.

"Fine, now follow me. I'll get us out of this, Domin." Eddy received no reaction from Grizz as he just stood looking at Eddy... studying him.

"Domin is dead. I am Grizz, and you can forget it!" Retaliated Grizz as he removed his pouch of explosives and tossed them down the length of the hallway toward the flames. "If it is not my way, it's the highway." Grizz began to run with his rope and mechanical grappler hook in hand. He picked up a lot of speed, before he lept out the broken window.

Eddy followed Grizz out the window, knowing the impact of the explosion would be too much for him to bear.

The apartment blew out at them from behind. Grizz tossed his mechanical grappler hook while in mid leap from the tenth story window. The hook caught the landing ski of the police surveillance helicopter.

The helicopter pulled away from the building as the entire structure collapsed. Grizz's weight began to tug at the helicopter. The search light swung around lighting their surroundings in the chaos. Aggressively climbing his cable to the cockpit of the two pilots, Grizz punched through the windshield with his studded black brass knuckles.

The police pilots of the helicopter panicked as Grizz opened the cockpit door. The officers shot at the intruder, but Grizz pulled them from their seats and dropped them from the helicopter. The two officers plummeted into the shallow waters of the strong and wide Fraser river. Grizz was left to pilot the helicopter alone, but not familiar with the controls, the air-craft steered aimlessly. Crashing into the river with a splash which sprung a spray of water fifty feet into the air, the rotors chopped into the river for a few beats, before they shattered apart. Pieces of metal rotor shards streaked through the air in every direction. Grizz struggled to get out of the helicopter. Eddy dropped toward the river to assist the pilots as well as Grizz.

After quickly rescuing the officers, Eddy dived under the water's surface and steadily swam to the helicopter. Clasping his arms and legs around the cockpit and applying pressure, the cockpit imploded. Grizz was not easy for Eddy to move underwater. Eddy pulled at Grizz with mighty strength, before he hauled him onto the sandy shore. Grizz slid off Eddy's shoulder and collapsed to the ground.

Eddy removed Grizz's helmet. Studying Grizz's scarred face for only a second Eddy placed his open hand onto Grizz's chest.

"Evon, warm this man and bring him around to consciousness." Eddy commanded his sertz. Eddy's sertz was a small but highly complex robot, about the size of a fly.

Eddy's strange energy gel suit increased in power as it became a very bright blue. Grizz coughed before he took a great gasp of air. Opening his eyes, Grizz looked at Eddy. Recognizing Eddy, Grizz pushed Him away and locked a questioning gaze with him as with wide wild eyes Grizz wanted to understand Eddy's intensions. Grizz's pupils were fully open and intense.

A long double edged blade sprang forth from the upper wrist of Grizz's gauntlet. Grizz swung the blade at Eddy as Eddy lifted his arms in defence. The blade struck Eddy's bulky fore arm device and the blue energy gel of his volk suit began to spill out through it onto the ground. A reaction caused by the damage to Eddy's arm device recalled the blue energy suit back into the unit where it spewed and sprayed out the open damaged slash on its side.

Grizz was certainly surprised and confused, when he saw the blue glowing energy gel drain out. With the intent to get away from the strange glowing ooze and escape Eddy, Grizz turned. Soaking wet, Grizz clumsily jumped to climb the rocky embankment but he collapsed on a wet boulder. Falling forward Grizz kicked back at Eddy's stomach. Grizz's heavy boot shattered a translucent disk secured to Eddy's abdomen. Eddy stumbled back and fell into the river. Splashing to regain his balance, Eddy watched as the pieces of the disk fell away, and floated down the river. He tried to gather the pieces as they were of some importance to the volk, but he soon gave up in disappointment. Eddy strode out of the water shaking his head slowly from side to side.

Grizz could tell he had shattered something dear to Eddy. Noticing Eddy stepping out of the river toward him, Grizz scampered up the hill. With a second glance Grizz caught sight of an anger flaring up in Eddy's eyes as he stood half naked, standing on the shore wearing only boxers. Eddy was more baffled than angry as his attention shifted to the device attached to his fore arm. Eddy examined just how badly his device was damaged.

The strange volk device appeared to be operational still. Eddy lifted his gaze to Grizz as Grizz climbed the rocks to the parking lot. Grizz's eyes were anxious and wide and his heavy armored suit was wet, which added to his awkward ability. Eddy picked up Grizz's metal helmet from the rocks and threw it at Grizz. The helmet struck Grizz at the center of his shoulder blades. The shoulder plates took most of the impact. The helmet bounced high off Grizz and landed amongst the vehicles of the parking lot.

Grizz turned and sneered at Eddy.

Eddy advanced by one step and Grizz felt threatened. Grizz recognized the look in the volk's eyes. Anger and power of the massive volk targeted him.

Grizz retaliated right away as he dislodged and rolled an impressively large boulder down at Eddy. With one hand, Eddy scooped up the boulder and tossed it over his head. A heavy '--thwump--' was heard as the river swallowed the boulder.

'Why hasn't Eddy attacked me yet?' Grizz wondered. Of course, Eddy could never hurt anyone. He

lacked the military experience and the training which only Grizz had. Grizz could see his advantage and he couldn't disguise it as he smiled with confidence.

"I would have killed you by now if that was my intention." Eddy began to crawl up the rocks. "Now, put your little knives away so we can get out of here." The volk looked so manipulative.

Grizz responded with a new insight to his situation, "Ohhh, you'd like that wouldn't you. I give you just a sliver of trust, then when I turn my back, you would attack!" Grizz had every reason to be very suspicious of Eddy, he was at war and everyone was a suspect.

"I'm getting tired of this." Eddy with words of a snake, "Would you rather we spend all night here on this embankment waiting for someone to come and kill us?" Eddy shook his head frustrated, before he charged up the river-side slope bearing down on Grizz. Grizz began to growl, warning Eddy of his dangerous action.

Eddy stumbled as he prepared for his immediate attack. Grizz stood up as he considered his options, before committing to one of them.

Winding his fist back, he threw himself forward delivering a deadly blow. Grizz was surprised by the volk's amazing speed and strength.

Eddy caught Grizz in the center of his stomach and sent him over the slight grade to the parking-lot. Grizz's upper back landed onto the hood of a silver corvette. A security alarm began to squeal irritatingly. Gaining control from the impact, Grizz snapped up and pushed himself away from the corvette. Grizz's long tangled hair quivered in the breeze, and he seemed to lose any sense of fear or rage. A tooth filled grin of satisfaction decorated Grizz's face, before he chuckled. "Eh-heh."

This was Grizz's ultimate challenge. Hungry to prove he was the greatest, even over volks, a stone cold expression settled over Grizz's jaw and his eyes began to burn. With a quick movement, Grizz had his samurai swords in hand. Speed and force came alive like fire as Grizz threw his arms around to slash Eddy with his blades.

"Easy, buddy." Eddy tried to calm Grizz as he lifted his hands up for him to stop. "Put your knives away so we can kill each other on equal terms?"

Grizz did not listen. Eddy's snap movements were proved to be incredibly fast as Grizz could not cut him. The volk also tried to pop Grizz with a quick shot through an opening, but Grizz displayed he had speed of his own and slashed Eddy's forearm.

Eddy placed his hand over the wound. Thick ruby blood began to seep through the volk's fingers. Grizz became a mad ninja butcher from the dark ages and he wanted to turn Eddy into a chopped sausage. Eddy turned and tried to run from Grizz. Grizz didn't pursue Eddy immediately, rather he went back to search for his helmet amongst the parked vehicles.

With long precise strides Eddy headed across the parking lot and back down the embankment to a nearby drainage tunnel. The opening was blocked by a welded re-bar mesh with gaps small enough to keep out small children and large animals.

Eddy wrenched on it to get an idea of how stable it was. A quick glance revealed Grizz was not going to grant Eddy time for numerous attempts to open the tunnel. Grizz found his helmet quickly as Eddy perceived thc way Grizz ran toward him was like a vicious mad bull clad in dark armor.

Astonishing, Eddy curled his fingers tightly around the bars and heaved with all he had. The concrete broke and the re-bar tore away. Eddy swung the heavy material at Grizz knocking him back onto the rocks but Grizz rolled with it and came back up on his feet. Eddy dived into the tunnel and tried to shimmy through it as fast as he could. Replacing the samurai swords in their sheaves, Grizz followed the volk. If he hadn't, the volk would likely disappear forever. Ahead of Eddy was darkness and behind him was the heavy cast iron boots of his predator, Grizz.

Grizz's blades clanged and scratched at the inside of the tunnel as his half growling, half breathing threatened Eddy's existence.

Grizz knew he was gaining on the volk. With a quick strike, Grizz clipped the heel of Eddy's volk boot with his gauntlet blade. The tight radius of the tunnel's space soon opened up to a much larger culvert. Eddy was the first to roll out of the pipe and stand up. Glancing behind, Eddy saw Grizz pulling himself out of the pipe.

Eddy instantly took off running down the dark shallow tunnel. The stench in the air was rancid as though there was a depletion of oxygen. Grizz used his other senses to guide him through the tunnels. Primarily he used his sense of sound to follow Eddy since the sense of smell was atrocious. Grizz picked up speed as he lumbered along, splashing with a wild vengeance.

Grizz could hear sounds of Eddy scruffling about just ahead. He was close.

Two lights came from above. Grizz knew it was a man hole, but the distraction was more than enough for Eddy who struck Grizz as he ran up beside him. Eddy threw his weight into Grizz as he jabbed his elbow into Grizz's side.

Grizz roared in pain. Eddy, lept up the rungs to the man-hole and pushed it up which brought him to the road above. An automobile of some sort flew over the man-hole and clanged its' tires against the metal cover. Eddy was lucky he didn't lose his arm.

Grizz tried to work through the pain and get up. He noticed Eddy was out of his mind as he poked his head out of the man hole only to find he was too large to get all the way through. The sound of rubber tires squealing along the road sounded as Eddy ducked back down right away. The left front tire of a commercial transport truck hit the open man-hole and the pin broke loose from its trailer. The flat-bed trailer, which was hauling steel beams, gouged into concrete. The beams ripped through the road throwing huge chunks of asphalt into the air. Tearing through the man-hole, the heavy trailer dug the opening out wider. The load bindings broke and the steel beams fanned out over the road. The beams carried with them great weight and velocity. They speared into oncoming traffic and knocked over street lights.

The detached semi-truck was forced to veer off the road colliding into the heavily occupied parking lot. Behind the devastated trailer and clutter of steel beams was a brilliant speeding sports car. Moving too fast and too close to the truck and trailer to stop, the driver's eyes grew as large as baseballs before he swerved to miss the accident. Entering oncoming traffic, the little red sports-car collided head on with a dump truck. The dump truck mowed over the sports car with ease before it turned off the road and drove up a practically vertical slope. When momentum would no longer carry the dump truck any further, it tilted and rolled down toward Grizz and Eddy.

The volk and Grizz turned and retreated further back into the sewer system. The thunderous noise was so loud they truly believed the tunnel would collapse in on them. They ran as fast as they could, deeper into the tunnel. They heard the heavy dump truck slam against the pavement behind them as its' load of gravel spilled out and buried the hole in the street.

Pitch black and through the silence which followed,

I heard the sound of gravel settling and Grizz's deep breathing. Grizz and Eddy paused in the darkness to catch their breath. Grizz could not see Eddy at all. He felt the volk was near, so Grizz searched the darkness with the palms of his hands and his arms held straight out at his sides. He wasn't certain what to do if he did find the volk. Grizz reflexively jerked left, then right as he sniffed the air and tried to get a fix on Eddy's position.

A distant squeak echoed. Like a sinister predator, Grizz snapped his head in the direction of the sound, but it was just a sewer rat scurrying in the dead of the dark, crypt-like silence within the dank bowels of Metro city.

Then the sound of the volk's voice was revealed, "Why fight?" Eddy coaxed Grizz. Grizz bent down low at the sound of Eddy's voice in an attempt to hone in on Eddy's exact location, but the sound of the voice echoed off the walls. If Grizz could find Eddy, he would hurt him real bad. Both of them walked in the near vicinity of one another. Eddy could see Grizz, but Grizz could only hear Eddy, "I remember you." Eddy spoke as they circled around in the cramped junction of the sewer. "You're from the Island." Grizz slipped a little as his foot caught on a ledge. He splashed to regain his balance from the curvature of the culvert. He swore under his breath at his own clumsiness. "What did they do to you, Domin?"

"I am going to make this sewer your tomb..." Grizz growled.

"Oh, come now, that is no way to talk to an old friend." Eddy attempted to lighten Grizz's mood.

Grizz let out a drawn breath of exhaustion, "I remember, Eddy." then Grizz crossed his gauntlets as his metal blades clash together. Speaking low under his sinister rough voice, "I've always hated you..."

"That's fine, I don't like you either, but I'm curious, what are you fighting for?" Eddy asked at point blank range.

Grizz was taken back by the question, for all his life he had a fight of some form or another and it was always for the same reason, "I fight to win!" Grizz spoke with a swagger.

"To win? Win what?" Eddy challenged.

"The fight you idiot! One wins and one loses. I don't lose." Grizz really wished he could see Eddy.

"I'm sure you don't. Listen, you are one of a kind, the last of your kind, right? I am the last of my kind as well."

"What about your mother? She's a volk as well, isn't she?" Grizz thought Eddy had made a mistake.

Eddy dropped his head though Grizz couldn't see it, from the silence he understood. "She isn't with us any more." Eddy finally told Grizz.

"I-I'm sorry Eddy." more silence, "Though I never knew her very well, she was my mother too."

"Domin, I fight for a purpose. I want to go home to my world where I belong. I have some information you would be very interested in."

"What kind of information?" Grizz demanded with a low snarl of skepticism.

"Secrets about the Knolix Island." Eddy answered with a gleam in his eye. Grizz perked up at the mention of not only the Island but its' name, *Knolix Island*.

Eddy must have something of value and he was willing to share it. *'Oh, what am I doing?…'* Grizz came to a new realization.

Filling his lungs with air, Eddy confidently said, "I invite you to join with me. Together we will be a force unstoppable and my chances of success increase considerably. Hold out your hand and we will shake on it. We will make a pact, you and I. Right here in this sewer we will become what we always have been, *Brothers*."

What had Eddy proposed here?

Grizz couldn't believe it. He was given a second chance to unit with his, *Brother*? Eddy was the twin of the volk he had such a connection to, though if only in a segregated way. To have Eddy as his Brother would be different because Eddy was a complete volk. Within himself, Grizz could feel his other Brothers speaking to him through the parts of his own body. *'Could it be? Nothing is lost, rather everything couldn't be more complete. Eddy was the missing piece to everything.'*

"We need to get out of here, together. Right now. Agreed?" Eddy asked the question which shook Grizz right out of his thoughts.

Eddy was the last of Grizz's Brothers. He would deeply regret hurting Eddy if he actually managed to do so. Without answering right away, Grizz replied, "Agreed... *Brother*..." came the echo from Grizz's deep rough voice. Extending his open hand into the darkness, Grizz expected Eddy to see it and take hold of it. With amazement and gratitude, Grizz found Eddy firmly shaking on their new understanding. The pact was sealed.

"Go back the way we came if you choose, but I am getting out this way." Eddy began digging through the gravel which had spilled out of the dump truck. Grizz cleared his head, it wasn't easy for him to let someone else call the shots. Grizz had a sense of what the right thing to do was in this filthy place of darkness. Grizz chose to help. Approaching Eddy from behind, Eddy's eyes shifted to the side as though he half expected Grizz to stab him in the back, but Grizz moved up beside Eddy and helped him to dig. When Eddy had punched through the gravel to the open hole in the road, he reached back down and grabbed Grizz by his armored glove and pulled him out. Their hearts were pumping out of their chest's.

Just beyond the parking lot's toll booth and row of

parked cars was a café. Everyone at the little restaurant had left their tables. Most of the people were doing what they could to help the injured while some women and waitresses remained peering out the windows at the accident. Eddy and Grizz jumped over and around the damaged vehicles of the accident. Eddy tore open vehicles so none of the injured would be difficult to get to. Grizz could see how Eddy was trying to help the scene by assisting rescuers who would soon be on the scene ready to use the jaws of life or other extraction means. Grizz assisted Eddy under the cloak of darkness. By opening the damaged vehicles they saved time for the casualties to be saved. After doing this, Eddy and Grizz approached the café. This caused quite a stir amongst the people at the scene.

The eyes in the windows staring back at Eddy and Grizz grew wide.

"Let's take a couple of these hogs." Grizz suggested as he made a gesture to the row of parked motorcycles.

"There's got to be a better way." Eddy said, no doubt the bikes were someone's prized possessions. In the distance, Grizz could hear the activity of people trying to assist with the vehicle accident.

"Take the hog and follow me, or stay and die. Don't argue with me, this game has no place for a goody-goody." Grizz declared with the intent to get moving before the authorities caught up to them.

"Get away from my bike you freak!" The voice of the motorcycle's owner cracked like thunder. Grizz refused to see a threat in the burly bikers.

Eddy stepped toward the biker with the palms of my hands held out toward him. The bearded biker was dressed in black leather and he looked like a hard man. Calmly, Eddy said, "Easy, man. We don't want any trouble."

Twenty devoted bikers came out of the café at once. They all shared the same Harley Davidson crests, emblems of eagles and fire along with gang colours. Someone snuck up behind Eddy whipping a chain across his shoulder. Grizz was smoking hot and mad as he was about to vanquish everyone and the restaurant as well. The angry bikers held hammers, knives and chains. Grizz was just about to go crazy on everyone when a loud voice came.

"All right, everyone put away your weapons." Eddy spoke loud and clear. "I told you, I don't want any trouble." The bikers just stared at Eddy in bewilderment. They did not understand what he was trying to tell them. From the biker's point of view, Eddy was evil and anything he said was only part of his plan to take their bikes. They could only speculate as to who the two huge people were and what they were doing there. If any of the bikers had listened to the radio recently, they would know Grizz and Eddy were dangerous. What was to happen next would determine a peaceful outcome or a mad brawl.

"Just a minute." One of the bikers said to the gang with his hand in the air. He stepped toward Eddy and opened his mouth as though he was going to ask him a question.

The bikers were just about to consider talking to Eddy when Grizz lifted his arms and took a step forward. With his hands held up like he was under arrest, Grizz spoke with a muffled voice from his helmet, "Oh, ya, we don't want any trouble... Hea-hea." his deep, menacing voice was saturated with a sense of deceitfulness as Grizz slightly turned his head toward Eddy and whispered. "Let's do this... Brother."

A few bikers who stood before the two Brothers moved in on Grizz as he stepped toward a couple of the parked motor cycles. Reaching out and grabbing two of the bikes by the front tires, Grizz dragged them from the curb and started swinging them around and around. The bikers who had surrounded Grizz began to back way off.

When Grizz released the bikes, one flew into the main front window of the café and the other one embedded itself in through the windshield of a nearby family mini van in the parking lot.

"Hey!" Eddy shouted at Grizz. "Stop this non-sense. We need to get out of here, right now!"

"My thoughts exactly." Grizz hissed back at Eddy. If Eddy was going to continue treating Grizz like he was a child, Grizz would have to define himself. Grizz turned back toward a few remaining parked Harley Davidsons. At the far end of the line of parked motor bikes, a couple of bikers were trying to start their motorcycles to protect them. Once their motors came alive with a chest pounding roar of thunder, Grizz swiftly moved in on them. Marching through the crowd, Grizz brushing people out of his way, back handing them with ease. Immediately, Grizz pulled the bikers from their Harleys. A few biker girlfriends screamed then decided to hold their breath after Grizz shot them a look.

Grizz hopped onto one of the bikes, and jerked his head expecting Eddy to follow, before he asked. "You com'n or not?" Grizz gave Eddy an anxious eye because they were out of time and most other options.

The sound of the sirens had grown very loud and the military surveillance helicopter made a *fly by* to report their position. Eddy headed toward Grizz as the bikers provided a wide path for Eddy to pass.

Considering how desperate their situation was, Eddy couldn't argue. The motorcycle's shocks strained under Eddy's weight as he dwarfed the size of the hog. Eddy rode passed the mad people of the cafe as they yelled and threw bear bottles at them.

Grizz led the way.

The thunderous noise of the motorcycles shook and echoed off the buildings in the wake of their high speed arrival. Throughout the streets of Metro city, Eddy followed close behind Grizz. The dark night skies deepened to heavier hues of purple and blue. An eerie smog lingered above the city streets. The warm interior lights of countless city dwellings decorated the tall buildings provided a calm in the tension of the moment.

Grizz, leading the way, steered them clear of roadblocks and search helicopters. They hid from their, would be captors, most of the time. Occasionally, the police surprised them but as long as Eddy tailed closely behind Grizz, they out smarted their pursuers. Driving through glass doors of large building complexes, they found Metro city had been evacuated. Crashing through the entrance of the Metro city mall, Grizz led Eddy through and out the back to an alley way to an underground parking lot of a neighboring building. Grizz's quick thinking and sharp maneuvers kept them hidden. Distracting the authorities they made the shadows their perfect cloaks. Sirens of police cars and fire-engines sounded off into the night. Deeper and deeper they went into the maze of Metro city. The sirens and rolling lights of the police seemed to diminish along with the average commuter vehicle. The army had successfully moved everyone out of the city. The situation became a strict military operation.

Running red lights of intersections in a desperate attempt to out run pursuing Boeing Sikorsky RAH-66 Comanche helicopters, the forces from the sky grew in numbers as the distance Grizz and Eddy covered through the city. Twin-turbine (tandem) armed reconnaissance helicopters came into play. These babies had stealth characteristics like retractable under carriage and weapons stubs, an angular over-all shape and engine exhaust slots under the fuselage. The main propeller hub was entirely covered, and the tail rotor is a ducted fan. Grizz liked a good challenge but he wasn't stupid. With monsters like these in pursuit, he knew the best defence was to run as far and as fast as possible if he and Eddy were to survive at all.

Grizz brought them to the out skirts of Metro city. The Comanche helicopters lost sight of them for a moment when they hid under an over pass. From there Grizz led Eddy into a quick detour through yet another back alley. As Grizz growled through his helmet, he could link his mind to the thoughts of the military. Like a map was built into Grizz's mind he steered them through the city avoiding the multitude of military vehicles on the road. Uncertain of their exact position, the city police in conjunction with the military were busy setting up more roadblocks closer to the heart of the city to keep Grizz and Eddy from getting out. Little did they know, Grizz and Eddy had already found a back door out of Metro city. Soon, Grizz and Eddy found themselves in a familiar industrial complex.

Before the Comanche helicopters found them again, They broke the lock at the gate of the chain link fence and drove into a huge old abandoned saw-mill yard. Grizz was already prepared for this sort of situation. He was back in his own environment as he entered the same industrial complex where the punk hide out was. Grizz, however, made a point to stay clear of the punk hide out itself. The industrial complex was large enough he could keep it a secret. Passing by the large field area where the brawl was, Grizz saw a few punks and rockers still remained in the area as they continued the difficult job of clearing out their people and belongings. Grizz knew to drive near selected warehouses on the east side of the complex where he kicked the doors in and broke windows.

'What was he looking for?' Eddy wondered. 'A place to hide? A friend who could help us? Or did he have some kind of mental imbalance I was not aware of?' At any rate, Eddy began to question the confidence he had in Grizz's ability. Grizz marched over to the high garage door and began lifting it. The lock broke before the door opened. They walked the bikes inside and closed the door behind them just as the spot lights of the surveillance helicopters washed over the building. They waited to see if they had been spotted. The helicopters did not stay long before they moved on, continuing their search. Grizz, familiar with his surroundings, pulled out an old dusty tarp and placed it over the two bikes.

"Follow me!" Grizz commanded. Within the warehouse, Eddy followed Grizz up the stairs of the filthy platform to a balcony which supplied a great overview of the saw mill below.

Eddy stopped half way up the stairs and looked at Grizz, "Don't even begin to consider me as some mindless follower you can pull around like a dog on a leash."

Grizz stopped in his tracks and turned to Eddy with a menacing slowness. "Sure, now keep up." he spoke facetiously.

Eddy's fist came down on the railing heavily, snapping it. "If I had never known you from the Island and if we weren't on the run, I would have been rid of you instantly."

Grizz looked down upon Eddy from the higher steps. "Quite a statement. What have I done to you to hate me so much?"

Eddy's emotions began to burn with anger. He felt he really did hate Grizz as Grizz tempted him to. "I find it hard to like someone who's entire personality is made of evil and hatred. You injure and kill innocent people without any regret."

"There are no innocent people. If those people were innocent they wouldn't have gotten involved and confronted me. It isn't me you hate, it's my military training."

"What kind of outlook is that? Killing is wrong, everyone knows that." Eddy let out a breath of fatigue. He was tired of Grizz's wild caveman like mentality.

"Espionage, assassin or defender of our nation, a Blackguard. Are you jealous you were not chosen for such training? You were not raised like me." Grizz grunted. "No one tried to make a secret weapon out of you."

"They wanted to!" Eddy told Grizz.

"That's just not the same. Now, are you coming or do you plan to continue boring me with your wining?" Grizz turned and stepped onto the upper level.

Eddy followed behind Grizz, shaking his head as he thought, *'None of this really matters. I must keep my focus on the goal, and the goal is to get home.'* then Eddy asked Grizz a new question. "How long can we hide out here before they find us?"

"I figure this location will last us the night at least." Grizz answered now with a swagger of attitude. "You saw me kick open some doors from warehouses at the east side of this industrial area? That was to set off the security alarms creating a strong decoy for our escape. Those alarm systems will encourage the military search party to concentrate on that area. From up here, I can keep my eyes on them. This warehouse is on my old turf. The alarm system was disabled long ago. Trust me, we're safe."

"You don't trust anyone, I get that, but I'm supposed to trust you? Just look at what you've done! Tripping those alarms will bring them here even sooner!" Eddy looked at the ceiling as he chewed his lip.

"I know. It's called a diversion to keep them looking where I want them to. As I said, I am able to monitor their progress and keep from being surprised by them."

"Suppose we are fully surrounded in the morning," Eddy asked suspiciously. "Then what would we do?"

"We'll take to the sewer."

"No! no more sewers for me." Eddy was disgusted.

"We are on the run!" Grizz snapped. "What kind of answer are you expecting from me? We don't have a lot of options. This is no special agent film. I can not conveniently fly us out of here at day break!"

Eddy looked at the motorcycles, he noticed all of the wood of the saw mill and the misplaced tools when an idea sprung to his mind.

After a long while where Eddy explained his idea of converting the motorcycles, Grizz finally gave into his request. Grizz figured, until he came up with a better plan, we might as well try out Eddy's idea. Grizz's questions and disagreements only proved how stubborn Eddy was about his plan. Grizz thought, *'At least your idea will be good for a laugh.'*

Carrying the motor cycles up the creaking stair case, they worked on the project together and talked. Grizz had many questions about the Island and he was amazed at how much Eddy knew about what was happening on the inside the Island. They learned a lot from each other's stories. Grizz was confident with the temporary safe house. Eddy was not so sure if they were as secure as Grizz let on but the communication seemed to break down some barriers and bring them closer to a shared

542

level of understanding.

"Hmph-hmph." Eddy heard a muffled chuckle from Grizz. "Funny, we were school mates yesterday and now we're going to war."

"We're not going to war." Eddy told Grizz sternly. "Could you pass me that wrench over there?" Eddy pointed. While Grizz reached for the wrench, Eddy continued. "Tomorrow morning, at day break, we're getting out of here." Eddy wanted to tell Grizz, *'I will go my way and you will go yours. The end.'* but like him or not, Eddy knew he had to take Grizz with him to the Ied era. Eddy glanced out the window to see if anyone was creeping around their complex. The area seemed secure. When Eddy turned back, Grizz placed the wrench in his hand.

"You have a plan, don't you?" The remark from Grizz surprised Eddy. "I know you well enough. You think like me. You don't aimlessly run from things and hope you don't get backed into a corner. You have a destination and I want to know where that is."

The wrench was one size to small. "It is not easy for me to respond. Not only do I think you won't understand, I think you won't trust me after I explain. You know I have been following you through the city, trusting you not to take us the wrong way, trapping us or getting us killed. Now, I need you to extend the same level of blind trust so I can take you to where we belong, but it won't be easy. I need a larger wrench, this one is no good."

"Oh, so after I saved your life and proven I can be trusted, you tell me I'm not smart enough to understand where we are going to go? Maybe we will live, maybe we will die, but you will always be an obnoxious volk to me, Ed-man, and that's the largest wrench I have so choke on it, pal."

"Obnoxious? I'm sure you had nothing but

543

compassion for the punk as you dropped him out a tenth story window. Besides all this pointless bickering, our lives are still at risk. Listen, I hope to return to the world of volks where we will no longer be hunted." Eddy gripped the bolt head with his finger tips and loosened them the hard way. In no time, Eddy removed and disassembled the front steering column.

"That's right, we are outcasts *here* in this world! Like you, Eddy, I don't fit into this world." I turned to look for shadows moving in the streets below but there was nothing. "Tell me... Am I right? Answer me! You and I are both victims of those psycho government scientist at the Island. We should be working together to bring them down."

"I am not interested in bringing them down. I told you, I just want to go home." With a sense of home sickness Eddy closed his eyes and turned away.

"By now, I have more volk blood running through my veins than I do human." With impressive strain, Grizz managed to bend a metal pipe as an example of his inhuman strength using only his bare hands and Eddy caught sight of Grizz's veins branching out over the tightened muscles of his arms. Eddy could actually see the dark blood pumping through enlarged veins.

"To live and see this volk world of ours, or to die trying, I'm ready, either way." I had the sense of an impending weight upon Grizz. *'What had he been through?'* Eddy wondered realistically.

Eddy removed the rear tire and chain before he proceeded to do the same to the other motor bike. As he did so, Eddy telepathically looked through a little bit of Grizz's memories to get a better understanding of his past.

Grizz knew Eddy was a telepath and that he was looking through his mind. It was like Narl was back from the grave with the only difference of painlessness. Allowing Eddy to have a look, Grizz said, "Sometimes I wish I was never created at all."

Eddy felt Grizz's deep sadness, "According to your file, from the Island's computer, you are the product of two babies who had, for natural causes, the worst start in life, but because of the pain you have endured, you're now one of the most powerful people on this planet. Through you, my twin brother lives."

Grizz turned his face to Eddy as though he were studying the volk. Feeling lighter from sharing, Grizz reclined into his chair comfortably.

"I never could understand who, or what, you were. Everyone knew you were a volk, but what does that mean? Are you an alien?" Felling closer to Eddy, Grizz expected an open and honest answer.

"I *am* from a different world. You and I can explore it together. It will all be new to me as well."

Grizz chuckled, "If we can get that far... Chances are you will get caught and your verdict will be death. Your cute little intrusion of this world will fill history books for years to come. By pushing your way into the public's eye, you will most likely become the most significant discovery of our time. There will probably be a museum built in your honor, filled with the strange broken utilities you have." Grizz pointed to my romstrunn. Eddy jerked it away before Grizz could touch it. Grizz smiled crookedly before he continued. "Your life history will be documented for all to read. If I'm lucky, I maybe briefly mentioned in the document. I certainly don't see how I can compete with the likes of you. The document will probably be placed on a stand in front of a couple of huge glass cased boxes. In one box will be your skin stuffed and positioned in a threatening manner to portray you as a beast. The other box will have your skeleton fused together at the joints."

"Nice." Eddy said trying to act as casually as he could. Grizz's prediction was not only compelling but quite possible. It was just the kind of thing Eddy fought to prevent. "I didn't know you were so talented at bed time stories." Eddy tried to stay as busy as possible and not let it show how Grizz's story actually gave him the willies.

Their work space was dark and cramped. There was no power available for power tools or light. Every little motion was enough to raise a small billow of dust. The dust got into everything. They choked on it and it irritated their eyes, even though their vision was already obscured by the darkness. Grizz was very messy and clumsy as he worked and he didn't follow Eddy's instructions very well at all.

"Just tell me. Where did you come from? How will you get to this world of yours?" Grizz pressed obtrusively.

"The how will require a great deal of trust on your part and I know that won't be easy for you. Our planet is called Verticus and we will have to travel through a great deal of both space and time to get there." Eddy tried to explained as basic as he could.

This was something... Something big, and Grizz understood how Eddy had difficulty explaining how they would have to travel, but if he and his mother made the journey without a scratch, Grizz was ready to do it. Grizz knew he might die trying, but it would be worth it, he was ready to die, "Believe it or not, I do trust you. I believe you, as well." Grizz stared at Eddy in all seriousness as Eddy looked up at Grizz half expecting to find a glimmer of fault in his comment. "You're not from around here and you had to get here, to this time and place, somehow.

Now you're going to back track and return to your world the same way you came here, right?" Eddy could see that Grizz understood enough about the journey they had to take.

Grizz had been watching the progress of the search efforts carefully. On occasion, Grizz would climb up onto the roof and with the use of his advanced sling-shot he targeted several structures in the industrial area. With perfect precision, Grizz hit the rickety structures and some of them fell over like skeletons breaking to pieces upon the ground. This was to mislead the searching military groups.

"I'm almost finished with these modifications." Eddy told Grizz in passing as Grizz looked bored and perhaps needed something to do. Grizz slowly leaned forward and studied the two disassembled motor cycles. "Why don't you give me a hand here?" Eddy asked as he was eager to finish his conversion project on the bikes.

Grizz didn't think Eddy's idea was going to work at all, "This is a waste of time. We've been at this for hours. The military's getting closer. I'm not tinkering with these bikes anymore and I need something else to do to prepare for when we have to fight our way out of this jam."

"Fine," Eddy told Grizz, "I need just a little more time. Why don't you find a way to distract the soldiers without getting us killed?"

"My pleasure." Grizz grinned like he finally had something fun to do. "I'll be right back."

Throughout the framework of long dead industrial buildings and rusty machinery, the military scouting groups were systematically securing individual complexes one by one. Many punks had been located and captured, but the level of aggression from the punks had escalated.

Grizz made his way to the area of the soldiers by way of one of his own old zip lines. Grizz and Kiki would use them at times for training or if they were late to the punk Lair. While Grizz was on the move, he thought about the new alliance he secured with Eddy, his new brother. Slipping through the night like an invisible ghost, Grizz wondered if he was dishonouring his original Brothers somehow. Eddy was no Blackguard, but he was certainly his brother. From above, hidden in the shadows, Grizz observed the military activity below him. Grizz knew he was only supposed to quickly check on the military and report back on their positions, but what Grizz saw was an opportunity to make an atonement for his deceased Brothers. In respectful memory of his Brothers, Grizz found a way to, not only honour their lives, but pay homage to each one of them with an act of consideration.

Within the make shift military encampment, the punk prisoners were being interrogated while a communications officer was busy speaking at his two way satellite radio.

Grizz listened to the communications officer for a moment while he observed the surroundings. "Field Mice are in position, sir, with eight civilians captured. They are punks, sir. Still no sign of the Blackguard..."

Near to the encampment, Grizz noticed a crane and a couple of bin removal trucks. A sign on the door of the dump trucks and crane read, 'Metro Scrap Metal Inc.'

Grizz jumped down to the crane to inspect it closer. The machine had a large electro magnet hung at the end of a cable. Examining the controls it was obvious the diesel engine would have to be started first before the magnet would have power. *'I can run this.'* Grizz assumed before he went back to rescue the punks and cause a well needed diversion.

"Don't even attempt to fool with us. We protect the nation but you? You're the scum of society. We know the Blackguard has had dealings with your lot. Tell us where he's hiding, now!" silence followed as the punks strained to be free of their bonds and glared eyes of revenge at the soldiers. It was not fear that consumed the punks, it was pure unquenchable rage.

The sergeant in charge turned from the interrogation to give his attention to the communications officer.

As the tough soldier was about to hit a punk with a club, a grappler hook dropped down from above and applied a powerful mechanical grip to the soldier's shoulder. With one grappler finger over the shoulder and down the chest, the two other grappler fingers tightened in at the soldeir's back. Lifted into the darkness above, quickly, the soldier cried out in excruciating pain. The sergeant turned back and noticed the interrogator was missing. Shouting at the punks the sergeant was furious without answers because the punks must have seen what happened to their companion. Nearby, the crane started up and moved the electro magnet next to the temporary encampment. When the sergeant threatened one of the punks with a pistol pointed at his head, the interrogator fell from above, flat on his front to the ground where he began to moan. The interrogator was messed up, due to his injuries.

Discreetly, Grizz sneaked up behind the unsuspecting field sergeant and tapped him on the shoulder. "You look'n fer me?" The sergeant turned around as Grizz upper cut him and he was out of the game. The sergeant's body was thrown right out next to the crane. "Grud, your powerful arms will continue on in glory." Grizz paid his respects to his brother's arms though it was brief. The other soldiers shot up to positions with a start as they clumsily pointed their weapons at Grizz. Giving a tug to a long piece of twine which was tied to a lever in the crane, Grizz activated the electro magnet.

The mobile crane was started and the powerful electro magnet pulled the rifles right out of the soldier's hands. "Gun's?" Grizz's voice penetrated the darkness, "That's cheating."

From out of the darkness, Grizz came swooping in swinging on his grappler line. Landing on a stunned soldier, Grizz took two other soldiers by their heads and slammed them to the ground. The communications officer came at Grizz swinging a metal rod behind his head to deliver a fatal blow. As he swung at Grizz, Grizz twisted around taking the rod from the officer's hand. With his leg jutting out in a quick turn, Grizz kicked the communications officer. The kick was so powerful, the body of the communications officer flew over the heads of the punks. "Stroy, your legs will continue with not only inhuman speed, but with the power of a mighty persuader."

Grizz examined the rod in his hands and thought of his brother, Narl. "Cunning and irritating, Narl, you had a gift of telepathy, though i don't have the same degree of such a gift, I am grateful for what I do have. You win, I suppose a piece of you will always be in my mind." Throwing the rod like a javelin, Grizz destroyed the communications radio.

Grizz relished in any opportunity to turn an enemy's weapon against himself. The soldiers, each one dazed, began to rise up moaning. One of the soldiers who had his head slammed to the floor had managed to get up and escape. Using his grappler, Grizz climbed high into the old structure above him. Looking out, Grizz could see the soldier had some wits as he was going to run all the way to the next closest squad and report. Grizz couldn't have that. Stretching back on his sling shot, Grizz arched his back and spread his wide chest before he took aim.

"With unpredictable, and uncontrollable rage, many more wars will be won, and I will owe it to you, Oblit." releasing the shot, Grizz fired one of his little solid football shaped bearings. The projectile hit the soldier square in his back with a solid muffled sound. Realizing the trooper was wearing a front and back bullet proof vest, Grizz was satisfied with how lifeless the soldier dropped. Grizz watched for a moment to be sure no one was going to get up again, before he turned and headed back. "I owe each one of you, my Brothers."

Grizz saw to it that the bonds which held the captured punks were quickly cut loose.

"Hey, Blackguard, we knew you'd come ta save us." Stab, who was one of the freed punks, spoke with both gratitude and attitude.

"Enough! More soldiers will be coming. You've had a busy night. Go home, take some vitamin B and get some well-deserved rest." Grizz told the punks.

At Grizz's instructions, the punks disappeared into the night.

Watching from the top of a tall scaffolding, Grizz was motionless as he saw the scouts discover the wounded soldiers. The military efforts doubled and Grizz knew from the direction the scouts were advancing, their time was up.

Grizz was not gone long on his solo venture before he returned to Eddy. "I have bad news." Grizz reported with a bleak tone in his voice. "The streets are full of vehicles heading out in one direction. They are coming to get us." Eddy seemed to be in deep thought as he continued to tinker with his project. Grizz was getting

551

worried about putting too much faith in a person who might be incapable of dealing with the situation.

Just finishing up the final examination of the motors. Everything seemed to be in perfect working order but Eddy would have liked to have tested his new creations. The time for truth had come. Without an opportunity to test the devices or practice simple maneuvers, Grizz and Eddy took on a much bigger risk than they wanted. "Your plan will take too long Ed-man." Grizz said. "This idea of changing motor cycles into flying machines is a waste of two vehicles and a lot of time and it won't work! We should have been working on a real plan, or even a back-up plan to get our butts out'a here! Now we have no time, and I for one am fresh out of ideas!"

"Are the charges set?" Eddy asked while busy trying to strap on one of the flight suits.

"Ya, but I feel like this is just another one of your ideas that'll back fire on us." between brothers, Eddy was able to let it slide.

"We are depending on each other's skills. It is possible things can fall apart in an instant, but we know enough about our own strengths and weaknesses that we are capable of beating the odds." Not looking away from his rigorous fine tuning of the motors, Eddy didn't even break concentration as he spoke.

"I agree, except I don't have any weaknesses." Grizz's words were self-righteous and bold, but Eddy just rolled his eyes in mocking disbelief. Both Grizz and Eddy had a much bigger game in mind than their own little quarrels.

The morning sun was just winking open at the distant horizon of Metro City's tall towers. Glistening dew drops on the dusty old glass with a golden warmth

Grizz recognized as a glimmer of hope to his otherwise dark life. Grizz sat at the window and watched as military infantry men, dressed in black fatigues, cautiously crept closer throughout the industrial warehouse yard outside. They broke into the warehouses one by one searching for the fugitives. The scouts who went out ahead of the other special agent soldiers, were very cautious and nervous. This was never more prevalent than when a rifle discharged within a nearby facility.

Within the saw mill, Eddy was busy completing some last minute adjustments and testing structure integrity. Eddy detached and discarded the rear wheel and most of the seat from the motor bike's frame. The joined front end fixture, which was the wheel, shocks, handle bars, gauges and headlights, were all removed and also discarded. The transformation of the motorcycles was complete. The two partners had converted the motorcycles into their new operational, flight suits, (in theory.)

Eddy strapped himself into the belts of one of the flight suit models. The harnesses were tightly secured around Eddy's shoulders and waste. The padded seat pressed against Eddy's upper back. The fuel tank was also padded and pressed against Eddy's lower back. The motor stuck out about two feet from Eddy's back with each wing having the span of twelve feet. Eddy attached a pole to where the rear wheel was originally supported. The pole stood straight up over Eddy's head. The propeller fanned out above him like a helicopter. Eddy had the handle bars connected to the pole. The bike chains were connected to a small sprocket which drove a larger pulley and belt which reached the propellers. With a metal bar attached to the gear shift they could change gears manually, while in flight. In order to control the steering, Eddy designed some wing attachments for their ankles. They would catch the air and allow them to keep their feet from dangling.

Noticing the troops heading for their complex, Grizz marched toward Eddy and said. "That's it! We're out'a time." Grizz began to strap his flight suit to his back. "Stay and tinker around with your gizmo as long as you want, I'm gone." Pulling the starter, the engine came alive with a roar as Grizz adjusted his choke and throttle.

"Okay, Grizz! I'm coming." Finding some old abandoned cover-alls and other old clothes left behind in lockers, Eddy had shaken the dust off and tried them on. Under the flight suit Eddy wore an old rustic brown jacket and he stretched his legs into a pair of dark green plastic rain pants.

As the soldiers reacted to the sound of the motors, Grizz and Eddy could hear the troopers entering the warehouse from below. Grizz set off the first stage of explosive charges and a section of the ceiling exploded at the far end of the room. Before the dust could settle, Grizz and Eddy hustled under the open roof. The debris was difficult to traverse but they managed to keep their balance.

Grizz clicked his flight suit into gear and began to lift off the floor slightly. Eddy pulled his lever and popped his flight suit into gear also. Placing a hand on a device mounted to a metal guard railing, Grizz flipped only a single switch with a quick snap of his fingers. The activated device started the second stage of explosives. Grizz cranked his flight suit, the motor sang like a viking woman before it shot out of the roof above like the sky was the vacuum of space. Grizz watched for Eddy, but he did not come with him. The detonators went off at the base of the building which started a chain reaction. Each explosion was followed by another and another as they worked around the outskirts of the warehouse. The walls cracked and the entire structure shook.

Grizz had set the last explosives to the base of all the main vertical support beams within the warehouse. While the entire warehouse collapsed as rubble to the earth, Eddy piloted his flight suit right out through the crown of the dust cloud. The warehouse was demolished. As Eddy rose higher into the sky, he glanced up and saw Grizz had achieved a great altitude above him.

Shots rang out at Grizz from below. Military snipers were scattered throughout the industrial complex. Looking out into the distance, Grizz could see the small silhouettes of military jet fighters join in formation and begin moving in his direction. Below, Grizz kept a sharp eye on Eddy's position. *'What is he doing so low still?'* Grizz wondered, *'Doesn't he know the danger he is in with the sharp shooters dug in throughout the area? We talked about this...'*

Eddy continued to fly low to the building tops. Contrary to Grizz, Eddy found, by staying low enough, he remained out of the gunners' sights.

Meanwhile, bullets ricochet off Grizz's armor. In an effort to take control, Grizz found himself tensing up throughout his entire body. Closing his eyes, Grizz began to concentrate. Grizz needed to get his head on straight if he were to survive the situation. Still flying straight up, Grizz let the flight suit lead him rather than take control.

Grizz shook his fist at the noise of the five jets as they passed with supersonic speed. Following the jets fly by came the loud boom in the wake of their faster than sound acceleration. Grizz took his hands away from his throttle so he could grab his incredibly large sling shot and a couple of ball bearings. Before Grizz was ready, a second squadron of five jets also passed him by. Grizz could feel himself begin to descend as he began to struggle to win back control. Eddy pulled up his trajectory sharply to begin moving in closer to assist Grizz.

The first squadron was F-35 joint strike fighters and the second squadron was F-22 raptors. When the jets passed Grizz and Eddy the first time, it was to identify them. The next time they passed would be to take them out of the sky permanently.

Grizz and Eddy had very little to retaliate against the air force's greatest strike fighters, but they were small with the potential and capability of incredible maneuverability. F-35s came up fast behind them and began to open fire with internal guns which had laser designators. The bullets narrowly missed Eddy as he rolled forward into a steep dive. The ammunition heavily pounded the surrounding buildings of Liberty town. Obviously, the air force did not care. Damage to an evacuated city could be repaired. Grizz shot a small black marble at an incoming jet and missed. He loaded his sling shot again and shot at the second jet. His aim was much more precise. Hitting the jet's cockpit windshield, did not have any effect on the jet.

When Grizz reached into his pouch once again, he accidentally tipped it up and all of the black ball bearings fell away out of sight. Grizz opened his hand and found one ball bearing left. Loading his sling shot for the last time to hit the last jet to pass, Grizz decisively picked his moment. When he released his shot, the black marble surprisingly pegged off the tip of an AIM-9 sidewinder missile under the wing. The jet detonated into millions of brilliant red hot hurtling pieces.

For Grizz, the moment of destroying the jet with his sling shot was an awakening. Grizz glared through the slits of his helmet at the other jets with ferocious anger accompanied with a new found sense of confidence. Throwing his long distorted sling shot away from himself, Eddy caught sight of the thing and watched as it fell to Liberty town. With a new sense of confidence, Grizz gripped his accelerator and pushed his flight suit into a twirling dive. With a playful vengeance, Grizz played a game of cat and mouse with the jets. Voraciously, an F-22 raptor pursued him. The fighter jets were much faster than the flight suits of course but it was only by Grizz and Eddy's hair pin maneuvering capabilities where they could stand a chance. Grizz and Eddy seemed to have a keen sense of predicting what the other was going to do. They flew with urgency as they maneuvered in and out, dodging and weaving throughout the towering skyscrapers of Metro city.

The F-22 raptor unloaded on Grizz with its' 20mm gatling gun. Tipping his wing as he made a sharp turn, Grizz's motor caught a shot from the 20mm shell. The raptor pilot thought he had Grizz when black smoke bellowed out from his engine. Playing into the role of the victim, Grizz dived and managed to trick the F-22 raptor into a collision course with an F-35 at an intersection midst the tall Metro city buildings. Anger became the buzz as the fighter jet wouldn't show signs of letting up and frivolously pursued Grizz in vengeance. Grizz's overwhelming, brawny maneuvers were cause enough for him to rise up above Eddy. Knowing he was in trouble, Grizz looked for a sign as to how Eddy expected to save him. Looking back, Grizz could see black smoke as the engine's cough worsened with each passing moment.

Unable to keep the flight suit in the sky, Grizz wound his way down to the lower levels of Metro city leaving a spiral of Black smoke trailing behind. The complex city was waiting below with a hunger to devour Grizz like a Venus fly trap, if his engine were to seize up.

Despite the pressure of the chase Eddy proved his faithfulness to Grizz and continued to stay in his near vicinity. One F-35 seemed to swoop in from out of nowhere and appear right behind Eddy. Eddy's flight suit slightly shook as he shifted gears before his engine roared. Eddy bolted forward just as the F-35 jet began to fire upon Eddy with thunder. Eddy had to react as he veered to the right around a sharp corner and on through a tight ally way. *'Catch me if you can!'* Eddy thought, but to his surprise the F-35 had short takeoff and vertical landing capabilities, or (STOVL). This allowed it to slow to a stop in midair, turn 45 degrees to Eddy's direction and with its' wingspan of 36 feet continue after him through the narrow ally. The last thing Eddy wanted was to let the F-35 get a target lock, so Eddy pulled up and performed a full loop which brought him down right on top of the fighter jet. Eddy landed flat on the F-35's cockpit window. Eddy became angry and he resembled Grizz as he gave the pilot his own wide eyed roar cry. With a final measure of anger, Eddy slammed his fists onto the bullet resistant glass. The powerful strike cracked the window. Grizz was impressed and Eddy knew spending too much time with Grizz would rub off on him eventually. The pilot of the F-35 took the opportunity to show of the maneuverability of his fighter. Eddy felt the jet under him lurch to the left and then it began to rise straight up.

Eddy twisted his throttle full open causing his flight suit to pull him away from the F-35. Again, Eddy found himself air bound, as he turned back, he saw how the wing tip of the F-35 clipped the brick wall of the ally accidentally and the momentum pulled the jet right into the building side. The jet fighter had lodged itself into the building structure where it began to burn. Eddy continued on as he rose high above the ally and found Grizz still twisting throughout the tall Metro city towers. Locating Grizz was easy as wherever Grizz went, he left a thick trail of black smoke to follow.

Though Grizz's flight suit was damaged, it still functioned for the moment. Through desperation and a willingness to survive, Grizz worked the controls of his flight suit, as an aggressive navigator. Picking up some speed then veering off toward a road, Grizz led them to the cleaner and more sophisticated part of Metro city. Eddy wondered, *'Where do you think you're taking us now?'*

The preceding jets came about and followed Grizz and Eddy, but they refrained from firing at them. Eddy looked to the city streets below and saw military vehicles scattered throughout the roads. Besides the fast moving U.S. army trucks, jeeps and motorcycles, Eddy and Grizz quickly caught a glimpse of multiple SmartTrucks, M109A6 Paladin Howitzers, stealth tanks, Surface-to-air missile trucks (SAM) and stationed Multi Launch Rocket Systems (MLR). Amongst the heavy artillery, soldiers ran, taking up positions and preparing for their next move. Because Grizz and Eddy were currently so close to the road and military traffic, no order was given to fire at them from above or below, however, the earthen governing powers on land and in the air were bent on tracking their every move.

To be continued in the parallel novel;
Genation Book 1 Earth Volk

ABOUT THE AUTHOR

Robert A. Hunt resides in his home land of Canada, British Columbia. A diehard story teller since for as long as he can remember. In between building and studying, Robert finds time to write science fiction fantasy which he contends may not be so fiction and unattainable after all. "We still have so much to learn about the world we live in." Robert, a full time author, has no plans of slowing down. When Robert is not writing, he is spending time with his family or exploring the beauty of North America because, for him, it is a great way to let his mind free.

Grizz Rise of the Blackguard is the back story of the Genation Character; Grizz, who is an essential character of the Genation series; *Earth Volk, Verticus, Insectivolk wars* and *Ultimate Power*. Other titles from Robert A. Hunt include; *Jasper*, The legend trilogy; *The Crater Mountain Sasquatch Legend, The Coalmont Legend* – are available now and *The Cross Breed Legend* – will be out in 2013.

Join the Epic Saga of Genation

Connect with Wordpainter Publishing and I on-line, simply look us up on the world wide web at:

http://tinyurl.com/bwr7dpg

http://tinyurl.com/cohbvjh

http://wordpainter-publishing.blogspot.ca

or look me up (Robert A. Hunt) on manicreaders.com, goodreads.com, amazon.com, Facebook or Twitter.

Genation

GRIZZ

Rise of the Blackguard

A boy born into the world without parents or even many important body parts, was chosen as the least likely to survive terrible surgical experimentations. With the untimely death of a new born alien being, specialists go to work in a frantic panic to find who they can aquire quickly to grapht the alien body parts to. An unimaginable and crazy situation unfolds as efforts are made to mold the most powerful warrior of our time. Discover the incredible events a young boy had to survive before he became known as, 'Grizz the Blackguard.' Surprises around every corner take you on a ride of rage and adventure through the life of Eddy Evon's long lost brother, popularly known as, Grizz.

Made in the USA
Charleston, SC
12 January 2014